FIONA GIBSON

Pedigree Mum

AVON
A division of HarperCollins*Publishers*
77–85 Fulham Palace Road,
London W6 8JB

www.harpercollins.co.uk

A Paperback Original 2013
1

First published in Great Britain by
HarperCollins*Publishers* 2013

A catalogue record for this book is
available from the British Library

ISBN-13: 978-1-84756-261-6

Set in Sabon LT Std by Palimpsest Book Production Limited,
Falkirk, Stirlingshire

Printed and bound in Great Britain by
Clays Ltd, St Ives plc

MIX
Paper from
responsible sources
FSC www.fsc.org **FSC C007454**

A big bark of thanks to Caroline Sheldon, Bryony Woods, Sammia Rafique, Becke Parker and the wonderfully talented and bushy-tailed Avon team.

Special tail-wags to Carolann for our daily head-clearing walks and to Dee for medical expertise (on what happens when children stuff small objects into ears).

Messy but hugely affectionate face licks to Jen, Kath, Cathy, Michelle and Wendy V – my lovely friends since we were young pups. Unlimited treats to Tania, Vicki, Amanda, Sam, Hilary and Pauline, collectively known as the Dolphinton Writers – truly an author's best friend.

Tons of love to my parents, Margery and Keith, and to my own gorgeous though rarely obedient family – Jimmy, Sam, Dex and Erin, plus our rescue dog Jack who's a bundle of loveliness, even when forced to wear an embarrassing head cone.

For the delectable Miss Wendy Rigg

PART ONE

Arrival

'Welcoming a new addition into your home is a decision not to be taken lightly. The impact on your family will be enormous.'

Your First Dog: A Complete Guide
by Jeremy Catchpole

Chapter One

So it actually exists. The perfect family day out, as peddled by the glossy magazines, featuring unfeasibly photogenic parents and children enjoying beach picnics in the sunshine – *it happens in real life,* Kerry realises. To her left, a family entirely populated by curly-haired blondes are tucking into a Niçoise salad from a huge transparent pink bowl. They've even brought salad tongs (pink to match the bowl) and it appears to be *fresh* tuna, not tinned. There's also a huge pastry oblong which looks like one of those savoury French tarts, with anchovies draped all over it – Kerry is amazed to see it being happily consumed by persons under eight years old – plus a dazzling array of fresh fruit.

At another gathering, kids in Breton tops are tucking into what looks like a week's worth of five-a-days at one sitting, and not your boring old apples and tangerines either. Kerry spots mangoes, papayas and gnarly little testicle-like things that might possibly be kumquats or maybe ugly fruits . . . God, she doesn't even know the names of the more exotic varieties. Is it any wonder she can't persuade her own children to acquaint themselves with pineapple? Here on Shorling beach, in the glorious April sunshine, no one is whingeing or picking out bits they don't like. There appears to be not one Cheesy Wotsit on the whole beach.

As for acceptable picnic attire, Kerry realises this is Petit Bateau territory, with a liberal sprinkling of Boden and Gap. It's also clear that Mia, who at seven years old favours scruffy denim shorts and has already splattered ice cream down her T-shirt, doesn't quite belong. And it's a miracle that Freddie, who's wearing the hideous black and orange tracksuit that's permanently welded to his lithe five-year-old body these days, hasn't been politely asked to leave the beach. Kerry might be feeling paranoid, but she's sure that kumquat-slicing mum over there is giving her children a look of distaste, as if fearful that they might pitch up beside them and start slugging Fanta and ripping open packets of Jammy Dodgers.

She chuckles to herself, focusing now on her husband Rob as he turns and motions for her to catch up. Their children are running along at the water's edge while Rob is marching ahead, laden with bags, having decided that the far end of the beach will be more suitable for kite flying. However, Kerry has lagged behind deliberately, swivelling her eyes from left to right in order to amass as much infor-mation as possible about the picnicking etiquette at Shorling-on-Sea. After all, they might live here one day. It's just a hazy idea, but still, research must be conducted in these matters.

At least Rob looks the part, she decides. Tall, dark-eyed, handsome Rob, who's been scouring the shops these past weeks for a top-notch kite, especially to bring today.

'Think this is a good place?' he asks as Kerry catches up with him. They have left the picnicking groups behind now, and she experiences a wave of pleasure as she surveys the sweep of flat, empty sand.

'Looks perfect,' she says. 'D'you think there's enough wind?'

4

'Yeah, 'course there is,' Freddie declares, unselfconsciously pulling off his sodden tracksuit bottoms. He points at a father and son over by the rocks who are expertly manoeuvring a box kite.

'*That's* impressive.' Rob grins at his son. 'Reckon we can do that, little man?'

'Yeah. Let me go first.' Freddie tries, unsuccessfully, to snatch the kite from Rob's grasp.

'You said *I* could, Daddy!' Mia declares, scampering towards them.

'Of course you can both have a go,' Rob says. 'It's for you guys, not me. Just let me see if I can get us started, okay?' Amidst the children's protests, Rob strides away while Kerry unpacks her own picnic offerings: ham baguettes, a little squashed, bananas having mysteriously blackened during the two hour drive from London to the south coast. But at least her blueberry muffins have endured the journey well. She almost wishes the anchovy tart mum would venture over and see them: *they're home-made, you know, and there's fruit nestling inside . . .*

Actually, no she doesn't, because all's not going well on the kite front. Having decided he does need assistance after all, Rob is urging Mia to launch the kite as he simultaneously charges away, gripping the spool as if trying to control an exuberant puppy. Kerry traps a bubble of laughter as, no matter how fast he runs or tugs ineffectually at the line, the bright yellow kite still smacks straight back down onto the sand.

'I really don't think there's enough wind,' she suggests, sitting cross-legged on a spread out towel.

Rob blows out air and glances at the father and son with the box kite. 'They don't seem to be having any problems,' he huffs.

'Yeah,' Freddie grumbles, 'why haven't we got one like that?'

Mia fixes her father with a thoughtful stare. 'Is it our kite's fault, Daddy, or is it you?'

Slinging the kite on the sand beside the picnic basket, Rob plonks himself down beside Kerry. 'Guess it must be me, sweetheart. Guy in the shop said even a dumbwit can fly this. It's guaranteed to fly like a bird, he said.'

'He lied then,' Freddie says.

'Can you get your money back?' Mia wants to know.

'Oh, I don't think I'll bother. Maybe I should leave kite flying to those alpha-dad types.' Rob grins, putting an arm around Kerry's shoulders.

'Well,' she says, 'that box kite probably took six weeks to build, and I bet he's president of some horribly competitive kite-flying club . . .'

'And the kid hates it,' Rob cuts in. 'He'd much rather be at home, plugged into his Xbox . . .'

'Have you noticed how he hasn't let the boy have a go?' Kerry has barely spoken when the man hands the kite's controls to his small, eager son who continues to manoeuvre it in majestic swoops.

'There must be some different kind of air pocket system going on there,' Rob says, taking a bite of a muffin. 'These are delicious by the way.'

'Thanks. New recipe.'

'Excellent work, Mrs Tambini.'

She laughs, kissing him lightly on the lips, relieved that she managed to persuade him to come down here today. The children are clearly enjoying it too, having wandered off back to the water's edge.

'D'you think it's okay,' Rob ventures, 'Freddie wandering about in his pants like that?'

'It's a beach,' she laughs. 'Of course it is, as long as no one realises they're from Primark. We'll probably be arrested if they do.'

Rob smiles. 'You really like it here, don't you?'

'I love it, even though it's gone posh. I always have, ever since I was a kid.' She glances at him, deciding not to ask him again whether they should take up her Aunt Maisie's offer of buying her home on the Shorling seafront at a ridiculously low price. Admittedly, the cottage needs work, but it's the perfect size, with a great primary school within walking distance. Maisie is keen to move to Spain where her oldest schoolfriend, Barbara, has an apartment. She's out there now, ready to embrace a new life, and Kerry feels she, Rob and the children are too. Rob has cautiously agreed that London is commutable – seventy minutes by train – and as a freelance songwriter, she could easily live and work here. And the children, who have now joined forces to build a sandcastle, would love it . . .

Rob strolls over to help them dig a moat, and Freddie squeals with delight every time a wave rushes in to fill it. As she watches the three of them digging frantically, Kerry is overcome by a surge of love for her husband. Rob seems to have been struggling at work lately, no doubt due to a clear out of virtually all of the old, faithful team. His new editor sounds utterly obnoxious, so is it any wonder he's seemed a bit distant and distracted?

Kerry gets up to join her family, helping to reinforce the moat's walls after each wave.

'We're winning against the sea!' Freddie yells until their castle finally melts away.

'Let's try the kite again,' Rob suggests, 'now that over-achiever with the box kite has gone.'

Perhaps because the pressure's off, this time the kite soars up easily – a canary-yellow diamond against a dazzling blue sky.

'Here, you try,' he says, passing the spool to Freddie while Mia claps delightedly.

'You did it, Daddy!' she cries.

'Hero,' Kerry murmurs teasingly. 'Kite maestro superstar.'

'Hey, it was nothing.' Rob chuckles, his smile dissolving as the kite spins erratically before dive-bombing a child-free couple who have just set out their picnic *à deux*. 'Shit, bollocks,' he blurts out, haring towards them to apologise profusely.

'It's fine,' the woman snaps. '*Don't worry about it.*' She extracts the kite from a fluted glass dish and hands it to Rob.

'Shit-bollocks,' Freddie sniggers into his hand as his father returns, brushing cous-cous off the kite with the flat of his hand.

It doesn't spoil the day though. The afternoon drifts by in a pleasant blur, and Rob is even persuaded by Mia to roll up his pristine Levi's and have a paddle. The muffins are devoured, plus delicious crab sandwiches from a nearby cafe. The children are engrossed in playing with a bouncy white terrier now, throwing a wrecked tennis ball for him with the approval of his elderly lady owner.

'I wish we had a dog,' Mia announces. 'Why can't we have one, Mummy?'

'Please don't start on about that now,' Kerry says, resting her head on Rob's shoulder.

He turns to her in the pinkish evening light and gently brushes a strand of hair from her eyes. 'This is beautiful, Kerry. I don't think I've ever realised how lovely it is to be by the sea.'

'It's been a perfect day,' she agrees. 'We should come down here more often.'

He nods, and there's a pause, as if he's taking care to choose the right words. 'You know what? I think we should do it. We should take up Maisie's offer and move here.'

She sits up and stares at him for a moment, wary of overreacting and causing him to backtrack. Then, unable to help herself, she flings her arms around his broad shoulders and kisses him long and hard on the lips.

'Are you sure?' she says finally. 'You're not feeling pushed into it, are you?'

'No, I'm not. Look at this place, and how the kids are here – it's so much better for them than a tiny backyard . . .'

'Well, *I* think so.' She swallows hard, watching as the yellow kite, now being flown single-handedly by Mia, darts gracefully, as if performing its own excited dance. The posh picnics have long been packed away and the beach is deserted apart from a couple of dog walkers in the far distance.

'Let's talk to her,' Rob says, 'as soon as she comes back from Spain.'

Kerry nods. 'Okay.' Closing her hand around his, she squeezes it tightly. 'It'll be great for us,' she adds. 'I can just feel it, Rob. I think it'll turn out to be one of the best things we've ever done.'

Chapter Two

Four months later

Certain activities should be left until the children are safely tucked up in bed. Sewing falls into this category. With all the swearing and blood loss involved, it's best not undertaken with impressionable young people around. Kerry has already acquired a repetitive injury from jabbing herself with a needle; all this to stitch a few name tapes onto school uniforms for the new term ahead. Could she get away with writing their names in biro on the wash-care labels instead? It's considered slovenly, Kerry knows this, but surely it's better than sending the children to their new school in blood-stained tops?

As a fresh scarlet bead seeps from the wound, Kerry manages to locate the first aid box from one of the many packing crates. These are still full and stacked precariously along one wall of the living room, like reinforcements against floods. Opening the tin of plasters, she selects one disguised as a bacon rasher (Freddie requested these last birthday; the set includes an egg, sausage and a blob of beans – a full English breakfast in plaster form). The name tapes are too thick, that's the trouble. The biro option hovers tantalisingly in Kerry's mind, even though she has already surmised that Shorling-on-Sea is a *sewn-in-name-tapes* sort of place.

The small, compact seaside town had a very different vibe when she spent childhood holidays here, in this very house where her Aunt Maisie used to live. Back then, the place bustled with visitors eating burgers on the seafront and children plucking tufts from pink candyfloss clouds. Where the town once smelt of fried onions, these days it's all organic bakeries and seafood restaurants. Apparently, more scallops and langoustines are consumed per capita in Shorling than anywhere else in Britain. Eating a doughnut in public would probably have you shot. The Gold Rush Arcade is now a Wagamama, the World's Biggest Museum of Tattoo Art has become a glass-walled restaurant filled with glossy people tackling crustaceans with an impressive array of little metal tools. The bleach-blonde ladies in velour tracksuits who once ran the numerous B&Bs – where did they all go, Kerry wonders? – have been replaced by glowing-skinned women with long, glossy hair, perfect teeth and children called Lottie and Felix.

Of course, it had been clear on kite-flying day that Shorling had gone upmarket. But it wasn't until they'd actually moved that the extent of the transformation had truly sunk in. Still, Kerry reflects, at least there's one final week of summer holidays. She'd noticed a sign advertising a children's end-of-summer beach party, and if Freddie and Mia could make some new friends, surely starting school would be a little easier. And what about her? Without lurking weirdly around the dog-walking women who hang out on Shorling beach, she hasn't the faintest idea how she'll meet anyone. Maybe it'll be easier at the school gates. Even more important, then, that Mia and Freddie's names aren't biro-ed on.

This flicker of optimism leads Kerry to picturing Rob selling their London home. Although it's on with an agency, Rob is adamant that estate agents are clueless, and that as deputy editor of a men's magazine, he is far better equipped

11

to point out its numerous Unique Selling Points. Reassuring herself that the house *will* sell, and that Rob will soon join them in Shorling, Kerry turns her attentions to the large, square chocolate cake sitting solidly on the table to her right.

In contrast to her pitiful needlework skills, Kerry can decorate cakes pretty nicely, even if she says so herself. Nothing fancy – no detailed scale models of a Loire Valley chateaux – just intricate piping that usually garners her a few brownie points at the children's birthday parties. For Freddie's last birthday she replicated an entire comic strip from one of his much-loved Tintin books, and when Mia turned seven she crammed the entire Simpsons cast, including many lesser-known characters, onto a ten-inch Victoria sponge. She even created a magazine cover to mark Rob's tenth anniversary of working at *Mr Jones* – 'The Thinking Man's Monthly', as the magazine's tagline goes.

This cake, too, is for Rob, but Kerry can't decide what to put on it. A simple 'Happy 40th Darling'? No, too generic. She could do a portrait in glacé icing but, while her beloved is undeniably handsome with his dark-eyed Italian looks, she wouldn't be able to resist exaggerating the long, strong nose and full, curvy mouth (trying to do a *flattering* portrait on a cake would be ridiculous, surely?) and she's not sure he'd appreciate that. As his new twenty-something boss has brought in an editorial team of equally youthful pups, Kerry senses that Rob is not entirely delighted about reaching this milestone. No – better tread carefully with this cake.

She ponders some more, deciding that if she doesn't get a move on the icing will set in the piping bag, leaving her with a cone of solidified sugar. Think, *think* . . . Taking a deep breath, and a gulp from the glass of now tepid char- donnay at her side, Kerry pipes carefully, transforming the cake into an elaborate book cover with delicate curlews all around its edges. In the centre, in her very best curly writing, she pipes:

ROBERTO TAMBINI
THIS IS YOUR CAKE!

Yep, pretty good. Kerry knows he finds exclamation marks vulgar, and is tempted to add more (CAKE!!!!!!!) just to wind him up, but manages to restrain herself. Anyway, he'll be delighted when she turns up to surprise him tomorrow morning at their London house. He'll be wowed by the cake, plus the smoked salmon, bagels and champagne she intends to pick up on the way for a special birthday brunch. The plan had been for Rob to head down to Shorling tomorrow afternoon, after showing more prospective buyers around their home. However, Kerry has arranged a far more enticing proposition. They'll celebrate his birthday by having a much-needed child-free Saturday together in London, *and* a night all by themselves (she has already de-fuzzed and selected reasonably racy black lingerie in readiness). Even now, after thirteen years together, the thought of lovely, unhurried sex with Rob sparks a delicious shiver of desire. Then on Sunday morning they'll pick up the children from her best friend Anita's, when they'll present Daddy with home-made cards and gifts.

It's just what he needs, Kerry reflects, clearing up in the kitchen before heading upstairs. She peeks into Mia's room where her daughter is sound asleep after an entire day on the beach. Picking up a bundle of sea-damp clothes, Kerry then steps quietly into Freddie's room where there's a curious odour. No, not just curious – rank, actually, like rotting fish.

'What're you doing, Mummy?' he asks sleepily.

'There's something stinky in here,' she whispers, her bare foot knocking against a plastic bucket half-tucked under his bed.

13

'They're my crabs.'

'You brought crabs home? I didn't realise. Ugh, they're *really* pongy . . .' In the bucket, fragments of crab shell contain the remains of flesh at various stages of decay.

'I was keeping them in the garden,' Freddie explains, 'but I didn't want them to be cold at night.'

'Oh.' She peers into the bucket again. 'But they're dead, sweetheart . . .'

'Yeah, I know,' he says brightly. 'I'm gonna make crab sandwiches with mayonnaise on like we had with Daddy.'

'What, you mean that day with the kite?'

'Yeah. They were yummy.'

'Er . . . yes, they were, darling, but I'm sorry – if you ate these, you'd be very, very ill.' Picking up the bucket, and ignoring his grumbles of protest, she plants a kiss on his forehead before making her way downstairs.

Even when the bucket's contents have been bagged up and deposited in the outside bin, the crabby odour still seems to permeate the house. Sloshing in extra orange-scented oil as she steps into her bath, Kerry decides that the smell's probably just in her head now – like her fears that things aren't quite the way they should be between her and Rob. She's probably imagining that too.

She'll get those name tapes sewn on tomorrow, and her plans will all come together beautifully. Yes, Kerry tries to convince herself – Rob's fortieth will turn out to be the best birthday he's ever had.

Chapter Three

'Planning to stay here all night?' Eddy calls good-naturedly across the editorial office of *Mr Jones* magazine. Rob looks up from his screen to where his new boss is pulling on his jacket.

'Just got a few things to tidy up,' he replies.

'Oh, c'mon, Rob. It's Friday night and it's gone seven o'clock. Come out for a quick drink. Nearly everyone else has been down there since six . . .'

Rob shakes his head. 'Thanks, but I'll just head off home. Got people to show round the house tomorrow, better make sure it's ship-shape . . .'

Eddy makes a bemused snort. 'Just a quick one. It'll do you good. What're you working on anyway?'

'Well, you said you wanted some alternatives to the magazine's strapline . . .' Secretly, Rob strongly believes that 'The Thinking Man's Monthly' does the job perfectly well, conveying the message: *Listen, mate, we run features on politicians and serious-looking leather briefcases. If you're looking for topless women you've come to the wrong place because we're Too Posh For Boobs.* However, Eddy thinks it's not 'dynamic' enough. *Mr Jones isn't supposed to be bloody dynamic,* Rob mouths silently as his editor banters with Frank, the art director. *That's the whole point. We once ran a four page feature on the history of Gentleman's Relish and that's what our readers expect.* Sensing tension radiating upwards from his back to his neck, Rob glares at the straplines he's managed to dredge up so far:

- *For men who mean business*
- *The discerning man's glossy*
- *The glossy man's best friend*

Jesus, what the hell is a 'glossy man'? And 'best friend'? That sounds like a dog. He ponders some more:

- *The magazine that was once respected and is now a bit shit*
- *No naked girls here – we're too refined for that . . .*

Then he adds, smiling to himself:

. . . Although we do feature the odd, deeply patronising sex tip which suggests that our 'thinking' readers aren't that hot in the sack.

He sits back, about to add to his personal rant when he realises with alarm that Eddy is lurking behind him, pink-cheeked like a baby and flaring his nostrils at the screen.

'Actually,' he says, 'I'm thinking of upping the sex content, Rob. We should run a few more features, practical advice, A–Z of foreplay . . .'

'Sorry?'

'You know – the usual get-her-into-bed stuff but delivered with a punchy edge . . .'

Rob blinks at Eddy. Try as he might, he cannot get his head around what an 'A–Z of foreplay delivered with a punchy edge' actually means.

'Well,' he says, frowning, 'if you really think our readers—'

'What, have sex?' Eddy guffaws. 'No, you're right, Rob. The uptight little farts probably aren't getting that much. All the more reason to give 'em a helping hand, eh?' He guffaws at his own joke.

'Er, I suppose so, yes.'

Eddy slaps a hand on Rob's shoulder. 'I don't mean we'd do it tackily. It'd be tastefully done . . .'

Nodding sagely as if taking all of this on board, Rob toys with the fantasy of opening a new document and typing out his resignation letter. How can he possibly do his job properly with a twenty-six-year-old idiot at the helm? The last magazine Eddy worked on was full of drinking games and Britain's Best Bum competitions. It's rumoured that the winner's 'prize' was to sleep with Eddy.

'*You* could write it,' Eddy adds, giving Rob's swivel chair an irritating jiggle.

'Oh, I don't think so. I've got a lot on and I'm sure we could find a freelancer, an expert. I could start putting out some feelers . . .'

Eddy shakes his head. 'You're the best writer here. On all the magazines I've worked on, I've never come across anyone as versatile . . .'

'Really?' Rob asks, flushing a little.

'God, yeah. You can turn your hand to anything, can't you? Interviews, travel, food, politics . . . You come across as this serious, keeps-things-ticking-along-nicely type, but actually you're a pretty intelligent guy!'

'Um, thanks, Eddy . . .' *Why don't you patronise me a bit more, you arsehole in your pale pink shirt and Dolce & Gabbana suit . . .*

'So don't tell me you can't knock out a monthly sex column. Under a pseudonym of course – we'd have to make out it was by a woman, a sort of "what's going on in her mind" type of thing.'

Rob jams his back teeth together, wishing Kerry were here to witness this. He's not sure he's managed to convey to her how awful things have been here lately.

'We could call you Miss Jones!' Eddy announces, triggering a bark of laughter from Frank on the other side of the office.

Rob squints at his boss. 'Or we could just commission an actual woman.'

'Yeah. Well, let's think about it. Anyway, that's enough about work – can I drag you out for that drink?'

'Yeah, come on, Miss Jones,' Frank sniggers, swaggering across the office from the art department.

Rob takes a moment to consider what to do next. He knows he should make an effort to socialise, as he did with the old team – the ones Eddy shunted off to the publishing group's less prestigious magazines like *Tram Enthusiast* and *Carp Angler*. He is also aware that he doesn't fit in with the new *dynamic* attitude which Eddy announced will replace the 'stuffy, gentlemanly tone', and that he's lucky to still have a job. In truth, though, the thought of going out drinking with these reptiles makes him want to gouge his eyeballs out.

'So? Can we drag you away from the coalface?' A smirking Eddy is beckoning him now, his loyal servant Frank looking bemused at his side.

'Well . . .' Rob hesitates before shutting down his computer. 'I don't see why not. Where are we going then?'

'Jack's.'

Rob nods approvingly, wondering how to negotiate this. He's not a member of Jack's, and is tempted to point out that he belongs to another private members' club – the one he, Simon and the rest of the cosy old team used to frequent. But now he's worried that even a casual mention of The Lounge will remind Eddy of his vintage, and he'll make a mental note to bung Rob over to *Horticultural Digest* first thing on Monday morning. When did life become so worrying?

The move to Shorling – that's started to concern him too. He knows it makes sense, and he was all for it that lovely day on the beach with the kite. Yet he can't help feeling a little anxious about the enormity of leaving the

18

city in which he's spent his entire adult life. Even Kerry seems slightly less enamoured with Shorling since she and the children moved down there, and he can't quite imagine how she'll fit in with those posh women with their haughty voices and BMWs.

'Er, I'm not actually a member of Jack's,' Rob admits as the three men head for the third floor lift.

'That's fine, you'll be my guest.' Eddy sweeps back his mop of fair hair and jabs the lift button.

'Great. Thanks.' Rob's mouth forms a tight line. The lift doors open, and they ride down in slightly awkward silence (despite the invitation, Rob suspects Eddy has only asked him out of politeness). It's a relief when they step out into the early evening bustle of Shaftesbury Avenue. The warm September evening, and the good-natured hubbub around him, raises Rob's spirits a little. He experiences a pang of missing Kerry and the children, and decides his one drink policy should mean he'll catch Mia and Freddie for a phone call before they go to bed. This time tomorrow, he reminds himself, they'll all be together. Maybe he'll treat his family to a special Sunday lunch at that seafood restaurant in the big glass cube, see what the kids make of the crustacean-crushing implements. That would be fun. Despite his anxiety about the move, he is heartily sick of being alone in London from Monday to Friday.

At Jack's, Eddy and Frank make a big show of being on first name terms with Theresa on the door.

'Has anyone ever told you you have beautiful eyes?' Eddy drawls, at which she chuckles indulgently and tosses back her glossy raven hair.

'Yes, darling. You, last week.'

'Oh, you play *so* hard to get. Isn't she a terrible tease, Rob?' Eddy emits a spluttery laugh, and Rob senses the tips of his ears turning a violent shade of puce. God, imagine having to be pleasant to wankers like this, every night of

19

the week. Rob almost wants to apologise on behalf of all mankind. *Just a quick one*, he reminds himself as the three men descend the narrow stairs to the basement, *so I don't seem like a stand-offish old bugger* . . .

His thoughts are cut short as he follows Eddy and Frank into the bar and realises that *all* of the *Mr Jones* editorial team are here – the clueless designers, the bewildering fashion team who describe clothes as 'pieces', and the writers who look like they've barely acquainted themselves with razors yet. Even Nadine, the young editorial assistant who doesn't seem to like him much, is smiling over the rim of her glass. And they're not only here, having a casual drink after work, but assembled before him in a rabbly semi-circle, all grinning and staring as they burst into song:

Happy birthday to you, happy birthday to you, happy birthday dear Robbeeeee . . .

Robbie? It sounds as if he's in a boy band. Rob's not a *Robbie*, but never mind that because here comes a cake, ablaze with candles and dusted with sugar (clearly, Jack's is too cool for the kind of garish iced creations Kerry creates), carried on a big silver board by a beautiful girl with red hair cascading down her back. Shock has morphed into pleasure as someone hands Rob a drink (how did they know he likes vodka and tonic?), and his colleagues cluster around him as the cake is cut.

'Well, thanks,' he blusters. 'I didn't think, I mean I didn't realise . . .'

'Hope you don't mind us hatching this little surprise,' says 'Stewie', the new features editor whose pallid complexion suggests he spends most of his free time huddled over a games console.

'No, of course not. Not at all.' Rob grins in disbelief. 'I've never had a surprise party before. I'm really touched . . .'

'Feel okay about the big four-o?'

'Oh yeah, it's fine . . .'

'And I hear you're going to be our new sex columnist!' exclaims fashion editor Ava, her severe black bob swinging excitedly.

'Er, it hasn't exactly been decided yet,' he says, a little less freaked out by the prospect now he's quickly downed most of his drink. How did she know, anyway?

'Eddy seems to think it has,' Ava says, raising an eyebrow. 'Once he gets an idea in his head there's no shifting it.'

'Well, I suppose I'll manage to, er . . .'

'You'll do a brilliant job,' declares Nadine, startling Rob with her friendliness. Usually, she regards him with cool indifference as if he's the maintenance guy.

'Er, thanks, Nadine. I'll give it my best shot, I suppose . . .'

She giggles, sweeping a hand over her cute gamine crop, and he feels himself blushing. Rob wonders briefly if she's teasing him. Perhaps she finds it hugely amusing that the oldest man in the office – the Granddaddy of *Mr Jones* – has been chosen to write a sex column. He's faintly relieved when Frank beckons him over to the bar to share a filthy joke.

No, he's just being paranoid, Rob decides, which is under-standable, considering the sweeping changes Eddy's been making. Anyway, he feels better tonight, now buoyed up by his second vodka and tonic. Nadine has reappeared at his side, and is telling him about working with Eddy – 'I follow him around like a little limpet,' she explains with a grin – and Ava is complimenting his jacket. As the evening continues with much banter and laughter, Rob decides to socialise more often, and to try to remodel his work persona, which he suspects comes across as too earnest for Eddy's 'dynamic' regime.

Rob might not be a member here at Jack's, and he might be hanging onto his job by the tips of his neatly-filed fingernails, but right now, turning forty doesn't seem so bad. And hours later – even though Rob rarely stays out late on a school night – he doesn't see why he shouldn't go along when someone suggests continuing the party at Nadine's Baker Street flat.

Chapter Four

'Mum. Mum! *MUUUUM!*'

Kerry snaps awake and peers at the alarm clock on her bedside table: 1.37 a.m. 'What is it, Freddie?' she croaks.

'Mum! C'mere!'

With a groan, Kerry hauls herself out of bed and blunders barefoot in a rumpled T-shirt and knickers across the landing. By the time she's in his room – which still retains its crabby whiff – she has already decided he sounds too perky to be ill or traumatised by a nightmare.

'It's the middle of the night, Freddie. What's wrong?'

'Can't sleep.' His brown eyes gleam in the dark.

'Why not? Did something wake you up?'

'Yeah.'

'What was it?'

'The sea.'

'The *sea*?' she repeats.

'Yeah.' He nods. 'It's noisy.'

Kerry kneels at his bedside and rubs her eyes. 'There's not an awful lot I can do about that, sweetheart. I mean, I can't turn it off.'

He scowls, radiating disappointment in her mothering abilities. 'Well, I can't sleep with it on,' he growls.

'You'll get used to it, love.'

'How long have we lived here?'

'Three weeks.'

'When will I be used to it?'

How is she supposed to answer that? *On September twenty-fifth at eight p.m. you will stop noticing those infuriating swishing waves . . .*

'Listen,' she says, mustering up a hidden reserve of patience, 'just close your eyes and think of happy things, okay? That's what I do and it really works. You'll soon be asleep.'

He's quiet for a moment. 'I'm thinking about a happy thing, Mummy.'

'That's good.'

Small pause. 'I'm thinking about when we have a dog.'

Kerry exhales loudly. 'Don't start on about dogs now, Freddie.'

'But you said, you promised—'

'I've *never* promised . . .'

'You did!' he shrieks.

'Shhh, you'll wake Mia—'

'You said we could have a dog when we're not in London and we're not in London now.'

'I didn't say definitely. I said maybe when you're older and can take him for walks by yourself and—'

'I'm older NOW!'

For God's sake. What would Rob say now, if he were here? He'd say she should have been one hundred percent firm about the dog thing, instead of her feeble 'maybe-one-day' wafflings. Rob is exceptionally good at pointing out what Kerry *should* have said after the event. It doesn't seem to occur to him that, as she has only worked part-time since having the children, she has had to make thousands more child-related decisions than he has.

'I'm going back to bed now,' she says firmly, tucking

24

Freddie's duvet, with its prancing Captain Haddocks and Snowies, around him.

'Mum!' Freddie cries as she leaves his room.

'Freddie, you'll wake your sister . . .'

'Can I phone Dad?'

'No, not in the middle of the night.'

'I wanna talk to him! I wanna say happy birthday . . .'

'It's not Dad's birthday yet, not till tomorrow.' Actually, it *is* tomorrow, she realises; it's nearly two a.m. and Rob is officially forty years old. But better not tell Freddie that. 'Good *night*, Freddie,' she says firmly from the landing, realising there's no point in going back to bed, as she is now shimmeringly awake.

Pulling on Rob's soft grey cashmere sweater over her T-shirt, Kerry heads downstairs into what used to be Aunt Maisie's dining room, and is now her designated music room. A music lecturer until cuts swept the university, Kerry is now trying to carve out a living as a freelance songwriter. While this might sound glamorous, her latest commission is for *Cuckoo Clock*, a long-established TV show for pre-school children (the over-zealous presenters wear bird costumes and sinister-looking rubbery yellow feet). The show is being given a facelift, including a whole stack of new songs, and at least they *want* her, Kerry thinks defiantly as she sits down at her piano. It might not be quite the illustrious future she'd in mind for herself at music college, but the money's good, and she also plans to teach piano from home. Isn't that the modern way of doing things – to have several strings to your bow, so to speak? And surely dozens of parents in a well-heeled town like Shorling are desperate for their little ones to learn the piano. Kerry doesn't have any pupils yet, but she plans to put ads on all the newsagents' noticeboards in the next day or two. God, she hasn't even finished unpacking or organising the house yet. It still amazes her, despite the fact that she should be used to it by now, how little you get done with children around. And the people at *Cuckoo Clock*'s production company don't seem to understand that even bouncy little bird songs can't be hammered out in five minutes.

It'll be easier when Rob moves down, she tells herself firmly. *Then we won't feel like cuckoos ourselves, stealing someone else's nest* . . . They'll also be able to *buy* Aunt Maisie's house, which will hopefully make it feel properly theirs. At the moment, thanks to her aunt's generosity and keenness to move, Kerry and the children are living here rent-free.

After taking a moment to gather her thoughts, she starts to sing and play quietly so as not to disturb the children.

Welcome to the cuckoo clock,
It's time to say to say hello,
What's behind the little doors . . .

'"What's behind the lit-tle doors?"' comes the mocking echo behind her.

She whirls round. 'Freddie! What are you doing out of bed?'

His lightly freckled face erupts into a wide-awake smile. 'What are you asking that for?'

'Because I told you, it's the middle of the night—'

'No, about the doors.' He rakes a hand through his dishevelled brown curls.

'Oh. Er . . . to build up tension, I suppose, so it's a surprise . . .'

'But it's a cuckoo, innit? *That's* what's behind the doors.'

Kerry blinks at her son. She is chilly now, despite the cashmere sweater, and goosebumps have sprung up on her bare legs.

'You're right,' she says flatly. 'It's a cuckoo. It really couldn't be anything else.'

Freddie grins triumphantly and starts swinging on the door. 'Ha, I knew it was. *Now* can I phone Dad?'

26

Chapter Five

Nadine's flat might only be forty-odd miles from Rob's new house by the sea, but the way he feels now, he might as well have landed on a different planet. The huge living room is girlie in the extreme, its sofa and chairs strewn with fluffy throws and an abundance of embroidered cushions. There are fairy lights, glowing red lamps and a multi-coloured chandelier. The effect, he muses as Nadine dispenses drinks (aided by a rather worse-for-wear Frank), is a little nauseating.

'So d'you like my place?' Nadine asks, curling up beside him on the vast purple velvet sofa.

'It's really, um, stylish,' he tells her, enunciating carefully in the hope of appearing sober.

'Thanks.' She smiles prettily. 'It's a bit of a mish-mash but I like it.'

'Yeah, but it's not yours, is it?' Eddy teases from his cross-legged position on the pink shag-pile rug. 'It's Daddy's.'

Nadine rolls her eyes good naturedly. 'Yep, but I'm here for the time being, darling. You don't think I could live here on an editorial assistant's salary, do you?'

'Thank God for Daddy,' Eddy guffaws, stretching the joke a little thin in Rob's opinion. He glances down at the gnarled oak table on which the remains of his birthday cake look a little ravaged on a plain white plate, wondering why he's suddenly feeling protective of Nadine. Her slight haughtiness in the office is, he suspects now, a desire to seem properly grown-up when she's barely emerged from her teens.

'So you're off to your new place tomorrow?' Ava asks Rob, rearranging her bony limbs on a giant floor cushion.

'Yes,' he says, 'after I've shown a couple of people round the house.'

She smiles, her teeth Tipp-Ex white against the blood red of her lipstick. 'I don't know if I could ever do that.'

'Show people around a flat, you mean?'

'No, silly! Leave London.' Ava winces.

'Well,' Rob says, 'it just seemed like the right time.' He can't explain about the education issue now, and how several friends have faked addresses and religions in order to get their children into decent schools. Mentioning that in front of all of these young things would make him sound about five hundred years old.

'What'll you *do* with yourself down there, Rob?' Nadine's voice cuts into his thoughts.

'Er, just get on with life, I suppose. Get fit, start running, go for long walks on the beach . . .' Agh, why is he saying that? Eddy will have him shovelled off to *Rambler's Monthly*.

'I love the sea,' Nadine says wistfully, 'but I can't imagine living away from all the shops and bars.'

Typical, he thinks without bitterness. Just the kind of thing a privileged girl with nothing to think about but chandeliers and cushions would say. Rob, whose father is Italian and his mother a straight-talking Yorkshire woman, is at least aware that life happens north of Watford – or south of Croydon, come to that.

'Well, I've been here for twenty years,' he explains

28

patiently. 'The noise, the traffic – I've had my fill, to be honest.'

Now he's sounding like Granddad again. Nadine nods, and at some point the others seem to drift away to different parts of the room, leaving just the two of them sitting very close on the sofa. She isn't his type at all – too girlie and *far* too young with her silver cowrie shell necklace which was probably acquired on some gap year jaunt, or maybe Daddy bought that for her too. In fact the thought of having a 'type' hasn't crossed Rob's mind since he met Kerry. But now, having drunk more than in recent memory, he can't help but notice how mesmerising her blue eyes are, framed by a sweep of dark lashes, and how her dainty nose is incredibly cute. For some reason, despite knowing the others for far longer, she has chosen to sit next to *him*. It no longer seems to matter that, while he was getting to grips with disposable nappies and jars of sludge-coloured baby food, Nadine was still in high school. *Exquisite* is the word that springs to mind now. This girl is exquisite, like a jewel.

'I hope you don't mind me saying,' she murmurs, shuffling even closer with her feet tucked under her neat little bottom, 'but you seem like your heart's not really in this seaside thing, Rob.'

'Er . . .' A wave of dizziness engulfs him as he blows out air. 'Yeah, it's freaking me out a bit. The *practical* side, the train and stuff – that'll be okay . . .' Hell, he *is* slurring now. Is he even making sense?

'But . . .?' She smiles sympathetically.

Rob blinks at her. 'God, I don't know, Nadine. It's half two in the morning . . .' She nods, encouraging him to go on. 'Am I ready to move? I don't know. It started off as a vague idea, something we might do when we were properly grown-up' – he laughs self-consciously, feeling a little sick – 'then wham, it's happened, Kerry and the kids are there already and there's this awful pressure to sell the London house . . .' *No, stop it, that came out all wrong. What about that lovely day on the beach with the kite? It had felt completely right then . . .*

Nadine is studying his face. 'Does Kerry know you're having doubts, Rob?'

'It's too late to stop it now. We've taken the kids out of their London school and enrolled them in Shorling. And anyway, she's convinced we can make it work. It'll just take time, she reckons . . .' He takes a big gulp from his glass, grateful that the others have wandered through to the kitchen in search of something to eat.

'You poor darling.' Nadine places a delicate hand on his knee. 'So you feel trapped . . .'

'Well, um, kind of . . .' Rob looks down at her hand, feeling no less startled than he would if a rare butterfly landed there. He can hardly swat it away, but nor does he feel entirely comfortable with her leaving it there for much longer. Anyway, why is he grumbling about the move? Is it the vodka, or a pathetic desire to say what he *thinks* he should say to a girl who can barely have turned twenty? Her hand is showing no sign of removing itself from his knee, and he wonders what the others will think as they come back into the room, armed with a lump of Cheddar and some crackers on a pink chopping board (clearly, neon pink is a theme around the flat). Of course, they won't think anything. Eddy's new team are always hugging and mauling each other. It's not unusual for Ava to give Eddy a languorous shoulder massage in the middle of a features meeting.

Rob swallows hard and tries to centre himself by picturing Mia and Freddie on the beach last weekend, sculpting a sand mermaid with seaweed for hair. He attempts to think of ordinary things: the numerous cracks and leaks he must fix in the Shorling house, and the lone nit Freddie made him examine with a magnifying glass as it writhed on a sheet of white paper.

By the time Eddy, Frank and Ava get up to leave, Rob realises he's even more inebriated than he first thought. Nadine springs up to fling her skinny arms around her friends before resuming her position on the sofa.

'So, Rob,' she starts, 'what are you going to do?'

He drains the last of his vodka and tonic. 'I have no fucking idea.'

'Well,' she says, 'for what it's worth, I have this mantra, okay? And it's that we should all be true to ourselves . . .'

Normally, Rob would snort at the kind of fluffy soundbite so beloved of women's magazines: *Follow your dreams. Life's not a rehearsal. Be true to yourself* . . . But it's approaching 3 a.m. and her eyes are incredible – piercing blue, emphasised with the kind of flicked black eyeliner which makes him think of sexy French girls in arthouse movies.

'You're right,' he blurts out. 'The thought of leaving London . . .'

'It's like leaving a part of yourself,' she suggests.

'Yes! That's exactly it. It's where I've lived and worked my whole adult life . . .'

'And you've done really well, Rob.'

'Oh, I don't know about that,' he murmurs bashfully.

'But you have! You virtually run the office . . . I've always found you a bit intimidating, to be honest.'

'God, I hope not.'

'No, that's just me being silly.'

'Well,' he says with a grin, 'I'll try to be less intimidating in future . . .'

And so the night goes on, Rob now too drunk to care about whether he's slurring or not, and sensing the little knots of tension starting to loosen in his shoulders and neck. He knows he should call a cab, but being here with Nadine is so much nicer especially as, with most of his family's possessions transported to Shorling, 'home' feels like a bleak shell with a bed and a sofa plonked in it.

'Look, Rob,' Nadine is saying, looking sleepy now, 'you can crash out here if you like. This is a sofa bed and I've got plenty of spare bedding.'

'I . . .' he starts, knowing he should continue: *Thanks, but I'd better go home.* But he can't. He is physically incapable of coherent speech because every fibre of his being is focused on Nadine's red lips.

They are getting closer and closer and Rob knows without doubt that she is going to kiss him. He also knows there is no way he'll be able to resist kissing her back. Then they *are* kissing – snogging, actually – the just-turned-forty-year-old father-of-two with undeniable talents in the Lego department, and the beautiful rich girl who lives in Daddy's flat and trots off to India whenever she feels like it. They pull apart, laughing in disbelief, and immediately she's up on her feet, making up the sofa bed while he stares into space, wondering what the hell just happened. Perhaps it was a hallucination. He's never kissed anyone but Kerry – not for over thirteen bloody years. But it's okay, it didn't mean anything . . .

Dizzy and overwhelmingly tired now, Rob is vaguely aware of saying goodnight to Nadine, then undressing to his boxers and falling into bed alone as the mauve-tinted dawn creeps into the room. Yet, when he wakes at 8.47 a.m., with his dried-out tongue gummed to the roof of his mouth, a tiny and naked Nadine is curled up on the sofa bed beside him.

Chapter Six

Kerry was up early – 6.35 a.m. – despite Freddie's nocturnal wakening and that *Cuckoo Clock* theme tune chirping away in her brain for much of the night. But at least she has been able to shower uninterrupted and even managed to blow-dry her hair. Normally she lets it dry naturally, which makes it sound like a considered move, in the way a celeb might share a beauty tip: '*I try to avoid exposing my hair to heat.*' However, it's more to do with the fact that, since having Mia, and *especially* since having Freddie, Kerry's 'beauty regime' (she can't help twitching with mirth whenever she hears that term) has been whittled down to a spot of Nivea on her face before bed. Rob is more high-maintenance than she is these days.

Kerry has also managed to unearth her old favourite red shift dress, plus glossy heels that match – not the dress, obviously (that would be too much red) but each other, which feels like a major achievement. It's a bit much for daytime, she suspects. But Kerry is hoping for maximum impact when she shows up to surprise Rob.

She's at the bathroom mirror now, applying make-up under the watchful gaze of Mia, who rarely sees her mother beautifying herself. *Teeth*, Kerry thinks a little late in the

33

proceedings, prompting Freddie to bellow, 'Why are you *sawing your mouth*?'

'I'm not sawing. I'm just cleaning the little gaps between my teeth.' She has a fleeting memory of a time when she could perform bathroom-related duties alone.

'Why?' Mia asks.

'Er, so my breath's nice and fresh.' Explaining about plaque and mouth germs seems a little unnecessary at this early hour.

A sly smile creeps across Freddie's face. 'That's 'cause you're gonna kiss Dad.'

Kerry drops her used dental floss strip into the bin. 'Yes, well, I hope so, sweetheart. That's the general idea, seeing as it's his birthday.'

'Can we phone Daddy now?' he asks, plucking her used floss from the bin and bringing it up to his own mouth.

'Freddie, put that back in the bin! It's dirty . . .'

He throws it down at his feet. 'Can I, Mum?'

'Yeah, I wanna call Dad,' Mia exclaims.

'In a little while,' Kerry says, brushing on mascara. 'It's only half eight and he might be having a lie in, seeing as it's Saturday.' She tries to remember what time he said the first people were coming round to look at the house. Around ten, was it? 'We'll call in about half an hour, okay?'

Mia sucks her teeth. 'You never let us phone him.'

'Sweetheart, that's not true. Ow.' Kerry jabs the mascara wand into her left eye, causing it to fill with tears. 'We speak to Daddy nearly every evening . . .'

'Yeah, but . . .' She makes a little *pfff* sound.

'Come on, darling. Dad'll soon be living with us, then you'll see him every day.' Dabbing her watery eye with some loo roll, she glances down at her children who are perched on the edge of the shabby enamelled bath. Still friendless in Shorling, Kerry has taken to counting the days until Rob comes home for the weekends. Yet, when he is here, she detects a sense of distance between them, almost as if they've forgotten how to fit together.

'Cause you're gonna kiss Dad. Freddie's words echo in Kerry's mind as she dabs away the mascara smears from around her eye and packs away her make-up. Actually, she can't remember the last time they kissed properly, and wonders how Rob will react to her black lacy lingerie. She's slightly worried that he might claim to be tired or, worse, not even react at all. What would she do then?

'So, can we have a dog, Mum?' Freddie asks as they all trot downstairs.

'Oh, Freddie, don't start that now . . .' She zips up the children's overnight bags which are packed and waiting in the hall.

'But you promised!' he exclaims.

Kerry sighs, calculating how much there's still to do – breakfast, washing up, the gathering together of the last of her own bits and pieces – before she can be granted her small blast of freedom.

'I can't think about getting a dog right now,' she tells him, filling two bowls with the only cereal her children will tolerate (virtually pure chocolate – *confectionery*, not breakfast, as Rob once pointed out).

'Why not?' Mia asks, fiddling with the banana-shaped hairclip at her forehead.

'Because I've got too many other things to think about right now.'

'What things?'

Oh, you know – getting this house sorted out and you two settled into your new school, not to mention figuring out how I'll earn enough money and make some friends – you know, have an actual adult to talk to occasionally . . .

'Just things,' she says, turning away to make coffee.

'Daddy would get us a dog,' Mia says with a sigh.

'Yeah,' Freddie snarls. 'We've got the meanest person on earth as our mummy.'

*

Anita is clearly *not* the meanest, most despicable person on earth, as Freddie and Mia are delighted to be having a sleepover at her place tonight. Having grown up in Shorling, where Kerry first met her during one of her numerous holidays to Aunt Maisie's, Anita and her family headed inland as soon as the Cath Kidston wellie brigade surged to the coast.

'Can't stand it,' Anita had announced at the time. 'It's all artisan-this, artisan-that. What if I want a completely un-artisan pint of milk or some frozen peas?'

The final straw had been trotting along to the cheap and cheerful kids' clothes shop, from which Anita had managed to kit out her four children, and discovering it had turned into a chi-chi boutique selling cashmere pashminas for babies.

'Wish they still lived in Shorling,' Mia declares as they turn off the main road and follow the twisting lane towards Anita's Sussex village.

'Me too,' Kerry says, more forcefully than she means to.

'Did they move 'cause *we* live there?' Freddie asks.

'No, of course not,' Kerry laughs, glancing back at him. 'They came here a couple of years ago, long before we thought of moving to Aunt Maisie's. Anyway, they're not too far away. Only forty-five minutes. Look – can you see the church spire in the village? We'll be there in a few minutes . . .'

'Yey!' he cries, unclipping his seatbelt in readiness and ignoring Kerry's barked command to put it back on again. Minutes later they are pulling up outside Lilac Cottage, the ramshackle house which Anita and her husband Ian plan to renovate, but haven't got around to yet.

'So it's the big surprise today,' Anita says, hugging her friend as their children greet each other in a whirl of excitable chatter.

'Yep.' Kerry smirks. 'Scare the socks off him, poor sod. He'll probably have a cardiac arrest.'

Anita laughs as all six children descend on a tray of just baked, as yet un-iced cakes. Cramming their mouths, they surge as one – tailed by Bess, an excitable spaniel – into the living room where the TV is turned on at deafening volume.

'Our mummy doesn't like dogs,' Freddie announces loudly, causing Kerry to laugh mirthlessly as Anita hands her a mug of tea.

'Bad, bad Mummy,' Anita teases her. 'Imagine, not wanting to be wading through great drifts of hair and being hammered with vet and kennel fees.'

'I know. I'm such a bloody kill-joy, aren't I?' She sinks into the faded sofa, nudging aside a distinctly doggie-smelling blanket. Everything about Anita's house is tatty but immensely comfortable. Armchairs and rugs are strewn with dog hair and toys, and scratched internal doors are further evidence of canine presence. Anita recently told Kerry with a resigned shrug, 'What we've done, you see, is the *opposite* of one those home make-overs.'

'Our goal is to actually destroy this place,' Ian had laughed with a roll of his eyes. Although his work as a marine engineer takes him away for weeks at a time, Kerry slightly envies their marriage. ('Oh, he ticks all the boxes,' Anita, ever the pragmatist, once joked.) Whereas she'd once found Rob at his laptop at 2 a.m., sweating over his Style Tip of the Month page, Kerry can't help thinking of Ian's job as *proper work*. Not that penning *Cuckoo Clock* songs could remotely be called that, of course.

Anita takes a seat beside Kerry and pushes back a mass of light brown curls. 'A home-made cake, your gorgeous dress and blow-dry . . .' she remarks. 'Poor Rob'll think you're having an affair.'

'Probably,' Kerry agrees. 'I've even booked a restaurant for tonight – a little Thai place where we went for our first proper date.'

'You two are *so* romantic.'

'D'you think so?'

'Oh, come on, Kerry. You know much Rob adores you. He'll be bowled over by this. What are you planning for tomorrow?'

'A long lie in, hopefully. Then we'll head back here to pick up the kids about two-ish, if that's okay with you . . .'

'No rush,' Anita says firmly. 'They'll be as happy as Larry all together. Just make the most of your weekend.'

Kerry glances over to where Ruby, Anita's only daughter, has wandered into the kitchen with Mia.

'We didn't win the sandcastle competition last year,' Ruby complains. 'It wasn't fair. Ours was the best, wasn't it, Mum?'

'It was pretty impressive,' Anita says. 'Why don't you join forces with Freddie and Mia this year? I'm sure you could come up with something amazing . . .'

'D'you still go back to Shorling for that?' Kerry asks, remembering her and Anita's unsuccessful attempts to win when they were their daughters' ages.

'Yep, never miss it, even though the stakes are much higher these days. Remember when it was just plain old castles? We're talking complex architectural structures now. Last year, the winners built Buckingham Palace and even had little guards in front with fluffy black hats made from glove fingers.'

Kerry shudders. 'Good God. That must've been the parents' work, surely.'

'Of course it was,' Anita says with disdain. 'Kids barely get a look-in these days.'

38

'Can't we do it together?' demands Mia, looking hopefully at Ruby.

'Well,' Kerry says, 'if it's okay with everyone . . .'

''Course it is,' Ruby declares.

Anita laughs. 'There you go then. Team Tambini–McCoy!'

'We can plan it today,' Ruby adds, while Mia crams another cake into her mouth.

Anita turns back to Kerry and grins. 'Just like us, aren't they, when we were that age?'

Kerry nods, overcome with a wave of affection for her friend.

'*Who's* just like you?' Mia asks.

'You two,' Kerry says, smiling. 'Anita and I were your age when we first became friends, did you know that?'

Mia nods. 'Uh-huh. You were on holiday and had no one to play with . . .'

'. . . And there she was,' Kerry continues, 'this wild little girl in a grubby T-shirt and knickers with a bucket of mussels that she'd collected. Hey,' she adds, 'maybe that'll happen to you too, Mia. You'll find a best friend just like that, the way I did.'

'Ruby's my friend,' Mia says simply, taking her hand.

'Of course she is,' Anita says. 'Anyway, maybe we'd better let Mummy get off to see your daddy now?'

'I suppose I should.' Kerry gets up, quickly brushing Bess's hairs from her dress. 'Thanks so much for this – I really owe you one.'

'Don't be silly,' Anita says firmly. 'And listen, you scrub up very well, Mrs Tambini. I have a feeling Rob's in for a pretty special birthday.'

Kerry glances down at her red dress. 'I just wanted, you know . . . a big ta-daaaa moment when I walk in through that door.'

'It's ta-daaaa all right,' Anita laughs.

It takes a full ten minutes for Kerry to say her goodbyes, and Anita and all six children come out to see her off. As Kerry finally drives away, she glances at the paper carrier bag on the passenger seat, containing Rob's birthday cake in its huge, square tin. Ignoring the twinge of doubt in the pit of her stomach, she tells herself that she's doing the right thing.

Chapter Seven

Rob is slumped over the washbasin in Nadine's bathroom, breathing deeply and trying not to throw up. It's gone ten and there are two missed calls from Kerry on his mobile. How did he manage to sleep in with the traffic noise and merciless sunlight streaming in through Nadine's huge living room window? Booze, of course. Far too much of it, on a virtually empty stomach too. All he ate last night was a meagre slice of lemon cake.

The thought of Kerry having phoned, and the prospect of explaining where he's been, causes Rob to retch painfully into the washbasin. So what *did* happen last night? He has absolutely no recollection. Oh, he remembers the early part all right – being made a fuss of at Jack's, like he actually belonged in the new team, then coming back to Nadine's and her quizzing him about moving to Shorling, then . . . just a big, fuzzy blur. Surely, he tries to reassure himself, the very fact that he can't remember anything would indicate that nothing went on? God, he hopes so. He has never once felt even the faintest urge to sleep with another woman and, despite Nadine's obvious attractiveness, the very possibility that it might have been on the cards hadn't even occurred to him last night. Perhaps she'd been drunker than she appeared, and had just happened to stumble onto the sofa bed and under the covers, wrapping her naked body around his entirely by accident. After all, mistakes happen. Eddy is always regaling the office with the time he peed into a former lover's clarinet case, and how he once tried to exit a girl's bedroom via her wardrobe . . .

Rob glances up dizzily from the plughole and focuses on a glass bowl sitting on the windowsill. It contains those effervescent ball things for the bath. Mia had some in her stocking last Christmas, he recalls with a twist of acute discomfort, containing secret glitter which clung to the sides of the bath for weeks. Nadine's chalky orbs are encrusted with shrivelled petals, suggesting to Rob what his traumatised liver might look like right now.

Oddly enough, gazing steadily at the bath bombs is helping him to untangle his thoughts. By now, he's managed to convince himself that he simply fell asleep last night. Yep, he'd definitely have been too drunk to manage anything else. Thank Christ for the withering effects of alcohol on a man's ability to 'perform', as they rather cringingly describe it in *Mr Jones* (it always makes Rob think of bounding into a woman's bedroom brandishing flaming torches, followed by a naked cartwheel).

We didn't do anything, he tells himself firmly, peering at his waxy reflection in the mirror. *Even if I'd been able to, which I definitely wouldn't, part of my brain would have yelled 'Stop!'* Yet there's still the tiniest, niggling doubt, and he needs to know for sure. Could he possibly think of a way of asking her without it sounding completely insulting? 'Er, I know we had a really nice time last night, but, um . . . would you mind filling me in on the details? It's just a bit . . . hazy.' Which leads him to picturing Nadine and Eddy having a good old chortle in the office first thing on Monday morning. They *did* have a bit of snog, Rob recalls now as bile rises in his throat, but that's not the end of the world. *I only kissed her*, he imagines himself confessing to Kerry, before the saucepan clangs over his head, rendering him unconscious on the kitchen floor.

Mopping a lick of sweat from his brow with Nadine's fresh white towel, Rob considers what to do next. Hell, he's already missed that first appointment. He'd better dress quickly, hurry home and get ready to show the next lot of people round the house. That would at least make him feel purposeful, which might help to cancel out the pool of unease currently simmering away in his stomach. They're due at one, he vaguely recalls, and he needs to clear up before they arrive. Then he can head down to Shorling and carry on with his weekend as if nothing has happened. He needn't even wake Nadine. Sure, it might be a little awkward on Monday, but he'll steel himself and just be casual with her and find out the actual facts then. That's Nadine sorted, he decides, inspecting his tongue in the mirror and deciding it looks corrugated. So what about his wife? He could confess everything (not that there's anything *to* confess), but what would that achieve? Despite being apparently 'good with words', according to Eddy The Patroniser, he doubts if he could fully convey what actually happened (especially as he still can't recall the details).

'Rob?' Nadine's voice makes his heart jolt. 'Rob? You okay in there?'

'Yeah, I'm fine,' he calls in an overly-bright voice through the locked bathroom door. No way he can disappear quietly now. He clears more foul-tasting gunk from his throat and spits it into the basin.

'Want some breakfast, sweetie?'

Sweetie? Good lord . . . 'Uh, no thanks.' He shudders and splashes cold water onto his face. Then, after patting it dry, he unbolts the door.

Nadine is standing there in the cool white hallway, a tiny

lilac T-shirt flung on over a pair of little fleecy tartan shorts. She's not wearing a bra, which is distracting.

'Hey,' she says with a sleepy grin.

'Hey,' he says, focusing firmly on her face.

'Are you *really* okay?' She raises a dark brow, and the flecks of last night's eyeliner around her cornflower-blue eyes are oddly fetching.

'Well . . .' He rakes back his hair and follows her into the living room. 'Guess I overdid it a bit.'

'It was your party, you're allowed to.' She takes his hand and leads him to the sofa which has already been folded away. 'It's okay, Rob,' she adds. 'It was really nice, actually . . .'

'Was it?' he croaks.

She laughs, showing perfect white teeth. 'Yeah, it was lovely.'

'Oh.' He senses a vein pulsating in his neck.

Nadine widens her eyes. 'You don't remember, do you?'

He shakes his head. 'Er . . . I'm really sorry, Nadine, but it's all a blur. I remember us talking, and me telling you I felt weird about leaving London and all that . . .'

'And then you went on to talk about your kids who sound adorable . . .'

A tidal wave of relief crashes over him until he remembers the kiss again, which definitely *did* happen.

'But, er . . .' He frowns. 'Are you saying . . . nothing else happened?'

She chuckles softly. 'You've got nothing to worry about, Rob.'

'But we did both, um . . . spend the night on here . . .' His neck reddens as he prods the sofa.

Nadine nods. 'My fault really. You were *so* sweet, and it was so late by then, I just wanted a cuddle and you said it was okay . . .'

'So . . .' Rob's breath catches in his throat. 'That was *it*?'

She nods. 'We just had a little cuddle as friends.'

'Oh.' Rob isn't entirely sure what that means, and is even less certain that it would go down well if Kerry were to find out – but, hell, things could be a lot worse. He just cuddled (as friends) this cute, ditsy girl who's turned out to be nothing like the frosty little princess he had her down for at work. And now . . . 'God, I'd better go,' he says quickly, checking his watch.

'Got to be somewhere?'

'Yes, I'm showing some people round the house and need to get it ready . . .' His new-found decisiveness is helping to shift the terrible gloom. After all, he is forty today: he must act his age and seize control of the day.

'You've got to clean the place?' she asks.

'Well, I just like to freshen it up when people are coming.' He swallows, hoping that doesn't sound too OCD. Secretly, though, he's itching to get home and polish the taps.

'Why don't I come along and help you?' she asks brightly.

'Oh, you don't want to waste your Saturday doing that.'

'I do, honestly!' She laughs huskily. 'It might sound weird but I *love* cleaning. I like all the products – the squirty stuff for the bath, all the little wipes and dimply sponges . . .' Rob smiles, unsure of whether she's having him on or not. 'And you can't spend your birthday all by yourself,' she adds. 'That would just be *too* sad.'

'Oh, I don't mind, and anyway, I'm off down to Shorling later . . .'

'You live in Bethnal Green, don't you?' Nadine cuts in.

'Yes, but—'

'Well, I was planning on heading over that way anyway. My friend Jade lives in Hackney. She's a hypnotist. She's helping me deal with anxieties.'

'Oh . . .'

'Come on, Rob, I'll keep you company and we can whip round your house with a J cloth. It'll be so much quicker if there's two of us.'

45

Rob nods, his hangover abating slightly as he thinks: *Why not? She only wants to help, and she'll probably get bored and head off after twenty minutes.*

'Okay,' he says. 'D'you think you could get ready quickly, though? I really need to make a start.'

'Sure,' she says with a grin. 'You know what, Rob? I really think you'll sell it today. I've a feeling I'll be your lucky charm.'

Chapter Eight

A few streets away from her old London home, Kerry pulls in and stops off for provisions. She is excited now, the way she used to be on her way to meet Rob, when she'd barely be able to eat for the delicious anticipation swirling inside her. Yet a seed of doubt is niggling too. Why wasn't he at home when she and the kids called him this morning to wish him happy birthday? They'd all been poised, ready to burst into raucous song – yet the answerphone had clicked on. Although they'd sung anyway, it had felt faintly pathetic, singing to a machine. And why hadn't he answered his mobile either? He was probably busy showing people the house, she reflects, loading her wire basket with smoked salmon, bagels and a bottle of champagne. Rob takes his house-selling duties terribly seriously, having clued himself up on the type of electrical wiring system they have – stuff which Kerry feels she *should* know about, but which overcomes her with ennui. As far as she's concerned, these things only warrant attention when they stop working. She finds Rob's earnestness endearing, though. It makes her want to hold him close and reassure him that everything will be okay.

At the thought of him opening the door to her, surprised

and perhaps even gasping in delight, Kerry's heart does a little flip. This weekend is just what they need to prove they still fancy each other. With his film-star looks, Rob is hard to resist . . . but does he still fancy *her*, now she's just a pusher of chocolate breakfast cereal and songwriter for grown adults who wear rubbery bird feet?

'Special occasion?' The middle-aged man at the checkout smiles flirtatiously.

She chuckles. 'Yes, it's my husband's fortieth. I'm buying a few treats to surprise him.'

He waggles a bushy eyebrow. 'Very romantic. He's a lucky man, love.'

'Well,' she replies with a smile, 'I hope so.'

This small exchange has buoyed up Kerry to the point of simmering excitement as she bags up her purchases. Why doesn't she do this more often? Their weekends in Shorling are filled up with practical talk about estate agents and the myriad of eccentricities of their new home. Is it any wonder they're feeling a little adrift, when all they seem to do is talk about radiators and stinky drains?

Kerry carries her shopping to the car, stashes it on the back seat and sets off, passing Freddie and Mia's old primary school. Although Freddie seemed fine – he'd only been there a year – Mia had been targeted by a mini thugette who, despite being called Peace Matthews, had a fondness for hitting, kicking and pushing other children off their chairs. And when Kerry had marched into school to discuss the issue, the teachers – known as 'Lucy' and 'Jane' and seemingly incapable of raising their voices above a timid whisper – had suggested 'all getting together and having a little chat'. Which had never materialised because, apparently, Peace was 'a little stressed at the moment'. So she bloody should be, Kerry thought furiously, when she'd picked up Mia with a ripped sweater and a graze on her cheek. (By then, she had added 'great schools' to her mental list of Reasons to Say Yes to Aunt Maisie's Unmissable Offer).

Their old terraced house is in sight now, pretty enough with its wooden external shutters and glossy black door, freshly painted by Rob to create a good first impression. The living room light is on, as it usually is, even during the day – without it, it's cave-like in there. This is her first visit back since the move, and Kerry is relieved to notice an absence of longing. Remembering Peace Matthews has made her absolutely certain they've done the right thing.

As luck would have it, there's a parking space outside the house. Kerry unloads her bags and stands at the front door. Would bounding straight in be more dramatic (the *ta-daaaa!* moment she's hoped for)? Or would it be better to knock instead, so Rob thinks it's just a delivery or one of those Jehovah's Witnesses who patrol this street from time to time? Unable to suppress the smile twitching at her lips, she gives the polished brass knocker a firm rap.

At first, there's nothing. Maybe Rob's upstairs, Kerry muses, showing people the bedrooms. Or perhaps he's on the loo.

'Come on, Rob,' she mutters under her breath, rapping the knocker again.

This time, she hears a voice inside. It's a girl – an undeniably young and rather posh-sounding girl whose voice Kerry doesn't recognise.

'Someone at the door!' the voice trills. 'Shall I get it?'

Something tightens in Kerry's chest, and she frowns at a lump of gloss paint on the door. No, she must have misheard. Perhaps it had come from next door . . .

'Robbie, want me to get that, babe?'

Robbie? *Babe?* Kerry has barely processed these words as the door opens. And she's no longer aware of her pinchy shoes or the carrier bag handles digging into her fingers

49

because a girl is there – a girl with short dark hair and red lips, tipping her head to one side.

'Can I help you?' she says in a breathy voice as a wild thought courses through Kerry's brain: *I've come to the wrong bloody house. Jesus. Writing those* Cuckoo Clock *songs has sent me mad . . .*

The girl is still looking expectantly at her when Rob appears – sorry, *Robbie, babe* – babbling, 'Kerry, hi! This is, um, Nadine . . .' His eyebrows shoot up, and he and Nadine step back into the house as Kerry follows them wordlessly in. 'A friend from work . . .' Rob is explaining, raking his hair with his fingers. 'Came over to help me spruce the place up . . .' Kerry sees him glance down at her flesh-pinching shoes.

'Really?' She frowns and places her bags carefully on the floor. This girl, this *Nadine*, is wearing a figure-hugging vest top and the tiniest denim cut-offs Kerry has ever seen – they'd barely fit one of Mia's Barbies – and looks about nineteen. 'What's going on, Rob?' she asks coolly, trying to cut out the girl from her vision.

'Nothing, I told you, she's just helping.' Rob clamps his mouth shut, and Nadine shoots him an alarmed look, as if expecting instructions on what to do now.

'You make it sound as if you've been living in squalor,' Kerry remarks. He's lying, she knows it; Rob cleans the cooker hob daily and replaces his toothbrush if so much as one bristle flares out.

'The place was looking a bit unloved,' he mutters. 'People are coming round, I've already missed the first lot—'

'Why?'

'Uh?'

'How come you missed them?'

'Er, I was just out . . . just popped out for a few minutes . . .'

'Really? Where did you pop out *to*?'

His dark eyes meet hers imploringly. 'Okay,' he says, exhaling forcefully. 'It was a big night last night. The guys at work had put on a bit of a party for me and I had too much to drink. Crashed out at Nadine's place because it was handy . . .' His bottom lip twitches as he tails off.

Kerry glances at Nadine, then back at Rob. 'So why didn't you just say that?'

'I knew what you'd think,' he mutters.

'We were just chatting, Kerry,' Nadine offers, her voice rising to even breathier heights. 'There was a whole gang of us from the office. It was just an impromptu get-together, a bit of a laugh, you should have been there . . .' She smiles nervously, then glances at the living room window as if considering launching herself through it.

'And then,' Rob cuts in, clearly getting into his stride now, 'Nadine said she'd come over and help me do some, uh, scrubbing . . . didn't you?' He turns to her and she nods over-enthusiastically.

'Yeah! Er, anyway, I think I'd better go. Really nice to meet you, Kerry.' Nadine flashes a wide, fake smile and hurriedly lets herself out.

'Um . . . bye,' Rob mutters to the floor.

'So,' Kerry says flatly when she's gone. 'What the fuck was all that about?'

Rob reddens. 'Nothing. I told you, she was just *helping*.'

Feeling ridiculous now in her dress and shoes, with her make-up carefully applied and that black lacy bra and French knickers underneath, Kerry wills herself not to cry.

'Don't insult me,' she gulps. 'It's absolutely obvious what's going on . . .'

'Oh, so I can't have female friends, is that it?' Rob barks. 'D'you know how hard it's been for me at work since Eddy and the new lot arrived, how stressed I've been about the move and the possibility of losing my job and—'

'Poor darling,' she snaps.

'Stop being like this!'

'Being like what, Rob? Do you *know* what I was, just ten minutes ago when I was buying champagne? Excited, that's what . . .' She gives the carrier bag containing the bottle a fierce kick. 'And I was excited putting on my red dress and heels—'

'You look lovely,' he blurts out. 'Very, er . . . done up.'

'Done up? What does *that* mean?'

'No, no . . . I mean nice. You look, er . . . sexy.'

'Really?' she barks. 'You know what *you* look? Post-bloody-coital . . .'

He shakes his head and rubs his hands across his face. 'That's ridiculous.'

'Is it?' she rages. 'Just tell me, Rob. Did you sleep with her?'

'Of course not!' he cries. 'God, Kerry, I can't believe you'd think—'

'Oh,' she cuts in, 'and I made you *this* . . .' She bends down to snatch the cake tin from its bag and whips off the lid.

'Er, that's . . . lovely. You're great at, um, icing . . .' He winces involuntarily.

'Don't bloody patronise me, Rob, after you've spent the entire night with a girl who must be half your age. Don't think you can make it all right by telling me what a great *icer* I am . . .'

'Kerry, please—'

'Happy birthday,' she snaps, accompanied by a gulping sob, the words ROBERTO TAMBINI THIS IS YOUR CAKE! mocking her now as she finds herself lifting the sponge from its tin. The tin falls to the wooden floor with a clang, and now Kerry is gripping the huge, squishy confection with both hands, registering her neatly-applied red nail polish for a second before the cake starts to fly, almost gracefully, in a strange sort of slow motion, hitting Rob squarely in the chest.

'For God's sake!' He looks down in horror.

She eyes him coldly. 'Oh, is that your Paul Smith T-shirt?'

'I don't care about the sodding T-shirt.' He stares at her, open-mouthed. The collapsed mound of sponge lies at his feet like a scene from a child's birthday party gone horribly wrong.

'Bye, Rob,' Kerry says, feeling eerily calm now. 'Enjoy the rest of your birthday.'

'You're not going, are you? This is mad, you've gone *insane* . . .' Kerry is aware of Rob saying her name over and over as she marches out to the street and climbs into her car.

'Kerry,' he mouths through the window as she turns on the ignition. Fixing her gaze determinedly ahead, she indicates and pulls away, revving violently and ignoring the angry toot from a black cab behind her. Glancing back just once, she sees her husband – deputy editor of the *Thinking Man's Monthly* – distraught on the pavement with chocolate ganache icing splattered across his chest.

'Stick that on your Style Tip of the Month page,' she yells as she drives away.

Chapter Nine

One week later

'*Why* can't we have a dog?' Freddie is standing, hands on hips, in nothing but a rather shrunken looking banana-yellow T-shirt.

'There are lots of reasons,' Kerry replies, assembling the picnic for when Anita arrives to whisk them all off to the beach. Thank God for her life-saving friend, offering to take all six children to the sandcastle competition, and allowing Kerry a precious couple of hours for a Private Talk with Rob.

'What reasons?' Freddie asks.

'Freddie, *please* put some pants on. We don't have much time . . .' She frowns at the food laid out on the table. Although Kerry won't be there, she feels it's important to raise her game in the picnic stakes; hence the big tub of strawberries, the sliced peaches and nectarines and the home-made brownies dusted with icing sugar. There are egg mayonnaise sandwiches too, made from rough-hewn brown bread instead of the usual white sliced which her children prefer. Could she get away with sneaking in a bunch of those peelable processed cheeses which the kids love?

Making no move to acquaint himself with pants, Freddie

stuffs a strawberry into his mouth. 'What reasons, Mummy?' he asks again.

'Time, for one thing,' she says briskly, packing the picnic into the hamper. 'Dogs take a huge amount of time and effort. We'd have to walk him at least twice a day, *and* train him, and I don't know anything about how to do that . . .'

'I do! You say "Good boy" and give him a biscuit.' He grins and reaches for a brownie.

'Leave the food *alone*, Freddie. It's for later. Anyway, there are loads of other reasons, like the vet's bills and all the medicines dogs need . . .' He frowns and prods at his genitals.

'Please stop playing with your willy.'

'Why?'

'Because you're poking about with the food, it's not very nice . . .' She glances up at the kitchen clock, a sense of dread pooling in her stomach as she realises that Rob is probably half-way to Shorling by now. Kerry has been so intent on maintaining a cheery demeanour in front of the children all week, she's barely had a chance to figure out how she feels about last Saturday's incident, and whether she's still furious with him for spending the night with a teenager. Actually, she's tried not to think about it too much – been in denial, probably. Which she suspects is terribly unhealthy and has probably triggered the start of an ulcer. Yet, even if he and Nadine *didn't* do it, as he has vehemently claimed during their terse phone conversations, she has to admit that it's still Not Right. In fact, the thought of being alone with her husband makes her feel quite nauseous.

Reluctantly, Freddie snatches a pair of pants from the radiator and pulls them on. 'Everyone else has a dog,' he mutters, reaching for his beloved black and orange tracksuit that's strewn over the back of a chair.

'You can't wear that tracksuit,' Kerry barks.

'Why not?'

'Because . . . because it's too hot out there. You'll be all sweaty and uncomfortable, *and* it needs a wash . . .'

'It's *fine*, Mum.' He rolls his eyes, already pulling the wretched thing on. As Mia appears, brandishing her carefully drawn design for a potentially prize-winning sand sculpture – 'That's fantastic, darling,' Kerry says distractedly – she realises she doesn't have the energy to cajole him out of it. Anyway, at least he's dressed.

'You didn't look at it, Mummy,' Mia huffs.

'I did! It's amazing. You've put so much thought and work into it . . .'

Mia scowls and slams her drawing onto the table. The jeans she's wearing finish at her ankles, Kerry notices, and her once purple T-shirt has faded to a chalky mauve. Is it worth trying to persuade her to change? Probably not. With the picnic packed, and a bag of towels, plus numerous buckets and spades in readiness by the door, Kerry checks the time again. Anita is due any minute now. As soon as she and the kids are all safely installed in the competition area of the beach, Kerry will hurry off to meet Rob in Hattie's, a chintzy tearoom at the far end of the seafront.

'Auntie Anita's got Bess,' Freddie reminds her as she grabs a big plastic bottle to fill with diluted orange. She realises that the other children will probably have little cartons of organic apple juice, but it's too late to worry about that now.

'Yes, well, that doesn't mean we have to have one, does it?'

'But I want one! You said if I was a good boy and I *am* a good boy . . .' He gives the elasticated waist of his tracksuit bottoms a fierce twang.

'We'd never be bored if we had a dog, Mummy,' Mia chips in. 'We'd always have someone to talk to and be our friend.'

Something twists in Kerry's stomach, and she busies

herself by swilling out the bowl she'd used to make the egg mayonnaise.

'But you do have people to talk to, sweetheart,' she murmurs. 'You have me and Daddy and all your old friends in London, and you'll soon make new ones here . . .'

'I won't,' Freddie says.

'Why not?' Kerry asks. 'What about those nice boys we were chatting to on the beach yesterday?'

'*They* had a dog . . .'

'Yes, Freddie, but not everyone—'

'I don't *want* new friends,' he barks at her. 'I ONLY WANT A DOG.' At which the doorbell pings, and Kerry almost weeps with relief as she rushes to greet Anita and her children at the door.

As she hugs her friend, amidst hugs and excitable chatter about multi-turreted sandcastles, she clearly hears Freddie muttering away in the kitchen.

'I hate egg,' he announces. 'It stinks and Mummy does too.'

Chapter Ten

Here she comes, Rob notes with a surge of relief, as Kerry crosses the road towards the tearoom where he's spent the last twenty minutes waiting for her. It's a breezy, early September afternoon, and she looks . . . *normal*, he's pleased to see, in jeans and a plain navy T-shirt – not that he didn't like her in that red dress and heels. Actually, no, he *hated* the red dress and heels because the image of her all done up is intermingled with the horror of her throwing that cake at him.

Kerry pushes open the teashop's glass door and marches straight for his table.

'Sorry I'm late,' she says briskly, dropping her bag onto the floor and plonking herself on the spindly wooden chair opposite him. Her face is slightly flushed and make-up free, her long dark hair tied back in a ponytail with a few stray strands poking out.

'That's okay,' he says, resisting the urge to reach straight for her hand. He can already detect a chilly vibe, which he'd expected, and is determined to do whatever it takes to put things right. This past week has been terrible. While he's managed to scrape through five interminable days at the office – relieved that Nadine has been perfectly friendly,

58

but not *overly*-friendly – he's missed the children dreadfully, and been unable to quell the persistent sense of dread that he's utterly screwed up his marriage. He's been unable to sleep, and trying to write his first sex column for *Mr Jones* caused him untold grief. He sat up for hours in bed with his laptop, trying to dredge up something to write about foreplay 'with a punchy edge', when all he could think about was his wife yelling and him ending up splattered in chocolate frosting. In desperation, he'd rattled out a column about using food during sex. (It was sprinkled with phrases like 'tasty treats' and 'finger-licking good'; the days of lengthy essays about classic Hitchcock movies were clearly long gone).

'Just an Americano please,' Kerry tells the waitress. 'You having another, Rob?' She eyes him coolly.

'Um, no thanks.' He glances at his cup of lukewarm coffee, knowing that a refill will make his nerves jangle even more alarmingly than they are now. The waitress glides away and a tense silence descends. 'So, er . . . are the kids okay?' Rob asks tentatively.

'Yes, Anita's with them on the beach.'

He nods. 'That's good of her. Um, but I actually meant, how have they been these past few days?'

Kerry smiles her thanks as the waitress places her coffee on the table. 'They're fine. They don't realise anything's happened, of course. Anyway, you've still spoken to them every evening.'

'Yeah, I know. I've just been . . .' He looks around, wishing she'd agreed to meet at the house, as he'd suggested, rather than in a cafe in the kind of town where you can't paint your front door without it being trumpeted on the front page of the *Shorling Advertiser*. 'I've been worried about them,' he adds, taken aback by the intensity of Kerry's green eyes. 'Anyway, thanks for agreeing to see me.'

'Of course I'd see you,' she says tersely. 'And the kids'll

be pleased to have some time with you later, especially with you being *ill* last weekend . . .'

This is what Kerry had told them: that a dreadful cold had caused him to stay in London last weekend, instead of seeing them on his birthday as planned. 'Don't make me feel worse than I do already,' he murmurs.

'Well, they were a bit put out that they couldn't give you the cards they'd made, and now you've got get well cards waiting for you too. Your correspondence is starting to stack up.'

Get well cards. God. The thought of Freddie and Mia busying away with their felt tips crushes something inside him.

'What else could I do?' she asks. 'I couldn't tell them what happened, could I?'

'Kerry,' he hisses, relieved that the other customers seem too engrossed in their own conversations to be listening in, 'I told you, it was nothing.'

Her eyes narrow. 'I still think it's weird. Why didn't you say straight away that you'd spent the night at her place?'

'Because I knew you'd blow it up out of all proportion . . .' A tall, statuesque blonde has wafted into the tearoom, and Rob's heart slumps as she smiles in recognition. Her blondeness is a little brassier than the usual refined Shorling look, her jeans a tad on the tight side and her patterned top daringly low-cut. She is clutching the hand of a small child with a tangle of light brown hair that would really benefit from a little involvement with a hairbrush.

'Hi,' the woman says with a big, bold smile, right up at their table now. 'I think I've seen you at Maisie Cartwright's house, haven't I?' She turns to her child. 'Remember you chatted to those nice children over the wall, darling?'

'Yes, that's us,' Kerry says warmly when the child fails to respond. 'I'm sure I've seen you too . . .'

'That's our favourite part of the beach,' the woman explains, 'right across from your house. I'm Brigid, by the way . . .'

'I'm Kerry, this is Rob . . .' Her chilly demeanour has evaporated. How do women do this, he marvels, switching on a smile so easily as the occasion demands?

'Not joining in with the sandcastle competition today?' Kerry asks the child pleasantly.

'Nah.'

'We decided to boycott it,' Brigid laughs. 'It's not really for the children anymore. It's just an opportunity for parents to show off.'

'Oh, I know,' Kerry agrees. 'It's ridiculous really . . .'

Please leave, Rob urges her silently. *My wife and I are busy trying to repair our marriage.*

'So how are you both settling in?' Brigid wants to know.

'Oh, we're loving it,' Kerry replies. As the women chatter on, Rob glances from Kerry to Brigid, wondering when they might run out of idle chit-chat.

'I saw your ad for piano lessons,' Brigid goes on while Rob clamps his back teeth together. 'How's that going?'

'I've had a few calls. Hopefully things'll start picking up once the children are back in school . . .'

'Bet you'll be inundated.' Brigid looks down at her sullen offspring. 'Would you like piano lessons, hon?'

'Nah.' There's a fierce shake of the head.

'Oh.' Brigid guffaws. 'Well, that's that then. Worth trying, I guess. Anyway, we'll leave you two lovebirds in peace.' With another huge grin, Brigid ushers her child of indeterminate gender towards two chrome stools at the high table by the window.

Now, Rob realises, it'll be impossible for him and Kerry to talk properly. Brigid and her ill-mannered kid are within earshot – in fact, the child keeps throwing him startled glances as if he might have something terrible growing out of his nose – and the companionable chatter from the other customers has died down to a murmur.

'Is that a boy or a girl?' he whispers to Kerry.

'A boy of course,' she hisses back. 'His name's Joe.'

'It's just, with that messy long hair . . .'

'Oh, for God's sake.' She exhales loudly. 'Lots of children have hair like that these days.'

Rob stirs his cold coffee, wondering how to steer the conversation towards the matter in hand.

'Anyway,' Kerry adds, 'the sandcastle competition finishes at around three. We should probably make our way down there soon.'

'But we've just got here,' he exclaims, feeling helpless.

'Well, maybe we should get there for the judging. They were planning to make this 3D treasure map. Mia's been drawing a plan and cutting out lots of little flags which she stuck onto toothpicks . . .'

Kerry's talking too fast, Rob decides. It's as if the faint staleness of a decade-long marriage has merged with the awkwardness of a terrible first date. The effect is hugely unsettling, and although Rob is trying to appear riveted, he couldn't give a damn about little toothpick flags right now. Clearly, she wants to get out of this tearoom – and away from him – as quickly as possible.

While Kerry rattles on, Rob tries to mentally transmit to Brigid that she and her snotty-nosed child must leave the cafe this instant because he *needs to talk to his wife.* He glances at his watch: half two already. Joe is now amusing himself by ripping open paper sachets of sugar and sprinkling their contents onto their table.

Glancing over, Brigid notices Rob's irritated glare. 'He's exploring texture,' she explains with an indulgent smile as Joe flicks a pile of sugar onto the floor.

'Oh, right.' He laughs hollowly.

'Well, I hope they win,' Kerry says.

Rob frowns. 'Sorry?'

'The kids. Haven't you been listening, Rob? I said I hope they win the contest . . .'

'Er, Kerry . . .' Rob begins, distracted again as Joe swipes his mother's teaspoon and drips coffee onto the sugary piles. What's he doing now – exploring how to make a bloody great mess?

'Oh, God, Joe,' Brigid cries. 'We'll have to go, you're meant to be at Oliver's party . . .' She rolls her eyes. 'Anyway, Kerry, we must get our boys together to play sometime.' With a big flashy smile, Brigid grabs Joe's hand as they clatter out of the cafe.

'I can't stand that,' Rob mutters as a sense of stillness descends.

'Stand what?' Kerry asks.

'*That*. Kids throwing sugar everywhere, mothers pretending they're engaged in some valuable learning experience when all they're really doing is being bloody infuriating . . .'

She laughs and shakes her head, and he senses the tension dispelling a little. 'God, Rob, when did you become such an angry old man?'

'Hey, less of the old . . .'

'Anyway,' she continues, 'ours aren't perfect either, remember. But yes, I know what you mean. Brigid seems nice, though, and I really need to get to know some people around here. I wish they were all as friendly as she is . . .'

'Kerry,' Rob butts in, reaching for her hand across the table. 'Let's . . . let's forget all this. Can we do that, please?'

She slides her hand out from under his. 'Last weekend, you mean?'

Rob nods. 'I know how it looked . . .'

'Oh yes, your friendly little cleaning lady.'

'. . . I want us to move on from this because we have to decide what to do.'

Kerry blinks at him. 'What d'you mean?'

'Er . . .' He plucks a sugar sachet from the bowl, accidentally rips it and quickly puts it back. 'The estate agent called me yesterday. That couple, the ones who came round to see the house after the, er . . .'

'What, last Saturday?'

'Yes, them. Well, they'd needed a few days to talk it over and they've decided they want it.'

'They've put in an offer?' Kerry asks, eyes widening.

'Yes.' He glances around the tearoom; even the fridge seems to have fallen silent now. 'The asking price too,' he adds.

'Really? Wow, that's great . . .'

Rob looks at his wife, thinking how lovely she looks today with her glossy dark hair pulled back and those few strands dancing prettily around her face. She looks relieved, too, about the London house. Rob is trying to seem pleased, but he also owes it to Kerry to be absolutely honest. He pauses, wondering how best to put it, knowing he must get it absolutely right.

Chapter Eleven

Around the corner from Hattie's, tucked away on a quiet cobbled side street, a new upmarket sandwich shop is struggling to survive. James Delaney, who's helping his son to get the place in order, was up this morning at 6.35 a.m. He's already walked his dog, Buddy, along Shorling beach, forced six-foot-three Luke out of bed and sliced a mountain of prosciutto, tomatoes and Emmental. He has also apologised numerous times for the fact that they don't have any rocket today. Luke messed up the greengrocer's order (again) so, while he held the fort, James raced around town, amassing as many acceptable lettuce varieties as he could manage. Although he failed to locate rocket, he did track down lollo rosso, butterhead, cos and lamb's lettuce – how many leaf varieties do people actually need? What would customers do if presented with plain old iceberg – burst into tears or attack him? It's one of the things that drives James mad about Shorling these days: this utter wankery about food. Which is unfortunate, really, as Luke's business idea – to set up a sandwich shop to out-posh all the others – was built upon the new residents' adoration of fine cheeses and hams nestling between organic sourdough.

With the main lunchtime period over – the term 'rush'

would be over-stating things – James pulls off his navy blue and white striped apron. Hanging it beside the enormous string of garlic behind the counter, he heads for the door of the shop. 'Just popping home,' he says.

'Okay, Dad,' Luke replies.

'I'll only be half an hour. Maybe you could clear the decks a bit, set out some more smoked salmon, chuck some lemon and black pepper over it . . .'

'Uh?'

'Pepper, Luke,' James says with exaggerated patience. 'You do know how to operate a pepper grinder. It's that twisty gadget with the little black things in.'

'Sure, Dad,' Luke says with an amiable smile. James blinks at his son, exasperated, yet unable to feel irritated with him for long. Luke is a handsome, stubbly-chinned boy who, while not wildly academic, has the knack of charming the pants off girls and money out of his wealthy friends' parents' bank accounts (hence being able to set up his own business at twenty-two years old). James can't help admiring his entrepreneurial streak; the way he managed to write a business plan, design the shop and amass the funds, when he'd felt sure the whole idea would come to nothing. Unfortunately, though, Shorling residents and day-trippers haven't gone mad for fillet steak with baby spinach and grilled artichoke hearts. Maybe, James reflects as he strides down the narrow street, it's just too much. After all, there's nothing much wrong with a plain cheese sandwich and a packet of crisps. He and Luke are virtually living off unsold food, their fridge crammed with leftovers. James has started waking up at night, nauseous after a supper of smoked trout, stilton and figs.

It also became apparent that, while Luke has never lacked enthusiasm, he needed someone with him in the shop to keep things running smoothly. As he can't afford to pay one of his floppy-haired friends, James saw no option but to step in, cramming his own freelance website design work into the evenings to get things on track. 'Just a few weeks,' he'd told Luke. 'Six at the most. Then you're on your own.' However, they both know that James will never leave Luke in the lurch.

James is back home now, and lets himself into the neat redbrick house with the not-so-neat dangly gutter, making a mental note to get it fixed.

'Hey, boy,' he says as Buddy charges towards him. 'Been on your own too long, huh? C'mon, just a quick walk . . .'

He clips on the lead, catching sight of himself in the small mirror in the hallway. God, he needs a haircut. He likes it short, no-nonsense, and before his involvement with Luke's (after much debate, his son decided the simplest option was to name the shop after himself), James would have regular trims at the old-fashioned Turkish barber's. Lately, though, such non-essentials have slipped off the radar. And, although he's glad to escape from the shop for a while, he's beginning to wonder if looking after Buddy is something he could do without too. Luke's on-off girlfriend Charlotte used to undertake dog-walking duties, but the status is definitely 'off' at the moment.

James sets off with Buddy pulling hard on the lead, panting and straining towards a dropped ice cream cone on the pavement. He barks suddenly at an elderly man on a mobility scooter, and James has to quickly haul him away before he pees against a bucket of fresh blooms outside the florist's. A woman with a wiry grey terrier – impeccably behaved – glares at him as she struts by. 'Should get him some training,' she mutters.

Oh, really? James wants to call after her. *Don't think I haven't tried that. We've even seen a behavioural expert – a dog psychologist – who diagnosed severe anxiety caused by trauma. He wasn't like this before my wife left, you know. Buddy was very much Amy's dog but, weirdly enough, she wasn't too keen on taking him when she moved up to Sheffield with her hairdresser – sorry, colourist . . . Said Brian 'isn't good with animals'.* Oh, really? James wasn't particularly 'good' with being dumped without warning either, but he'd had to deal with that.

Halting his racing thoughts – the tutting woman has long since disappeared – James takes a short cut through the alley towards the beach. While Buddy stops to investigate a damp patch on the pavement, James glances at the glass-covered noticeboard on the newsagent's wall. *Sandwich Express*, he reads. *Bespoke buffets delivered to your workplace. Contact Gary for a slice of the action.* Hmmm. Should he and Luke start a delivery service? It seems over-ambitious seeing as they're struggling to keep the shop afloat, but every little helps.

Buddy is pulling again now and starts barking sharply, startling a passing teenager on a bike who gives James a two-fingered salute. Since Amy's departure, Buddy has become fearful of cyclists, motorbikes and lorries – most vehicles, come to think of it. Despite the fact that he's gripping Buddy's lead, James hopes that, if he keeps staring ahead, any passers-by will assume that this dog has nothing whatsoever to do with him. He fixes his gaze on the newsagent's ads. Most are offering boats for sale, holiday cottages to let, and essential services such as chakra realignment and 'a full feng-shui survey to breathe life into your home'. Then a small white postcard catches his eye: *Piano Tuition.*

There's a burst of laughter from down on the shore. The beach is packed with children, he realises; must be the annual sandcastle competition, which Luke won with an impressive marble run construction when he was seven or eight (he'd been able to charm a whole horde of people to help him, even back then).

James turns back to the noticeboard.

All levels, abilities and musical styles – in your own home or in my music room in Shorling. Whether you wish to work towards ABRSM exams, or learn to play purely for fun, call qualified tutor Kerry Tambini on 07776 456 896.

He smiles. A little hobby to slot in is the last thing he needs, but still . . .

Without considering what he's doing, James slips the loop of Buddy's lead over the bollard at the end of the alley and delves into his jacket pocket. He's forgotten his phone, but he does have a crumpled shopping list scrawled on a paper napkin. He pulls out the tiniest stub of a pencil and scribbles down the number, thinking how mad it is, assuming he'd be capable of learning anything new at forty-three years old. Anyway, hadn't he planned to sell Amy's piano, seeing as she clearly doesn't want that either?

Another barking outburst interrupts his thoughts as Buddy starts leaping wildly, clearly furious at being tied up. The sight of a small dog across the street – one of those poochy creatures with a bow at its fringe – has sent him into a frenzy. James hurriedly lifts his lead off the bollard, simultaneously making apologetic gestures to the dog's owner in her prim floral dress while snapping, 'That's *enough*, Buddy. Calm down.' Shooting him a furious look, the woman scoops up her quivering pet, as if fearful that Buddy might savage it. About to explain that he's just nervous, defensive, or whatever you want to call it, James momentarily loses concentration, enabling Buddy to break free from his grasp and charge across the road in a blur of black and white fur, red leather lead flying behind him. The woman shrinks back in fear, but Buddy is no longer interested in her yapping hound. He's now pelting down towards the beach with a cursing James in pursuit.

To his horror, Buddy is heading straight for the sandcastle competition, paying no heed to the fact that most of these structures have clearly required weeks of careful planning and complex architectural plans.

'Buddy!' James cries, carefully stepping around what looks like a scale model of the Sagrada Família with wet sand dribbled over its majestic spires. 'Come here *right now*.'

Buddy stops for a moment, investigating the remains of a picnic spread out on a rainbow-striped blanket. A bearded man who might have stepped out of the Toast catalogue shoos him away, and a bunch of children yell in protest as Buddy scampers over a mound of sand with little flags stuck all over it, like some kind of gigantic pin cushion.

'It's ridiculous!' someone cries. 'That dog's out of control.'

'Sorry, sorry, sorry,' James mutters as he tears after his dog, who has now cocked his leg against the judges' trestle table for a hasty pee before continuing his explorations of the beach.

'Could the owner of this dog *please* remove him from the area,' a male voice booms over the PA system. 'A Beach Buddy has already been informed . . .'

Ah, the illustrious BBs, jumped-up volunteers in lilac T-shirts who appear out of thin air on the rare occasion that someone dares to stub out a fag in the sand. They don't take kindly to dogs venturing into the wrong zone – as James has been reminded on several occasions by a zealous-dad type with a shiny 'BB' button badge, who clearly derived great pleasure from having the authority to tell people off.

At least Buddy has left the competition now, and is prancing delightedly in the shallow waves. James marches towards him, not realising that the paper napkin with the piano teacher's number has fluttered away behind him and is being carried away by the light breeze. By the time he's marched Buddy back to the promenade, wondering if 3 p.m. is too early for strong alcohol, he has forgotten that he even wrote it down.

Chapter Twelve

Kerry had always assumed that a mid-life crisis involves the purchase of an enormous motorbike and ill-advised leather trousers. But now she thinks maybe they're more complicated than that. More like a forty-year-old man gets monumentally pissed with younger colleagues, stays over at the flat of some little princess, then announces that perhaps moving to the south coast wasn't such a great idea after all, despite being one hundred percent certain that blissful day with the kite. And that now he's had time to 'really think things through', and despite the fact that they have an offer on the house, maybe they should hang onto their London home for a while longer, as a sort of . . . 'base'.

'What d'you mean, a "base"?' Kerry asks. She and Rob have left the tearoom and are waiting at the pedestrian crossing to cross the road to the beach.

'Just . . . somewhere I'd stay,' Rob says, 'one or two nights a week instead of commuting every day, until we're sure about selling it.'

'But I thought we *were* certain,' she points out. 'I seem to remember you saying, "Let's do it, tell Maisie we want to go ahead."' She looks at him expectantly, baffled by this new development. 'And now you're completely backtracking,' she adds. 'I don't know what the hell's going on with you, Rob.'

For some reason, Kerry is finding it hard to breathe. Aware that in just a few minutes she'll be required to be all perky and smiley in front of hordes of mothers at the sandcastle competition, she exhales fiercely and starts to cross the road.

'I've just been mulling things over,' Rob says, hurrying to keep up with her.

'Well, I don't see how we can afford to run two homes – not with your job being so precarious and me just starting freelancing. We've got to buy Maisie's place sometime. We can't expect to live rent-free forever.'

Rob presses his lips together as they reach a group of shiny blonde teenage girls dressed in skimpy shorts and Abercrombie sweatshirts, talking in loud, braying voices.

'Anyway, when you say you want a "base",' Kerry adds as they make their way along the seafront, 'do you mean a shag pad?'

'Of course I don't mean that. For God's sake, that's ridiculous.'

'So why would you need it, unless this thing with Nadine—'

'There's no *thing*,' he snaps. 'I thought I'd finally managed to get that across to you . . .'

She glares at him, wishing she wasn't obliged to spend another moment in his company. 'Why d'you want to keep the house, then?'

'I'm just trying to think practically,' he mutters. 'It *is* quite a schlep every day . . .'

Kerry throws him a baffled look. 'But you said you'd be fine with the train, and you can always stay over with Simon or Phil if there's something on after work . . .'

'I . . . I just think,' Rob starts, 'maybe we're being a bit

72

hasty in selling it. It all feels a bit sudden, that's all. Maybe we'd be better renting it out instead?'

'I wish you'd have the courage to admit you're having cold feet about moving,' she replies bitterly.

'No, I'm not. I just think . . . this might be a more sensible option, for us not to burn our bridges, you know? You've said yourself how you haven't managed to make any friends yet, and I was thinking, perhaps that's why last Saturday happened. I'm not making excuses, but maybe I'm not quite ready to make a complete break, and that's why I went out and drank too much and crashed out at Nadine's like a fucking idiot. Maybe it's just been building up and I needed to let it all out . . .'

'*What* did you need to let out?' Kerry barks. 'Your sperm?'

The woman in the creperie kiosk stares at them, brandishing her spatula in mid-air.

'I can't talk to you when you're being like this,' Rob hisses, quickening his pace. 'That's really going to help us settle in around here, isn't it, shouting about sperm in public?'

'Well, *you* obviously don't want to settle in, so what does it matter?'

'Kerry, listen to me.' He grabs her arm and they stop and glare at each other. 'Just forget what I said about the house. Let's accept the offer – I'll ring the agent first thing on Monday, okay? And once I've done that, can we please just forget this whole thing?'

She focuses hard on his handsome face, which looks as tired and stressed today as it had during the early parenting years when sleep was snatched in hour-long segments. Kerry inhales, feeling her anger fading slightly and deciding she has to get over this. Rob is far too prim and proper for a one-night stand; in all their years together, she has never seen him even flirting with anyone. As for the house cleaning incident – *Cif-gate*, as she and Anita have named it – Nadine

73

is probably nurturing some mild, Daddy-type crush on Rob, and insisted on tagging along. A woman would have to strip naked and launch herself, missile-like, at Rob for him to realise she found him attractive. 'Come on,' she says coolly, shrugging away his hand. 'They'll all be waiting for us at the beach.'

Spotting his parents treading gingerly between the sand constructions, Freddie leaps up and waves frantically.

'It got run over!' he yells.

'What did?' Kerry hurries towards Anita and the children.

Anita pulls a wry smile. 'Well, Sand Island looked great until a dog ran right across the top of it.'

'Oh *no*.' Kerry frowns at the collapsed mound, its tooth-pick flags scattered everywhere. Daniel, Anita's youngest, has burst into tears, and Anita pulls him onto her lap.

'I'm sure it doesn't matter,' Kerry tries to console him. 'The judges probably looked at the sandcastles before the dog came—'

'No they didn't,' Freddie thunders.

'Dogs shouldn't be running about loose on the beach,' Rob declares.

'Oh, I'm sure it wasn't deliberate,' Anita explains. 'Some guy was chasing it, it must have got loose . . .'

'Then it was his responsibility to keep it under control,' Rob huffs as Kerry and Anita exchange glances.

'My mummy won't let us have a dog,' Freddie bleats loudly to anyone within earshot.

Sitting beside Kerry on Anita's tartan rug, Rob takes Kerry's hand in his and squeezes it. 'Quite right, Mummy,' he whispers with a smile.

The tinkle of a brass bell from the judges' table calls everyone to attention.

'After that unfortunate little incident,' announces an elderly lady, her gold-rimmed glasses glinting in the weak sunshine, 'it's time to announce the winners of the annual Shorling sandcastle competition. Everyone ready?'

'Yeah!' Freddie yells. Kerry removes her hand from Rob's slightly clammy grasp.

'Okay. It's been a tough decision but, in third place, I'm delighted to announce . . . Team Tyler-Jones for their fabulous Hogwarts!'

'Boring,' chime Freddie and Anita's boy Jacob.

'Shush, Freddie,' Rob hisses.

The judge tinkles her bell again. 'Second prize . . . Team Marshall's amazing Eiffel Tower!'

'Show-offs,' Anita whispers with a grin. 'Their dad did the whole thing anyway, barking orders at his children like Hitler in a yachting cap.'

Kerry snorts with laughter, sensing the tensions of the past, miserable week starting to drift away, despite the fact that Freddie appears to be the only child here in a tracksuit.

'And first prize . . . Team Crawly-Jones and their amazing replica of the Sagrada Família . . .'

Mia's face droops. 'What's a Farm-ear?'

'Just some old church,' Kerry murmurs.

'I wouldn't quite put it that way,' guffaws the yachting cap man. 'I think you'll find it's Gaudí's architectural masterpiece although, granted, there's been controversy over the more contemporary aspects of the restoration . . .' He smiles smugly and pops a shiny black olive into his mouth.

'Has there really?' Kerry asks, feigning wonderment as the woman at the judges' table calls the assembled crowd to attention.

'Everyone?' she calls out. 'We just had a quick chat among ourselves and decided to award a very special prize to the team who put in so much effort, only to have it all destroyed . . .'

Mia and Freddie gawp at their mother expectantly.

'. . . Team Tambini-McCoy with their treasure island – at least that's what we *think* it was before the unfortunate event – so if the children would like to come forward . . .' All six surge towards the judges' table, their rowdiness garnering the odd look of disdain as they return, delighted, with their booty.

Admittedly it's just an ice cream token each, but Rob is dispatched to the old-fashioned red and white striped kiosk with the children dancing around him as if they've scooped a major prize.

Anita stretches out her slender honey-tanned legs on the blanket. 'So . . .?' she says when Rob is out of earshot. 'How did it go?'

Kerry pulls off her canvas plimsoles and digs her toes into the warm sand. 'Okay, I guess. He's still adamant that nothing happened.'

'Which is feasible . . .'

'Yes.'

The small pause is filled with the blur of children playing, and there's a palpable sense of relief among the kids now the competition is over. Kerry glances at her oldest friend, the one who made all those summers in Shorling so special, and to whom she'd write excitable letters in multi-coloured felt tips during the long months until her next stay at Aunt Maisie's. When Kerry turned seventeen, her parents had been filled with a new sense of adventure, perhaps relieved that they no longer felt obliged to take their only child back to Shorling every summer. Her father bought an ugly beige campervan – nothing so stylish as a VW camper – and he and her mum took to trundling around France while Kerry started holidaying with friends. The year it had happened – the motorway crash just south of Bordeaux – Kerry and Anita had been in a rowdy resort in Crete. As the red sports car had cut up the campervan, and Kerry's dad had braked suddenly, veering into the forest below, Kerry and Anita were probably downing fierce cocktails in the Banana Moon bar. What if Anita hadn't suggested the trip, and Kerry had gone on holiday with her parents instead? She still plays the 'what if?' game occasionally.

'Kerry?' Anita says gently.

'Uh-huh?'

She indicates the small crowd clamouring around the ice cream kiosk. 'Look at poor Rob. The kids are probably confusing the hell out of him. Imagine, having to remember *six* ice cream flavours all at once.' They laugh as, surrounded by children, he throws up his hands in mock surrender. 'You do believe him, don't you?' Anita adds.

Kerry nods. 'Yes, I suppose I do. I've only been here a month, but maybe I've already lost touch with the real world, you know? I mean, the fact that people make friends in the office and go out after work. It's all perfectly normal, isn't it? You socialise with the other teachers . . .'

'Yes, of course I do.'

'Though you don't have sleepovers.'

'Er, no.' Anita gives her a wry smile. 'No one would dare. You wouldn't believe what staffroom gossip is like.'

Kerry chuckles. 'It's different for Rob. He's had an awful time since his new editor arrived, and I think he just had to let off a bit of steam.'

'We all need to do that sometimes,' Anita says.

Rob and the children are heading back towards them now, the two girls charging ahead of the pack.

'I still can't believe what I did to him, though,' Kerry says, shaking her head.

'God, I know,' Anita laughs. 'What a bloody great waste of a cake.'

Chapter Thirteen

Jack's, three weeks later

Jack's might be thronging on a Friday night, but on a rainy Monday evening at the start of October it's an entirely different story. Nadine, who's been pleasant enough since Rob spent the night at her place, had hung around in the office after everyone else had left.

'Not like you to work late,' Rob had remarked, which had come out sounding ruder than he'd intended.

'Are you implying I'm a slacker?' she'd responded with an arch of her brow.

'Of course not,' he'd replied quickly, before adding, 'You okay, Nadine? You seem a bit fed-up today.' She didn't seem to be working, at least not on anything obvious. She was just sitting at her desk, rearranging her novelty pens with the fluorescent gonks on their ends and flicking idly through the latest issue of *Mr Jones*. Then she'd closed the magazine, and her eyes had met his across the office.

'Um, actually I'm *not* okay, Rob,' she'd said. 'D'you have time for a quick drink?'

So here they are – even Nadine is a member of Jack's, it transpires – with Rob waiting to be served in the basement bar. At a quarter to seven, they are the only customers in the place. Apart from Theresa with her clipboard on the door, there's no sign of any staff either.

Standing at the elegant, curved bar, Rob glances back at their table and wills someone to materialise and serve him. He's only planning to stay for a quick one, just to be nice; he'll hear her woes (she really does look miserable now, all pale and hunched in the corner) then get home sharpish. In fact he isn't entirely comfortable about being in a drinking establishment with Nadine at all, not after last time. He's managed to smooth things over with Kerry by the skin of his teeth. He's accepted the Ramsays' offer on the house and, after making an utter arse of himself, now feels ready to embrace that new life on the coast.

Ah, there are signs of life from the nether regions of Jack's. From a back room emerges the stunning red-head who'd presented him with his birthday cake, and he waits for her to recognise him.

'Yeah?' she says blankly.

'Er, a Kronenbourg and a tomato juice please.' Weird drink, a tomato juice. No pleasure in it as far as he can work out. It probably has negligible calories, though, which is clearly high on Nadine's agenda. Come to think of it, he isn't entirely sure she actually eats. Maybe she gleans her nutrition from the garnishes in drinks.

'Here you go.' The red-head places the drinks on the bar – Nadine's has a sliver of celery stuck in it – and takes his money without thanks or any hint of being human. Perhaps she's an android, Rob reflects as he carries the drinks back to the table. Or maybe there's a secret rule that over-thirties aren't supposed to be in here.

'So,' he says, taking the seat opposite Nadine.

She pulls a tight smile.

'Everything all right?'

'Like I said, not really.' She twizzles the straw in her drink.

'Er . . . is it something to do with Eddy?'

'What?' She looks aghast.

'I mean . . .' Rob scratches his chin, relieved that the red-head has disappeared into the back room again. 'I just wondered if it was something to do with work, if you were worried about—'

'I'm not *worried*, Rob,' she says sharply.

'Oh! Well, that's good. You shouldn't be. I know you're only the editorial assistant but—'

'*Only* the editorial assistant?' she repeats.

Shit, this is hard work. He'd give anything to be down in Shorling now, snuggled up with Kerry and the kids, watching a movie together.

'What I mean is,' he explains, 'you're just starting out and I know things are a bit shaky in the company at the moment. But Eddy's obviously really happy with you and I'm sure your job's secure . . .'

Nadine purses her lips and shifts in the plush red seat. 'Well, I am worried but it's not about work.'

'So what's—'

'I'm *pregnant*, Rob.'

'Are you? God!' He emits a strange combination of gasp and laugh and glances down briefly at her stomach, which appears to be frying pan flat, then back up at her face. Her expression has settled into one of extreme distaste, as if a terrible odour is drifting up from her glass. 'That's er . . . amazing,' he adds. 'That's really incredible news. Wow!'

Nadine blinks slowly. 'Yes, that's what I thought too.'

Rob bites his lip, wondering why she's selected him, alone, to share her news. 'I didn't even know you had a boyfriend,' he adds, regretting it instantly: since when was Nadine's love life any of his business?

'I don't,' she says.

'Well,' he says with a stilted laugh, 'I might be ancient but as far as I remember it does take two people to make a baby.' Nadine looks down at her drink and stirs it unnecessarily. Poor girl, he muses. It was obviously a one-night stand, and maybe the heartless git has left her in the lurch. 'Um,' he goes on, 'are you sure you really are pregnant and it's not just a false alarm?'

I did the test at the end of last week,' she replies flatly, 'and I've thought of nothing else all weekend.'

'Of course,' he says, relaxing a little and quickly deciding that the role of sympathetic older, wiser colleague is the one to adopt. 'It's a huge thing, Nadine. I mean . . . you're only twenty, aren't you? It's a big, big change. If you ever want to talk, or grab a coffee or something . . .'

She raises her brows in mock amusement. 'To talk about what, Rob?'

'Uh, the pregnancy, having a baby . . .' He shrugs lamely.

'You've had a lot of experience of that, have you?'

Jesus, he thinks, there's no need to be like that, to keep arching those brows in such a, such an . . . *arched* manner. He's only trying to be a friend, when he could be at home packing up the last bits and pieces.

'I know my kids are older now,' he says huffily, 'but I can just about remember the baby stage.'

'Oh, right.' Her voice wavers and her eyes mist, causing Rob to place a hand over hers on the table without even thinking about it. 'You mean,' she croaks, 'you can give me some tips on nappies and feeding and burping and all that. Yeah, that'd be great, Rob. Cheers . . .'

'Nadine,' he murmurs, shaking his head, 'are you sure you actually want to go ahead with this?'

'Of course I do, Rob. It's my *baby*. God.'

I only bloody asked, he thinks bitterly. 'It'll be okay,' he adds quietly.

'Will it? How d'you know?'

'I . . . I'm sure you'll be fine. It's just the shock, that's all. Like you said, you've only just found out . . .' He keeps his hand on hers, feeling strangely protective of this poor, accidentally pregnant girl. Imagine, though, having a baby at twenty years old. It doesn't bear thinking about . . .

Nadine slides her hand out from under his. 'That depends,' she says.

He frowns. 'On what?'

'On you.'

'I don't understand . . .' Something shifts in him then, and he senses the lighter, happier mood of the past four weeks dispersing into the slightly stale air of Jack's basement bar.

Nadine gives her tomato juice another stir and looks up at him. 'It's yours, Rob,' she says. 'It's *your* baby.'

Chapter Fourteen

James lifts a tray of unsold rare breed pork and leek sausages from the oven and flips them onto two plates.

'I've arranged to have another three hundred flyers printed,' Luke tells his father as they sit down at the kitchen table to eat.

'We can't afford printing costs at the moment,' James reminds him. 'Remember, we're only just managing to meet the suppliers' bills.'

'Yeah, I know. I had a chat with Marcus's dad and he's going to run them off for us for free.'

James grins as Luke picks up the new squeezy ketchup bottle and shakes it ineffectually over his sausages and mash. 'How did you manage that, then?'

'Just explained that we need to raise our profile, and as we can't afford to advertise the next best thing is to distribute flyers in all the right shops. They'll be on thick, matt card and I've put a special taster offer on, too.' He pauses and frowns at the apparently malfunctioning sauce bottle.

'Yes, I understand the theory,' James says, 'and it's great – but how do you manage this?'

'Manage what?'

'To persuade people to do things for you for free.'

Luke laughs. 'Just my natural charm, I guess. Anyway, there's nothing wrong with what we're offering, Dad. It's the location, I think. Too tucked away. I know we couldn't afford the seafront but we need to work harder to let people know we exist.'

James nods thoughtfully. 'You're probably right, and I think the flyers are a great idea. Here, give me that bottle.' Taking it from him, James removes its top, peels off the foil seal and replaces the stopper. 'There. Think you can manage now?'

'Oh, thanks, Dad.' With a smirk, Luke squirts ketchup noisily all over his plate and proceeds to shovel in his dinner with enthusiastic chomps and slurps. Christ, James thinks, he's capable of thinking creatively and blagging all kinds of favours and freebies, but he still needs his dad to open a new sauce bottle. And he eats like he's at a trough in a farmyard, not at a kitchen table – yet is capable of engaging in extremely noisy sex under this very roof.

James blinks down at a bowl of leftover potato salad, trying to forget the terrible rumpus he heard last night, signalling that Luke and Charlotte had got back together. He should be happy for his son – he suspects that Luke is deeply in love with her – but, like buffalo copulating or people being cut open in hospital, he doesn't feel it necessary to be subjected to every gruesome, sick-making detail.

Although James likes to think he's a reasonably modern man, he couldn't help thinking: *What would Amy make of this?* She adored her only child, coddling him like a delicate egg. (James isn't quite sure what a coddled egg is, but it's surely not dissimilar to a younger Luke who was still having his fish fingers cut up into dainty pieces at ten years old). But she's been out of their lives for two years now – Luke was so aghast that he's shunned all attempts at contact – and James is left with the task of trying to ease his transition into being a capable grown-up man. Sure, he's full of ideas and enthusiasm. It's the practicalities – like remembering to order butter and clean the meat slicer – that he's not so hot on.

Pushing his plate aside, James glances down at Buddy, taking a few seconds to register the rich odour which is beginning to permeate the kitchen. It definitely isn't sausage or potato salad and, as far as James is aware, nothing is rotting in the bin.

'Look, Dad,' Luke exclaims, jabbing his fork in the direction of the cooker. There, sitting in front of it, is a large turd.

'I don't bloody believe it.' James leaps up, sending his chair clattering backwards, at which Buddy scoots out of the kitchen.

'That's disgusting,' Luke observes as his father clears it up. 'Why did he do that?'

'Because he needed to go,' James snaps.

'Did he?'

James stomps out to the back garden, drops the carrier bag-wrapped gift into the bin and marches back inside. 'Luke,' he says sternly, 'we had an agreement, right? I do the morning and lunchtime walks and you do the evening—'

'We wouldn't have to,' Luke interrupts, 'if you put up a higher fence that he couldn't jump over. Then he could just have a little wander about in the garden.' Ah yes – another of Buddy's newly-developed quirks. For years, he had pottered about happily on the lawn, without showing any desire to escape.

'I don't exactly have time to build another fence right now, Luke.' James frowns at his son, wondering if he plans to place his dirty plate and cutlery in the dishwasher or – the favoured tactic – expects them to spirit themselves into the appliance all on their own.

To avoid the issue, he wanders through to the living room and sinks into the sofa, overcome by a wave of exhaustion.

He starts to flick through the newspapers he brought home from the shop. It had been Luke's idea to add two small tables by the window, plus a rack of newspapers, to encourage customers to linger over a coffee and snack. So far, they've been the only ones to read them.

'Dad . . .' Luke has appeared in the doorway. 'I was just thinking, maybe we should take Buddy to a trainer again.'

James looks up at him. 'Remember what they said last time? That he seemed to have trouble grasping basic commands. That was a polite way of saying he's a hopeless case.'

'What'll we do then?'

James studies the handsome young man who turns heads every time he saunters through town. Luke has inherited his grey eyes, but Amy's striking cheekbones and long, rangy build.

'Um . . . what would you think if we found him another home?' he asks hesitantly.

There's a beat's silence as Luke studies his fingernails. 'I'd feel bad but . . .'

'Yeah, I know. Me too.'

'I mean, I love him,' Luke adds, 'and he's a great dog, but . . .'

Buddy trots into the room and arranges himself comfortably at James's feet. 'I just don't think he gets enough attention from us two,' he says, reaching down to tickle behind his ears. 'Maybe that's the real problem. He's playing up because he's lonely.'

Luke nods sadly. 'He was Mum's dog really, wasn't he?'

James starts to speak, horrified that his eyes have started to water.

'Hey, Dad.' Luke lands beside him on the sofa and puts an arm around his shoulders. 'Maybe it's the best thing to do.'

'You really think so?'

Luke's phone bleeps with an incoming text, but he has

the decency to ignore it. 'Yeah. Sometimes I reckon Buddy doesn't really like us very much.'

'We're too male for him,' James suggests.

'God knows what it is. If we advertised him, though, would we mention him being scared of everything and occasionally crapping on the floor?'

James musters a weak smile, enjoying just being here with his son, and Buddy lying at their feet. 'I think,' he says carefully, 'we might just keep those little details to ourselves.'

Chapter Fifteen

It's a bleak, wet Tuesday and Rob has called in sick. He never throws a sickie, and he despises those who do, such as fashion editor Ava who had the audacity last week to claim she'd 'caught something' the morning after she'd been to the lavish PR party she'd spent all afternoon getting ready for. Eddy doesn't seem to mind skivers. Perhaps that's all part of the new 'dynamic' attitude: being so 'out there' that sometimes you can't be arsed to go to work.

This morning, though, Rob couldn't face the office so he called in, feigning a migraine. Which was true, sort of. The terrible reality – that Nadine says she's having his baby – is creating a terrible tension around his frontal lobe, as if his brain is in danger of bursting out of his skull. And now, hell, Kerry is phoning his mobile.

'Hi,' he croaks, digging a fingernail into the well-worn corduroy sofa.

'Hi, hon, sorry to call you at work, hoped you'd be on your lunch break—'

'Is everything okay?' It's his knee-jerk reaction. Any time Kerry calls during the day, he fears that one of his children is being stitched back together at A&E.

'Yes, it's fine, it's just . . . I know this sounds stupid, but

I've just been out for a walk to clear my head. Been working on those *Cuckoo Clock* songs all morning . . .'

Nadine's having my baby rings loud and clear between his ears.

'. . . Anyway,' Kerry continues, 'I spotted this ad on the noticeboard at the newsagent's and . . . God, you're going to think I've gone stark raving mad . . .'

A baby. A real live baby. So what's it to be – suicide by downing the entire contents of the bathroom cabinet? As far as he can recall there's only some ancient Sudocrem and a mangled tube of Anusol in there . . .

'I just think it might be good for us,' Kerry continues, sounding slightly breathless as if she's walking at a brisk pace. 'I know we're okay here but . . . I don't know . . . it feels like there's something missing, Rob. Well, *you*, obviously . . .' She chuckles. 'God, we can't wait till you're here, you know. Only a couple of weeks to go now . . .'

'Yeah,' he says dully.

'Why don't you just move down properly next weekend? You could hire a van, couldn't you, and get Simon to help? I mean, it's not as if there's anything to stay for now, and the kids miss you so much . . .'

'I miss them too,' he says, feeling as if he might cry.

'Anyway,' Kerry continues, 'that's not what I called about. I just wanted to tell you . . .'

Rob is incapable of tuning in to what she's saying. He is replaying what Nadine told him in Jack's last night: 'Maybe I should have been honest and told you we'd had sex. But you're a lovely, decent guy and I knew you'd feel terrible about Kerry . . . I just didn't want to put you through that stress . . .'

'So what d'you think?' Kerry asks.

He grips the phone. 'About what?'

'Rob, have you been listening to me at all?'

He's sweating now, his entire head tensing as if being

slowly crushed by some kind of enormous clamp. 'Sorry, Kerry, just got a few things on my mind . . .'

She lets out an exasperated sigh. 'That's okay, you're at the office, you should have said instead of letting me prattle on. All I was saying was—'

'I'm not at work actually. I'm at home, not feeling very well . . .'

'Oh, what's wrong?' Her sympathetic tone makes his insides twist with shame.

'Just . . . a migraine.'

'Aw, never had one of those before, have you?' *No, and I've never had a twenty-year-old who I barely know suddenly announcing she's having my child . . .*

'No, I don't think so.'

'Taken anything for it?'

'Er, just paracetamol.'

'You could probably do with something stronger.' *Yes, too bloody right, like something to render me unconscious for a very long time, perhaps until the blessed release of death . . .* 'Anyway,' she adds perkily, 'all I was saying is, I've just seen an ad for a dog that some guy wants to rehome – family-friendly, lovely with people and other dogs, sounds perfect. There's a photo of him and he looks adorable – a big, shaggy, cuddly thing. And I thought, seeing as I'm based at home now, and considering the kids are struggling to make friends . . .' She pauses. 'I think,' she adds softly, 'they deserve it.'

'I, er, dunno,' Rob mutters.

'You mean you don't think it's a good idea?'

He tries to clear his parched throat. 'I, um, don't see the point . . .'

'Of course there's a point! He'd be *theirs*, they could learn how to look after him. Animals are good for children, everyone knows that . . .'

'No, I know there's a *point* to dogs, if you're blind or in the police force or need drugs sniffing out but—'

Kerry bursts out laughing. 'You're mad, Rob. But yes, dogs can be useful, which just shows how intelligent and easily trainable they are.'

'Kerry, I . . .'

'Think how excited they'd be!' she cuts in. 'Oh, I know that picking up poo with the little black bag isn't hugely appealing but I'm sure we'd get used to it. It's probably like baby poo. You know how changing other people's babies' nappies is completely disgusting?' *God, can't she tell there's something terribly wrong here? How can she go on and on like this as if everything's normal?* ' . . . But your own – well, that's different. When it's come out of someone you love, it sort of loses its disgustingness, doesn't it? Isn't that weird, Rob, don't you think?'

Not half as weird as me allegedly making a girl pregnant and having absolutely no recollection of doing it . . .

'Not that I'm saying it'll be like having another baby,' Kerry laughs, clearly oblivious to his pain. 'I suspect it'll be a *tinier* bit easier than that. Like, there's no weaning or night waking, hopefully, or strangers marching up to you and telling you he should have a hat on or a warmer jacket . . .'

Stop it, stop it, stop it. Please stop talking about babies . . .

'D'you remember all that?' Kerry asks fondly. 'You'd come home from work and I'd be ranting on about some woman in the park who'd told me to put brandy in Mia's bottle.'

'Er, yeah . . .'

'And you were *really* helpful,' she sniggers. 'You said, just tell them to fuck off.'

'Er, Kerry, I really need to talk—'

'So, listen, shall I phone that guy from the ad?'

'Which ad?'

'The dog one! Oh, go on, let's do it . . .' She pauses, and he can tell she's smiling. There are faint street noises in the background and he pictures her green eyes shining, her dark hair blowing messily in the breeze. Tears spill onto his cheeks and he quickly wipes them away. 'If we do,' Kerry adds, 'let's make it a surprise and not say anything until the dog's actually here. You won't tell them, will you?'

'No . . .'

'God, I'm so excited! Oh, Rob . . . this just feels right, you know? *Everything* feels right. I've had a few enquiries from my ad, did I tell you? I just need to spruce up the music room, then I can start booking some pupils in.'

'Er, that's great.'

'Well, it all feels positive anyway.' She pauses for breath. 'It's still lonely here without you but soon we'll all be back together, a proper family . . .' She tails off, but this time Rob can't respond. 'Sorry, sweetheart,' she adds. 'I'm ranting on and you're stuck at home with a horrible migraine. I'll shut up now and let you get some rest . . .'

'Okay,' he says dully.

'And Rob, I love you, you know that, don't you?'

He opens his mouth, but more tears are falling and all he can do is make a strange, puppy-like yelp.

'Rob? Are you okay?'

He clears his throat, his face now utterly wet as he says, 'Kerry, I'm so sorry. There's something you have to know.'

Chapter Sixteen

They say grief comes in stages. Maybe it does, if it's the kind associated with running out of eye cream or scuffing the toe of a favourite shoe. Not a husband saying, *I know how this sounds but I promise you I can't remember a thing . . . yes, it does seem impossible but it has happened before – er, yes, with you . . . Only once or twice during the early days when we'd been out and come home drunk – no, of course I didn't admit it, you'd have been horrified . . .*

And that had been that. Thirteen years together melted away in an instant, like candyfloss on a tongue. As for the 'stages' – anger, grief, depression in whichever order they're supposed to come – Kerry hasn't had time for anything so orderly. The rest of yesterday had passed in a blur (she was too blown away to even cry). Rob had called twice more, sobbing inconsolably and begging to drive down and see her; she'd had no option but to cut him off mid-flow. After collecting the children from school, she'd spent an hour on the phone to Anita, and the rest of the evening had been spent Acting Normal in front of the children. It was only later in bed that she'd allowed herself to cry – and, once she'd started, she'd feared that she might never be able to stop. And now, at 8.10 a.m. on a grey Wednesday morning,

93

Kerry must continue to behave as if nothing untoward has happened. Her marriage may be over but she must still brush hair, put out juice and cereal and locate gym shoes and playtime snacks deemed acceptable at Shorling Primary (e.g. little pouches of dried apricots from the wholefood store; crisps, it would appear, are regarded as the devil's work).

The landline rings and, without thinking, she grabs it. 'It's me,' Rob croaks.

'What d'you want?'

'I need to talk to you . . .' His voice is thick and hoarse, as if he's been up all night.

Kerry blinks rapidly. 'I can't, not now . . .'

'Please listen to me,' he implores her. 'Okay, it happened, but you have to believe that I can't remember anything—'

'Does that mean it doesn't count?' she snaps.

'No, of course it does, I didn't mean . . .'

'Mummy, who's on the phone?' Mia demands from the breakfast table. '*What* doesn't count?'

Kerry rubs her eyes and growls, 'I've got to go,' before abruptly ending the call.

'Was that Daddy?' Mia asks, grinning.

'Yes, darling.'

'Why did he phone?' Freddie wants to know.

'Oh . . . he just wanted to check something . . .'

'Why didn't he want to speak to me?' Mia tosses her spoon into her empty cereal bowl.

Kerry blinks slowly. 'He was in a rush, sweetie.'

Mia nods, apparently satisfied with this. 'Remember it's the feast today, Mummy.'

'What feast?' Kerry asks, hoping her pink, swollen eyes will continue to pass unnoticed.

'The *feast*. I need my stuff, Mum. It said in that letter.'

'What letter?' Kerry chooses to ignore the fact that Freddie has picked up his bowl and is noisily slurping chocolate-tinged milk.

'That letter from school,' Mia says with a roll of her eyes. Ah, yes, Kerry vaguely remembers now. How remiss of her to allow torturous thoughts of her husband having energetic sex with a girl who was born in something like 1992 – she's not even old enough to remember Britpop, for God's sake – to take precedence over preparing for Miss Pettifer's Egyptian banquet. Now, as she focuses hard, she vaguely recalls Mia's teacher's request for the kind of delicacies people would have enjoyed four thousand years ago, but she's darned if she can remember what they are. The letter doesn't appear to be lurking in the teetering pile of unattended-to mail on top of the microwave. Nor is it hiding in what Mia has christened the 'everything drawer' which, although they've only lived here for six weeks, is already jammed with take-away menus, matted hairbrushes and any random small item which has yet to be allocated a proper home.

'We'll have to forget about it,' Kerry says briskly. 'I'm sure everyone else will bring lots of things to share. I'll write a note to Miss Pettifer saying I'm sorry but I totally forgot.'

Mia stares at her, aghast. 'You *can't* do that.'

'Why not?'

'I'll be the only one!' Mia's mouth crumples and her dark eyes fill with tears.

'Darling . . .' Kerry puts an arm around her daughter but is abruptly shrugged off. 'I'm really sorry but it's quarter past eight and there isn't time to get anything together.'

'No one'll let me share,' Mia cries. 'They're not my friends . . .'

'What makes you think that, hon?'

'They're just not!' she shouts. 'I've *got* to take something. We can buy stuff on the way to school . . .'

'We could,' Kerry says, feeling helpless, 'but we don't know what to buy.'

'Stuff the Egyptians liked,' Freddie offers helpfully.

'I know, Freddie, but I don't know *what* they liked.'

'Why not?' He throws her a disdainful look.

Because, sweethearts, your father has made someone else pregnant. Although I know that's a shoddy excuse and, if I were a proper mother with one of those hyper-efficient maternal brains, I'd still be able to locate a typical menu from a pharaohs' feast . . .

'I can't remember,' she says, feeling horribly close to crying herself. The landline rings again; Kerry lifts the receiver and bangs it straight back down again.

'Google it then,' Mia commands.

Kerry tries to blink away the moisture that keeps blurring her vision. She thought she'd been doing so well today, breezing through the morning routine as if nothing untoward had happened. Now she's hastily Googling 'Egyptian food' but all she can find is a theme restaurant called Cleopatra's in nearby Sandhead where it appears that the waitresses wear gold crocheted headdresses.

Now Mia and Freddie are both looming over her as she scowls at an image of Lamb Koftas – 'poos on sticks', Freddie announces delightedly – on her laptop. With the best will in the world, these cannot be knocked together in the thirteen minutes before they must leave for school. Kerry flicks through other options: rice-stuffed pigeon. Yoghurt pudding with fried onions and a puddle of chicken broth. Honey and cinnamon pie . . .

'You could take a jar of honey,' she announces. 'I read that someone discovered some from Ancient Egyptian times and it was still fine to eat . . .'

Mia shudders. 'No, ew, it'd be dirty.'

'No, *ours* wasn't dug up. It's from the Co-op. But it'll still taste just like the kind they used to have—'

Mia shakes her head. 'Don't wanna take honey.'

'What about fruit then? They must've had fruit . . .' But

when she Googles 'Egyptian fruit', all that pops up are Egyptian fruit bats for sale, £250 for a breeding pair.

'Look, Mummy,' Mia exclaims, jabbing the screen. 'Figs.'

Kerry sighs. 'If you moan about the apricots I give you for playtime, then I don't think you'll like figs.'

'That's 'cause those apricots are brown,' she retorts. *Yes, angel, because they're from the hideously expensive whole-food store, i.e. sulphur dioxide-free, which is more important, apparently, than them being a prettier shade of orange . . .*

'Are you crying, Mummy?' Freddie asks with interest.

'No, I've just got something in my eye.' She pulls a fake smile and rubs her leaking eyes on the sleeve of her top.

'Figs are nice,' Mia says levelly. 'We had 'em at Nanny and Nonno's with ham.'

Ah, Rob's foodie parents who have always been unswervingly kind to their grandchildren, and almost like a surrogate mum and dad to Kerry. What will *they* make of the impregnation when he dares to tell them?

'So,' Mia says, having perked up now, 'can we go to the fruit shop?'

'Not at half-eight in the morning, no. Sorry, love. Come on now, you two – shoes on. We've got to go *now*.' Amidst protests, Kerry switches off her laptop, crams small feet into shoes, hooks schoolbags onto their backs and grabs lunchboxes. She ushers them out and bangs the front door shut, realising that Freddie's school trousers have a smear of mud on one leg but it's too late to do anything about it now. Mia continues to protest, and Freddie refuses to hold Kerry's hand as they cross the road.

'Everyone else'll have stuff,' Mia grumbles, dragging her feet.

'Yes, and I'm sure Miss Pettifer will make sure it's all shared out . . .'

'No, she won't.'

'Why d'you say that? You were telling me yesterday how kind she is . . .'

'I hate it here!' Mia announces, stopping in her tracks. 'I *hate* it. I want to see Daddy and I want to go back to London.'

'Mia, please . . .' Her daughter's eyes flood with tears, and Kerry bobs down to hug her tightly. 'Come on, darling. You've been so good about moving . . .'

'WHY CAN'T I HAVE FIGS?' she roars, pulling away from Kerry, her cheeks flaming. Kerry stands there, feeling as if she's been punched in the stomach.

'Mia,' she mutters, 'please stop this . . .'

'It's not fair! I told you about the feast . . .'

Yes, and quite a lot has happened since then . . . A few metres ahead, a couple of mothers – each with an immaculate daughter – have turned back for a gawp, because not much happens in a genteel seaside town. (Kerry has noticed this: the way people stop and gaze when something of mild interest occurs, like a car exhaust backfiring or a plane flying overhead). Grabbing Mia and Freddie's hands, she marches onwards, past the staring women – one auburn, one pale blonde, both wearing what would be termed 'fun skirts' in the Boden catalogue.

'Did you hear that?' one of the women hisses. 'I can hardly believe it. That little girl was yelling for *fags*.'

Kerry turns to face them. 'No, she wasn't. She's seven years old. She said *figs*, for the Egyptian feast at school.'

'Oh!' At least the auburn-haired one has the decency to blush. 'Sorry, I didn't mean . . .'

'It's okay,' Kerry says tersely.

'That's Mia, Mummy,' the woman's daughter announces. 'She's in my class.'

'Hi, Audrey-Jane,' Mia says shyly. 'Hi, Tabitha.' The blonde woman's daughter grins, showing missing front teeth.

The auburn mother musters a smile. 'Er, I'm Lara, this is Emily . . .'

98

'Kerry.'

'Nice to meet you, Kerry,' Lara says rather coolly, as if still unconvinced over the fags issue.

'You've moved into Maisie Cartwright's house, haven't you?' Emily asks. Christ, does everyone know everything around here?

'That's right, she's my aunt actually. She's moved to Spain . . .'

'So I heard. Is she enjoying it?'

Kerry casts her mind to the postcard she received this morning which she could hardly bear to read: *I'm so happy that you, Rob and the children will be living in the cottage. I hope you have many happy years there . . .* 'Um, yes, she seems to be.'

'Lucky woman,' Emily says with a prim smile as they all start marching briskly towards school. 'So, how are you settling in?'

'Oh, we're doing fine, thank you,' Kerry says blithely.

'My mummy forgot the Egyptian feast,' Mia murmurs to Audrey-Jane.

'God, so did I,' Emily exclaims.

'Me too,' adds Lara, seemingly unconcerned, 'but I'm not sure about food-sharing in the classroom anyway. I mean, you can't be sure where everything's come from . . .' She winces at Kerry as if expecting her to agree, and the two friends fall into a discussion about various crimes against nutrition. Diluted cordial at the school Christmas party, fun-sized Mars Bars hidden during the Easter egg hunt . . . that's the thing about living somewhere like this, Kerry realises. Everything's so damned policed. You have those Beach Buddies, scanning the shoreline for so much as a discarded ice lolly stick, and mothers checking each other out as their ravenous children surge through the school gates at home time to be handed punnets of cherries and bottles of water.

As they turn into a side street, Kerry glances at the chalk-board propped up outside a sandwich shop. *Char-grilled mozzarella and figs on lightly-toasted walnut sourdough . . .*

'Figs!' she blurts out. 'Look – FIGS!'

'Sorry?' Lara gives her a quizzical look.

'Figs! They have figs here, *and* they're open . . .' And that's not all. *Manchego cheese with dates and Serrano ham . . .* 'Are dates Egyptian, Mia?'

'Er, I think so. I don't like 'em . . .'

'It doesn't matter what you *like*,' Kerry says quickly. 'Oh, and look, they do chargrilled chicken with spinach and honey and pomegranate dressing . . .'

'The Egyptians had pomegranates,' Tabitha exclaims as Kerry marches into the shop.

The gangly, dark-haired boy behind the counter couldn't be sweeter, allowing her to buy an array of fruits and seeming unperturbed by the fact that she doesn't require them to be turned into a sandwich.

'You've just saved my life,' she says, clutching the bulging brown paper bag.

'Any time,' he says grinning.

'Well, thanks again. I'm so glad I spotted your shop. I hadn't even noticed it until today.'

Outside, she shows Lara and Emily her purchases. 'Well, that was very slick,' Lara remarks, 'but now we're late and you know what Miss Pettifer's like if they miss the bell.'

Be like that then, Kerry muses as they march onwards in a tense, stony-faced group. *Pour scorn upon my Egyptian offerings that I managed to pull together less than twenty-four hours after my marriage went tits up.*

*

Perhaps, Kerry surmises later, she *has* managed to pull off a small feat today, and not just for the school banquet. She has, after all, survived the first morning after Rob's announcement. She may have shed a few tears but she hasn't lain weeping with the children stepping over her in a puddle of gin on the kitchen floor. And when Anita arrives that evening, having driven down to Shorling straight after work, Kerry has already decided that, somehow, she'll find a way through this thing that's exploded in her face.

'He's the last person I'd have thought would do this,' Anita declares, sipping tea in Kerry's kitchen.

Kerry nods. 'I know. Nice, reliable, respectable Rob – maybe it serves me right for being so complacent.'

'But it's insane, Kerry. It's as if he went mad that night. You don't think he's ever done anything like this before, do you?'

'No,' Kerry says firmly. 'I really don't . . .'

'And . . .' Anita pauses. 'I don't suppose you can forgive him?'

'How can I possibly when she's pregnant?'

'But . . .' Anita pauses. 'What if she's lying and it's not his?'

Kerry rubs her hands across her face as the sound of *The Bare Necessities* drifts through from the living room. 'The thing is, it *could* be, and he's certainly assuming it is.'

'Why, though? He can't even remember it happening. She might have made the whole thing up. Maybe they didn't even do it—'

'Oh, he's got a history of being unable to remember whether he did it or not,' Kerry cuts in bitterly. 'Said it happened with me.'

Anita frowns. 'Like some kind of blackout thing, you mean?'

Kerry nods miserably, the tears flowing unchecked now as Anita envelops her in a hug.

'I'd want to kill him,' her friend murmurs. 'I can't believe the stupid sod has done this . . .'

101

'Me too, and you know what the worst thing is right now – the thing I'm most dreading?'

'Yes,' Anita says softly. 'How you're going to tell the kids.'

And so later that evening, bolstered by Anita's mercy dash, Kerry sits with Freddie and Mia on Freddie's bed. 'Listen,' she begins, resting the storybook on her lap, 'you know Daddy's been staying in London these past few weeks?'

Mia nods while Freddie investigates his left ear with a finger. 'Yeah. Read the story,' he commands.

'In a minute, darling. It's just . . .'

'Are you getting revorced?' he cuts in.

'Why d'you ask that?' Kerry's heart judders.

'Tom's mum and dad are getting revorced. He told me at school. He's gonna have *two* bedrooms.'

'Oh,' Kerry says as Mia throws her a startled look. 'Well, er, the word's actually *divorced*, honey, and I don't know. I mean, yes, maybe . . .' Her children's dark eyes are upon her, radiating alarm. 'Daddy-has-a-new-girlfriend-they're-having-a-baby,' she blurts out in a rush.

There's a startled silence. 'They made a baby?' Mia exclaims.

'Um, yes.'

'How?' demands Freddie.

'They just . . .' She clears her throat. 'They just did, like we made you.'

'With kissing?' Freddie asks.

'Er, I expect so, yes . . .' Kerry is aware of Mia snuggling closer and wrapping her arms around her.

'Is Daddy gonna live with the new baby,' she whispers, 'and not us?'

'I don't know, darling,' she says, pulling both of them close. 'We'll have to see.' Silence seems to fill the small room with its jumble of books and games piled messily onto shelves. Kerry can't even hear the sea.

'I know what men and ladies do,' Freddie says, brightening. 'They take their clothes off and bounce on the bed.'

Mia glares at him, then up at her mother. 'No they don't. It's seeds and eggs. I read it in a book.'

'That's right, sweetie. It was in that bodies book I gave you.'

'Daddy did that,' Mia adds, turning to her brother. 'His seed met her egg.'

Freddie frowns. 'Where?'

'In London,' she says knowledgeably.

'In . . . in her body actually,' Kerry says firmly.

'Whose body?' Freddie asks.

'His girlfriend's. She's, um . . . called Nadine.'

Cupping a hand over her mouth, Mia leans in to whisper into Freddie's ear, making him dissolve into giggles. 'What's that, Freddie?' Kerry asks.

'She said it's in her vagina.'

'Yes, that's right.'

'The baby's in there, in her vagina.'

'Well, not exactly but you're nearly right – it's not too far away from there and that's probably where it'll come out . . .' Kerry blows out air and feels herself sweating. 'Anyway, enough about babies. I don't suppose you're hungry, are you? Would you like a treat before bed?'

'Can I have Coco Pops?' Freddie asks, as if startled by his good luck.

'Coco Pops?' Mia repeats. 'Are we allowed them at bedtime after our teeth?'

'Sure. Why not?' Kerry says. 'In fact, I'm going down to get two bowlfuls right now and you can both eat them in bed.'

'Yeah!' Freddie exclaims. 'And I'm not doing my teeth again neither.'

Kerry gets up, relieved that her children have been so easily cheered up after her shock announcement. She's grateful, too, to have a simple task to occupy her, even if it is only filling two bowls with contraband cereal. In fact, right at this moment, it feels like *exactly* the right thing to do.

'Mummy!' Freddie shouts as she makes for the bedroom door.

'Yes, Freddie?'

'Will he still be our daddy?'

She frowns. 'D'you mean when the new baby comes?'

'Yeah.' He nods solemnly.

Kerry bites her lip, willing herself not to cry, at least not until she's reached the sanctuary of the kitchen. 'Of course he will,' she says. 'Don't worry, darling. Daddy loves both of you and nothing will ever change that.'

Chapter Seventeen

'Migraine better?' Eddy enquires as Rob saunters into the office on Thursday morning.

'Yes, much better thanks.' He plans to get the pleasantries over with as quickly as possible so he can hide behind his screen and at least pretend to be working.

'Unusual for one to last for two days,' Eddy adds with a smirk.

'Er, yeah. Anyway, I'm fine now,' Rob says, marching towards his desk with what feels like a ridiculously bouncy walk in order to display his wellness to all. Does everyone know, he wonders? Surely Nadine hasn't said anything yet. During their brief, slightly terse conversations during the past few days, she's assured him that she has no intention of 'making a grand announcement', as she put it. She's at her desk at the far end of the office, prim and expressionless in a dress with tiny purple flowers all over it. Hair neat, red lipstick immaculately applied. She flicks her gaze up at Rob, then quickly back down to her screen.

Rob switches on his computer and stares at it. His first task today is to write his second Miss Jones column, although at this moment it feels as insurmountable as building a cathedral with his bare hands. On this grim, drizzly October morning, the very concept of sex seems appalling; dirty, misguided, leading only to cake-throwing and despair. Yet he has no choice other than to get on with it. Having missed two days of work, and being incapable of switching on his laptop at home, he's hopelessly behind with everything. He needs to talk to Kerry but, understandably, she either cuts him off or won't pick up the call. How can he possibly write a coherent sentence with all of this whirling around in his brain?

Gazing at his blank screen, Rob tries to force his brain into writer mode. As they work three months ahead – they are already planning the January issue – his first Miss Jones column has yet to provoke any reader response, so he has no idea if he got it right with the food-in-the-bedroom one. For this issue, Eddy has suggested the topic of 'Why women sometimes go off sex'. How the hell should Rob know? He's not a woman, as he's reminded his editor on several occasions. 'Think like a woman then,' Eddy instructed him with a snigger.

Okay, think. *Think*. It's not easy, considering his wife has left him and God knows when he'll next see Mia and Freddie. He also can't quite believe that Nadine plans to go ahead with this pregnancy, but Rob can't allow his thoughts to venture down that sorry route now. Using all his faculties to tune out the background chatter, Rob tries to think himself into being a woman. Right. He is now not only a woman but a woman who has *gone off sex*. More than frigid, she is virtually deep-frozen. She would rather have a cup of tea or an episode of *EastEnders* – anything rather than her boyfriend's mauling hands all over her.

How has Rob's life ended up like this? This isn't how he'd envisaged himself as a rookie journalist nearly twenty years ago. He'd imagined travelling to war-torn countries, crafting insightful pieces and making a name for himself. Rob glances around the office in mild alarm. Catching Nadine's eye, he quickly turns back to his screen. It's only six hundred words, he reminds himself. Get on with it, idiot. *Before we talk about what you can do,* he types quickly, *we need to look at why I might not be in the mood right now. Maybe I'm stressed at work and you're not paying me enough attention when I come home, shattered, after a terrible Tube journey . . .* These days it's assumed that Mr Jones's entire readership lives in London. 'Why live somewhere that tries to be like London but is smaller and crapper?' Eddy once remarked. 'Crappier,' Rob yearned to correct him.

Damn, now he's lost his thread. A small photo in a silver frame eyes him from his desk. It's of Mia and Freddie on a Majorcan beach a couple of summers ago; they'd been thrilled by the tiny fish that had darted around their legs. What are they doing right now, he wonders? Has Kerry told them yet? If they were terribly distraught – as he imagines they were – perhaps she's kept them off school and they're all huddled on the sofa, discussing what a despicable father he is. Rob blinks at the photo again before placing it carefully in his desk drawer.

When he looks up, Nadine is strolling towards him. 'Hi,' she says, her eyes flicking towards his screen and a small smile crossing her lips.

'Er, hi, Nadine.' He wills her to go away and play with her gonk pencils or something. Instead, she starts reading the text on his screen. '"Maybe I'm not in the mood right now",' she teases in a breathy voice. '"Maybe you need to pay me a little more attention instead of coming home and spending an hour offloading about work . . ."'

Rob feels his cheeks burning. 'Yeah, well. Got to get into character, you know.'

'Hmm. Anyway, I just wondered what you're doing for lunch today, now your *migraine's* gone?'

'No plans,' he murmurs. 'Shall we, er, grab a sandwich or something?'

107

She nods curtly. 'I think we should.'

He glances quickly around the office to check no one's listening in. 'I have tried to talk to you,' he whispers. 'I've called you so many times but you always seem—'

She nods, already turning away. 'Let's have lunch.'

Now it's impossible for Rob to concentrate on the wretched column. Yet he ploughs onwards, suggesting more possible reasons for this poor female's libido to have plummeted, and by the time he's arrived at the 'what you can do bit' he is barely capable of focusing on the screen.

So lunchtime, when it finally rolls around, is almost a relief. Having brazenly left the office together, he and Nadine have settled upon a new deli-cum-cafe they've never been to before, having carefully avoided the team's usual haunts. They have chosen the table furthest from the window, yet Rob still wishes there was a screen or something, to shield them from prying eyes.

'So . . . how are you feeling?' he asks glumly.

'All right,' Nadine says with a weak smile. 'Still shell-shocked, I guess.'

'Have you told many people yet?'

'No, just my closest friends – my besties.'

'Right.' He grimaces at the waitress as their orders arrive; hers a neat grilled chicken salad, dressing on the side, his a gargantuan salt beef sandwich.

'You haven't told your parents?' he asks.

She shakes her head.

'How d'you think they'll react?'

'Er . . . Mum'll be fine, I think. Dad maybe not, but we'll see.'

Rob nods and glances down at his plate, realising he's not remotely hungry. These past few days he's barely eaten a thing, surviving on black coffee and the odd cigarette, the first he's smoked since giving up a decade ago.

'Nadine,' he starts, his stomach tightening as he tries to

formulate the right words, 'please don't take this the wrong way. It's just something I have to ask you, okay?'

'Uh-huh,' she says, pursing her lips.

'It's, um . . . definitely mine, isn't it?'

'Jesus, Rob,' she hisses. '*Yes*. Whose d'you think it is?' Her eyes flash angrily, and a blotchy rash appears instantly on her slender neck.

'I don't – well, I just . . .'

'There hasn't been anyone else. It's *yours*, whether you believe that or not—'

'Okay, okay,' he says quickly. 'I just wanted to be sure . . .'

'Well, now you can be.'

Rob nods and they fall into a tense silence. 'Look,' she murmurs finally, her voice softening, 'I know this is a horrible mess for you . . .'

She looks so small and vulnerable, he reaches for her hand instinctively. 'It's not your fault,' he murmurs.

'No, what I mean is . . .' She musters a smile then – her first genuine smile since that night at her flat. 'I'm single, Rob. Okay, I'd never imagined having a baby at my age, but I started to think . . . why not? How hard can it be?' Rob wants to cut in and say *It's bloody hard, Nadine. If you think it's all reading picture books and making coochy-coo noises you're in for a shock* . . . but manages to stop himself. It's not the time for a lecture from a been-there, done-that dad.

'I'll help you. I'll do anything I can.' As soon as the words are out of his mouth, Rob knows he means it. Despite Kerry, the children and the whole mess he's made – or perhaps because of it – he has to prove to himself that he's capable of being a decent human being. *A baby*. Bloody hell. It'll be the size of a tangerine pip or something, but it's still his flesh and blood. 'Nadine, listen,' he continues, 'I know none of this is ideal, and God knows what's ahead of us, but I want you to know I'm here for you, whatever happens.'

Her eyes widen. 'That's a nice thing to say, Rob.'

'Well, I didn't say it to be nice, so you'd think I'm some kind of decent guy. I said it because it's true.'

She nods, carefully placing her cutlery on her plate. Her lunch, and his, remain untouched.

'Did you think I'd leave you in the lurch?' he asks.

'I didn't know what to think. I've been terrified actually.' She lets out a small, mirthless laugh.

'Well, of course I won't.'

'Um . . . thanks,' she says as he squeezes her hand. 'But what about your kids, your wife . . .'

'We'll have to see. I don't know what Kerry's told them, and I can only hope they won't hate my guts, that they'll still want to see me . . .'

'Oh, Rob,' Nadine exclaims, 'I feel so bad. That's what I meant, you see – I'm young, I can have a baby and carry on with my life. It's more complicated for you.'

'I guess I'll have to figure out some way to deal with it all,' he mutters. He doesn't mention the fact that, until today, he has plagued Kerry with texts and calls to the point at which she made it clear that his begging and pleading was pointless.

As they stroll back to the office, Rob notices that Nadine's demeanour has changed. She seems brighter and happier, heightening the fact that she must have spent the days since the pregnancy test in a state of terror. She is also strikingly beautiful, he notices, perhaps for the first time. Sure, he'd always thought she was cute, but now he sees men giving her the odd quick, appreciative glance, checking her out, hoping for a glimmer of eye contact. One passerby – young and handsome in an expensive-looking suit – gives him a quizzical look, or perhaps one of envy? Rob swallows hard, feeling himself blush. A homeless man with a filthy blanket over his knees is sitting in a disused doorway and, when he extends his hand for money, Rob pulls out his wallet and presses a tenner into his palm, as if that might somehow undo some of the damage he's done.

You're forty years old, he reminds himself as he and Nadine turn into Shaftesbury Avenue and their faceless office block comes into view. *You had everything going for you – a beautiful wife and children who loved you, a new house by the sea, and you've gone and got a girl pregnant who's precisely half your age, you stupid bloody fool . . .*

As they approach the main entrance, he is aware of being spotted by Frank, who's striding towards them while forking noodles into his mouth from a carton. *If ever there was the time to start behaving like a proper adult*, Rob decides, greeting him with a nod and a stoical smile, *it's right now.*

Chapter Eighteen

Kerry can hardly believe she's about to call a man about a dog. It feels like one of those rash things people do post-break-up, like sleeping with a platonic male friend or having an extravagant tattoo. Of course, her dog-owning credentials are impeccable: *Not averse to walking/being outdoors. Not especially house-proud so won't freak out at sight of odd dog hair/muddy paw print. Works from home so dog won't be left alone for long periods. Has two dog-loving children so lashings of affection and fuss guaranteed . . .*

Yet what if Buddy doesn't like fuss, or children for that matter? He sounds perfect – 'Adorable, loving and well-behaved dog seeks happy family home', the ad read – but say they don't click? Over a week has passed since Kerry scribbled down the owner's number. In the aftermath of Rob's announcement, and being unable to face him last weekend – even though he wanted to come down to Shorling for 'a proper chat' with the children – her energies have been consumed by trying to maintain a sense of normality, while dealing with Freddie and Mia's persistent questions about when they'll next see their dad.

'Soon,' she keeps saying. 'Daddy and I just need to talk, then we'll figure out the regular days you'll be with him.

You'll still see him lots, I promise. It won't be that different from before.' Yeah, right.

In fact, Kerry had forgotten about the dog until she'd discovered the scrap of paper bearing the phone number in a jeans pocket this morning. Unable to face making lunch, she taps out the number.

'Hello?' The male voice is abrupt.

'Hi, erm . . . I'm probably too late about this,' Kerry starts, 'but I saw the ad for your dog . . .'

'Oh yes, he's still here if you're interested . . .'

'Could you possibly tell me a bit more about him?'

She hears an intake of breath. 'Why don't you just come over and meet him? Are you local?'

'Yes, we're down at the seafront . . .'

'Sorry,' he says briskly, 'I'm just taking a quick lunchbreak – would tomorrow be okay? I can arrange to be at home if I know you're coming.' Kerry pauses, rapidly losing her nerve. 'If you think he might be right for you, you can have him on loan to see how you get along,' the man adds, which to Kerry's mind sounds like the equivalent of meeting for coffee on a blind date, rather than committing to a whole evening in a restaurant.

'I have a feeling that, once my children meet him, there'll be no question of handing him back.' She laughs, expecting a hint of warmth from this man who hasn't even introduced himself. Yet there's none. He's clearly eager to finish the call.

'Could you come around six-ish tomorrow?' he asks.

'I'd like to make it earlier, if that's okay. If he seems right for us, I'd love to be able to surprise the children by taking him with me when I collect them from school . . .' Now, surely, he'll thaw a little.

'Right . . . well, I suppose I could leave the shop for an hour or so . . . would two o'clock be okay?'

'That's perfect. I'm Kerry, by the way. Kerry Tambini.'

'James,' he says. And that's that. God, Kerry thinks; he's *rehoming his dog*. The way he spoke, anyone would think he'd advertised a dining table.

Their cool exchange replays in her mind as she tries to pick up the melody she started to write this morning. Barely three bars of 'Spread Your Wings', her latest *Cuckoo Clock* offering, have been written, and now she is finding it impossible to focus. Buddy is threatening to bankrupt them before he's even joined their family.

At one thirty, her first pupil arrives, a reed-thin woman in a grey shift dress and heels, her fair hair secured in a neat French plait. After several minutes, Kerry surmises that she dutifully worked her way through the early grades as a child.

'What made you want to start playing again?' she asks, registering Jasmine's perfect, peach-tinted manicure.

'Oh, my modern dance classes have moved to another day,' she says airily, 'so I suddenly had a gap to fill on Thursday lunchtimes.'

'Right.' Kerry smiles, conscious now that the top she's wearing is a little bobbly from the wash, and her own nails conspicuously bare. She sees Jasmine glancing around the music room, taking in the dated wallpaper with its pale lime floral design, and Aunt Maisie's sun-faded blue velvet curtains, which had seemed perfectly acceptable this morning when she did a speedy Hoover and dust, but are now bleating 'Replace me.'

'It's a funny old house, isn't it?' Jasmine asks as the lesson draws to a close.

'Yes,' Kerry agrees. 'I know it so well, though, I suppose I'm kind of immune to its faults. It was my aunt's place, you see. I spent most of my holidays here as a child.'

Jasmine gives her an inscrutable look. 'Well, I hope your husband's good at DIY,' she says with a chuckle.

'Er, yes, he's pretty handy.' *With twenty-year-old editorial*

114

assistants, especially. Shame he wasn't as efficient at knocking up IKEA wardrobes in all the years we spent together . . .

'He's got his work cut out then,' Jasmine observes.

'He certainly does,' Kerry says jovially, having acquired a twinge in her jaw from maintaining a perky smile. Jasmine pays her, hooks a cornflower-blue patent bag over her shoulder and steps over Freddie's discarded Wagon Wheel wrapper which Kerry had omitted to pick up earlier.

'Roof looks a bit of a worry,' is Jasmine's parting shot as Kerry sees her out.

No, Kerry thinks as she closes the front door, *that's the least of my worries, actually, as long as it doesn't fall off and crush someone . . .*

Realising that any attempts to continue with her 'Spread Your Wings' melody will be futile now, she stuffs her hair into a ponytail, throws on a baggy sweater over her top and heads for the town centre. It's a breezy afternoon with a colourless sky and, with the main holiday season finished, Shorling has an air of stillness, as if something is definitely over. Kerry realises, too, that now she's here among the numerous boutiques and gift shops, there's nothing she actually needs or, crucially, can afford to buy. A sole, bleak thought – that she appears to have become a single parent – gnaws away at her brain as she glances at window displays of dead-eyed seagulls carved from driftwood. Why would anyone covet a hand-made model yacht with a price tag of £850? She considers stopping for a coffee instead of all this aimless ambling, but is wary of being spotted by one of those school gate mothers who have so far greeted her attempts to make conversation with chilly indifference.

With a start, Kerry realises that she never used to worry so much about what people thought of her. However, these days she'd prefer to avoid being seen whiling away an empty afternoon in a cafe on her own. She can just imagine the murmurs as she waits outside school: *That's her, just moved into that clapped out old cottage that really needs a lick of paint. If we're going to be in with a chance of winning Britain's Prettiest Coastal Town she'd better sort it out . . .*

As faint rain starts to fall, Kerry finds herself being lured into the dusty warmth of the charity bookshop. This being Shorling, it's posher than most new book stores, and the moss-green velvet sofas and aromatic candles raise her spirits a little. As everything's meticulously categorised – none of your usual charity shop mish-mash – it's easy to locate the pet section. Kerry retires to the plush reading area with *Your First Dog: A Complete Guide* by Jeremy Catchpole, installing herself in a squishy armchair. There's a montage of extremely cute pups on the cover, but from that point things skid rapidly downhill. Kerry's eyes light upon *Behaviour and aggression: Remember that ANY dog is capable of snapping and biting if provoked.* While she's not planning on 'provoking' Buddy, that doesn't sound good. She flips to the health chapter: *Parasites: An infection of roundworms can lead to bloating and chronic gas.* Delightful. *Tapeworms can be spotted in stools and occasionally glimpsed inside your dog's ears. Certain parasites can be ingested when your dog consumes faecal matter . . .*

Kerry bites her lip, now a little concerned about the irreversible nature of this dog project, despite James's suggestion that Buddy could be returned, like an ill-fitting sweater. Once upon a time, she had despised people who likened the trials of early parenthood to pet ownership. 'Ooh, I know what you mean,' her old colleague Clemmie had sympathised when Kerry had mentioned her chronic sleep deprivation when Freddie was a baby. 'Ginger drives us crazy too when he wants to go out at night.' *Please don't compare a politely mewing pussy with the nocturnal roars of a six-month-old human baby*, Kerry had wanted to snap. But now, she's beginning to understand the similarities. Dog, baby: both say, 'RESPONSIBILITY' and 'DO YOU REALLY THINK YOU'RE UP TO THIS?'

Her mobile rings, and she pulls it out from the pocket of her faded denim skirt with an abrupt, 'Hello?'

'Hi, is it a good time?' Rob always says this, realising, of course, that there is never a good time to converse with the Impregnator.

''S'pose so.' The book is lying open on Kerry's lap. Her eyes alight upon a picture of a dog attempting to mount the leg of an elderly lady sitting in a winged armchair.

'You sound busy.'

The picture is captioned *Inappropriate Sexual Behaviour*. 'I'm just out,' she murmurs.

'Right, well, I won't keep you a minute. It's about this weekend . . .'

'Uh-huh . . .'

'Er . . .' Rob sighs audibly. 'Look, I know how you feel, Kerry.'

She frowns so hard, it makes her head hurt. 'Do you?'

'Well, no, I didn't mean it like that. I just know you don't want to see me, and I understand that, but I have to talk to the kids, okay? I need some time with them. I can't tell you how awful I—'

'Spare it, Rob,' she cuts in, glaring down at a paragraph on post-operative mood changes: *His over-eagerness to mate with every passing female will diminish immediately, following castration.*

'I, er, thought maybe I could come down on Saturday morning and take them over to Mum and Dad's,' Rob adds. 'They could spend the night there with me, if that sounds okay.'

Kerry considers this. While her inclination is to say no – for reasons that she cannot begin to articulate – she is keenly aware how much Freddie and Mia are missing their father.

117

'I suppose so,' she mutters, 'as long as your parents are fine with it.'

'Of course they are. They love seeing the kids. This has been so hard for Mum and Dad and you know how fond of you they are—'

'All right,' she snaps.

'Sorry.' He pauses. 'Are the kids okay, d'you think?'

'Well, they'll be happy tomorrow,' she says tersely. 'I'm collecting a dog.'

'Are you? So you're really going ahead with it?'

'Yes, why wouldn't I?' Out of the corner of her eye she sees a statuesque blonde woman entering the shop. It's Brigid, clutching the hand of Joe, her sugar-scattering little boy.

'There'll be all the walking,' Rob points out.

'I *can* walk, you know. I am capable of forward motion.'

'I know, it's just . . . I wouldn't want you to rush into anything,' Rob mumbles.

'Sorry?'

'I mean—'

'You wouldn't want *me* to rush into anything?'

'I just mean,' Rob blusters, 'it'll be a hell of a tie for you . . .'

'Like having a baby?' she blurts out, unable to stop herself.

'No, no, that's totally different . . .'

'Because you've obviously thought that through really carefully,' she charges on, keeping her head down and praying that Brigid doesn't spot her. Luckily, she seems to be engrossed in the mind, body and spirit section while Joe spins a rack of charity gift leaflets with unnerving speed.

'Kerry, please—'

'You've obviously taken a really measured view of things,' she continues, her cheeks burning, 'and decided that, when

118

you had a little wobble about moving to the coast, the most sensible course of action was to impregnate the intern.'

'Er, she's the editorial assistant,' he mutters.

'I don't give a damn what she does, Rob. She could be expected to clean the urinals with her tongue for all I care.' Kerry clamps her mouth shut, heart thumping against her ribs. An elderly woman in the poetry section peers over and frowns.

'Anyway, good luck with the dog,' Rob says dully as they finish the call.

Aware that her face is still scrunched into an unbecoming frown, Kerry allows herself a moment to picture Buddy attacking Rob when he shows up on Saturday. All dogs are capable of biting, after all. Perhaps, having bonded immediately with Kerry, Buddy will sense that this tall, dark-eyed man has wronged her in the most terrible way and go in for the kill. As Brigid continues to peruse the shelves, Kerry cheers herself up by imagining Rob staggering out of her house, his favourite Aquascutum trousers ripped at the shins and splattered with blood.

How is it possible to spend thirteen years with someone and not realise what an absolute dick they are? Kerry muses. You'd think there's be signs – iffy sexual preferences, or worrying political views. But there was nothing. Sweet, well-meaning, bit-on-the-earnest-side Rob, with the head-turning good looks. What went wrong?

'Kerry?' With a start, she looks up to where Brigid is towering above her in a dangerously short T-shirt dress and flat pumps.

'Oh, hi, Brigid.' Although she's pleased to see her again, she doesn't know if she's capable right now of coming across as the kind of woman Brigid might want to be friends with.

'Sorry, you're reading. I didn't mean to disturb you. God, I know how lovely it is when you can steal a few minutes with a book.'

'Mummy-I-want-that-book,' Joe mumbles.

'Just a minute, darling . . .'

'You're not disturbing me at all,' Kerry says brightly. 'I was just having a quick browse . . . aren't you well today, Joe?'

He frowns at her and shakes his head. 'He's supposed to have a tummy ache,' Brigid says with a roll of her eyes, 'but by ten o'clock he seemed to have made a full recovery.'

'*I want that book*,' he barks.

'Well, I'm not buying it, sweetheart. I'm *not* having it in the house. Anyway,' Brigid continues, indicating the hardback on Kerry's lap, 'can I assume you're planning on getting a new family member?'

Kerry smiles. 'Yes, I am. You probably think I'm completely mad . . .'

'Not at all,' she exclaims. 'We love dogs, don't we, Joe?'

'I WANT THAT BOOK!'

'Sorry, absolutely not.' Brigid grins conspiratorially at Kerry. 'Anyway, maybe you'd like to meet ours sometime. We could walk them together. I always think it's good for dogs to socialise, don't you?'

'I don't actually know,' Kerry admits with a smile. 'He'll be our first. I've arranged to pick him up tomorrow.'

'Oh, I'm so excited for you.' Brigid's cheery demeanour has made Kerry's prickliness over the conversation with Rob fade away. Her gold hoop earrings and cluster of jingly bracelets are a little glitzy for Shorling, Kerry notes approvingly. How pleasing to meet someone who doesn't appear to conform to the type.

'Thanks,' she says. 'I'm pretty excited too.'

'We're going for a quick walk right now,' Brigid adds, 'to blow away the terrible virus that Joe reckoned was about to strike him dead about five hours ago. Don't suppose you fancy joining us, if you're finished in here?'

'Sounds great.' Kerry leaps up from the armchair,

hurriedly pays for her book and leaves the shop with Brigid and Joe, to find their gleaming brown and white Staffy waiting patiently outside.

*

'She was a rescue dog,' Brigid explains as they follow the worn stone steps down onto the sand. 'We don't know her exact age but we reckon around ten or eleven.'

'Is that really old?' Kerry asks. 'I keep realising how little I know about dogs.'

'Oh, Roxy's a veteran all right,' Brigid says, casting her a fond glance, 'and the softest girl in the world, despite Staffies' reputations.'

'Well, she's still got her looks,' Kerry says. 'She's a real beauty.'

'She's nearly as old as Mummy,' Joe announces, all traces of ill-humour having now disappeared.

'In dog years, she's more like Granny's age,' Brigid laughs.

'Well, I hope Buddy's as good-natured,' Kerry says.

'Where are you getting him from?'

Kerry fills her in on the ad, and the owner's brusqueness on the phone. 'If that was my dog, I wouldn't just hand him over to the first person to call,' she says. 'I'd want to make sure they were suitable. But he didn't ask me anything – whether anyone's at home during the day, or if we have a garden . . .'

'Strange,' Brigid agrees.

'It's as if he just wants to be rid of him.'

'He's a lucky dog then,' she says as Joe tears away to the rock pools, dishevelled hair flying in the light October breeze. Brigid lets out a snort. 'So much for him being ill. He knows I'm a pushover, that's the problem. A soft touch that he can wrap around his little finger, being just the two of us.'

Kerry looks at her and smiles, suddenly picturing Brigid as a younger woman; partying in Ibiza or Goa with a bunch of similarly bronzed, leggy girls. And she finds herself telling her all about Rob: his fortieth birthday night out, the Impregnation, and the terrible days that have followed.

'That's awful,' Brigid exclaims. 'I'd never have imagined, Kerry – not even that day I saw the two of you having coffee in Hattie's. God. You seemed so *together*.'

Kerry smiles wryly. 'I imagine they're engraving my name on that Oscar right now.'

'Well, I think you're amazing.'

'Not at all,' Kerry says briskly. 'If it was just me, alone, I'd be lying on the sofa with a bottle of gin and the curtains shut. But you can't, can you? Children have to be up for school and dressed and fed. It's *good* for me, actually. They force me to carry on because, however wretched I might feel, it's not just about me. They're affected as well, and that's the main reason I'm getting Buddy.'

'It's something new and positive,' Brigid remarks, nodding. 'I can understand that.' She gives Joe a little wave – he's now soaked to the knees from jumping into the rock pools – then turns back to Kerry. 'I lend Roxy out sometimes, you know. To friends, I mean.'

'What for?'

'Oh, she always gets the guys.'

'You mean male dogs? Still up for that, is she?'

'No, no, I mean *men*,' Brigid laughs. 'Think about it. Apart from babies – which are a pretty powerful man-deterrent, let's face it – what's the best conversation opener you can think of?'

Kerry shrugs. 'No idea.'

'Being out with your dog, of course. You'll be amazed how many people you meet. You know that just about everyone has at least one around here – it's almost mandatory . . .'

Although Kerry doesn't want to overstep the mark and scare off the sole tentative connection she's made here, she is desperate to ask about Brigid's love life. She likes the fact that the custard-yellow bag slung over her shoulder is rather battered looking, and would be considered a little trashy around these parts. She enjoys her loud, throaty laugh, and the fact that her child clearly isn't impeccably behaved.

'So have *you* met anyone that way?' she ventures. 'Using Roxy as a sort of matchmaker, I mean.'

Brigid chuckles. 'I have actually. There was David with the King Charles spaniel – sweet, but a disgustingly noisy eater – then Jason with the Labradoodle, who'd never got over his ex, and the last one, Mike with the Doberman pinscher, typical posh boy – you know how they are around here . . .'

'Wow,' Kerry marvels. 'That's pretty impressive.'

'Told you, Kerry, a dog's a wonderful thing. For children, too – they're a special friend they can talk to.'

Kerry nods, her throat tightening at the thought of Freddie and Mia perhaps confiding in Buddy about their father's departure and new baby. Although they seemed to accept the new information, Freddie's question about Rob – *Will he still be our daddy?* – still rings hollowly in her ears.

'Well,' she says, checking her watch, 'guess I'd better head off to school.'

Brigid smiles. 'It's been really nice bumping into you today.'

'I've enjoyed it too. Thanks for cheering me up.' She waves goodbye to Joe, then adds, 'What book was it, by the way? The one Joe wanted in the charity shop . . .'

'Oh, that,' Brigid laughs. 'It was one of those Thomas the Tank Engines. I can't *bear* them in the house, can you? Gordon and Henry and the Fat Controller. God . . .' She shudders.

'Yes, we had a year when Freddie would have nothing else at bedtime.' Kerry laughs dryly. 'Maybe that's what drove Rob into the arms of another woman.'

Brigid smiles, then gives her a quick, unexpected hug before adding, 'Listen, you can call me any time, okay? I only work three days a week, in the library. A lot of the time we're just pottering about, especially at weekends. Let's exchange numbers.'

'Great,' Kerry says, whipping out her phone. As they part company, she turns to see Joe throw a stick for Roxy as Brigid strides towards them. Despite all that's happened, Kerry feels a little lighter as she makes her way to school. She's certain now that getting a dog is completely the right thing to do, for all the reasons Brigid mentioned. But also, she realises with a smile, because Rob is most definitely *not* a dog person.

Chapter Nineteen

'She doesn't even *like* dogs,' Rob tells Simon, clutching his bottle of beer and a cigarette outside the Soho pub. 'It's so out of character. She's not one of those people who stops and strokes them in parks. In fact she's always been a bit nervous of them, ever since one nipped her on the ankle when she was a little girl . . .'

He can sense Simon, his old editor and friend, appraising him over the rim of his glass of red wine. It's disconcerting, being regarded with a mixture of incredulity and barely-disguised disapproval.

'I don't see why this is a big deal,' he says levelly.

'Well, I just don't think she's thought it through.'

Simon blinks at him. Although his neatly-cropped hair is far more salt than pepper these days, he's looked younger – and certainly happier – since he was kicked off *Mr Jones* and shunted down to *Tram Enthusiast*'s basement offices. It's as if time operates on a different system down there in the bowels of the building. In contrast, Rob feels as if he has aged with astonishing speed these past few weeks. His heart feels leaden, his intestines a mass of knots and tangles, and his gut aches with a dull, heavy pain from missing Kerry and the children.

'After everything that's happened,' Simon remarks, 'I don't think the dog issue is something you should be worrying about.'

'I know, but—'

'Sorry, Rob, but Kerry can do whatever she likes now. She could get a herd of buffalo if she wanted to.'

'Tell it like it is,' he murmurs, wishing he was one of the happy, smiling people around him who are enjoying this pleasant October evening. Of course, Simon's right, that's the worst part of it. Rob is vaguely aware that, in directing his focus on a minor aspect of the proceedings – Kerry's impending acquisition of a crotch-sniffer – he's attempting to avoid the bigger ones. Like how it'll be when he sees Freddie and Mia this weekend, the first time since 'it' happened. Whether his mum will speak to him or concuss him with her meat cleaver. And, beyond that, Nadine's pregnancy – culminating in a baby, obviously – and how he intends to deal with that. Birth, nappies, reading bedtime stories to a child whose genetic make-up isn't fifty percent Kerry's . . . not to mention impending bankruptcy when he finds himself supporting two families. Right now, these things feel gargantuan. Who could blame him for fixating on a dog?

'So how are things with Nadine?' Simon is asking.

He shrugs. 'Okay, I guess. Sort of . . . polite.'

'So you haven't, *you* know . . .' He waggles a brow.

'No,' Rob hisses, shaking his head in disbelief. 'It's not like we're together, in a proper relationship or anything. It was just that one time. Just a stupid, drunken, flukey thing.'

'Blimey,' Simon mutters with a shake of his head. 'And there's no way you can, you know . . . fix things with Kerry and get back together?'

'No, I've tried everything. She won't even consider it, not even for the kids . . .'

Simon pats his arm consolingly, and they fall into an

uncomfortable silence as Rob lights up another cigarette. He'd looked forward to this drink after work and the chance to talk to someone who's known him for years, with whom he doesn't have to put up a pretence of being young and dynamic and remotely interested in some surgically-enhanced model from a TV reality show. He'd imagined making his friend laugh about the terrible Miss Jones column he's being forced to write, after which they'd launch into an extremely satisfying character assassination of Eddy, Frank and the rest of the team. Rob had also planned to ask if he might be able to stay with Simon if the need arises when he has to move out of the house in a few weeks' time. Now, though, he's decided to wrap up the evening as quickly as possible.

'So,' Simon ventures, 'does anyone at work know yet?'

'No, thank God. She's only told her close friends, and she's just broken the news to her parents . . .'

'Ah, your new in-laws.' Simon smiles ruefully. 'Had the pleasure yet?'

He shakes his head. 'They live in Zurich and don't seem to have any plans to come over, as far as I can gather. Nadine said she's had some pretty intense chats with her mum on the phone, but her dad doesn't seem that involved.'

'Until he comes charging at you with a big stick,' Simon chortles, 'or a bucket of boiling oil or a bread knife . . .'

'Yeah, okay.' Rob laughs dryly.

'. . . And chops your knackers off.'

'Hmmm.' Rob blinks at him.

'Back on the fags, then,' Simon observes.

'Yeah. Gonna quit, though,' he says, stubbing it out. 'Fancy going inside? It's a bit nippy out here.' In truth, Rob doesn't feel entirely comfortable standing out in the street so close to the office.

With a resigned shrug, Simon heads inside, where they grab the only free table and sit in silence for a few moments, sipping their drinks.

127

'Um . . . can I ask you something?' Rob starts.

'Sure, fire away.'

'Have you ever had a rough patch with Louise? A really bad one, I mean, when you thought you might break up?'

Simon frowns. 'Nope, never. Love her to bits, mate.'

Rob takes a moment to digest this. 'I don't mean *that*. I know you do. I mean . . . have you ever done something you really regretted, that could have ruined everything?'

Simon thinks for a moment. Surely he has, Rob reflects. Everyone makes mistakes, don't they?

'Oh, yeah,' Simon says finally. 'I was painting the garage – you know, with a roller – and it was really windy and when I looked round, one side of her brand new Audi was completely speckled in white.'

Rob frowns at him.

'I know, you're speechless, right?' Simon guffaws. 'Can you imagine Louise's face?'

'Yes, I can,' he says, shaking his head in disbelief – not about the car, but the fact that, even with his old friend, he has to act like a phoney idiot. What does he care about a speckled car?

'Anyway, another drink?' Simon is already out of his seat.

Still feeling a little stung over that knackers quip, Rob shakes his head and quickly drains his glass. 'No, better get home. Still got that bloody column to finish.'

'Oh yeah, I heard about that,' Simon sniggers as they squeeze their way out of the now bustling pub. 'Not the best timing, is it?'

'To be a woman? No.'

'I mean to start dishing out sex advice.'

'You could say that.' Rob musters a laugh.

'Yeah, well, I'm sure things'll work out,' Simon says, giving him a firm pat on the back as they part company. Rob looks back just once, catching his friend's concerned glance as he pulls out his packet of cigarettes and lights up.

*

Although he intended to go home, Rob finds himself not heading for the Tube but following random streets, not really considering where he's going until he arrives in Baker Street. It's almost 9 p.m. when he buzzes Nadine's bell.

'Hey,' she says through the intercom, 'this is a surprise.'

'Hope you don't mind?'

'No, it's fine – come up.' She buzzes him in and, when he arrives at the door to her flat, he realises all he wants is company with someone who won't make jokes about hot oil, or go on about how bloody perfect their relationship is.

They don't even talk about the baby, not really. Nadine makes him tea, and they chat companionably about her upbringing in Berkshire – horses, lavish dinner parties, all the trappings of the wealthy English countryside – financed by her banker father. Granted, she's not the most fascinating person Rob has ever encountered – and he's a little perturbed to discover that her bijoux CD collection consists entirely of chart compilations. Talking to her is like falling into conversation with a pleasant young person on a train, he decides as she goes to refill their mugs. It's relaxing and enjoyable – but you're not exactly devastated when they get off at Crewe. *You're not sitting next to her on a train, idiot*, he reminds himself sternly. *You're having a child with her*. He rearranges his expression into a perky smile when she reappears with tea and toast, thanking her profusely and complimenting the bland abstract print on the living room wall.

'It's Mummy's actually,' she says. 'I think she got it in Debenhams.' *Jesus fuck*.

'I really like it,' he says, wondering where these hitherto undiscovered reserves of fakery are coming from.

Nadine smiles warmly and checks her watch. 'You can stay tonight if you like. It's been lovely, chatting with you. Nice and normal after all the craziness.'

'Well . . . if you're sure it's all right,' he says hesitantly, overcome by a wave of fatigue. He knows he shouldn't really. When he said he'd be there for her, he meant in the supportive and financial sense, not that he had any intention of them ever sleeping together again. Yet . . . she's an enchantingly beautiful girl. And the thought of heading out into the cold, damp night and back to his depressing house now seems unbearable. Kerry can barely bring herself to speak to him, so really, what's the harm in staying here? And so he spends the night, not on the sofa bed this time but in her vast, extravagantly-carved double bed. His finds himself kissing her soft, young mouth as she wraps her slender limbs around him, and it feels good, not being alone with his torturous thoughts. He's too exhausted to care that he'll have to show up at work in the same clothes tomorrow. Instead, he holds this sweet, pretty girl who likes chart music and Debenhams art, and this time, he doesn't forget a thing.

Chapter Twenty

When Kerry arrives at the redbrick terraced house, James greets her with a brief smile and his mobile jammed to his ear.

'I manage to run things when *you're* not there,' he barks, beckoning her into the hallway. *Sorry,* he mouths with a broad shouldered shrug, turning to march into the kitchen and motioning for Kerry to follow as he continues his conversation. He jabs at a chair, indicating that she should sit. She does so, like an obedient hound, wondering if she might also be offered a biscuit.

As Kerry waits for him to finish, feeling a little stranded, she takes in the undeniable maleness of the sparse and functional room. These days, whilst she no longer registers the clutter in friends' houses (it's as unremarkable as chairs or carpeting), she never fails to register the absence of it. No children live here, that's for sure. And that's good, she decides, having wondered how she'd feel if a little boy or girl were being forced to part with their beloved pet.

'So, there's a queue,' James barks into his phone. 'I'd hazard a guess that they're customers, Luke. I'd say that's good. Yes, I know it's hard to keep up with the orders but that's the whole point, isn't it? If they wanted quick they'd buy a pre-packaged sandwich in the newsagent's . . .' He glances at Kerry with another apologetic grimace and pushes back his slightly untidy light brown hair. Grey eyes, Kerry notes: kind eyes that crinkle appealingly, despite his current ill-humour. He's a little older than her, she guesses – maybe early-to-mid forties. 'I know Ben's your friend,' he goes on, 'but we're *not* hiring now, okay? No . . . no. Well, we'll just have to manage, Luke. Look, I can't discuss this right now.'

There's a movement in the kitchen doorway, and Kerry turns to see a large, shaggy-haired, timid-looking black and white dog standing there. He is observing her with an amber-eyed gaze.

So this is Buddy. Part bearded collie, mostly unknown, according to James when she'd called again for more information, feeling unsatisfied by their initial exchange. Six years old, likes to run, play, fetch sticks and balls and be made a fuss of. Has been snipped, as James put it, so uninterested in passing females. (This relieved Kerry; she had been trying to erase the mental image of that dog from the book getting frisky with the old lady in the winged chair).

'Hello, Buddy,' she says gently, getting up to greet him as his owner goes on, apparently reminding the person on the phone to add basil to a greengrocer's order. Buddy eyes Kerry nervously as if he's just arrived at a party and is unsure about walking in.

'Hey, boy,' she says, his cue to turn and quickly pad away. 'Buddy?' she calls ineffectually into the hallway, but he fails to reappear.

'Sorry about that.' James has finished the call and shakes her hand rather formally.

'That's okay.' She smiles.

'I see you've met him.' He glances over her shoulder into the hallway.

'Yes, he seems a bit shy actually.'

'Oh, he'll be fine. Hang on a minute . . .' He disappears into another room, returning with Buddy trotting timidly at his ankles looking up at James, as if fully aware that Kerry isn't some random woman who has happened to drop by, but the person who's come to take him away – forever.

'Oh, he's lovely,' Kerry says, keeping her distance in case she startles him again.

'Yes, he's great. Very affectionate as I said on the phone . . .'

'I have to admit, I don't know anything about dogs, apart from what I've picked up from books and the internet. To be honest, most of it seems to be about the millions of things that can go wrong . . .'

'Well, we've never had any problems,' James says quickly as Buddy settles into a curled up position, not just at, but actually *on* his feet.

There's an awkward pause which Kerry feels compelled to fill. 'Er . . . how often d'you walk him?' she asks.

'Couple of times a day. I do a quick walk first thing, then another early afternoon . . . apart from that, he'll potter about quite happily in the garden. He's pretty low-maintenance really. You'll hardly know he's there.'

Another silence. *Ask me if I have a garden then*, Kerry muses. *Say something to show you actually care where he's going, and what his life will be like.*

'And he's never aggressive?' she asks. 'There's no biting or snapping or anything? I'm sure he'll be fine but I have to be sure. You see, I have two young children and I know some dogs can be weird around kids, especially if they're not used to them.' She doesn't know that at all; she's just saying whatever pops into her head.

'No, he's fine with children, and he's never shown any aggression.'

'And he's trained and everything?' Now Kerry feels as if she's interviewing *him*.

'Oh, yes,' James says quickly.

'I mean in the doing-his-business sense.'

'He's fine with all that. No problem at all.'

Kerry frowns. It doesn't seem right, managing the hand-over in such a cold-hearted manner. But then, maybe James is desperately upset, and worried he'll lose it if there's a long, drawn-out goodbye. Perhaps, she decides, this chilliness is his way of coping.

'He seems a bit nervous,' she observes.

James bends down, ruffling behind Buddy's soft, floppy ears. 'He's fine, aren't you, boy? So how are you taking him? D'you have a car?'

'No, I'd rather walk him home, it's only fifteen minutes away. I thought it'd give us the chance to get to know each other.'

'Right.' James checks his watch. *All right, all right, we're going*, Kerry thinks with a prickle of irritation. 'If you give me your address,' he adds, 'I can drop off his basket, his food and everything later. All his info's in there.' He indicates a cardboard folder on the kitchen table labelled 'Buddy'. 'Veterinary records, vaccinations, pet insurance . . .'

'MOT?'

'Sorry?'

'Has he been MOT'd?' Kerry asks with a bemused smile. 'I'm sorry, James. This feels a bit like handing over a car. Are there any quirks I should know about? Is he a good runner?'

'Oh,' James emits a dry laugh. 'He's certainly that.'

'And I take it that's his fuel.' She indicates the big bag of chicken and vegetables in dry biscuit form on the table.

'Yep, he has a cup in the morning and another for dinner . . .'

'Well, um . . . I suppose we'll be going then. You've got my number in case you think of anything else I should know . . .'

134

'Yes.'

'Here's my address.' She takes a scrap of paper and pen from her bag and scribbles it quickly. Looking down at Buddy, who is gazing mournfully up at her from his curled up position on James's feet, Kerry feels a rush of affection for this unwanted pet. 'Come on then, Buddy,' she says softly. Buddy glances at his ex-owner, then gets up and potters slowly to the front door.

'Here's his lead.' James hands it to her and she clips it onto his collar.

'Well, thanks,' she says.

'No, thank *you*.' He checks his watch again. 'Er, I really should get back to work now . . .'

'Oh, of course. Um . . . can I just ask why you're re-homing him?'

He looks at her, and she sees tiredness clouding those soft grey eyes. 'Circumstances have changed,' he says with a shrug.

'Right. Well, you don't have to worry about him. My children have been asking for a dog for years, driving me mad, coming up with names . . .' She stops abruptly as he's clearly not interested. 'We'll be off then,' she adds.

James nods and says goodbye without addressing Buddy at all, then steps back into the house.

Kerry takes a moment to gather her thoughts in the small front garden. It was clearly once well-tended, its rectangular borders edged with scalloped tiles, but has now grown indistinct beneath a light covering of weeds. The paint on the front door is peeling, a piece of guttering is dangling down, and tiny pink flowers are sprouting in the cracks between the paving slabs. Kerry waits while Buddy sniffs a dandelion, half-expecting James to burst back out of his house and crumple to the ground for a last, heartfelt hug with his beloved dog. But there is nothing.

'Heartless shit,' she mutters under her breath, turning

away and making her way down the quiet residential street with Buddy trotting meekly at her side.

As they walk together, Kerry notices a small shift, assuming at first that it's the freshness of the breezy October day. She feels lighter somehow, and is conscious of a kernel of excitement fizzling inside her as she realises what's happening.

She isn't walking alone.

Of course, she and the children spend huge chunks of their weekends on Shorling beach these days, but Freddie and Mia tend to run off and dabble about in the rock pools or shallow waves. They don't walk together, like this. And during these past couple of weeks, it has felt as if they don't walk to and from school together either. As soon as she spots Audrey-Jane, Mia tears ahead to catch up, trying to ingratiate herself with excitable chatter which, to Kerry's consternation, seems to be largely ignored. Meanwhile, Kerry feels obliged to engage in polite chit-chat with Lara and Emily, who seem inseparable and are clearly not keen to let her in. Even Freddie will do anything – lag behind, or tag along with any boy who's roughly his age – to avoid walking at his mother's side.

She keeps glancing down at Buddy as they walk, scarcely believing she's now in sole charge of this living, breathing creature who will require regular feeding, play and exercise. *He depends on me now.* Both thrilling and terrifying, the thought lodges itself in Kerry's mind. Still an hour till school pick-up, when she plans to bring Buddy with her to the school gates. She has it all figured out: how she'll adopt a casual stance, so Freddie and Mia won't suspect anything when they first spot her from a distance. They'll wander across the playground towards her, not paying much attention. Then they'll spot him and – the rest is a blur. It makes Kerry's heart race just thinking about it.

Picturing James's handsome but distinctly beleaguered face at the handover today, she glances down and says, 'My circumstances have changed too, Buddy. I think we're going to get along just fine.'

Chapter Twenty-One

Harvey Chuckles is standing on a small stage in a draughty community hall, knowing without a doubt that every child in this room would give anything to be somewhere else.

'Wanna play outside,' a boy complains, triggering a ripple of dissatisfaction.

'Make him go away,' a little girl shrieks from the front row of chairs.

The woman sitting behind her taps her on the shoulder. 'Hush, sweetheart. Don't be rude . . .'

'But I don't like him. Tell him to go, Mummy!'

'Just be quiet and watch, Cordelia,' the woman snaps. Harvey blunders on through his act, producing his dove pan, an ingenious device the size of a saucepan which enables him to make small objects disappear. By this point, he is wishing *he* could crawl into the pan and magic himself to a place where strong alcohol is administered. He has juggled beanbags, ridden his unicycle and played jaunty tunes on his one-man-band. Yet his doleful audience look as if they've been forced to watch one of those late night Open University programmes on BBC2. Why did they hire him, he wonders? Is it that this particular bunch of pre-schoolers would prefer a freestyle party with no entertainer, or that he is a particularly substandard clown?

Think, think. Balloon animals – that always delights them (well, it works with Sam, Harvey's four-year-old nephew, though maybe he's just been humouring him). With a rush of determination he kicks his dove pan aside.

'Now,' he announces, 'I want you to come up with the most outrageous animal you can think of and I'll make it for you . . .' His yellow clown wig is making his head itch and the children are growing more restless by the minute. Whatever made him think this was a good idea? Before his recent incarnation as a children's entertainer, Harvey had led a reasonably healthy, functioning life, grabbing whatever small acting job came his way and keeping mind and body in shape with regular runs along the long, flat sweep of Shorling beach. He'd never realised that small people, who are barely capable of going to the loo unaided, could be so bloody hostile. Performing in front of a roomful of young strangers is *nothing* like entertaining Sam, who laughs at anything he does.

'Anyone think of an animal yet?' he asks, sweating a little.

'A dog!' chirps one of the mothers.

'A dog. Great! That's an easy one. While I do this' – he starts twisting the sausage balloons between clumsy fingers – 'the rest of you can think of something more challenging for me . . .'

'Mummy . . .' whimpers a little curly-haired girl, dissolving into quiet sobs as Harvey finally manages to fashion his sausage balloon into a dog, yes, but a dog with an unsightly bulge between its back legs, like elephantitis of the testicles.

'Bit of a malfunction there,' he sniggers, aware that it's wrong to laugh when a child is weeping just six feet in front of him. 'Now, can anyone think of any other—'

'Er, excuse me!' trills the malnourished-looking woman who booked him for this birthday party. 'Would you mind doing something musical again? I think . . .' She winces apologetically, 'the little ones might enjoy that more.'

'Oh.' He adjusts his slightly-slipped wig. 'Yeah, that's . . . that's fine.'

'It's not that we don't like your animals,' she adds quickly.

'No, no, music's great, that's an excellent idea . . .' He drops his unused balloons by his feet and struggles back into his one-man-band contraption. It's home-made, constructed during his student years, and seemed funny and quirky back then. Now, strapped to the fully formed body of a thirty-three-year-old man, it seems . . . ridiculous.

'Play "Cuckoo Clock"!' the curly-haired girl commands, having miraculously stopped crying. Relieved, he starts to play a vague approximation of the theme tune he hasn't heard for decades. 'That's the *old* one,' she complains.

'Uh?'

'They changed it,' one of the mothers offers, 'last week. It's more, er . . . *modern* now.'

Harvey stops playing. 'I'm sorry, I haven't heard it.'

'Haven't you?' the woman asks. 'I'd have thought, with this being your job—' She emits a small, withering laugh.

'Nope, no idea.' At this point in the game, there's no point in pretending.

'He doesn't watch *Cuckoo Clock*,' the curly-haired girl gasps.

No, he thinks, *because I'm an adult, you see, and the only reason I'm doing this is because my agent just told me there's nothing on the horizon – I think she's building up to dropping me actually – and unless I can rake together a couple of hundred quid I'll never make this month's rent . . .*

'Well, er,' the skinny woman says, glancing at the other mothers anxiously, 'maybe that's enough for today? What

140

does everyone think?' There are a few nods from the adults, and an air of relief fills the room.

With difficulty, Harvey unstraps his one-man-band and places it carefully on the scuffed parquet floor. The skinny woman appears beside him, addressing the audience with a rictus grin. 'That was great, wasn't it, boys and girls? Now let's all put our hands together for Charlie Chuckles!'

'Harvey,' he corrects her, but she fails to hear. He checks his watch. He was booked till four, and it's only twenty past three.

*

Of course, his name isn't really Harvey Chuckles. He is Harvey Galbraith, an actor who grew up in Cumbria before heading south, and who has spent the past decade feeling ridiculously grateful for whatever crumb of work has fluttered his way. For a few years, he nabbed parts in enough TV dramas and plays to convince him that this was a career worth pursuing. Yet things dwindled away and, during especially barren periods, he resorted to doing a little modelling. There was the odd catalogue, or women's magazine at the less glamorous end of the spectrum, in which he'd invariably be cast as the 'husband' in fashion shoots, kitted out in Aran sweaters and chinos, often accessorised with a Labrador on a lead. But even that has dried up now. 'Sorry, Harv,' Lisa, his old modelling agent told him. 'You're still a good-looking guy but you're not striking enough to make it as the Mature Hunk.'

So here he is, packing his clowning gear into the boot of his five-year-old Punto in Shorling community centre's car park. On this blustery Friday afternoon, he hasn't even bothered to change out of his costume or take off his face-paint. This isn't like him at all; when he started this six months ago, he vowed that no one would find out what

141

he was doing. No one who mattered, anyway. Harvey has been single for a criminally lengthy period, and he suspects that, if any woman finds out what he does, he'll have no chance of meeting anyone. What kind of adult female wants to go out with a clown, for God's sake? Oh, maybe once – just for a laugh – but there'd be no possibility of anything serious, anything *real*. A sharp wind whips through the springy yellow curls of his acrylic wig as he closes the car boot. Scraps of litter twist and dance across the car park, and there are bursts of laughter from the children inside the hall. *Now* they're having fun, charging up and down like a pack of raucous hounds which is all, frankly, children really want to do. They don't want to watch a small metal bird disappear into a dove pan.

Spots of rain are starting to fall. Harvey climbs into his car and turns on the windscreen wipers, watching their back-and-forth motion for a few moments. A scrap of white paper is trapped under one of them and doesn't appear to be dislodging. Clicking the wipers off, he steps back out into the rain and pulls it out from beneath the wiper.

'Look, Mummy, a clown!' a little girl yelps from the pavement. Harvey turns and gives her a half-hearted wave; she waves back, beaming delightedly. Still clutching the damp piece of paper, he realises he can't just chuck it on the ground – not in front of the only non-hostile child he's encountered all day. 'I like your wig,' she calls out, giggling.

'Thank you.' He bows graciously as she and her mother wave again and make their way down the street. Harvey glances down at the soggy fragment in his hand. Although it's smudged and barely legible, he can just make out a single word: 'piano'. Carefully avoiding tearing the paper, he unfolds it and reads: PIANO TUITION KERRY, plus a mobile number.

Piano lessons. It's raining harder now, causing Harvey's diamond-patterned satin trousers to cling to his legs. But he's stopped noticing the cold and imagines himself sitting in an elderly lady's front room, perhaps being offered tea from a china cup. The room would be warm, with a sleeping cat on the rug, and the piano teacher would teach him to play something beautiful. It doesn't matter that Harvey doesn't know anything about classical music, or that the nearest he's come to playing the piano is tinkering about on his ancient Casio keyboard at home. Because right now, the music that fills his head is making this wet October day feel a little less bleak.

Imagine . . . not playing the wrong *Cuckoo Clock* song on his one-man-band but something *lovely*, like rippling water. What would it be – Handel, Chopin or another of those dead guys? Harvey has no idea. But he knows that being able to play would be an escape from all of this – something of his own. The clowning has to stop, he decides, climbing back into his car and pulling out his phone from the pocket of his baggy red jacket. He places the tiny, sodden piece of paper on the passenger seat. Then, with a swirl of excitement in his stomach, and making a mental note to switch back to his normal voice – not his Harvey Chuckles voice – he taps out the piano teacher's number.

Chapter Twenty-Two

As soon as Kerry takes the call, Buddy zips across her path, pulling urgently on his lead. Until now, he'd been walking obediently at her side but, like a small child taking exception to his mother making a phone call, he seems to resent not having her full attention.

'That's great,' she tells the well-spoken man, keeping a firm grip on the lead as Buddy strains ahead. 'Yes, I still have some spaces, I'm sure I can fit you in . . .'

Mothers – plus the odd dad – are converging on the school gates. Despite the light rain, hair is neat and outfits look thought about rather than flung together in haste. Kerry feels suddenly self-conscious in her scruffy brown jacket.

'I'm an absolute beginner,' the man adds.

'Well, that's fine because I work with all abilities—' Her words are drowned out by an outburst of barking. Buddy appears to have spied another dog – a small, fluffy black thing, like a Mongolian cushion, with no discernible features that Kerry can make out. It glides along beside its owner, as if on casters, paying no heed to the cacophony of barking several metres to its left. Apart from a quick frown in their direction, the owner hasn't acknowledged them either. She strides on in her blue linen dress and camel trenchcoat, heels clicking as Buddy scrambles to get towards them.

'Buddy, stop it,' Kerry hisses as he continues to bark and lunge, nails scraping frantically on the pavement.

Now the cushion's owner has stopped. 'I'm not sure *he* should be going to school,' she remarks over the racket.

'Buddy, *stop*. He's just . . . new,' she explains. 'I only picked him up half an hour ago. He's probably a bit unsettled . . .'

'Huh. Is *that* what you call it?' the woman scoffs, dark bob swinging around her pointed chin. 'I'd say he's completely out of control. Is he aggressive?'

'No, of course not,' Kerry exclaims, realising that, actually, she has no idea. That man – James – said he wasn't, but then, if he was desperate to rehome him, he was hardly likely to say, 'There is a small chance he might savage your children.'

She realises she's still gripping her phone. 'Sorry, call you back,' she shouts over the barking, not sure if the caller is still there or not. Quickly shoving her mobile into her jacket pocket, she grips Buddy's lead with both hands.

'That dog shouldn't be around children,' the woman says sharply, trotting off with her docile hound and merging with the other parents at the gate.

Kerry exhales fiercely. Great. First day as a dog owner and already she's failed. Should she have primed herself to spot other dogs before Buddy did, and made a point of avoiding them? She'd always assumed dogs enjoyed mingling with others of their kind, with all the butt-sniffing that goes on. Relief floods through her as, with the other dog out of sight now, Buddy's barks gradually subside. Now he's just panting, which still doesn't look especially friendly, but at least it's unlikely to alarm small children when they come out of school.

Now Lara and Emily have appeared at her side. It's spooky, the way they appear inseparable, always patrolling as a pair.

'Ooh,' Lara remarks. 'I heard all that commotion. Got a new friend, I see.'

'Yes,' Kerry says with a grin, 'this is Buddy . . .'

'Oh, he's very sweet. Bit nervy, though, isn't he? I'd say he has *issues*.'

'I don't think—'

'He was only barking,' Brigid exclaims, striding towards them in a garish pink mac, her hair piled up messily and secured with a giant plastic tortoiseshell claw. 'That's what dogs are designed to do, Lara.'

'Yes, but that one doesn't.' Kerry indicates the cushion dog lurking beside its owner, and quickly repositions herself to block it from Buddy's vision.

Brigid has bobbed down to ruffle Buddy's fur. 'He's adorable, isn't he? What a gorgeous dog! And he'll soon settle down. He's just trying to assert his authority.'

'Well, I hope so.' Kerry checks her watch, willing the minutes to flash by and the children to rush out of school so they can meet Buddy and go home before he attracts any more sour looks.

'Oh, is he new?' A woman in a sky-blue running top and startlingly tight shorts grins down at Buddy.

'Yes, I've just picked him up today.'

'Bet the children love him.'

Kerry grins. 'They haven't met him yet. He's a surprise for them, can't wait till they come out . . .'

'Ah, that'll be nice for them after all they've been through.'

Kerry blinks at the woman. 'Er, well, they've been begging me for years to get one. It's been a long, intense campaign and I finally crumbled.'

The woman makes big, patronising eyes at Kerry and pats her arm. 'That's wonderful. I have to say, I think you're all coping very well, considering.'

'Do you?' Kerry frowns, aware of Brigid regarding the woman with mild horror.

'Oh yes. It must be *so* hard . . .'

What, to have your husband impregnate the work

146

experience – sorry, editorial assistant? It's shocking, the way details about your life spread around here, Chinese-whispers style. Kerry has mentioned her situation in passing to Lara, Emily and a couple of others, but is floored by this sudden outpouring of sympathy.

'We're all doing fine, thanks,' she says firmly, making a point of turning away to cut that woman, with her *you-can-tell-me-all-about-it-dear* therapist's voice, from her vision. Not much happens around here, that's the problem, so any small event is leapt upon and gleefully discussed. And now that woman is murmuring to a friend, 'That's the one who . . .'

'That's right,' Kerry wants to scream, 'and you know what else? His new girlfriend is twenty years old. That's *seventeen years younger than me*. She is astoundingly pretty with huge blue eyes and small, sticky-out, modelly breasts. and I know this because I've not only met her, albeit briefly – but I also went out and bought that stupid magazine, *Mr Jones*, and when I saw her pouty picture on the contributors' page I nearly threw up all over it . . .'

Thankfully, Brigid has swiftly engaged the two gossiping women in a conversation about plans for improving the playground. Kerry should probably join in, perhaps ingratiating herself by offering to make several hundred cupcakes to raise funds, but she doesn't have the energy right now. She glances down at Buddy, wondering if this is how her life will be now: hanging out with a black and white mongrel with an aversion to cushions. Well, at least he's being sweet, pressed up lovingly against her legs, the pleasing warmth from his furry body permeating her jeans. And the benefits, she suspects, will be many. Unlike a husband of ten years, he won't moan about the office or the fact that Freddie has crayoned his trousers or squirted his man moisturiser into the sink. Dogs don't have jobs, trousers or expensive skin-care. Their needs are simple: food, water, exercise and love – ah. And the other thing. The thing that appears to be

147

happening now as Buddy shifts away from Kerry's legs and assumes a squatting stance on the pavement.

For one brief, optimistic moment, she wonders if he's merely . . . *flexing*. When Freddie was a baby, she'd signed up for a course of yoga classes in the hope of becoming one of those serene, dreamy mums who reacts to spilt milk-sodden Weetabix with a beatific smile. In fact, she'd only made it to one class, and Buddy's tensed, slightly trembling pose reminds her of the only position she could manage: on hands and knees, bum to the ground, as if pooing.

Only, in this case, not 'as if', but actually dumping a load. 'Oh, God,' Kerry mutters.

She glances around at the glowy-faced parents in the hope that, by the time she looks back down at the ground, the mighty deposit will have miraculously disappeared, or at the very least have slipped discreetly away down a pavement crack. But no. It's still horribly, conspicuously there, almost glowing like neon. Could she blame it on that cushion dog? She spots him through the gathering of parents, snuffling at the ground. No, he's tiny compared to Buddy. Anything that drops out of his bottom will be no bigger than a chickpea.

'Brigid,' she hisses as a couple of mothers turn to glare at the mess.

Brigid breaks off her conversation and hurries over. 'You okay, Kerry?'

'Not really. Look.' She points at the ground and grimaces.

'Oh dear. Not a good place for that.'

'I know, and I don't have a bag with me. I didn't even bring my shoulder bag, I just shoved my purse and phone in my pocket . . .'

Brigid groans. 'I don't have a thing on me. Sorry.'

'Er, I've got this.' With a withering smile, Lara holds up a lilac paper carrier bag with a ribbon tie and 'Dilly's Bakery' printed on it in elegant script. 'It's got macaroons in it,' she adds. 'They're our regular Friday treat but I guess you could have the bag, if you're desperate . . .'

'No, I can't use your lovely macaroon bag for poo.' Kerry pulls out her purse and flicks through its cluttered interior. Much as she'd like to pretend otherwise, there's no way she'll be able to pick up Buddy's rank deposit with a WH Smiths receipt.

Cushion dog's owner is at her side now, pursing her lips and extracting a little black plastic sack from her handbag. 'Here,' she says with a tight smile.

'Thank you. I must be better prepared next time.' Kerry quickly bags up the poo and knots it tightly, privately marvelling at how weighty it is. At least Buddy hasn't started barking again, even though the other dog is beside them now, sniffing him with great interest. Distance seems to be his trigger, Kerry observes. 'Guess I've got a lot to learn,' she adds with a forced laugh. 'If he starts that crouching thing again, I'll know to put a cork in it, haha.'

The woman eyes her with distaste and takes a step back. But Kerry no longer cares what anyone thinks, because Brigid is exclaiming, 'Look – here they come!' The rain has stopped, and the playground is wet and shiny in the weak afternoon sun as the children surge out of school. Kerry spots Mia first in her tomato-red sweatshirt and grey pleated skirt, swinging her battered Horrible Histories lunchbox. Spotting her mother, she smiles and waves; she hasn't registered Buddy yet. Then she does, and there's a small hesitation as if she can't quite believe what she's seeing, or perhaps she's thinking, *Oh, that's a cute dog sitting near Mummy*. Her smile brightens as she hurries towards Kerry, then Freddie appears, registering Buddy immediately and zooming towards them like a rocket.

'Mummy!' he yells. 'Whose dog is this?'

'He's ours,' Kerry laughs.

'Really?' Mia exclaims, tears springing into her dark eyes. 'Ours to keep, forever?'

'Yes – yes, of course, sweetheart.' Kerry realises she's not just laughing but crying too, as her children bob down to hug Buddy.

'Is it a boy or a girl?' Mia wants to know.

'He's a boy, about six, his owner didn't want . . .' She tails off, as Freddie and Mia are too excited to absorb any information right now. Other children push forward, and soon Buddy is surrounded by a delighted crowd. Kerry knows she should warn them to be careful because he still seems a little unsure, but she doesn't want to spoil the moment and anyway, his tail is wagging so much, it looks as if it could spin off.

'He's a hit then,' Lara observes with a wry smile.

'Yes, looks like it.'

'He's a beauty,' Brigid says, 'isn't he, Joe?'

'Yeah, he's great.' Her son digs at the lump of gum in his mouth, stretches it out and pops it back in again.

'Oh, Mummy,' Freddie blurts out, throwing his arms around her. 'I love him, thank you, thank you!'

'This is the best day of my life,' Mia declares. 'What shall we call him?'

'Well, he's called Buddy at the moment but we can change it if you like, if you can both agree on another name . . .'

'No,' Mia insists, 'I like Buddy . . .'

'Me too,' Freddie declares, his expression changing to one of puzzlement as he looks up at his mother. 'Why are you crying?'

'Oh, don't worry,' she says quickly, 'these are happy tears.'

They turn to leave with Brigid and Joe, plus a gaggle of children all clamouring to hold Buddy's lead. Swinging her knotted poo bag, Kerry murmurs to Brigid, 'I think he might be a bit of a handful actually.'

'Don't worry.' Brigid gives her arm a squeeze. 'The most interesting men always are.'

Chapter Twenty-three

'Come over again if you like,' Nadine had murmured in the tiny office kitchen this afternoon. 'I'm having a low-key night in.' Hmmm. Well, that had sounded okay: a couple of hours at her place, perhaps staying over again, then up with the lark, back home to change and make himself look like a respectable dad on his way to pick up his children for the weekend. (*I'm a weekend dad now* . . . the phrase had been turning over in his mind all day.) So he and Nadine had jumped in a cab back to her place.

'You don't need to cook for me,' he says now as she starts busying away in the kitchen.

'Oh, I'm just getting a few bits and pieces together. They like something to nibble with their drinks.'

Rob frowns. *They?*

'They're coming over about half eight-ish,' she adds.

'Er, who?' he asks lightly.

'Just a few friends.' There's the clink of crockery, and the sound of a packet being ripped open.

He gets up and peers into the kitchen. 'A few friends? You never said . . .'

She smiles prettily, clutching a large glass bowl of tortilla chips. 'It *is* Friday night, Rob. Don't you normally do something fun at the weekend?'

'Er . . . yes, I suppose so,' he fibs.

'Well, since I've been feeling a bit tired and queasy I haven't really been in the mood for going out.'

'I can understand that,' Rob says. To his shame, he realises he hadn't known she'd been feeling under the weather.

'So I thought I'd ask the girls round. You don't *mind*, do you?'

'Of course not. God, Nadine. It's your flat and, like you say, it's Friday night . . .' His mind starts to whir as he tries to conjure up an excuse as to why he must leave right now.

She puts down the bowl on the worktop and starts removing pink glasses from the wall cabinet to line up on the worktop. One . . . two . . . three . . . four . . .

'Do they, um . . . know?' he asks as a fifth glass joins the others and the cupboard is, mercifully, shut.

'About the baby?' She laughs. 'Of course they do, Rob. They're my best friends.'

'But isn't it a bit early? I mean, you haven't had a scan yet, I'd have thought you'd want to keep it quiet . . .'

'Rob, these girls are *the most important people in my life*,' she declares. 'Why wouldn't I want to share it with them?'

Rob is momentarily stuck for words. *Because it's too early, anything could happen . . .*

'Wouldn't it be more, er . . . comfortable if I wasn't here?' He checks his watch, willing her to say yes.

'No, of course it wouldn't.' Nadine sighs, fixing him with those gorgeous blue eyes which have the effect of stirring something within him, despite the almighty mess he's found himself in. 'Last night was really nice,' she offers hesitantly, touching his arm.

'Yes, it was.' He musters a smile.

'You were very sweet.'

'Er . . . thank you.' *This doesn't mean I'm ready to meet*

your friends en masse . . . He swallows hard. While he's slowly getting used to Nadine's extreme youth, the thought of spending an evening with a bunch of similarly-aged girls is quite terrifying. What will they talk about – clubbing, the tribulations of teenage complexions or, heaven forbid, chart music? The Top 20 hasn't bothered Rob's consciousness for at least a decade.

'Come on, Rob,' she chides him, 'cheer up. This is a special night for me – a sort of celebration. And they're so looking forward to meeting you.'

'Really?' He frowns.

'Of course they are! We're going to be parents, Rob, and they want to share that.' Her eyes sparkle like sequins.

Although it's tempting to snatch his phone from his pocket and announce some fictional crisis, he forces a grin and says, 'Okay, if you're sure.'

'Great, I'm so pleased. You know, you're not nearly as stuffy as people think.'

*

'You're adorable, Rob,' Sasha gushes as he stands in the middle of Nadine's living room, clutching two drinks.

'Gorgeous,' agrees Jade, pulling up her knees to her chin on the sofa and exposing several miles of tanned limb beneath a diaphanous turquoise dress.

'I told you, he's not so bad,' Nadine says fondly, while Harriet flops a head onto her shoulder. Sasha, Jade and Harriet are Nadine's friends from 'way, way back' – which probably means about eighteen months, Rob surmises. Unlike Nadine, with her chic make-up and neat crop, these girls are all of the glossy-lipped, swishy blonde hair variety, like some girl group thrown together for a TV talent show. Rob feels as if he has accidentally stumbled into a branch of Claire's Accessories.

'I can't believe you're having a baby, Nads,' Sasha announces, clutching her pink glass. 'It's the best thing I've ever heard in my life.'

I very much doubt that, Rob thinks darkly, crunching a cashew.

'It's amazing,' gushes Jade. 'How d'you feel, Rob? Are you *so* excited?'

'Of course,' Rob replies. 'It's absolutely terrific.'

Harriet giggles. 'You're going to have an adorable little baby. Look at the pair of you – you're so lovely together. I know it's all happened really quickly but don't you think,' – she looks around at the others – 'that some things are just meant to be?'

'Oh, yeah,' Jade declares, already appearing a little tipsy as she drains her glass. The girls are drinking 'Pink Ginger', a mocktail of Nadine's invention consisting of ginger beer (to counteract nausea), elderflower and rhubarb cordials, plus a generous splosh of vodka for her friends. To Rob's mind, it tastes like liquid seaside rock.

Jade fixes her large, rather scary kohl-rimmed grey eyes on Rob. 'So what names are you thinking of?'

'Er, we haven't yet,' he replies.

'How about Joshua?' Harriet offers. 'I always thought Joshua was sweet, or Freddie . . .'

Nadine laughs huskily while Rob busies himself by straightening up the little bowls of snacks on the low table. 'He has a Freddie already,' Nadine explains, 'so that's kind of out.'

'Whoops,' Jade giggles, clasping a hand over her mouth.

'I like those natural names,' Sasha muses, 'like Summer or Autumn or Rain . . .'

'Hail would be good,' Rob mutters under his breath, striding back to the kitchen. 'Or Thunder. Yep, Thunder Tambini has a certain ring . . .' He blinks at the open shelves Nadine has arranged with all manner of quirky 'finds', as she calls them: little tin vehicles, a green crocheted frog, a glass paperweight with Dolly Mixture sweets trapped inside. While he found her single-girl's flat a tad too cutesy for his taste on his first visit, it now feels claustrophobic. Horribly un-baby-friendly, too, with all her itsy-bitsy chokeable trinkets all over the place. *Rain*, he reflects. Great, if you want your child to be in psychotherapy by age six.

He is a little drunk, too, he realises now as he leans back against the baby-blue fridge. The kitchen is strewn with fairy lights – it's like being in a bloody grotto – and Rob is overwhelmed by a pang of missing his old life. He craves Kerry and his children, all crammed around the slightly too-small table in their old kitchen in Bethnal Green, with its naff faux-teak units and the children's drawings Blu-Tacked wonkily all over the cupboards.

The unrecognisable music has been turned up now, and the girls are shouting to be heard over it. He rejoins the group and tries, gamely, to join in, but they keep talking over each other and it becomes impossible to follow their conversational threads without bellowing, 'Sorry, what did you say?' like some wizened old man with an ear trumpet.

Escaping to the bathroom, Rob lands heavily on the loo seat and fishes out his phone from his pocket. Without considering what he's doing, he calls Kerry's number.

'It's me,' he whispers.

'Rob? What d'you want?'

'Um . . .' He realises he has no idea what he intended to say. He just wanted – no, *needed* – to hear her voice. 'I er . . . wanted to say sorry for being so negative about the dog thing. Just wondered if the kids were excited when they met him?' He puts his head in his hands, realising that what he really wanted to say was, *I love you, Kerry. I love you so much and I want you back*.

'Hmmm,' Kerry murmurs. 'Yes, of course they were delighted. They'll tell you all about it tomorrow and you'll

155

see him – Buddy – when you pick them up. Don't worry, though – he's been briefed not to home in on your crotch.'

'That's good, haha.'

There's a small, tense pause. 'Where are you?'

'Um . . . at, er . . . the flat.' He clears his throat. 'Nadine's place . . .'

'Sounds like a party.'

'It's . . . a sort of girls' night in.'

Kerry snorts. 'What, like a sleepover?'

Rob senses himself flushing, and some part of that drink – the rhubarb component most likely – fizzles chemically at the back of his throat. 'Not exactly, no . . .'

'Are they painting their nails and applying face packs?'

'No, they're just . . . playing music and chatting, and I just wanted to call—'

'Er, Rob,' Kerry cuts in. 'I'm kind of busy.'

'Oh.' His stomach slumps. Christ, the girls are singing now, punctuated by bursts of high-pitched laughter. He thinks of Kerry curled up on their knackered old sofa in Shorling and almost chokes with yearning.

'You can't do this,' she adds.

'What?'

'Phone me out of the blue like this, just because you're feeling out of your depth or whatever it is, and want something old and familiar.'

He frowns so hard, it causes his skull to throb. 'You're not old and familiar, Kerry.'

There's a bitter laugh. 'I'm going now.'

'Oh . . . okay.'

'*Please* don't do this again. It's not fair and it's not very good for me right now.' Her voice trembles as they finish the call.

Now Rob feels even worse. He didn't plan to upset her – it's the last thing he wants. He just wanted to say something nice to the woman he loves, and all he could think of was to praise her for going ahead with the dog thing. *You've done the right thing*, he'd wanted to say, *if it makes Freddie and Mia happy after all they've been through. Christ, get them a whole bloody pack of hounds if you want to, and I'm sorry, so sorry for everything – for Nadine and the baby and fucking up so badly, and if I could do anything to make it not have happened, then I would . . .*

But it's too late for that. What Rob must do now is go back into the living room where the girls will have decided that his unborn child should be called Fern or Crocus. For a short while he'll have to pretend to be enjoying himself, just to be polite. Then he'll feign another migraine and take himself off to his cold, empty house, feeling as if his heart could break.

Chapter Twenty-Four

It's gone ten by the time Kerry has finally coaxed the children to bed, having persuaded them that, yes, they still have to go to Nanny and Nonno's with Daddy tomorrow, but it's only for one night. And yes, of course Buddy will still be here when they get back on Sunday.

'It's not one night,' Freddie bleated. 'It's *two whole days*.'

And now with the children in bed it's just Kerry and Buddy, sharing the living room sofa (her no-dog-on-furniture rule lasted approximately five minutes). When she goes through to the kitchen he trots at her heels, his gaze unwavering as she extracts the wine bottle from the fridge and pours herself a glass. He tails her to the music room, sitting expectantly at her feet as she starts to play the piano. And when she gets up from her stool to select a piece of music from her files, he looks up, following her every movement.

'It's okay,' she says, patting his head. 'I'm just going to the loo. Back in a minute.' She hopes Buddy's expression indicates that that's okay (it's impossible to tell). Yet, as soon as she's shut the bathroom door behind her, his distressed whine quickly morphs into urgent barks. With a sigh, she lets him in, leaving the door open and trying not to feel under surveillance as she attends to business with him staring at her.

The flush of the loo seems to terrify him, and he shoots out, coming to a panting standstill at the front door.

'D'you need to go out?' she ponders, clipping on his lead and stepping out into the small, gravelled front garden. 'Yes, I guess you do.' There, just outside the house, she spots Buddy's bag of food, document file and a couple of bowls all packed neatly into his basket; James must have dropped everything off without knocking. Just as well it hasn't rained. *Thanks a lot*, Kerry mutters, deciding he clearly wants as little communication with her as possible. She circuits the garden several times until Buddy pees, then takes him inside, praying his barking doesn't wake the children as she dashes back outside to retrieve the basket.

Is he exhibiting separation anxiety, like babies and toddlers have? Placing his basket in the corner of the living room and plumping up its paw-patterned cushion, she tries to coax him into it. He jumps up onto the sofa instead, wriggling to get comfortable, and when she sits beside him he rests his head on her lap. Now Kerry can't fetch her wine or even reach the TV remote. She is trapped, and there's nothing for it but to sit here with her now-sleeping dog, listening to the faint rush of the waves in the distance.

Her trilling mobile makes Buddy flinch, and she snatches it from her jeans pocket.

'Kerry? It's James.'

'You mean Buddy-James?'

'Yes.' He chuckles. 'Look, I'm really sorry to call you so late . . .'

'That's okay. Is something wrong?' A thought strikes her: he wants Buddy back. That brusqueness – it was all a cover-up, and he's realised he's made a terrible mistake.

James clears his throat. 'I should have explained. You see, I'm helping my son with his business – he has a

159

sandwich shop – while trying to keep up with my own website design work. Things have been incredibly hectic lately, but this evening, when I started to think about Buddy . . .' He tails off.

'I did wonder,' she says carefully, running a hand over Buddy's soft fur. How on earth will she tell Freddie and Mia that Buddy has to go back? Rob was right – it *was* a rash move. Even if this hadn't happened, all kinds of things can go wrong: illness, accidents, death . . . Buddy opens an amber eye and looks at her. She no longer cares about his barking outburst or the fact that he pooed outside school; it's *just what dogs do*.

'. . . He has a few issues,' James is saying, 'since, er, something happened at home.'

'Oh, I see.'

'He gets really anxious,' James goes on, 'like if he sees or hears another dog that he can't greet and sniff, and if a truck goes by – any large vehicle really – and there's been some chewing and the odd, er, little accident . . .'

'I'm sorry to hear that,' she murmurs.

'No, *I'm* sorry. I wish I'd been more honest with you from the start.'

Kerry bites her lip. His voice is lovely; warmer and friendlier than the clipped tone he'd adopted when she'd been at his house. 'You can come and pick him up tomorrow if you like,' she says flatly.

'Oh. Er . . . right. Okay.'

There's a stilted pause, and Buddy shifts position so as to edge further onto Kerry's lap. 'My children will be away with their dad then,' she adds, 'and I'd rather it happened when they're not around. The sooner the better, I suppose, before they get too attached.' Some hope of that. The entire evening has been filled with cuddling, grooming and playing with Buddy, and he seemed to relish the attention.

'Er, I only want him back if he's too much for you,' James says.

'No, *I* didn't say he was too much. I thought you said you'd made a mistake . . .'

'Did I?' James sounds baffled. 'No, I just wanted you to know what he's like – his little quirks, I suppose. I thought you should know what you're taking on. But he'd never hurt or bite anyone and he loves people. He's just . . .'

'A handful?' Kerry says, laughing now and overcome with relief. 'Oh, of course I don't want you to take him back. Absolutely not. My children are thrilled and we all think he's fantastic – in fact he's asleep with his head on my lap right now.'

'He's doing that with you already?' James sounds as if he's smiling.

'Yes, he is.' Buddy opens an eye again and she's filled with a rush of warmth for him. 'I'm sure we can cope with his quirks.'

'I'm really glad. I just felt, you know – a bit guilty . . .'

'A sort of Trade Descriptions Act thing?'

'Yeah.' He chuckles. 'Well, maybe I'll run into you sometime when you're out walking him.'

Kerry pictures James in his empty-feeling house, with a space in the hall where Buddy's basket used to be, and it's on the tip of her tongue to arrange something. But he clearly has too much on his plate right now. 'I'm sure he'd like that,' she says. 'And thanks, James. He's the perfect dog for us.'

Later, when Kerry goes to bed, Buddy follows her upstairs and leaps up onto her bed, settling on the lower section of the duvet. It's tempting to let him stay there; the bed has felt huge since she moved here, and seems to have expanded even more these past few weeks. But she can't let Buddy sleep here, as some kind of husband substitute; it would be too sad, too *poor-dumped-wife* to contemplate. Yet he wants

161

to be near her, so she fetches his basket from downstairs and places it in the corner of her bedroom.

He curls up in it instantly. Soon she hears his deep, steady breathing, and as Kerry drifts towards sleep herself, she already feels a little less alone.

PART TWO

Settling in

'There are bound to be a few small hiccups during the early days. Building a new relationship requires much time and patience.'

Your First Dog: A Complete Guide
by Jeremy Catchpole

Chapter Twenty-Five

December 1, the first snowfall

'SNOW!' Freddie charges into Kerry's bedroom where she's still submerged in duvet and launches himself on top of her.

'Ooof,' she cries, catching her breath. 'What is it, Freddie?'

'Snow, Mummy, snow!' Mia appears in the Mickey Mouse pyjamas Rob's parents bought her, much to his distaste. Commercial tat, he reckons, but who cares what he thinks these days? It's childish, yes – but Kerry now derives untold pleasure from the children enjoying the things Rob regards as either 'tacky' (contraband chocolate cereals, all things Disney) or 'potentially dangerous and certainly troublesome' (dogs). She knows she shouldn't waste brain space by considering Rob's likes and dislikes; it's been two months since the split, after all. Yet she can't ignore a frisson of delight as she reflects how much he'd hate a bounding, panting animal on the bed, shedding his fur and biting playfully at a pillow. It's astounded her, how quickly she's fallen in love with Buddy, and how he and Freddie are providing all the male attention she needs right now (despite Brigid urging her to pounce on attractive male dog-walkers). Anyway, it's not as if she's being besieged by offers. At the current time, Buddy is the only male trying to lick Kerry's face around here.

Freddie, Mia and Buddy are all on her bed now, peering out through the window as fat snowflakes fall from a colourless sky.

'Come and see, Mummy,' Mia commands, her face pressed up against the glass.

'I can see from here, sweetheart . . .'

'Come and see *properly*.'

'Okay, okay,' she laughs, glancing at her alarm clock as she squeezes in beside her children at the window. At 7.48 a.m., Shorling is waking to its first snowfall of the year. The row of beach huts and the ice cream kiosk are already thinly coated in white. The sea view from Kerry's bedroom has helped to soothe her during these past eight weeks, and it's all the better for being shrouded in fresh, storybook snow.

'Hey, you've already got your boots on,' Kerry remarks, spotting a flash of silvery rubber peeping out from Freddie's PJ bottoms.

'Yeah.' Freddie's wellies are as sparkly as disco balls, bought for him during his last visit to Rob's parents. Rob told her he'd spotted them, glinting in their come-hither way in a shop window (as far as Mary is concerned, whatever the grandchildren desire must be theirs).

'He slept in them,' Mia announces, 'like, *all* night.'

'You can't have,' Kerry says as Freddie starts giggling.

'I did,' he says proudly. 'I sleep with my wellies on every night.'

'What, every night since you were at Nanny and Nonno's last week?' Kerry asks. 'But I always tuck you in and you're never wearing them then . . .'

'He waits till you've gone,' Mia offers, with a pause for effect, 'then he puts 'em on in secret.'

'Oh, *Freddie* . . .'

'So I'm always ready for snow,' he announces with a grin, and Kerry feels her spirits rise as she, the children and Buddy all bound downstairs.

They're lucky, she reflects over a hasty breakfast. Kerry has, if she says so herself, managed to remain remarkably adult throughout the whole Rob debacle, if only because she's been unable to think of anything which would cause him maximum inconvenience and humiliation and not have her arrested. Yet it's the children who have emerged as the real stars of this New Situation. While their friendships here are still a little tentative, the announcement that Daddy has spread his seed to produce a new poppet triggered, after the initial confusion, a distinct air of – well, not *excitement* exactly, but curiosity. And right now, Kerry reflects, Nadine is likely to be vomiting noisily into the washbasin and cursing Rob for ruining her young life.

*

An hour later, after a frantic search for gloves, hats and scarves, the children are whizzing on sledges down the slopes of Thorny Park in the crisp sunshine. Soon they're joined by Brigid and Joe, who busies himself by bossing Freddie and Mia around, demanding turns on Mia's 'faster' sledge and lobbing snowballs at his mother. The fact that her children accept Joe's superior role hints, Kerry suspects, that they are impressed by his cocky attitude. Meanwhile, Roxy seems happiest sitting regally on the sidelines, observing Buddy tearing around in circles, as if running just for the joy of it. She loves that about him: how easily pleased he is, delighting in being free.

'It's funny,' she tells Brigid, 'but I can't imagine being without him.'

Brigid smiles. 'It happens amazingly quickly, doesn't it?'

'It really does. I know there's all the walking, and we still have barking outbursts and he's terrified of the toilet flush *and* there's been the odd pee on the kitchen floor. But in other ways he's so . . . undemanding.'

'And there's the man-attracting thing I told you about,' Brigid adds.

'Oh, I'm sure you're right, but I'm so not looking for anyone right now.'

Brigid raises a brow. 'Not even casually?'

'No, not even that. God, I just feel . . . I don't have the headspace for that.'

'Not even just a quickie in the afternoon while the kids are in school?'

Kerry bursts out laughing. 'God. No. No, thanks.'

'Well,' Brigid says, 'maybe you should.'

Kerry looks at her and frowns. 'Why? Do I seem . . . I don't know . . . as if I sort of *need* it? Like I'm frustrated or something? Don't tell me I'm giving off desperate vibes . . .'

'No, I just mean, it'd be *nice* for you. You're either teaching or writing your songs or looking after the children and, well, we all need a little treat sometimes.'

Kerry turns this possibility over in her mind. Even if she were to meet someone – and God knows how she'd do that – would she be capable of desiring a man, of unearthing her libido when her head is filled with shopping lists, school forms, *Cuckoo Clock* and teaching? When she forces herself to think about sex, she can't imagine it ever feeling like a lovely, natural thing to do. If it were on the cards, she'd have to regard it as a project – like lagging the boiler – and mentally prepare herself for it.

'I don't have a sex drive any more,' she confides. 'Maybe it's the whole Rob thing, or work – I mean, it's hard to think about being naked with someone when you're desperately trying to figure out lyrics about birds flying off to Africa for their winter holidays. It kind of kills it for me.'

Brigid eyes her solemnly. 'Yes, I can imagine, but you still have *needs*, Kerry. You owe it to yourself.'

Kerry chuckles. 'No, I think I'm going to turn into a

withered old lady with a crocheted blanket over my knees, doing the puzzles in *Woman's Weekly*.'

'Oh, for God's sake. You're only thirty-seven. Men are always checking you out, you know.'

'Really? I hadn't noticed.' Kerry laughs witheringly and glances down the hill where the children are patting snow onto their snowman's belly. In the distance, a tall figure is marching purposely along the whitened path; spotting him, Buddy tears away from the children and races towards him, leaping up in delight. 'Oh, God,' Kerry blurts out, charging down the hill, already apologising, then realising, as the man turns toward her, that it's James. 'I guess he's just pleased to see you,' she says with relief.

'Hey, Buddy-boy. Good to see you too.' James smiles and bends down to ruffle his fur.

Hot on Kerry's heels, Brigid flashes James a big, bold smile as he straightens up.

'Brigid,' Kerry says, 'this is James, Buddy's previous owner.'

'Nice to meet you, James.' She tosses back her abundant fair hair. 'Buddy's such a character.'

'Well,' James says hesitantly, 'he's been through a lot over the past couple of years.'

'Oh, what happened?' Brigid asks, and Kerry flinches at her brazenness.

'Um . . .' James pauses, picking up a stick and throwing it in a huge arc for Buddy to chase. 'I guess it started when we lost Suzie, then he got even worse when . . .' He tails off and shrugs, as if having second thoughts about sharing it.

'Oh.' Kerry glances at Brigid, willing her not to fire any more questions.

'Were they really close?' Brigid fixes him with wide, concerned eyes.

'Yes, inseparable really.' He looks down at Buddy, who's

brought the stick back to him and dropped it at his feet. 'It was very sudden, you see. The worst part was, it was completely my fault.'

Kerry frowns. 'God, James, how awful for you.'

'I reversed over her,' he adds quietly.

'What?' Kerry blurts out. 'That's terrible . . .'

'You poor, poor man,' Brigid exclaims.

'Oh,' he adds, throwing the stick again, 'it *was* awful, and of course I wish it hadn't happened. But she was getting on a bit, she had terrible arthritis and was incontinent . . .'

Kerry blinks at him, unable to scrabble together an appropriate response. So James ran over his wife, yet is implying that, as she had health issues, it wasn't such a tragedy? She looks over to where the children are gathering up twigs for their snowman's hair. Adding a pleasing finishing touch, Joe manages to locate a dropped cigarette butt – possibly the only one in Shorling – and jabs it into the snowman's mouth.

'So I guess Buddy had a lot of readjusting to do,' Brigid murmurs.

'Yes, that's right,' James says.

Kerry catches Brigid's eye, wondering how to shift the conversation towards lighter territory, like how things are going at the sandwich shop.

'I did think about getting another one,' James adds.

'Another *wife*?' Kerry gasps. 'Well . . . I suppose there's nothing wrong with wanting to meet someone else. I, er . . . guess you had to move on . . .' She wants to leave the park now, maybe head for the seafront and treat everyone to an extortionately priced hot chocolate with whipped cream. She realises James is studying her intently, a look of incredulity in his soft grey eyes.

'No,' he says carefully, 'I mean, I thought of getting another *dog*.'

Kerry blinks at him. 'Did you think that might help? Getting another pet, I mean, after losing your wife . . .'

'I didn't *lose* my wife,' he says levelly. 'She left. Met someone else.'

'Oh, I thought you meant you'd run over her!' Brigid exclaims with a great barking laugh.

'So did I,' says Kerry, blushing furiously, 'and that maybe it was for the best what with her arthritis and incontinence and . . .'

James gawps at Kerry and Brigid in turn. 'You think I reversed over my arthritic, incontinent wife?'

'Well . . . yes.' Kerry tries to trap a laugh. 'I misunderstood. I'm sorry.' Her shoulders are shaking now, and she's convulsing inside while trying to maintain a ridiculously solemn expression.

'You assumed I'd reversed over my wife,' James says, 'and thought that was *okay*?'

'No, no of course not,' Kerry splutters.

'Suzie was a King Charles spaniel,' he says levelly.

'Oh, I'm so glad,' Kerry exclaims. 'Not that she died, of course, but because, er . . .' She is filled with relief when Freddie runs over, demanding, 'Who are *you*?'

'Freddie,' Kerry says quickly, 'that's a bit rude . . .'

'I'm James,' he says, thawing a little. 'Buddy used to be mine.'

'We love Buddy,' Freddie announces. 'Why didn't *you* like him?'

'Er, it wasn't quite like that,' James says briskly. 'Anyway, I'd better get back, make sure Luke hasn't burnt the place down trying to make a panini . . .'

Brigid flashes another beaming smile. 'Well, hopefully we'll run into you again sometime, James. It's been lovely meeting you.'

'Yes, hope to see you around,' he says unconvincingly, before virtually sprinting away.

'God.' Kerry grins as Freddie scampers back to join Mia and Joe. 'That dead wife thing.'

'I know.' Brigid shakes her head. 'Gorgeous, though, don't you think? Lovely eyes.'

'Er . . . yes, I did notice that.' She grins.

'You should call him,' Brigid adds.

'Oh, sure, after implying that he not only killed his wife but thought it was probably for the best, seeing as she had some toileting issues . . .'

They start laughing again, prompting the children to turn and look at them quizzically. 'I'm sure he wouldn't hold that against you,' Brigid sniggers.

'What about you?' Kerry asks. 'You were in full-on flirt mode unless I was misreading the signs . . .'

'Oh, that was just to remind you how it's done. Go on – you still have his number, don't you? It's almost as if it's meant to be, you two meeting through Buddy like that. I told you dogs were good for that kind of thing . . .' Then an oversized snowball hits Kerry on the side of the head, and soon she and Brigid are under siege, screaming and laughing beneath a hail of missiles, all thoughts of James forgotten.

Chapter Twenty-Six

Snow has been falling in soft flurries since Saturday, but Rob barely registers the white rooftops as he and Nadine leave her flat on Monday morning. It's proper snow, too, the kind that Mia and Freddie love: fluffy and light, demanding to be caught in mittened hands.

'*More* snow,' Nadine remarks.

'Uh-huh,' Rob says, although he couldn't care less about the weather. Today, rather boldly, they have taken the same day off work, because they are going to see a scan of their baby. The pavements are slushy and, without thinking, Rob takes Nadine's stripy-gloved hand protectively in his. He's startled by the realisation that he wants – no, *needs* to look after her. Just a week ago he was still wishing the baby wouldn't happen: that it would fade away, sadly but also – he hates to admit this – conveniently too. Although he wasn't naïve enough to believe that this would magically fix things between him and Kerry, it would certainly be easier than having a child with a girl with whom he'd exchanged less than a dozen words prior to his fortieth birthday. However, Rob is ashamed of this now, and determined to man up about the whole business. As they step into the packed Tube carriage, with him managing not to ask someone to give Nadine a seat as she is *with child*, he simply wants reassurance that the baby is okay.

By the time they reach the hospital, Nadine has become chattier, like an excited girl. She is all buttoned up in her black wool jacket with a soft blue mohair scarf at her neck, plus a little pull-on black knitted hat and her customary red lipstick. She looks lovely, Rob thinks. He must hold it together for her sake.

'I don't want to know the sex, do you?' she asks as they make their way along the bland, beige corridor.

'No, I'd rather not,' Rob agrees.

'But what if we see?' she asks excitedly. 'What if there's, you know – a tiny little willy swinging about?'

'I honestly don't think we'll see at this stage.' Rob chooses his words carefully; he knows how sensitive she is about him having gone through this twice before (although what is he supposed to do – pretend Mia and Freddie don't exist?).

'Yes, but what if we *do*?'

'Well,' Rob says, 'we'll just pretend we haven't. Anyway, it's pretty blurry and hard to see anything in real detail.'

Nadine shoots him a look as they take a right turn through swinging doors towards the reception desk. 'I wish you weren't so blasé,' she murmurs.

'I'm not, I'm just saying . . .'

'Well, I think it's a pretty big deal,' she retorts in earshot of the receptionist as she whips the appointment card from her bag.

They are directed to a waiting area where Rob pushes coins into the vending machine (coffee for him, nothing for her; these days she only tolerates mint or fennel tea). He carries it to his seat, trying to think of safe conversational topics that won't have Nadine accusing him of being blasé, or convey that he is in any way anxious. He is, though, mainly due to Nadine's tiny, bird-like body.

While Kerry breezed through both pregnancies, looking more magnificent by the day, he fears that Nadine will struggle to carry the child once it's beyond the size of a crumpet.

'So,' he says, perching on the seat beside her, 'd'you think they'll be speculating about why we've both taken the day off?'

Nadine shakes her head. 'I wouldn't think so.'

'Don't you think they must have an idea, though? I mean, Frank and Eddy have both seen us coming back from lunch together. I know we don't talk much at work but surely they must have picked up on something?' He takes a sip of gritty Americano from the cardboard cup, reflecting on how quickly he's fallen into a pattern of staying over at her place every second night or so.

'Well, I've told Eddy,' she says.

'*What?* You mean you've told him we're seeing each other?'

'No . . . I mean he knows about the baby.' She blinks at him, a small smile fluttering across her lips.

'Really?' Rob blows out a big gust of air. 'God. When did you tell him?'

'On Friday when you were out at the dentist's.'

'What, three days ago and you haven't mentioned it to me?' Rob glances around the waiting area. Three other couples are chatting happily, clearly unencumbered by the prospect of workplace scandals.

'You were with your parents most of the weekend,' she says coolly.

'I was back last night, Nadine.' Rob shoots her a vexed sideways glance. He doesn't know what disturbs him more: the fact that Nadine chose not to mention this, or Eddy knowing the whole of Friday afternoon, but still managing to act normally – asking him to sort out some budget issues, and praising his last Miss Jones column. His editor might be an utter buffoon but he is, clearly, a pretty fine actor too.

'Look,' Nadine says with a shrug, 'I'm sorry, Rob. You know me and Eddy go back a long way. I just felt he should know, that's all, and I had to talk to someone . . .' *What about your three best friends – wouldn't they have sufficed?*

'What did Eddy say?' Rob asks huffily.

Nadine smiles. 'He thinks it's great.'

'Really?' *So he doesn't think I'm a dirty old man?*

'Yes, of course. He likes you, respects you . . . said it's made him see you in a whole new light.' *Hmmm, bet it did . . .*

'Nadine Heffelfinger?' A young blonde woman with a neat, slicked-back ponytail has appeared in the waiting area. Nadine leaps up eagerly. She and Rob follow her down another short corridor and into a small room, where the sonographer greets them with an automatic smile.

'Hi,' she says, 'I'm Kirsty, now if you could hop up please, Nadine . . .' Jacket and hat are quickly handed to Rob. He takes a seat as Nadine lies down, with belly exposed and a faint curve of a baby bump, or is Rob imagining that? And in an instant it appears on the screen: a blur of white like the snow outside and there, as clear as day, his child. Head, legs, arms. A beating heart.

'Look,' Nadine murmurs, her eyes wet with tears as she turns to him. 'Look at our baby.'

'I can see,' Rob manages to say, although he's finding it hard to speak. So it's real. It actually happened, that night with the lemon cake and all that vodka.

'We've got a good, strong heartbeat here,' the sonographer says, dragging the white plastic gadget across Nadine's blemish-free skin.

'Oh, thank goodness,' Nadine says. Without thinking, Rob reaches up to grasp her small hand; she coils her fingers around his and squeezes. How could he have wished that this wouldn't happen – that they'd come here to be told there was no heartbeat at all? 'Rob, are you okay?' Nadine smiles at him.

'Yes. Yeah, I'm fine.'

'Well, everything looks as it should be,' the sonographer says, 'but I know it's an emotional time for both of you.' She smiles kindly, this freckle-faced girl who barely looks older than Nadine, and nothing about her suggests that she's judging Rob for fathering this little blur in the snow. Here in this darkened room, he doesn't feel judged or ashamed. If only, he thinks wildly, they could stay here until the baby comes.

He and Nadine are still holding hands as measurements are taken and dates calculated, and for those few moments, Rob can't imagine wanting to be anywhere else.

Chapter Twenty-Seven

'Is it a boy or a girl?' Mia asks, making her rubbery mermaid plunge through the meringue-like suds in the bath. She and Freddie are still happy to share bathtime, for which Kerry is hugely grateful; so much easier to sluice them both down at once.

'It's a girl, stupid,' Freddie retorts from the tap end. 'Mermaids aren't boys. They have boobies.'

Kerry is perched on the loo seat while Buddy dozes on the bath mat at her feet. She is aware that, if she were truly efficient, she would be using this opportunity to fold towels, or scrub out the bath toys box where slimy stuff lurks. Instead, she is leafing sleepily through a nine-day-old Sunday supplement. She flicks to the food page, studying a celebrity chef's 'warming family lunches'. Mia and Freddie would probably delight in pumpkin risotto with crispy sage if she were a proper mother who'd trained them to enjoy such sophisticated flavours from birth. On this count, she's failed. Most of Freddie's vegetables are abandoned or flicked off his plate, and what hope is there if he won't even tolerate sweetcorn? It's bright yellow – and sweet, for God's sake. The perfect child-friendly food.

'I don't mean mermaids,' Mia says carefully. 'I mean Daddy and Nadine's baby.'

Kerry shuts the magazine. *Nadine*. The mention of her name triggers a small, sharp pain, like a little tinfoil spear being jabbed into her teeth. Freddie and Mia have yet to meet her, and of course they'll have to at some point, as Rob seems to be 'seeing her' properly now. Spending most of the week at her place, by the sound of it. 'I'd rather be honest with you,' he'd said, during their last brief conversation, as if expecting one of the 'well done' stickers which Mia is always so proud to receive at school. Yet, maybe things will be easier when they have met her, as at least the questions will stop: *What's Nadine like, Mummy? I really don't know . . . When can I meet her? Soon, darling, I promise . . .*

'I said, is it a boy or a girl?' Mia repeats, scowling up at her mother.

'I don't know,' Kerry murmurs. 'We'll have to wait and see.'

Mia scoops up a handful of bubbles and blows them in Freddie's face. 'I don't *wanna* wait.'

'I want a boy,' Freddie announces.

'Well, I want a girl,' Mia counters.

'We don't know yet,' he adds sagely, glancing at his mother, ''cause it's in her tummy.'

'That's right, sweetheart.' Kerry blinks rapidly, hating the fact that she still loses control of her tear ducts occasionally, always without any warning.

'How big is it now, Mummy?' Mia wants to know.

'Er, I'm not sure. About the size of a grape, I'd imagine.' Kerry kneels down on the floor to scrub at a lump of hardened toothpaste with a wodge of loo roll.

'When's it out?' Freddie asks.

'Oh. Um . . .' How long until the joyous birth, he means, when Kerry will have to pretend to be at least *interested*, if not awash with delight, this child being a little half-sister or brother to Mia and Freddie. How will she pull off that one? What if he or she looks just like a newborn Freddie or Mia, despite having nothing whatsoever to do with her? 'I'm not sure exactly,' she replies finally, picking off the last of the toothpaste with a fingernail, 'but there are a few months to go yet. They had a scan at the hospital and saw its heart beating.'

She sweeps her hands over her eyes on the pretence of brushing hair out of her face. A week ago now, Rob called to tell her about it, sounding all choked up and emotional. She still can't shift the image of a blurry scan from her mind. What had he expected her to say – congratulations, or, 'Ooh, I'd love to have a look sometime, if Nadine wouldn't mind?' Maybe she should. That would be the modern approach, wouldn't it? She could start knitting some little baby bootees while she's at it . . .

'What's a scan?' Mia asks.

'A picture of the baby in the mummy's tummy,' Kerry says curtly.

'Can I see it?' Freddie asks.

'Er. . . . it's not really up to me, Freddie.'

He glares at her, as if slowly deciding that she's not quite the fabulous mother he'd once thought she was. 'Why not?'

'Because . . . it's *their* baby. You'll have to ask Daddy if you can see it.'

'I wanna see it!' he yells. 'I wanna see the picture.'

Taking a deep breath, Kerry strokes the top of Buddy's head. 'Fine,' she mutters. 'I'm sure you can.'

'How do they do it?' Mia muses. It's only now that Kerry realises her daughter has been carefully snipping away at her mermaid's hair with the nail scissors. Synthetic blonde clumps are floating on the soft clouds of foam. 'Do they put a camera in her, Mummy?'

'No, it's a special gadget that can sort of . . . see through skin.' Kerry is sweating now, whether due to the steamy bathroom or the children's line of questioning, she's not sure.

'How?' Freddie demands.

'Er . . .' Kerry tries to figure out an explanation, even though she's never been especially adept at telling the children the things they really want to know: how the TV works, why the sky is blue, where planets go in the daytime.

'Does it make her bleed?' Mia asks.

'No, darling, it doesn't *actually*—' Kerry is relieved to snatch her ringing mobile from her pocket.

'Hi, Kerry? My name's Harvey. I called you a couple of months ago about piano lessons . . .'

'Oh, did you?' She frowns. 'Sorry, I'm pretty fully booked now, don't think I can take on anyone else . . .'

'We were cut off,' he interrupts, 'and I meant to phone you back but stupidly, I just had your number on a soggy scrap of paper and lost it . . .'

'Well, I can save your number now and get back to you if anyone drops out, if that's okay.'

'Oh.' There's a small silence as, still gripping her phone, Kerry coaxes Mia and Freddie out of the bath and into the pyjamas that have been warming on the radiator. It's not entirely true that she can't squeeze in another pupil. Yet right now, after being quizzed about scans and babies, she can't rouse the enthusiasm to make arrangements. She doesn't even know where her diary is.

'I've spent weeks trying to track you down,' Harvey adds. 'The newsagent had taken your card off the noticeboard and didn't have your contact details. Then a friend of my flatmate's mentioned that her daughter's started coming to you – Chloe Watson?'

'Yes, she's had a couple of lessons . . .' In Freddie's room now, with Buddy sniffing about at her side, she surveys the explosion of books and toys on the floor.

'When she said it was a Kerry, I knew it must be you. I hope that doesn't sound too bizarre,' Harvey adds with a self-conscious laugh. 'It's just, I'd had a really shitty day doing, er, some work things. I was sitting in my car, having a moment to myself, when this tiny piece of paper – like a bit of napkin or something – blew onto my windscreen with your name on it.'

'That *is* weird.' Kerry motions for Freddie not to wear his wellies tonight, but they're already being pulled on amidst sniggers as he tumbles into bed. 'So it was sort of like a sign?' she adds with a weary smile.

'I don't know. Yes, maybe it was.'

Wandering through to Mia's room now, Kerry takes the brush from her dressing table and works through her daughter's wavy caramel hair in sweeping strokes. 'Well,' she says, 'maybe I could fit you in on Saturdays, if that's good for you.'

'Er, that's my busiest day unfortunately.'

'What's your job, Harvey?'

'I, er . . . sort of organise events. Parties, conferences – that kind of thing.'

Nice, friendly voice, she decides. There's a trace of a northern accent, although not one she can entirely place. 'Right. Well, I'm sorry but that's the best I can do. I'm pretty full up during the week.'

'Okay,' he says firmly. 'Saturdays would be good – I'm sure I can sort something out.'

'Would you want lessons at your house or could you come here?'

'Oh, my flat's not suitable,' he says quickly. 'I'll come to you, if that's okay.'

'Of course it is. Most pupils do. D'you live in Shorling?'

'Yes, up by the golf course.' Kerry puts down the brush and motions for her daughter to choose a story book. Mia chooses to tip out her vast collection of Sylvanian Families animals out of their battered shoebox instead.

'So, what I'd normally do,' Kerry continues, still clutching her phone as she helps her to line up the badgers and bears, 'is suggest that you come round for a chat before we arrange your first lesson. I don't charge for that, obviously. It's just so we can talk about the kinds of music you like, and whether you'd prefer to follow a structured course, and work towards exams, or have a more relaxed, free-form approach. It's also,' she adds, absent-mindedly tickling Buddy's ears as he nuzzles against her, 'so you can be certain that I'm the right teacher for you.'

'Oh, I'm sure you will be.'

Kerry can't help smiling at his childlike eagerness. 'Well, we'll see.'

'So when could I do that?' Harvey asks.

'Um . . .' She frowns. 'I'm teaching all day tomorrow, then on Thursday I have a meeting for a show I work for. Friday's a bit hectic so maybe next weekend, if that suits you?'

'Oh.' His disappointment is palpable. 'I don't suppose tonight would be okay?'

Kerry pauses, carefully placing Mia's favourite rabbit at the helm of the large toy narrowboat which she's extracted from under her bed. God, he's keen – perhaps *too* keen. What kind of person spends weeks trying to track down a name from a soggy piece of paper when Shorling is awash with music tutors? If you wanted your child to learn the marimba, there'd be someone local to teach them. Kerry fears that, since the split with Rob, and her mainly fruitless attempts to befriend Emily, Lara and the rest of the school-gate clique, she's lost her ability to suss out whether someone is a decent person or not. Yet she's also . . . *intrigued*.

'Mummy!' Freddie yells from his room. 'Hurry up and do my story. I've been waiting *hours*.'

'In a minute, hon,' she calls back. 'Er, okay,' she tells Harvey. 'It's 82 Ocean Drive, the white house at the end. The one with the scruffy front garden that's probably going to wreck Shorling's chance of winning Britain's Prettiest Seaside Town this year. You'll easily spot it.'

'Right,' he chuckles. 'See you in half an hour then?'

'Could you make it an hour? I'm just about to launch into the bedtime story routine.'

'Oh. Um, yeah. Okay.' He sounds rather perturbed as Freddie bursts into song in the background. It's more of a taunt, actually, bellowed out to the tune of *Stop the bus, I need a wee-wee*, but with substitute lyrics: *Daaaa-ddy's baby is a bo-ooy . . .*

'See you at half-eight,' she says quickly before ending the call.

Such musical talent at five years old, Kerry reflects, snatching a random picture book from the buckling shelf in Mia's room. She could be one of those mothers who's forever boasting about her gifted children – if it didn't make her want to squash a pillow over her head and cry.

Chapter Twenty-Eight

Buddy's urgent barking announces Harvey's arrival. While Kerry is slightly regretting arranging to see him tonight, at least someone is keen to spend time with her around here. It's come to something when, apart from being ridiculously grateful for seeing Brigid once or twice a week, Kerry has become reliant on pupils for adult company. She has even found herself looking forward to Jasmine arriving in a cloud of expensive perfume on Thursday afternoons, despite the fact that piano lessons are merely filling a gap until yoga starts up again.

'Hi.' Harvey's face breaks into a grin as Kerry welcomes him in. 'Thanks for making time to see me.'

'That's okay,' she says, taken aback by the fact that his phone voice and appearance don't entirely match. She'd figured mid-twenties tops, gangly and puppy-like, but the man who stands before her in her cluttered kitchen is towering above her, a proper strong-looking man with dark, almost black wavy hair, playful deep blue eyes and a hint of stubble. Buddy is now sitting obediently on his cushion in the corner of the kitchen, as if in readiness for being judged.

'Nice dog,' Harvey offers. 'Loves people, obviously.'

'We've only had him a few weeks,' Kerry explains. 'We're still new to the whole dog business.'

He smiles, casting Buddy a fond glance. 'Nothing to it, not once you tune into what they're all about.'

'You're a dog person then?'

Harvey nods. 'Always had them, until about a year ago when my flatmate moved in. He's allergic, unfortunately.'

'That's a pity.'

'So how's he settled with you?'

Kerry pauses, tempted to gloss over Buddy's quirks, but decides there's something about Harvey that compels her to be honest. 'He's brilliant with us, loves being off the lead and charging about on the beach. But he barks like crazy at other dogs and hates being left alone in the house. He has a bunch of neuroses.' She shrugs. 'I guess he's just a little needy.'

Harvey nods. 'Separation anxiety's pretty common. Maybe he's had some sort of trauma or loss.'

'Er, yes, his previous owner mentioned something like that . . .'

'But dogs are like humans,' he adds. 'Pretty resilient. It just takes time.'

For a moment, Kerry is stuck for words, as if it's not Buddy he's talking about, but her. *It just takes time*. How long, exactly? She hates it, the way she can be fine one moment and utterly grief-stricken the next. A hazy picture, of a smudge of baby in a womb, floats into her consciousness.

'I'm sure you're right,' she says quickly. 'Anyway, let's go through to the music room and we can talk about what you'd like to do.'

As he follows her out of the kitchen, Kerry silently curses the Impregnator for turning her into the kind of woman who could, literally, blub at anything.

'So have you played much before?' she asks, clearing her throat as they sit side by side at the piano.

186

'Er, only an old Casio keyboard I have at home. I know middle C and the C major chord but beyond that I'm pretty lost.'

She glances at him, deciding she likes this smiley, amiable man; his eagerness is refreshing, especially after the gloomy twelve-year-old boy she taught this afternoon.

'So what kind of music d'you want to play, Harvey?'

He shrugs. 'Oh, anything really.'

'Really? You don't have a preference?'

'Well, maybe not death metal.' He grins.

'How about I play something now, and you improvise here' – she indicates the upper reaches of the keyboard – 'just to get a feel for it?'

'Um . . . okay.' She starts to play, and after a few moments' hesitation Harvey starts to pick out notes, tentatively at first, then relaxing a little.

'Mummy?' comes the small voice from the doorway.

Kerry turns to see Mia, pink-faced and sleepy with pillow-mussed hair. 'Sweetheart, what are you doing out of bed? It's gone nine, you've got school tomorrow . . .'

'Got a tummy ache.'

'Oh, have you? Come here, darling.' Mia's gaze remains fixed upon Harvey as she strides over and hops up onto her mother's knee. 'This is Mia,' Kerry adds.

'Hi, Mia, nice to meet you.' He smiles and raises a hand in greeting.

'I know you,' she announces with a sly grin.

'I don't think you do, Mia,' Kerry says. 'He's just come to talk about piano lessons.'

'I *do*, Mummy.' She turns to him. 'You're Harvey Chuckles and you came to my school.'

'Harvey Chuckles?' Kerry repeats.

'Er . . . it's sort of my professional name,' he says quickly. 'They booked me last minute at school when the other entertainer couldn't make it . . .'

187

'But I thought you said you organised conferences?'

'Well, er . . .'

'These conferences are for under-eights,' she says with a smirk.

'Er . . . I suppose so, yes.'

'You had a yellow wig on,' Mia continues, clearly in her stride now, 'but we saw you take it off, *and* your face-paint, and make yourself back into an ordinary man.'

Harvey is laughing now, and blushing; the effect is curiously endearing, Kerry decides.

'You weren't supposed to see that part,' he tells Mia. 'Anyway, do you play the piano? I expect you do . . .'

'Yeah, Mummy teaches me.'

'We're sort of doing it casually,' Kerry explains.

Mia grins at him, swinging her legs from Kerry's lap, stomach ache evidently forgotten.

'We play together,' she says proudly, 'and it's not boring learning like at school. Every time I get better 'cause that's what Mummy does. She makes it fun.'

'Well, that sounds great,' Harvey says. 'That's exactly what I'd like to do too.'

'D'you like being a clown?' Mia asks him.

'Um . . . I do,' he replies, clearly fibbing, 'although I wouldn't say it's what I'd like to do for the rest of my life.'

'Yeah.' She nods thoughtfully. 'You don't get old man clowns.'

'Mia,' Kerry cuts in, 'you really must go to bed now. Come on, sweetheart.' She lifts her daughter from her lap, carefully stepping over Buddy who's been gnawing his rubbery hamburger toy at her feet. 'Sorry about that,' she tells Harvey as Mia reluctantly makes to leave the room, yet still lurks, clearly intrigued, in the doorway.

'That's okay. Maybe I'd better leave you in peace, though. I've taken up enough of your evening already.' He smiles and, once again, Kerry finds herself warming to this affable man who seems to have attached some curious significance to a scrap of paper stuck to his wet windscreen.

'See you next Saturday then,' she says. 'Is two thirty good for you?'

'Yes, looking forward to it.'

'If any conferences come up,' she adds, 'we can always rearrange.'

At least he's able to laugh at himself, she notes as she sees him out, with Buddy barking in protest, seemingly grief-stricken at his departure. Still, that's probably an essential quality for a clown.

'I felt sorry for Harvey Chuckles,' Mia murmurs as she and Kerry head upstairs. 'Audrey-Jane was mean to him and I don't want to be her friend.'

'Oh, honey.' Tucking her in and perching on the edge of her bed, Kerry gently brushes a crinkle of her daughter's hair from her face. 'I thought you liked Audrey-Jane. Didn't you say she was being much friendlier at school?'

'Yeah, sometimes. Dunno.'

'Well, maybe we could ask her around for a playdate soon, or anyone else you'd like to play with – you don't have to be friendly to someone who's not very nice to you . . .'

Mia scowls, her bottom lip wobbling. 'She doesn't like me. Nobody does.'

'Darling, they do,' Kerry murmurs, aware of Mia's beating heart as she holds her close. 'You're a lovely girl and you've got to know lots of people already . . .'

'I don't have a *best* friend.' She sniffs loudly.

'I know, but these things happen naturally when you get to know people properly. We'll start planning your birthday party soon, okay? And you can invite as many people as you like.'

Kerry kisses her cheek, then clicks off the bedside light,

189

aware of Mia's large, dark eyes fixed intently upon her. 'No one'll come,' she announces.

'Of course they will. Why wouldn't they? We'll make it really fun and I'll do you a really special cake . . .'

'Will Daddy come?'

'Er . . .' Kerry clamps her back teeth together. 'I'm sure he will.'

'Can Harvey Chuckles come too?'

'Oh, darling, we hardly know him and it probably costs an awful lot to hire a clown . . .'

As Mia falls silent, Kerry gently strokes her hair, wishing she had the power to make everything all right.

'Tabitha threw a sweet,' she murmurs sleepily, 'and it hit him on the head.'

'Poor Harvey. That wasn't very kind, was it? Come on now, love. I've got a song to finish tonight.'

Mia nods, but before Kerry has even reached her bedroom door, she calls out, 'Mummy?'

'*Yes*, Mia?'

'Can I have my birthday cake from a shop please?'

'Oh.' Kerry frowns. Following the Egyptian theme which has gripped Mia's imagination, she has started making tentative plans for a sarcophagus cake covered in gold paste icing and studded with jewels. 'Why d'you want a shop cake, sweetheart?'

''Cause everyone else has one.'

'I'm sure they don't.'

'Yeah, they do! I've seen pictures.'

Pictures of birthday cakes – because she wasn't actually invited to see them for real. 'Um . . . whose cake did you see a picture of?'

'Cassandra's.'

'Just Cassandra's?'

'Yeah.' *We're not talking 'everyone', then.* 'Will you cuddle me?' Mia whispers.

190

'Of course I will.' Forgetting work, Kerry slips into the single bed, surrounded by a soft toy menagerie and holding her daughter close until she is breathing deeply, fast asleep.

Chapter Twenty-Nine

It's true, Harvey does know about dogs. Since he was a little boy, he's instinctively known how to develop a mutual trust and understanding, leading to a sense of security: crucial for any animal if he's to be a fine companion and not make a spectacle of himself, like Kerry said Buddy does from time to time. He seemed like a real character, though. As he climbs the steep hill with the huge, posh houses which leads up to the golf course, Harvey reflects how much he misses owning a dog of his own. The walks, the games and companionship – all those rituals are good for a person. However, it would appear that those days are over. Harvey has let his spare room to his friend Ethan, who leaves a scattering of worn socks, pants and other small, unsavoury items in his wake. A pain, yes, and Harvey would far rather have the place to himself. But unfortunately, dogs don't pay a share of the rent.

'How did your lesson go?' Ethan asks, peering up from the sofa in the small, neat living room that's lined with Harvey's books, CDs and the vinyl he can't quite manage to part with. Ethan's wiry red hair is unkempt, his mouth full of last night's home-made chicken curry which is visible as he speaks. On the coffee table, a gummy-looking bottle of mango chutney rests on Harvey's treasured copy of *One Flew Over the Cuckoo's Nest* – original seventies edition – and a small bowl is perched on Ethan's lap.

'It wasn't a lesson,' Harvey says. 'Just a chat to see how we got on.' He senses Ethan studying him with small, dark eyes – the eyes of a creature who rarely ventures out into daylight – as he hangs up his jacket on the hook by the door.

'What was she like?' Ethan asks.

'Nice, y'know. Friendly. Interesting.' Harvey shrugs, registering his flatmate's naan bread draped over the arm of the sofa like an oily antimacassar. He could ignore this or snatch it away, inspecting the inevitable greasy patch beneath it and give his flatmate a lecture about his slovenly ways.

'Old, was she?' Ethan enquires.

'No, not old. About our age, hard to tell really . . .'

'Not one of those craggy old teachers who slams the piano lid on your fingers when you play a wrong note?'

'Jesus,' Harvey sniggers, deciding to let the naan thing go. 'Did you have a teacher like that?'

'Yeah, old battle-axe. Stank of violets and death. Still have the scars here.' Ethan waggles his chubby hand, which Harvey knows to be scar-less because they've been friends since they were eighteen and started at drama college together. 'So why are you having these lessons again?' he enquires. 'I thought you were skint.'

'Just fancied it,' Harvey says lightly.

''S'pose it could come in handy with the act,' Ethan teases him. 'A little musical interlude, make a change from the old one-man-band . . .'

'Yeah, maybe.'

Ethan wipes a blob of mustard-coloured sauce from his chin. 'Was she fit, then?'

'Who?'

'The *teacher*.'

193

Harvey blinks at Ethan, wondering whether to mention Kerry's lovely green eyes and dark brown, wavy hair that tumbled around her slender shoulders. He wouldn't have hesitated when they were younger. He'd have mentioned that strange moment in her kitchen, too, when it looked as if she were about to cry. How fragile she seemed, despite her breezy demeanour. Now, though, with no escape from Ethan and his arse-scratching tendencies, Harvey guards his privacy jealously.

'She was nice-looking, yeah,' he mutters with a shrug.

'Married?'

'Er, no, I don't think so.'

'Oh, so you *noticed* then.' A bit of chicken flies out of Ethan's mouth, which Harvey also chooses not to comment upon. The little shits who pelted him with sweets at the last party he did had better table manners.

'Only because I was watching her hands while she was playing, okay?'

'And you *just so happened* to check out her marital status.'

'No, I wasn't really thinking about that.' Harvey rolls his eyes.

'Oh, come on. Didn't you want to make beautiful music with her?' Ethan guffaws loudly and swigs from a bottle of beer. 'You did, didn't you? It's obvious you fancied her . . .'

'What's obvious? Tell me one thing I've said that makes you think I was remotely attracted to her.'

'That's why it's obvious,' Ethan declares. 'You're being all guarded and secretive, going over there to talk about, um, Chopin or whatever. You don't even *like* classical music . . .'

'Oh, fuck off.'

Ethan smirks and picks up the naan bread, ripping a chunk out of it with his teeth. Harvey was right; the sofa arm now looks as if it's been licked by a huge, oily tongue.

'So are you going to ask her out?' Ethan wants to know.

Harvey glowers at him. 'How old are you again? She's going to be *teaching* me, for Christ's sake. It's a professional relationship.'

'Oh, is that what you call it?' Ethan calls after him as Harvey escapes to his bedroom. 'It's about time you found yourself a decent woman, Harv. I worry about you. There's got to be *some* desperate bird out there who'd be willing to do it with a clown.'

Sinking onto the edge of his bed, Harvey takes a moment to compose his thoughts. *Lighten up*, he tells himself. *He doesn't get out much. Don't rise to the bait . . .* Plus, Harvey realises, he's bloody starving, having forgotten to eat in his eagerness to meet Kerry. He gets up and pokes his head around the living room door. 'Any of that curry left?'

'Huh?'

'The curry I made last night. Any left for me?'

'Aw, no,' Ethan says, dumping his empty bowl at his feet. 'Sorry, mate, that was the last of it. But if you're heading for the kitchen, could you get me another of those cold beers?'

Chapter Thirty

Rob knew he'd been expecting too much for Eddy to keep Nadine's pregnancy secret. There was no big announcement, no collective gasp: just the office grapevine yacking away, triggering the odd bemused 'congratulations', plus a sense, Rob notes, that he has finally been accepted by the new team. As if he's not the stuffy old duffer after all, and that being a cheat and a liar and making a girl half his age pregnant has somehow made him more . . . *interesting*. He's aware of Ava throwing him a bemused look as she stuffs her 'Chocotastic' Pop Tart into the office toaster, and Frank and Eddy halting their murmured discussion as he saunters past. Meanwhile, Nadine has acquired a dreamy demeanour. In fact, she seems to have given up working at all in favour of aligning her pots of pens with their various neon rubbers and fluffy gonks on their ends.

Although he tries not to stare openly, occasionally Rob sees her take a brush from her red patent bag and actually groom a gonk's hair. *I'm going out with a girl who collects novelty pens*, he muses, although 'going out' doesn't really describe it. For one thing, on the nights he stays over at her place, they rarely venture out. They still don't have a great deal to talk about, he realises. But they've watched a few movies, and she has taken to cooking strange meals – not triggered by any particular cravings but because, as far as he can gather, she's never actually cooked much before. Last night she made some kind of Mexican beany starter, leaving an explosion of vegetable choppings and little puddles of bean juice in her wake. 'I love cooking for you,' she announced, reaching across the table to squeeze his hand as his eyes watered from all the chilli.

Then they went to bed. Rob has felt so wretched these past two months, it's been a relief to lose himself with a sweet, young girl with a beautiful, delicate little body who seems, amazingly, to want him. What will happen, though, when the Bethnal Green house sale goes through? Although she seems to expect it, the thought of living at her place full-time makes him uneasy to say the least.

It takes an enormous amount of willpower for Rob to switch his attention back towards the half-written feature on the screen. His intro reads: 'It's Spring – get a six-pack in the time it takes to scoff a burger.' Despite the gaudy Christmas lights winking outside, the issue they're working on now is all 'spring clean your body' and 'put the spring back into your love life'. (Eddy, ever fond of a cliché, has gone overboard for the 'reinvent yourself' angle.) Two issues containing Rob's sex columns have already been on sale. To Eddy's delight – 'see, I said you'd be a natural, Robster!' – they've provoked a flurry of emailed questions from readers, some of such a technical nature that Rob is flummoxed as to how to respond.

By 6 p.m. he's almost finished the feature. It's Thursday – late night shopping – and Nadine, who's looking impatient now, wants to start checking out buggies and cots. It takes another half hour before he makes his way over to her desk.

'Sorry about that,' he says.

'That's okay.' She smiles prettily, having reapplied her

cherry-red lipstick (how does she always get it so immaculate? he wonders) and customary eyeliner flicks in preparation for the shops. As they head for the lift, Rob can't resist taking Nadine's small hand in his. God, this is weird, he thinks, a thought that darts across his brain without warning several times a day. Here we are, virtually a couple now, having a baby. A couple who, less than an hour later, have taken possession not just of a buggy but a car seat, cot, bouncy chair, play mat and wall hanging featuring hand-appliqued gambolling bunnies, all to be delivered within the next five working days.

'Oh, look at that!' she cries. He'd been trying to casually manoeuvre her out of the baby department of the store before his credit card melts in the machine.

'We don't need that, do we?' He eyes the cripplingly expensive quilt.

'Well, I suppose it's not *essential*, but we don't want our baby sleeping under a tatty old blanket, do we?'

'No, of course not, but I'm sure there are cheaper—' He stops abruptly as she picks up the quilt. The bags he's clutching already contain a changing mat, several fleecy rompers in gender-unspecific lemon and mint, plus a knitted toy mouse in a scratchy red coat which doesn't look terribly baby-friendly to Rob (but hey, what does he know?). And now Nadine is choosing a rotating night light which projects pictures of sheep, and cooing over a hand-painted wooden trolley filled with bricks (which the child won't be capable of pushing until he or she is at least a year old – but again, he says nothing). Rob is flagging now, but Nadine is showing no sign of ever wanting to stop. He chews his lip as she browses anti-stretch-mark oils in a mums-to-be boutique off Oxford Street, and stuffs his traumatised Visa card back into his wallet as she chats with the salesgirl.

'Massage in the oil at least twice a day,' the woman advises her. 'That way, you'll keep the skin supple so it'll accommodate your growing bump.' She beams at Rob. 'You'll do that for her, won't you?'

'Of course,' he blusters, sensing himself flushing. At least she didn't assume he was her dad, dragged out on bag-carrying duties.

'God, you're so uptight,' Nadine chastises him as they leave the shop.

'What d'you mean?'

'Looking all embarrassed when that woman said you should massage me.' She laughs disparagingly. 'It is natural, you know, to take care of your pregnant girlfriend . . .'

The carrier-bag handles are biting into Rob's hands, and he dumps them on the pavement as he scans Oxford Street for a cab. 'I'm not embarrassed. It just a bit public, that's all.'

'Hmmm.' She narrows her eyes at him. 'Maybe it's just an age thing. I guess men of your generation just aren't that comfortable with nudity.'

Rob snorts involuntarily. 'Oh, right, so I've become a man of *my generation* now, have I? Well, I'm sorry but there's not much I can do about that.' Funny how his age didn't seem to matter while she was ravaging him in his drunken stupor. He glances down at the numerous shopping bags at his feet. 'Those night lights are rubbish,' he adds. 'Mia had one and it broke within two days.'

'Well, we'll be more careful, won't we?'

'No,' he insists, 'I mean they have a design flaw. The rotating bit rests on a little spike and it's just not sturdy enough to withstand any knocks—'

'Rob,' she cuts in, 'I don't feel too good.'

'There are other kinds of night lights,' he continues, still scanning the street for a cab. 'They're little glowing things to plug in which seem to work better and are less complicated . . .'

'My stomach hurts,' Nadine murmurs.

He looks down at her, realising now how pale she is, and how fragile-looking in her little black jacket and red knitted dress. 'Maybe it's that bean thing you made last night. To be honest, I've been a bit, um, flatulent in the office . . .'

'I'm not *flatulent*,' she snaps, waving as a cab approaches while Rob gathers up their bags. 'I've got a pain in my stomach, okay? I'm worried, Rob. This doesn't feel right.'

'You don't think something's wrong with the baby?' He feels sick with panic as the cab pulls up alongside them.

'I don't know. I've just got these pains . . .'

Something changes then, and Rob no longer cares that she's chosen a silly sheep night light or seems overly hung-up about stretch marks as they climb into the cab. He puts an arm around her and holds her hand tightly as they speed towards the hospital.

Chapter Thirty-One

Whenever Rob is due to pick up the children, Kerry experiences the same dilemma. Should she be polished and fully made-up, suggesting that she's swishing off on a lunch date followed by copious afternoon sex the instant his car's pulled away? Or slump to the door in scabby jogging bottoms, hair unwashed and face raw from sobbing? Reminding herself that trying to project some kind of image would imply that she actually *cares* what he thinks, she quickly pulls on a corduroy skirt, pale grey sweater and brushes on mascara and tinted lipgloss. Harvey-the-Clown is coming for his first proper lesson today and, after her watery-eyed moment last time he was here, it feels important to present herself as a properly functioning human being.

Rob, who's arrived now, *does* look different these days. While he still favours his usual weekend attire of smart jeans and expensive-looking cotton sweater, there's also a cloud of tension around him.

'Is he always like this?' Rob asks from his cross-legged position on the kitchen floor as he tries to bat Buddy away from his crotch. Disconcertingly, instead of dashing straight off to his parents with the children, he has chosen to hang around to help Freddie with his Great Wall of China, an ambitious Lego construction which now bisects the kitchen.

'You know what's strange?' Kerry says tersely. 'He might not be the best-behaved dog in the world, but he's actually never done this to anyone but you.'

'Well, that's nice,' Rob says as Buddy continues to investigate his nether regions. 'Suppose I should be flattered, then.'

As Kerry regards him with distaste, sitting there pathetically on the floor, she is overwhelmed by an urge to kick him hard in the shins. She can't, of course – not with Freddie beside him, carefully placing a yellow brick on the top of the wall. She must *behave nicely*. God. The effort required triggers a strong desire for wine, and it's only 11 a.m. . . .

'Maybe it's a smell you're giving off,' she adds.

'What d'you mean by that?'

'Well,' she says dryly, 'perhaps you're giving off a powerful testosterone scent that only dogs can detect. Maybe it's an age thing – you know, your final hormonal surge.'

Rob makes a small grunting sound.

'Or,' she continues, quite enjoying herself now, 'you've brought it on yourself because you've got this *thing* about dogs homing straight for your toilet parts and it's become a self-fulfilling prophecy.'

'You're deranged,' he mutters, shaking his head.

'I don't think I am, Rob.'

'Look,' he says tetchily, 'could you just call him off me please?'

Call him off, as if he's a savage police hound. Kerry snorts in derision as Rob tries to push him away, which has the effect of making Buddy sit obediently at his side and offer him a paw.

'He's giving you his paw, Daddy,' Freddie observes.

'Is he? That's nice.' Rob shrinks away a little.

'Don't you *like* Buddy?'

'Of course I do, Freddie. He's, ah . . . a real character.'

Kerry turns away, wondering if these handovers will become easier with time, and if she'll ever stop wanting to physically hurt him. *Please leave now*, she urges him silently. *Just fuck off out of my house.*

'Buddy's fine with all the other men who come round,' she says before she can stop herself. Oh, the murky depths she's plummeted to now. *All the men who are desperate to ravish me, you arse, and who are thrilling in bed, unlike you who – I have to say this – was a pretty bloody tedious lay with your, 'Ooh, give me a little scratchy first' routine* . . .

The years of her life she wasted, dutifully running the tips of her nails up and down the jerk's back. And the baby voice he used when he asked her! Ugh, she could puke right here on Aunt Maisie's floral-patterned lino. How had she forgotten *that*?

Kerry clears her throat. 'Freddie, could you please go upstairs and tell Mia that Daddy's ready to leave now?'

Mercifully, he scatters a handful of Lego on the floor and charges upstairs as requested while Rob straightens up, somewhat *creakily*, Kerry is pleased to note. However, if he's distraught by the possibility of her entertaining copious gentleman callers, he certainly isn't showing it.

Perhaps to distance himself from Buddy, who has rolled onto his back anticipating a belly tickle, Rob has now positioned himself at the kitchen window. He looks, Kerry decides, like someone who's just arrived at a rented holiday cottage and is assessing the view. She feels idiotic now for trying to make him jealous. After all, the prospect of going to bed with anyone ever again is highly unlikely. Sex has become like golf to her, or fly fishing – something other people do, and she can't for the life of her see what's so enticing about it. Last time she slept with a man who wasn't Rob, mobile phones weighed roughly the same as a bag of sugar and she could have redecorated the house in the time it took to log on to the internet. What would happen now, if she were to find herself in bed with someone? Would candid shots of her naked body be broadcast across the globe?

Even *thinking* about sex with Rob in the vicinity feels wrong. Pointedly refusing to break the awkward silence, Kerry busies herself by pretending to sort through an enormous stack of paperwork from the top of the fridge.

'We were at the hospital on Thursday night,' Rob murmurs, still facing the window.

'Oh. What was wrong?' She keeps her voice flat, emotionless.

Rob exhales forcefully. 'Er . . . Nadine had some pains. Thought she was going to miscarry . . .'

Why the hell is he telling her this, and how does he expect her to respond?

'So what happened?' Kerry asks flatly, aware of the children chattering upstairs – no, arguing, actually. Mia has apparently 'stolen' Freddie's wellies.

'She was scanned, everything was fine – seems like it was just a warning. Doctor says she's got to take it easy, she's probably just been doing too much . . .'

'Mmmm.' Kerry flicks through a wodge of paper – a reminder to have Mia's eyes tested, something from the bank, a new contract from *Cuckoo Clock*, a questionnaire asking her how she plans to boost Shorling's chances of winning Britain's Prettiest Seaside Town . . . *If there are windowboxes at your property, are they: well-tended/ requiring attention/empty at present (please tick box) . . .*

'She's . . . er . . . coming to Mum and Dad's this weekend,' Rob adds. 'I hope that's okay with you.'

Kerry blinks at the piece of paper in her hand. *If you are able to get involved during the week prior to judging, what kind of help can you offer? Litter picking/exterior painting/tending communal gardens . . . please tick box.*

'It's none of my business really,' she replies, so relieved when Mia runs into the kitchen that she could hug her.

It's Rob who's bestowed with cuddles, though. Kerry watches, feeling momentarily redundant as Mia exclaims, 'I didn't know you were here, Daddy! Freddie didn't tell me . . .'

'Me and Mummy were just having a chat,' he says. 'I love your hair in those little plaits, by the way. Very pretty. So what have you been up to this week?'

Her face crumples. 'Audrey-Jane was mean to me at school.'

'Aw, what did she do, sweetheart?'

'She said I could play, and we *were* playing, then Tabitha came over and they ran off and told me to go away . . .'

'Oh.' Rob, who finds the intricacies of girls' friendships baffling, clearly doesn't know how to respond.

'They said we're poor,' she adds.

'Silly girls,' he blusters. 'What a load of nonsense. They're just spoiled rotten, okay? Anyway, I heard you've been doing really well in class . . .'

'Yeah. Got to read my story out.'

'That's fantastic, darling. Well, the others are probably just jealous.' Freddie has reappeared now, and Kerry quickly checks their overnight bags to ensure that essentials haven't been discarded in favour of yet more cuddly toys.

'All set then?' She glances at Rob. 'It's just, I have a pupil due in ten minutes.'

'But I wanna finish my wall.' Freddie glares down at his Lego construction.

'Sorry, we need to go now,' Rob says gently, taking his hand. 'Come on, Nanny and Nonno are so looking forward to seeing you.'

Thank God for Rob's parents, Kerry thinks, not for the first time since the break-up. Rob is using their place as a base for when he has the children, which means they're still getting Daddy-time – she isn't so peevish as to deny them that – without having to stay in the London house, where they don't even have beds anymore. Or, worse still, *her* flat where, presumably, Rob will soon be living full-time. Despite her determination to be fair and reasonable, Kerry isn't sure she can handle the idea of them staying there. At least, not yet.

'Can we take the wall,' Freddie asks hopefully, 'and finish it at Nanny and Nonno's?'

'Of course not, stupid,' Mia crows. 'It'll break.'

'No it won't.' He blows a farty noise in her face.

'I'll keep it safe for you,' Kerry says quickly, 'and you can finish it when you get back, okay?'

'*Don't* smash it up.' He fixes her with a fierce stare.

'Of course I won't, darling.' *Although, if you were to construct a Lego model of your father's face . . .*

They're leaving now, and at the sight of Kerry hugging the children, Buddy leaps for the door as if trying to block their exit.

'He gets a bit stressed when people leave,' Kerry says over his fretful barks.

'A dog with a separation anxiety?' Rob pulls a wry smile.

'Yes, well, he has abandonment issues.' Restraining Buddy by his collar, she steps outside with Rob and the children, shutting the door firmly behind her.

A car has pulled up, and Harvey climbs out, looking mildly taken aback by the small group who are clambering into Rob's car, and the urgent barking from inside the house.

'Hi, Harvey,' Kerry says with a smile, glancing back to see Buddy who's on the back of the sofa now, steaming the glass with his breath. 'Just saying goodbye,' she adds. 'Won't be a minute.'

'Yeah, sure.' No need to introduce him to Rob, she decides as he buckles the children's seatbelts and climbs into the front. For all he knows, this handsome young man has come round to whisk her off to that glass cube seafood restaurant, followed by an afternoon in bed. She tries to transmit the message: *I am fully intending to have hot sex with this man*. But she can't even do that. With all the barking going on, Kerry is incapable of dredging up a lewd thought. Anyway, Mia has lowered the rear window and is shouting, 'It's that clown man again! It's Harvey Chuckles!' Which causes Harvey to blush and Rob to smirk, infuriatingly, before driving away.

*

Harvey, it turns out, is a joy to teach. Keen and attentive, he picks up simple chords and melodies with ease, and soon Kerry starts to feel halfway human again.

'So you do children's parties,' Kerry says after his lesson.

'Yep, for my sins.' He steps gingerly over the Great Wall of China in the kitchen and ruffles Buddy behind the ears.

'Well, I admire you. Two birthday parties a year are enough for me. I can knock together a cake and organise a few games, but there's always that sense that everything could spiral out of control at any minute . . .'

'I know that feeling. Last one I did, some kid pelted me with barley sugars.'

'Who gives out barley sugars at a children's party?'

'God knows,' he laughs. 'I suspect they were handed out as ammunition – you know, make me work for my fee.'

'I don't suppose . . .' She pauses. 'No, I'm sure you'll be busy – it's the Saturday between Christmas and New Year . . .'

'What is?'

'Mia's birthday party. We're having it here, planning to invite a few of her class . . .' She breaks off again, wondering how much to tell him. 'It'll be her first birthday since we moved here, *and* since her dad and I split up,' she explains, 'so I really want it to go well for her. I don't suppose you'd be free that day, the twenty-ninth?' She sees him hesitate and regrets putting him on the spot.

'Fine, I'm sure I could do that.'

'Well, if something else comes up . . .'

'No, I'd like to do it,' he adds firmly.

She smiles, relieved. 'I don't know why I didn't think of booking someone before. It's probably because Rob wouldn't have considered it. How feeble does *that* sound?' She laughs. 'Sometimes it feels as if I'm still getting used to being on my own, you know? And when things need seeing to – like horrible stuff bubbling up in the shower – I need to think, okay, don't panic, just call someone who knows what they're doing . . .' She stops abruptly, conscious of babbling on. Since when did she become incapable of conducting herself like a normal person?

'Well,' he says, 'I'll do my best. Maybe, um . . .' He glances down at the garish orange floor. 'Would it be awful of me to suggest doing it in exchange for a couple of piano lessons?'

'Sure, but more than a couple. Say . . . five, does that sound okay? Would that cover your normal fee?'

'Oh, *more* than. That's very generous of you.'

'That's a deal then.' She grins, feeling her spirits rise as she sees Harvey out. And, although it's immensely tempting to text Rob to tell him she's just booked a children's entertainer, with steely willpower she manages to resist.

Chapter Thirty-Two

'I can't believe you still buy him an advent calendar,' Nadine tells Mary, Rob's mother. 'That's the *cutest* thing I ever heard.'

Rob watches in tight-jawed silence as his girlfriend fixes his mum with a beaming, red-lipped smile which has yet to be returned.

'He's always had one, hasn't he, Eugene?' Mary flicks her gaze towards Rob's father, who merely nods and looks down at his plate. 'I gave it to him last weekend,' she adds, 'in time for the first of December. But he left it here.'

'That's even better,' Nadine goes on, 'because today's, what – the eighth? So you've got eight chocolates to eat, Rob, you lucky man!'

Rob darts a look at Nadine, trying to transmit the message that she must stop this immediately, that his parents' rather stiff and formal dining room is no place to start wittering on about advent calendars and taking the piss out of him. Conversations here tend to orbit the same safe territories: the children, his job, his father's pickle business and his mother's latest triumphs at the WI.

'Oh, I love advent calendars, don't you?' Nadine is addressing Mia and Freddie now, who are regarding her with astonishment, as if she's just burst out of a cake. She picks up her glass of sparkling water and beams around the table. 'They're one of the best things about Christmas, aren't they? Do *you* two get them?'

Mia nods wordlessly, and Freddie picks at a nostril. Rob glimpses his mother's terse face and calculates how much he might possibly get away with drinking without making a complete arse of himself. Clearly, Nadine feels out of her depth here. Mia and Freddie are still gawping at her, now pushing green beans and sweetcorn around their plates. Rob knows he should try to take charge of the situation, but doesn't want to make the atmosphere worse by telling them not to stare or demanding that they eat their vegetables.

Eugene is slicing his pork chop with such delicacy that he could be performing a delicate operation on a human kidney. Mary's entire face looks as if it might crack, even though it was her who'd insisted, 'Of course we want to meet this Nadine, seeing as you're having a child with her.' She'd pronounced it '*Nay*-deen' in her strong Yorkshire accent, wincing slightly as if she'd meant to say, 'tumour'. 'We want to welcome her into our family, Roberto,' she'd added stoically.

'Oh, I'm in a pretty menial job at the moment,' Nadine is explaining (one of his parents must have asked her a question, Rob isn't sure which). 'It's not what I really want to do, though. What I'm *really* interested in is interior design, making spaces fun and inspiring, and after the baby's born I hope to pursue that.' She stabs a bean with her fork and pops it into her mouth.

'So who'll look after the baby?' Mary asks while Freddie mutters that he's ready for pudding now.

'Sorry?' Nadine frowns.

'In a minute, Freddie,' Eugene says kindly, refilling his grandson's glass with orange juice.

'I mean, who'll take care of your child,' Mary asks, 'when you rush off back to work?'

'Er, a nanny or childminder or nursery,' Nadine says, in an *isn't-that-obvious?* voice.

'Oh, so you're planning to do that, are you?' Mary counters.

'Mum,' Rob cuts in, 'we haven't decided any of that yet.'

Nadine throws Rob a confused look, then focuses back on his mum. 'Er . . . I will want to go back to work, Mary, so, yes. I can't imagine being a full-time mother.'

'Can't you?' Mary exclaims.

'No, I imagine it'd drive me mad,' Nadine replies with a small laugh.

Shut up, shut up, shut up, Rob wills her, glancing fretfully at his mum in her violently-patterned purple floral dress, with her lipstick applied a little too thickly today. He needs to talk to Nadine alone and explain that Mary is of the opinion that if you don't willingly spend every moment of eighteen long, hard years tending to your children's every need, then really, why did you bother having them? 'I looked after Roberto and Domenico,' Mary says carefully, 'and I'd never have done it any differently. I'm their *mum* . . . isn't that right, Eugene?'

'Yes, Mary,' he mutters.

'Well, I'll still be the baby's mummy—' Nadine starts.

'And Kerry gave up everything to be a full-time mother to Mia and Freddie,' Mary adds. 'Devoted, she was, from day one . . .'

'Mum, *please*,' Rob barks. 'We're capable of figuring it all out, you know. There's still plenty of time.'

'Not *that* much, Roberto.' Mary's gaze drops to Nadine's belly.

'What did Mummy give up?' Mia asks thoughtfully, the first words she's spoken over lunch.

'Nothing, sweetheart,' Rob murmurs.

'D'you mean her job at the university, Nanny?'

Mary's face softens a little. 'Er, yes, love.'

'She still went to work,' Mia adds helpfully, 'but not every day. Some days we went to nursery and some days we did fun stuff like Play-Doh and drawing.' She grins expectantly at Nadine.

'My mummy's a piano teacher,' Freddie announces loudly.

'Er, yes, so I've heard.' Nadine clears her throat.

'Can I have pudding now?' he adds. 'I want pie.'

'Yes, of course you can, Freddie.' Mary springs up from her chair, clearing mounds of plates without any offers of help, and beetles towards the kitchen.

Sorry, Rob mouths to Nadine, but her attention has been diverted by something Freddie appears to have done. 'Er, did you just put sweetcorn in your ear?' she asks lightly.

'No?' He phrases it as a question.

'I'm sorry' – she frowns at Rob – 'I thought I just saw him. In fact, I'm sure he did . . .'

'Well, I didn't,' Freddie snaps. 'She's *lying*.'

'Freddie!' Rob hisses, 'that's very rude. Apologise to Nadine right now.'

'No!'

Rob takes a big gulp of wine, wondering how far to take this.

'You wouldn't do a silly thing like that, would you, Freddie, love?' Mary calls through from the kitchen.

'No, Nanny.' Freddie folds his arms and smiles smugly. 'Can I have toffee pie?'

Only now does Rob dare to reach for Nadine's hand under the table and give it a small squeeze. *Sorry*, he wants to tell her again. *Sorry for Freddie's horrible behaviour and for not standing up for you about the going-back-to-work thing. It's just Mum, just her way, she's not that bad really* . . . He can't, though – not in front of his father and children who are sitting glumly at the table, as if awaiting trial.

Instead, he tries to pretend everything's normal, and quizzes his dad about new additions to his pickle line, while marinating in his own shame.

*

Food and wine keep coming all afternoon, all the better for Rob to anaesthetise himself with. Thankfully, there is no further discussion over Nadine's plans to abandon her firstborn in favour of a glittering career in interior design. Eugene has also perked up, and is waxing lyrical about onions – 'Pearl pickles in balsamic, shortlisted for the small producer's award' – which doesn't seem too controversial until Freddie pipes up, 'Onions stink, Nonno.'

'Freddie.' Rob rolls his eyes at him. 'I'm sure you'll like Nonno's onions when you're older because they're very special.'

It's true, Tambini's Pickles has flourished for four decades, and at seventy-two, Eugene seems to have no intention of loosening the reins on his baby.

'D'*you* like onions?' Freddie turns to Nadine.

'Um, I used to,' she says carefully, 'but since I've been expecting the baby I haven't liked them at all.'

'Why?'

'Um . . . your tastes change,' she explains. 'Things you used to like suddenly taste weird, and you start craving other foods instead.'

'What's "crave"?' Freddie asks, glowering at her as if she might have made a terrible smell.

'When you want something so, so much, that you have to have it.' Nadine smiles at Rob, and he feels a rush of affection – or is it pity? – for her. Poor girl, trapped in his parents' stuffy dining room with its dark wood panelling and his hostile kids, gamely trying her best. He wants to tell her she's doing great and he's proud of her, and for his

213

mother to stay where she is, out of harm's way in the kitchen. But here she comes, whipping away dessert plates, then reappearing with a cheeseboard bearing a pungent Camembert and a melting wedge of Brie.

'What's with the French stuff, Mum?' Rob asks. 'Why not the usuals?' Taleggio and Gorgonzola, he means – his father's favourites.

'Domenico's been managing a project in Lyon,' Eugene says. 'Didn't he tell you?'

'Oh yes, I think he mentioned it . . .' *Of course, despite life being a little full-on right now, it's essential to keep up with my brother's schedule . . .*

'Brought these back for us,' Mary adds, eyes gleaming with pride. 'So thoughtful, even though he was ever so busy with meetings.'

'That's nice, Mum.' Rob looks dolefully at the wooden board. They're only cheeses, but they seem to symbolise the gaping chasm between the high flier at the helm of some kind of global call centre operation, and him, the big brother, whose career has been reduced to pretending to be a woman who goes on about sex a lot.

'I'm sorry, Mary,' Nadine says, 'but I can't eat those.'

'Why not?' Mia asks.

'Er, because they're unpasteurised,' Rob explains.

'That means they might have germs in,' Nadine adds, 'that could harm the baby.'

'Yeuch!' Freddie recoils from the table.

'No, they're okay for *you* to eat,' Rob explains. 'Come on, you've always liked trying different cheeses . . .'

'Don't want germy cheese,' Freddie announces, jumping down from his chair even though he has yet to be granted permission (Rob's parents are extremely hot on table etiquette).

'*What* is wrong with Freddie today?' Mary turns, pale-faced, to Rob.

214

'Sorry, Mum. Freddie, come and sit down this minute—'

'DON'T WANT GERMY CHEESE!' Freddie blasts out, stamping his foot.

'But they're not germy,' Mary insists. 'They're *fine*, Freddie, love . . .'

'*She* said it.' Freddie jabs a finger at Nadine.

'She's not *she*,' Rob says sharply, getting up from his seat, grabbing his son by the sleeve and marching him back to the table. 'Her name's Nadine and no one's forcing you to eat cheese so stop making such a bloody great fuss.'

The room falls silent. Eugene clears his throat and Nadine pokes at something in her eye.

'It's just the pregnancy, Mum,' Rob murmurs. 'Nadine can't be in the same postcode as Brie.' All adult eyes swivel towards him as he adds, 'Joke.'

Lunch is cleared away quickly then, with Mia and Freddie wisely deciding they'll have more fun hanging out with Nanny and Nonno in the kitchen. Nadine excuses herself and slips off to the loo. Finding himself alone for a moment, Rob slips out to the back garden and extracts his cigarettes from his pocket.

'Hey.'

He turns to see Nadine at the patio door. 'Hi,' he says wearily.

'I thought you'd stopped.' She steps out onto the lawn and sits beside him on the worn wooden bench. The garden looks dead now, bordered by a spindly fence and endless rolling Kent countryside beyond.

'Just been having the occasional one,' he says.

'Oh, Rob. When the baby comes—'

'Don't worry, I'll hang out of the window. You can hold onto me by my ankles while I dangle upside down.'

She shakes her head, exasperated.

'It's just a little lapse,' he adds, inhaling so hard it makes his head spin. 'I'll stop way before that.'

'Well, I hope so. Oh, and . . . I don't think I'm going to stay here tonight, Rob. Would you mind calling me a taxi to the station?'

'What – you mean you want to leave?'

'Yes, I think it'd be best, and I know you've been drinking . . .'

'Only a tiny glass,' he fibs, studying her pale, flawless face that looks somehow illuminated, and the clear blue eyes fixed upon his. 'Look – are you sure you want to go? I know it's not easy but Mum's okay when you get to know her. She's just a bit prickly today. It's been quite tough for her, the whole break-up and everything, and I think the kids are just a bit weirded out . . .'

'It is real, you know, the thing about unpasteurised cheeses,' Nadine interrupts. 'I didn't make it up.'

'I know that, but Mum's from a different generation. When she was expecting me and Dom, she probably ate nothing *but* pâté and soft cheeses and had the odd fag and glass of wine, and we've turned out okay . . .'

A smile tweaks her lips. 'That's debatable.'

'Oh, come on.' He crushes his cigarette butt with his shoe, then nudges it under a plant pot where his mum won't see it. 'Dom and his wife and the kids are coming over later. You'll really like them. It'll be more fun then . . .'

She shakes her head. 'Maybe it's just me, Rob. I'm not used to scenarios like this. I don't manage family things very well.' He takes her hands and wraps his fingers around hers. Nadine's parents are a bit of a mystery to him. While her mother calls fairly regularly, sounding frightfully posh and nervy on the phone, her father seems to show zero interest in her, apart from providing a steady cash flow into her bank account.

'I'll ask Dad if I can take you on a factory tour if you like,' Rob cajoles with a smile. 'Not many people get one of those.' Nadine looks down at her shiny black shoes. 'Honestly,' he adds, 'the weekend's going to get better, I promise.' But there's no persuading her and, half an hour later, having explained to his parents that she doesn't feel well, Rob and Nadine are in a taxi on their way to the station.

'You needn't have come with me,' she says, staring gloomily out of the window. I'm not an invalid, Rob.'

'I *know*, Nadine. I just wanted to keep you company.' He takes her hand, relieved that she hasn't bad-mouthed his mother in the cab. The driver knows his parents (Eugene Tambini is something of a minor celebrity around here) and has already spent ten minutes enthusing about 'that apple chutney with the raisins and nuts – and I'm not even a pickle man'.

Rob murmured his agreement, his mind more on his mother's vinegary treatment of Nadine and how he might go about making amends. Maybe it was a bad idea to invite her down this weekend. He should have coaxed his parents to London instead, and treated them to dinner and a hotel stay; that would have impressed Mary so much, she wouldn't have had it in her to be rude.

Something else is worrying him too. Did Nadine mean it about going back to work pretty much straightaway? And what's all this about a career change? Full-time child-care will cost a fortune, and Rob is already dispatching a hefty chunk of his salary to Kerry, not just because he knows he should, but also in an attempt to cancel out his guilt (a big fail on that score).

'So,' the jovial grey-haired driver says, pulling up outside the station, 'I guess when it's time for you and your brother to take over the business, there'll be one of those almighty family feuds over who's boss . . .'

'Erm, I don't think so,' Rob replies with a tight smile. 'They're not really my thing, pickles.'

'Ah, you're the high-flying journalist one.'

'Uh, that's right.' He pays the driver and grabs Nadine's

bag, making a mental note to never move to the countryside, even by accident, where everyone knows everybody else's bloody business. At least the driver has dispersed the tension between him and Nadine. She's sniggering now, and mutters, 'High-flyer, eh?' as they reach the platform.

'Ha. Yes, he obviously doesn't know as much about my family as he thinks he does.' An icy wind whips against his cheek.

'Oh, don't be fed up, Rob.'

'Well, it's just been a pretty duff weekend so far.'

Nadine sighs. 'Look, I had to meet them sometime and it was never going to be easy, was it? I'm sure we'll get to know each other. I just . . . wasn't really up for it today.'

He nods and kisses her red lips as the train approaches. Minutes later, his girlfriend and unborn baby really are in a different postcode from Brie.

Chapter Thirty-Three

After Harvey's lesson, followed by an eager nine-year-old girl whose mother constantly texted from the armchair, Kerry heads out into the breezy afternoon. She has arranged to meet Brigid, who is delighted that she has started to accompany her for dog walks. With Joe despatched to a friend's house, they have just Buddy and Roxy for company as they stride along the wide, flat sweep of Shorling beach.

'Buddy's making great progress,' Brigid observes.

Kerry smiles. 'Thanks. Sometimes I dare to think, I'm not too bad at this. Being a dog owner, I mean.'

'He seems so much happier and more settled . . .'

'Well, it's been at least two weeks since he peed indoors,' Kerry adds, 'and now he only barks when a really huge, loud vehicle goes by. He's usually fine with anything on four wheels. God, I hope I don't sound like one of those awful boasting parents. You know – "Oh, Juliette's doing so well with the oboe, she's going to skip through the exams and go straight to grade eight . . ."'

Brigid lets out a big, gravelly laugh. 'I'd say you're allowed to give yourself a pat on the back once in a while.'

'Well . . . maybe.' Kerry glances down at Buddy. 'He's doing *me* good, too. It would drive me mad, being stuck in that little music room all day, but of course, having a dog forces you out into the real world.'

'How's work going?' Brigid asks.

'Eight songs done, five to go, and after that they want three new ones a week so it's a sort of ongoing thing . . .'

'What, indefinitely?'

Kerry chuckles. 'Sounds like it – till the end of time. God, what a thought . . .'

'You're such a grafter,' Brigid marvels. 'Twenty hours a week at the library are all I can manage. And I'm glad you're a dog person now. You know what Shorling's like – pretty and all that, but not the friendliest place if you don't quite fit the mould. It can be a bit lonely sometimes.'

Kerry glances at Brigid. She knows Joe's dad disappeared years ago, deciding that Goan beaches held more appeal than his newborn son, which struck her as heartless beyond belief. She is aware, too, that Joe isn't always invited to classmates' parties, and has seen some of the school gate mothers giving Brigid's clingy tops and skimpy dresses disdainful glances.

'Same for me,' she says. 'Without our walks, my weekends would feel really strange and empty when the kids are with Rob. I suppose that's why I cram in as many pupils on Saturdays and Sundays as I can.'

'Clown guy coming along okay?' Brigid grins.

Kerry laughs as she unclips Buddy's lead. 'He's only had one proper lesson but yes, seems ultra-keen.'

'Keen on *you*, I bet.' She raises a brow.

'I've told you, I'm not looking . . .'

'Right, now you've got Buddy instead . . .'

They stop and perch on the rocks as the dogs potter around together.

'Don't knock it,' Kerry laughs. 'I was all over the place when Rob left and now, well . . . it's as if Buddy's given our lives some kind of shape and order. And it's great watching him home in on Rob's crotch like a heat-seeking missile . . .'

'Kerry,' Brigid nudges her, 'I think you'd better call him back.'

Hell, Buddy has taken off, and is pelting across the wet sand, paying no heed to her calls.

'Buddy!' she yells, heading towards the sea where he's leaping through the shallow waves, sending up a spray of water behind him. If he weren't showing her up – several dog walkers are watching with interest as she calls him ineffectually – she'd delight in his exuberance. He turns inland then, pelting towards the dunes. Kerry spots a small figure in a pink coat who shrinks back as Buddy leaps up at her.

'Buddy, get *down*,' she calls out, breathless as she catches up with him and clips on his lead. The woman glares down at the wet splodges all over her coat.

'I'm *so* sorry,' Kerry exclaims.

'He's out of control,' the woman splutters, her small, immaculately-clipped dog – Kerry has yet to be able to identify breeds – sitting neatly beside her.

'I'm *really* sorry,' Kerry repeats. 'He just loves people and—'

'You shouldn't have a big dog like that if you can't control him.'

'But he's only . . .' Kerry falters, instantly pinged back to a terrible moment in the Co-op when she'd taken her eye off Freddie – who was just a toddler then – for just long enough for him to clamber onto a freezer, extract a packet of potato waffles and fling them across the store like a frisbee, hitting an elderly man on the neck. Of course, she'd apologised profusely. Sometimes it feels as if she spends her *life* saying sorry for things she hasn't actually done. *Women like that*, she heard the man mutter as he stomped away, *shouldn't be allowed to have kids*. Like there was a series of child-rearing tests you had to pass in order to be 'allowed' to make them.

'I can control him actually,' Kerry fibs, glowering at the woman, 'and there's no need to be so unpleasant.'

'I think *you'd* be a little annoyed,' she splutters, 'if your coat was dry clean only.' The white dog twitches its nose at the woman's feet.

'Tell you what, then,' Kerry retorts. 'I live at 82 Ocean Drive. Have your coat cleaned and send me the bill, okay?'

The woman growls something unintelligible as Kerry marches back to where Brigid and Roxy are waiting by the rocks.

'Take it she gave you a hard time?' she asks.

Kerry sighs. 'Oh, I suppose she was justified. You don't see any other dogs leaping up at strangers, and her coat *is* dry clean only.'

'Who'd wear something like that to walk their dog?' Brigid scoffs. 'Come on, it's freezing out here. Let's grab a coffee and a snack.'

Kerry hesitates. 'Buddy doesn't like being tied up outside and I don't fancy another scene, to be honest.'

'Oh, I know just the place. We can sit right by the window so he'll be able to see you. We're both child-free, aren't we? Let's make the most of it.'

*

The cafe Brigid has in mind is Luke's, the sandwich place which came to the rescue with the Egyptian feast, and which has two tables by the window overlooking the narrow cobbled street.

'I love their Emmental and spinach on wholegrain,' Brigid enthuses, scanning the chalked menu above the counter.

Kerry glances outside. 'Just look at him, Brigid.' She

222

indicates Buddy's mournful face at the glass. 'He looks like a pitiful orphan waiting for scraps.'

'Rubbish,' Brigid retorts. 'I've never seen a happier, healthier-looking dog. Anyway, he's got Roxy for company. Now, what are you having? My treat.'

'Um . . . an Americano and a chocolate brownie please.'

'That's my girl.' Brigid gives their order to the floppy-haired boy behind the counter – the one who saved Kerry's bacon with his figs – and carries their tray to the table. Outside, Roxy is sitting politely, almost motionless, like one of those model dogs with a slot in their head where you can post coins for charity. Beside her, Buddy gazes in at Kerry, radiating adoration.

'So I had my first encounter from that dating site,' Brigid is telling her.

'What – grownupandsorted.com?'

'That's the one. God, what a disaster that was.'

'What happened?' Kerry asks.

'Ugh.' Brigid shudders. 'Have you ever noticed how off-putting it is to watch a man eating salad? Like, when *you're* not eating – we were only supposed to be meeting for coffee – and you've got this big, strapping man in front of you cramming lettuce leaves into his mouth . . .' She makes a chomping rabbit face, and they're both sniggering as Kerry's mobile rings.

She checks the screen. 'Damn, it's the Impregnator . . . hi, Rob? Everything okay?'

'Yeah, yeah,' he mumbles vaguely.

'Are the children all right?'

'Uh . . . yes. I, um . . . I'm just sitting in Mum and Dad's back garden having a fag.'

'A fag? But I thought you stopped years ago.' Kerry throws Brigid an exasperated look.

'Yeah, well, no. I've sort of started again.' He pauses. 'I just . . . wanted to call you. Things, er . . . didn't go too well over lunch. I've had to take Nadine to the station . . .'

Kerry takes a moment to process this. 'Did something happen with her and kids? Did she *upset* them?'

'No, no,' he says quickly. 'It wasn't that. It was more between her and Mum, they didn't quite see eye-to-eye—'

'Rob, why are you calling me about this?' she cuts in.

'I . . . just thought . . .'

'Well, *don't* think,' she snaps. 'Having to listen while you tell me about things that have gone wrong . . . it's just not in my job description anymore, okay?'

'I'm sorry, I just—'

'And I'm actually with someone right now,' she adds firmly. 'I'm *busy*, Rob.'

'Oh.' There's a baffled silence, as if he fully expects her to spend these long, child-free weekends gawping bleakly at daytime TV, or perhaps chipping limescale off the toilet bowl. Across the table, Brigid is sniggering silently.

'So it's not the best time for me,' Kerry adds, barely stifling a laugh.

'I'm *really* sorry,' Rob blusters. 'You should have said.'

'Well, I'm saying now.'

'Right. Okay. See-you-tomorrow-about-fourish,' he barks before ringing off, at which Kerry and Brigid dissolve into laughter.

'He thinks you're in bed,' Brigid hisses.

'Good.'

'And now he's torturing himself, imagining you naked with some hot man.'

Kerry snorts, wishing now that she'd fully exploited the moment, perhaps by murmuring, *Hang on, darling, just let me get my ex off the phone* . . . 'When actually,' she adds, 'I'm just caressing a sexy little brownie.'

'It *is* sexy,' Brigid agrees. 'Look at it, giving you come-hither looks from its plate.'

'Mmmm, I love it.' Kerry strokes it suggestively before

224

taking a nibble. 'God, you're *such* a foxy little brownie.' She emits a dreamy *mmmmm* sound.

'Glad you like it, Kerry.' James has marched into the shop, brandishing a large cardboard box. He nods in recognition to Brigid and breaks into a grin.

'Hi, James . . .' Kerry feels her cheeks flaming.

'I bake them myself, you know.'

'Do you? This is your place, is it?'

'Well, Luke's officially.' James indicates his son behind the counter, then glances towards the dogs sitting outside. 'Looks like you're making good progress with Buddy. He'd never have sat waiting patiently for me like that. Would have made a complete spectacle of himself by now . . .'

She frowns. 'Don't you think he looks abandoned, though?'

James goes behind the counter and starts slicing ham. 'He has a needy face. That's just his look, isn't it, Luke?'

'Yeah,' Luke laughs, and Kerry can see the striking father-son resemblance: same soft grey eyes and angular jawlines. A sprawling family has burst into the shop, and she marvels at the extensive list of exotic sandwiches they're asking James and Luke to prepare. Mia's party is still some weeks off but, as well as requesting a bought cake, her daughter has already decreed that 'we will *not* be having sandwiches'.

'Oh, I booked clown man for the party,' Kerry tells Brigid.

'Great, that should take the pressure off. Is he single by any chance?'

'God.' She bursts out laughing. 'I have no idea. I thought you were dating salad man anyway.'

'Absolutely not,' Brigid snorts.

'And, er . . . clowns do it for you, do they?'

'Um . . . possibly,' she says, unfathomably. They get up to leave the shop, and Brigid is already untying Buddy's lead outside when James emerges from behind the counter.

'Erm, Kerry,' he says as Luke banters with the customers, 'I wondered if you'd like to meet up sometime? I kind of feel I was never really clear about Buddy, never explained things properly. It's great to see him looking so happy' – she glances out and sees that he's still wearing his orphan face – 'and I'd like to say thanks.'

'Oh.' She smiles, registering something she hadn't noticed about him until now: a pleasing grown-up-ness – not in a Rob way, not the poncey grown-up-ness of *Mr Jones* magazine, but someone sweet, kind and infinitely capable. 'I'd really like that,' she says.

'So . . . can I call you?'

'Sure, of course,' she says, then strides out to join Brigid, murmuring, 'My God, it looks like I've got a date.'

'He asked you out?'

'Er . . . well, sort of. Yes, he did.'

Brigid grins approvingly. 'Told you dogs were useful for all sorts of things.'

Chapter Thirty-Four

The mood has lifted at Rob's parents' place, not only as a result of Nadine's departure but also the arrival of his younger brother Domenico, plus Dom's wife Jessie and their two children. Dom and Jessie are big on banter and laughs, delighting Freddie and Mia with boisterous tickling games on the living room floor, while their sons Ollie and Marcus tear into the remains of Mary's toffee tart and the cheeses, despite the fact that another gargantuan meal is just around the corner.

'Shame we missed Nadine,' Dom tells Rob as they find themselves alone in their parents' kitchen.

'Yeah, she was looking forward to meeting you all.' Rob starts unloading the dishwasher.

'Er, Mum said she wasn't feeling well?' Dom wipes his hands on a dish towel. Only eighteen months younger than Rob, he could easily pass for a disgustingly handsome thirty. Rob sometimes wonders if he's ageing in reverse, like a bloody better-looking Dorian Gray.

'She was just feeling a bit off-colour,' he murmurs.

'Um . . . yeah. I heard about the Brie.'

Rob sighs, knowing that whatever he says is unlikely to get past his brother's razor-sharp bullshit detector. And so it all spills out, not only about the suspected Tambini plot to poison her unborn child, but the way he's stumbled into her life of girlie get-togethers and abominable cooking, as if he's in a first-night performance of some terrible play, and no one thought to give him a script beforehand.

'Fuck, Rob,' Dom mutters, raking back his abundant dark hair. 'I was shocked, you know, when it happened. I'd never realised you and Kerry had problems . . .'

'Well, we didn't. That's the whole point.'

Dom frowns at him. 'So why . . .?'

'I'd rather not go into the ins and outs,' he blusters, choosing to ignore his brother's flamboyant eyebrow wiggles. 'I fucked up, okay?'

'Er . . . just a bit, Rob.'

'Yeah. Well, it's happened and I'm not going to walk away from Nadine and the baby. I'm . . . you might find this really hard to believe, but I'm trying to do the decent thing here.'

'I know you are.' Dom's voice softens.

'Anyway,' Rob says with forced jollity, 'here I am. One minute, happily married, about to move into a pretty little cottage by the sea. Next thing, living in a flat strewn with fairy lights like Santa's fucking grotto.'

'So you're living together now?'

Rob pauses to extract a carton of orange juice from the fridge and takes a big swig from it, a small gesture that both brothers know drives their mother insane. 'Kind of half-and-half at the moment, but we're about to complete on the sale of the house. It seems crazy to rent a flat of my own when she'll need me there.' He senses his kid brother studying him, as if he's an interviewer, not entirely sure that Rob is cut out for the job.

'What's it like at work, the two of you being in the same office?'

'We sort of . . . orbit each other.'

'Like planets.'

'Yeah, with the feeling that a meteor's going to smash right into us.'

Dom laughs dryly, adding, 'You'll have to give up this porn shit when there's an innocent little baby toddling around.'

Rob sniggers, slightly regretting having told Dom about his Miss Jones column. 'Can't afford to at the moment, not with things so iffy at work.'

'Hmmm.' Dom smirks. 'Have to say, it's quite . . . believable actually. You as a woman, I mean.'

'You actually *read* it?'

'Well, I don't pore over it but, y'know – they usually have a copy lying around at the barber's. And I might have a quick look, if it happens to fall open at the right page.' He grins, and Rob is overwhelmed by a feeling of gratitude that his brother made the journey today, despite the fact that he's still emitting an air of slight disapproval and bewilderment.

All four children, plus Rob's parents and sister-in-law, are playing a rowdy game of Pictionary in the living room. The tense atmosphere of lunchtime has made way for a comforting sense of bonhomie, and the rest of the evening passes pleasantly amidst a steady flow of wine and chatter.

'I'm *fine*,' is all Nadine will divulge when Rob calls her before heading upstairs to bed.

'Are you sure? I still worry, you know, after that scare you had . . .'

'I'm just tired, Rob. I am in my second trimester, you know.' Hmmm. As far as Rob recalls, the first few weeks are the exhausting part. Come her second trimesters, Kerry was full of energy, glowing and gorgeous with hair all glossy and . . . no, he *mustn't* think about that.

It'll all be okay when I'm back in London, he reassures himself as he climbs into bed. Yet, despite trying to think soothing thoughts, he realises there is no possibility of being able to drop off to sleep tonight. What had possessed him to call Kerry today, just for a chat? He must stop doing this. She was obviously in bed with someone, or at the very least in a state of undress – he can picture the scene right now, which triggers a wave of queasiness. It's not good for his digestion, imagining his wife in the throes of passion with someone else, especially after two slices of his mum's toffee tart and a whacking great slab of that Brie.

Rob is starting to sweat now beneath the thick, hairy blanket – Mary remains suspicious of duvets, they're far too modern and convenient – and burps loudly. His stomach is in turmoil and he feels as if he's gained half a stone since arriving here. He sits up, wishing his parents didn't keep the house so hot, but realising it's far too chilly on this bitter December night to open the window.

What kind of father are you to do this to your children?

The question has lodged itself firmly in his brain, and he wipes a lick of perspiration from his brow.

You've messed up your entire family. What sort of man do you think you are, shacking up with a twenty-year-old?

Tears spring into Rob's eyes, and he dabs them away with a corner of the blanket. God, he has to snap out of this. No point in going over and over it, torturing himself in the middle of the night. What good will that do Mia and Freddie?

Rob slides out of bed and clicks on the bedside lamp. He needs to distract himself from these terrible thoughts, and the only thing he can think of is to turn on his laptop and try to focus on work. If he can just finish his column, it'll be out of his hair and he won't need to think about it when he gets back to London tomorrow night. Nothing makes him feel more phoney and ridiculous than writing his latest Miss Jones despatch in Nadine's flat, especially when she keeps peering over his shoulder, giggling and suggesting teasing little touches for him to add. 'Well, I am a woman,' she's reminded him on numerous occasions. *Only just*, replied the voice in his head.

Pillows propped up behind him, Rob is now back in bed with fingers poised over his keyboard. This month's column is addressing all those men out there who are under the illusion that nipples should be twiddled like old-fashioned radio knobs. *My breasts*, he types, *are what I think of as fun pillows, so take your time and enjoy* . . . What did that cab driver call him again? Big shot journalist? *My nipples*, he continues, *are the supercharged epicentres of a zillion tingly nerve endings* . . . Yeah, Eddy will love that. Plus, miraculously, spilling out such ridiculous prose is helping to chase away those gloomy thoughts . . .

'Daddy!'

Rob's heart lurches.

'*Daaaad!*'

Shit. Freddie's awake. Something must be really wrong. He never wakes in the night here, he loves his cosy bed in the huge spare bedroom . . . Hurtling out of bed and across the landing, Rob manages to locate Freddie's bed in the semi-darkness.

'What's wrong?' he whispers, instinctively reaching out to touch his son's clammy forehead.

'I had a dream, Daddy.'

'Shhh. It's okay, darling. We're at Nanny and Nonno's, remember? Everyone else is asleep, we mustn't wake them . . .'

Across the shadowy room, Marcus shifts beneath his covers on the bottom bunk, while Mia mutters quietly in the bed above. Ollie, who's on a camp bed at the far end of the room, doesn't even stir.

'I can't sleep.' Freddie sniffs into the sleeve of his PJ top.

'I'll lie with you for a little while,' Rob whispers. 'Move up a bit. But we've got to be very quiet, okay?'

'Yeah. I had a really scary nightmare, Dad.'

'What about?' Rob is now in bed with his son, stroking his hair. It's been so long since he's lain close to one of his children, it causes an ache in his heart.

'Bad cheese,' Freddie mutters.

'What?'

'Cheese with germs in.'

'Oh, love.' Curling an arm around Freddie, Rob pulls him close. 'That was just Nadine. There are certain things you shouldn't eat when you're having a baby but you needn't worry about that.'

'Yeah, only ladies have babies.'

'That's right. Now hush, try to go to sleep.'

'It comes out their vagina, Mummy said.'

'Um, yes.' *Christ, how about we wake everyone up and have a little where-babies-come-from talk right now?*

'Can you see germs?' Freddie whispers.

'What germs?'

'The cheese ones.'

'No, not just by looking with your normal eyes. You'd need a microscope . . .'

'It is germy then!' Freddie exclaims.

'*Shhhh!*' Rob sighs, feeling suddenly, achingly tired, as if his bones could crumble like the thin, salty crackers his father likes. 'Well, there are good and bad germs.'

'I wanna see the germs in Nanny's cheese.'

'Freddie, *please* go to sleep . . .'

'Can I have a microscope?'

'Shush!' It's gone 2 a.m., and Mary will be rousing everyone at eight thirty for her customary Sunday breakfast: eggs, salamis, a great mound of pastries and amazing coffee he's never managed to replicate at home, despite investing in various hideously expensive gadgets. Picturing his

232

mum's breakfasts, coupled with the steady rhythm of Freddie's breathing, gives Rob a warm feeling inside. As he finally drifts off, the day's worries start to float away and he's a proper dad again, before the split – before Shorling, even – when they all lived together in Bethnal Green in a rather gloomy little house, but happy as anything.

Rob is properly asleep now, back with Kerry at home, and his old mate Simon in the editor's chair. In his dreams, Rob is carefully crafting a lengthy feature about vineyard tours in Umbria, and all is right with the world.

Chapter Thirty-Five

Mary Tambini loves nothing better than having her boys here, her beautiful Roberto and Domenico and all the children, who bring this big old house to life. She's worried, though, which is probably why, at 2.47 a.m., she decides there's no point in tossing and turning in bed, and pads lightly downstairs to the kitchen instead. Here, waiting for the kettle to boil, she mulls over the day's events. Rob's bedroom light was on, she noticed as she passed his door on the landing, resisting the urge to check he was okay. *He's a forty-year-old man*, she reminded herself, *not a little boy anymore. He can stay up as late as he wants.*

Now, as she sits at the kitchen table, her hands cupped around her mug of tea, what happened today seems even stranger and more impossible to figure out. Yes, she's had a few months to get over the shock of Roberto leaving Kerry and taking up with that girl – that *Nay*-dine – yet it still seems . . . ridiculous. There'd been no warning whatsoever. He'd just blurted it all out on the phone, leaving her and Eugene shocked to the core. When Mary had called Kerry she, too, had sounded stunned, but also strong and determined, and had tactfully avoiding saying anything bad about

Roberto. Not that Mary would have blamed her. God, she could wring his neck sometimes, the silly, silly boy . . .

She's not angry now, though – more concerned, because she has never seen him looking so stressed, not even when that new editor arrived and all his old friends were thrown off the magazine. *And* he's started smoking again. He might be able to fool the children with his minty gum and mouthwash but she detected it straight away.

Is he still awake, she wonders? Would it be completely wrong of her to go up and try to talk to him? She doesn't see why she shouldn't. After all, the family will still be here tomorrow so she's unlikely to have the chance of a private chat. The central heating pipes judder ominously as Mary gets up from her chair and treads softly upstairs.

His light is still on, and she taps the door gently. 'Roberto?' she whispers. No reply. Another tap. 'Roberto? Are you awake?' Still nothing. She hesitates before pushing the door open, then reassures herself that he must have fallen sleep – while reading, probably – with the light on. But when she steps into the room, Roberto's not there. The covers have been thrown back, as if in haste, and his laptop is sitting open on his bed.

Mary is a modern woman; she shops online and is on Facebook, mainly to keep in touch with Eugene's side of the family in Verona. Roberto has been working on a document, she notices, and his laptop is running on battery power. Should she save the document and shut it down for him, or is he planning to come back and work on it? It'll probably save automatically if it runs out of power, but she wouldn't want to risk him losing anything important. Mary gets up and checks the bathroom – no one there – then peeps around the door of the biggest bedroom where all four of her grandchildren are sleeping soundly. Ah, there's Roberto, fast asleep with Freddie in his arms. The image of the two of them snuggled together causes a lump to form in her throat. This is what it's about, she thinks, her vision blurring. This is *family*. Mary wishes Nadine could see this. Maybe then she'd be less keen to dump her baby with a stranger and have an almighty strop about cheese . . .

Mary pads quietly back to Rob's room and perches on the edge of his bed, turning the laptop towards her. She's about to press save, but can't resist a little peek at what he's been working on. Such a talented writer, Roberto – although he's recently stopped sending his father copies of *Mr Jones*, she's noticed. 'It's taken a different direction,' he explained. 'Not sure it'd be your kind of thing anymore.'

Mary's eyes flick across the screen. *So many men give my breasts a cursory tweak before moving onto the main event*. She squints at the text, as if she might have misread it. *My super-sensitive nipples*, she reads on, *are not radio knobs . . . kiss and lick my lovely sumptuous . . .* At that, Mary stops. Why is he writing as if he were a woman – the kind of woman who refers to her breasts as 'pleasure centres'? The phrase 'fun pillows' leaps out at her. Mary shivers in her apricot Marks & Spencer's nightie. Is this what he's lowered himself to now – writing pornography? Is he desperate for money these days?

She stares at the screen, seeing just a haze of type now as her mind races. Perhaps this isn't a magazine feature after all, but a fantasy. Maybe Rob is one of those men who – she can hardly bring herself to consider the possibility – thinks he was born the wrong sex. After all, it's written in the first person – 'fondle *my* domes of love'. Mary's throat feels dry and tight, and she wants to run through to Eugene to tell him what she's just read. Does this mean their baby son, who loved his rusty old Tonka truck and Scalextric set, is one of those men who doesn't feel right until he's had his body pumped with female hormones and his penis removed?

Mary feels dizzy and nauseous as she saves the feature

and shuts down the laptop. Taking a moment to compose herself, she gets up to turn off the light, then makes her way back to her own room. She slips back into bed beside Eugene, deciding that, no matter how much she loves her husband with every cell of her being, she can never tell him that their darling son would like his bra to be removed by someone's teeth.

Chapter Thirty-Six

'Eddy? Hi, it's me, Nadine.'

'Hey, how you doing?'

'Fine, I suppose.' She frowns and shifts position on the sofa. There are frequent kicks now, and she loves the feeling, imagining her baby dancing or somersaulting.

'Still with the in-laws?' There's a trace of amusement in his voice.

'No, I'm not. It didn't go very well, to be honest, so I've come home early. Caught a train this afternoon.' She slides a hand over her small bump, wondering if the baby can sense it there.

'Why? What happened?'

'Oh, the dad was okay – wasn't exactly the fun, jolly type that Rob had made him out to be, but at least he didn't fly off the handle when I dared to suggest that I might go back to work one day, or make a big fuss because I wouldn't eat their unpasteurised cheeses . . .'

'They didn't try to force-feed you, did they?' Eddy sniggers. 'Maybe they were just concerned. After all, you *are* supposed to be eating for two . . .' There's a babble of voices in the background, and music, and Nadine senses that he'd like to wind up this call as quickly as possible.

'It's not funny, Eddy. His mum was horrible – a dried-up old cow who kept calling me *Nay*-dine.' She slips into a Yorkshire accent: '"Ah can't see the point of having children unless you're going to spend eighteen years wiping their bums and strapped to the sink." Old bitch!' She blinks away a tear. 'And to think she's going to be grandma to my baby . . .'

'Well . . .' He pauses. '. . . You *think*.'

Nadine blinks at the star-shaped fairy lights – her only concession to Christmas decorations this year – which she's artfully draped around the Debenhams print. Part of the strand is dangling down but she doesn't have the energy to put it back up.

'I told you, Eddy, it probably *is* Rob's.'

'Well, let's bloody hope so.'

'That's nice,' she says coolly, remembering Eddy's lack of concern over the split condom that last time.

He sighs, and she senses exasperation gusting down the phone. 'Oh, sweetie, I didn't mean it like that. But I'm sure you're right – it is far more likely, the way I've treated my body these past few years . . .'

'I don't think it comes down to how much drink and drugs you consume, Eddy—'

'Of course it does!' He guffaws. 'It's in every magazine you read, isn't it? Including ours. It's a pretty safe bet that I've annihilated ninety-eight percent of my sperm by now.'

God, he's such an idiot. Why did she never realise what an absolute self-centred little jerk he is? Just as well she's with Rob now . . .

'It's working out with you and Robster, though, isn't it?' he asks.

'D'you really care if it is or not?'

''Course I do.'

She sniffs loudly. 'Um, yes, I think so. . . . I mean he's sweet to me and everything . . . but there's his kids – what

239

am I going to do about them? They hardly said a word to me today, and I don't know how to behave with them, whether to try and make friends or just leave them be . . .'

'They're probably a bit freaked out. I'm sure they'll be fine . . .'

'And what about his mother?' she charges on, feeling her heart rate quicken, which can't be good for the baby. 'It wasn't just the childcare and cheese thing, Eddy. She *hated* me, I could see it in her eyes, the way I've ripped her perfect son's marriage apart . . .'

'For God's sake, Nads, she can't have been that bad.'

'She looked like she wanted to stab me with that cheese knife!'

'Oh, babes.'

Is that all he can say? It's easy for him to be dismissive when he's sitting in a bar surrounded by friends with a drink in front of him. Her bottom lip is wobbling now, her vision fuzzing through tears. She'd never imagined that pregnancy would make you feel like this – highly emotional, prone to dramatic mood swings – or maybe that's just her, and the situation she's found herself in. She just needs someone to talk to. Sure, Nadine has plenty of friends, but while they still come over for the odd girlie night, she's noticed that they've become slightly less keen to hang out with her. 'We didn't think you'd want to come,' Jade said the other day when it transpired that she, Sasha and Harriet had been out shopping together. Why wouldn't she? Pregnant women still buy clothes. They still meet up with friends to gossip and chat . . . don't they? Or are they supposed to wear rags and live as hermits?

'Anyway,' Nadine tells Eddy curtly, 'I'll let you get back to your night out.'

'I'm at home actually, just having a few festive drinkies with Frank and Ava and a few others.'

'Oh. So, er . . . they heard everything you said just then.'

'No, of course they didn't . . .'

'Well,' she says coolly, 'say hi for me.' *You could have invited me*, she thinks as she finishes the call; but of course, she was supposed to be at Eugene and Mary's grand old house in Kent, charming these supposedly lovely people to the point at which they'd get over the Rob/Kerry break-up and welcome her into their family.

Nadine places her phone on the table. She pictures Eddy and the others all lolling around in his beige, minimalist flat, with his ridiculously huge Christmas tree (silver baubles only) where she used to spend the night occasionally until that last time, three days before her encounter on the sofa bed with Rob.

Don't be so bitter, she tells herself out loud as she undresses in the bathroom in preparation for a lovely long soak. *Negative feelings can't be good for the baby*. Eddy gave her that first big break, after all, when she barely had a qualification to her name. There she was, just eighteen years old, with a paid junior position on a trashy little soft porn magazine called *I'm Hot*, whereas most of her friends had ended up doing unpaid internships for what felt like forever. Making it clear that he fancied her, Eddy then took her with him to a short-lived free weekly magazine, teasing her that if she didn't make the grade, she'd be the one handing it out at Tube stations in the pouring rain. Finally, when he landed the editorship of *Mr Jones*, he forced out that hatchet-faced assistant and brought Nadine in instead.

She'd felt blessed, even when it had become clear that he was sleeping with Ava as well. 'What's the problem?' he'd asked, all big, innocent eyes when she'd confronted him. 'You're a sweet girl, Nadine, but it's not like we're a couple. I've never lied to you.'

Revenge – that's why she'd orchestrated the thing with Rob. That and the fact that he's gorgeous, of course (she's always had a thing for older men with dark Italian looks).

241

Anyway, what was good enough for Eddy was good enough for her, so she'd gone for it, even though Rob had been off his face and the sex had been a bit of a non-event. The worst thing was, he'd talked in his sleep that night on her sofa bed. 'Kerry,' he'd muttered, 'you've got all the duvet again.' In the morning, Nadine had reassured herself that he wouldn't have stayed if everything had been rosy at home, so none of this was her fault really. In fact, she's probably done him a favour in making it possible to escape a life sentence in the dreary seaside town she's only been to once, with her grandma, where everyone looked about eight hundred years old. Rob hadn't wanted to move. Didn't he admit it that night?

She steps into the bath and sinks into the soothing warm water. Yes, she decides, examining her sugar-pink toenails as they poke through the suds, Rob Tambini probably thinks she's the best thing that ever happened to him.

Chapter Thirty-Seven

Now Kerry remembers why normal people go out, as in, venture beyond the boundaries of their own home when on a date (she is trying not to think of tonight as a date, but what else could it be, really?). That way, the state of your house doesn't matter. You can turn up all freshly showered and blow-dried and no one will guess that your kitchen is strewn with sheet music, plus the numerous Christmas cards and home-made decorations which have yet to find a home. However, tonight, Kerry hasn't had a choice. Asking Brigid to babysit would have meant her having to bring Joe along too, or dropping off Freddie and Mia at Brigid's (not ideal on a school night although, intrigued by his surly attitude – a teenage boy in a four-year-old's body – they would have enjoyed the arrangement hugely). With a hollow feeling in her stomach, Kerry realised she had no one else to ask.

Still, her anxieties turn into a kind of fizzling excitement as she does a speedy clear-up and answers her ringing phone.

'All set?' Anita asks.

'Yep, I think so.' Kerry grins. 'The place still looks a bit shabby but that's probably a good thing, makes it seem more relaxed.'

'Shabby's fine,' Anita agrees. 'You don't want him to think you've spent all day cleaning for him.'

'Well, no chance of that. Anyway, I'm thinking candles to make it cosier . . .'

'Yes, go for candles.'

'You don't think it'll look like I'm trying too hard? It's just the kitchen light's horribly bright and pore-illuminating . . .'

Anita laughs. 'Candles are *not* trying too hard. They're not a big deal. They don't say, I want sex.'

'Hmmm. I just don't want him to think I'm this desperate dumped woman who's planning to hurl myself at him.'

'You are, though, aren't you?' she teases. 'I mean, the hurling part.'

Spotting Buddy's favourite chewed-up blanket lying by the fridge, Kerry grabs it and stuffs it into the walk-in cupboard. 'Hmmm, maybe. The thing is, though, even if there's a *remote* possibility that it might happen, the kids will be asleep upstairs.'

'I know. He sounds nice, though.'

'Yes, he is. He's . . . the kind of man you wouldn't expect to be single, you know? Like, he'd be the good-looking dad at the school gates with a little gaggle of flirty mums around him.'

'But his son's grown-up?'

'Yes, they run a sandwich place together.'

Anita pauses and Kerry knows her friend's smiling. 'Maybe I shouldn't say it, but I have a really good feeling about this guy.'

Kerry sniggers. 'Um . . . maybe that's why it took me all afternoon to dig out something even vaguely suitable to wear.'

'Just be casual, don't worry about it. What are you cooking, anyway?'

'Um, *casual* seabass, a *casual* salad and I've got a couple of bottles of decent sauvignon . . .'

'Perfect.'

Kerry grins, rounding up the odd stray plastic cup and placing it in the dishwasher. 'I've actually got a good feeling too. The kids have been great – didn't even notice I'd hauled their bedtime forward, although Freddie did complain that I'd raced through *The Tiger Who Came to Tea* in about ten seconds flat.'

Anita chuckles. 'Well, good luck, and don't forget to file me a full report tomorrow.'

An hour later, at 8.30 p.m., Kerry is wearing a simple blue shift dress and ballet pumps, with minimal make-up and a huge smile on her face as she welcomes in James. He has also, she notes, taken the casual route in dark jeans and pale linen shirt, and looks all the lovelier for it.

*

'That was delicious, Kerry,' James says, placing his cutlery on his plate. 'I don't want to sound pathetic but there's something *so* nice about being cooked for.'

She laughs. 'I know what you mean. Doesn't Luke ever cook for you, after all the help you give him at the shop?'

'You've got to be joking,' he retorts. 'Anyway, I'm starting to think it's time he got his own place. We really need our own space.'

'Driving you mad, is he?'

James smirks. 'God. I don't know if I should tell you this. He's just got back with his girlfriend, Charlotte, and let's just say they were a bit . . . vocal last night.'

'Really?' Kerry sniggers, refilling their glasses.

'I'm actually surprised *you* didn't hear them.'

'No, well, I sleep like a log – out cold, like a dead person.' She takes another sip of wine. 'Did you mention it this morning?'

'No chance. Charlotte was still there, wafting around in Luke's T-shirt . . .'

'Bet that was awkward . . .'

James nods. 'And we've been busy all day so the moment's kind of gone, you know?'

'And I suppose he *is* a proper grown man,' Kerry offers.

'Yes, well, at his age I was married but our bedroom wasn't about six feet from my mum and dad's.'

She gets up to make coffee and unwrap posh chocolate brownies from the new bakery, a tip-off from Brigid. They are delicious, James agrees; almost as good as the ones *he* makes. How pleasing, Kerry thinks, to see a man tucking in and relishing food. Rob never seemed to care much about what he ate, perhaps due to being plied with delicious Italian cooking from birth and then spoiled with those endless account expense lunches. He never seemed to stop and appreciate anything he put in his mouth, so to speak.

'I hope you don't mind me asking,' Kerry says hesitantly, 'but when did you and your wife break up?'

'Um . . . two years ago now.'

'And there was no warning at all?'

'Not any that I picked up on, no. That was probably the worst part – that there must have been signs, and I just didn't see them.'

Kerry nods. 'Well, you shouldn't blame yourself. I didn't see it coming either . . .' Perhaps it's the bottle of wine they've shared, or the fact that they're not in a restaurant, on a *date*-date, but Kerry finds herself telling him about Rob and Nadine and the baby. He listens attentively as she describes the achingly miserable handovers of the children, and chuckles appreciatively at the thrown birthday cake incident.

'God,' he says, 'you've had a lot on your plate. You seem to handle it so well, though . . .'

'Well,' she says with a shrug, 'I guess I'm just about

emerging from the fug. Um . . . shall we open another bottle?'

James smiles. 'Why not? I walked here anyway. This is a really lovely evening, Kerry.'

She fetches the wine from the fridge and opens it. 'It's nice for me too. I was actually surprised when you asked to meet up. I'd thought you were a bit, well . . . distant and distracted until then.'

A small shrug. 'Well, you did imply I'd run over my incontinent wife . . .'

'James, I'm *so* sorry about that . . .'

'No,' he chuckles, 'it's fine. Anyway, by the time I saw you in the shop, drooling over my brownie, I'd figured out who you are. And it was such a coincidence, I thought, well, why not just ask?'

She frowns. 'What d'you mean?'

'Oh, you're getting pretty well known around Shorling, you know. I hear customers talking about you . . .'

'Really?'

'It's that kind of place, isn't it? French tutors, piano lessons – kids around here aren't allowed to be idle for a minute.'

'Oh yes, the hot-housing. I'm sure I'm going to be reported for not signing up Freddie and Mia for at least three activities a day . . .'

'Well, you probably couldn't have picked a better place to teach piano. And you know what's funny? I was going to call you about lessons a couple of months ago. I'd scribbled down the number from your ad, then Buddy went mad – one of his barking outbursts – and I must have dropped it . . .'

'So you wanted to play?' Kerry asks.

He grins. 'Well, I do play, a bit. Then I thought, who am I kidding, with the shop and everything – when will I have the time? Anyway,' he adds, 'the piano's Amy's.'

247

Kerry nods. 'So you'd feel strange playing it . . .'

'I don't know, maybe. I haven't, not since she left.'

She studies his face, and as his kind, grey eyes meet hers she finds herself asking, 'Why don't you play mine?'

James shakes his head. 'I haven't played for two years, Kerry. I'm beyond rusty. More like completely seized up . . .'

'I won't judge you,' she says firmly. 'In fact, I promise I won't comment at all. I'd just like to hear you play.'

He smiles then. 'Okay, then you'll play something for me?'

'Agreed.'

They head through to the music room, and as James starts to play, missing notes and muttering apologies, Kerry wishes she hadn't asked him. She's on the verge of asking him to stop, as he's clearly not enjoying this – but how can she do that without sounding like some mean-spirited judge on a talent show? Then something changes, and his shoulders relax, and she can almost *see* the tension leaving his arms, hands and fingers. And what he's playing is . . . lovely. It's not perfect, there's still the odd slip-up, but it's a sweet, pure melody, and all the more moving for being so simple.

He stops and gives her a sheepish look. For a moment, Kerry doesn't know what to say. 'That was lovely,' she murmurs finally. 'Sorry, I said I wouldn't comment but . . .'

He blushes and smiles. 'Thanks.'

'Um, I don't think I know it.'

'No, well, I wrote it.'

'Really? You wrote that? It's beautiful, James. Would you play it again?'

He shrugs and starts to play. This time, Kerry can't help sneaking a look at his handsome face with those soft grey eyes and full lips. And she wants – the realisation almost makes her tumble off her stool – to kiss him. Should she? Her lips haven't been in close contact with anyone's apart from Rob's since last century and, God, they hadn't exactly

248

done much kissing before the split. She *really* wants to kiss James, though, and not just because he is undeniably easy on the eye. It's seeing him play, a little uncertainly but so sweetly; it's acting as a powerful aphrodisiac. Some women are turned on by watching a man cook, or emerging from the sea, James Bond style in snug swimming trunks. But for Kerry, watching a man play the piano is the thing . . . God, what would happen if he launched into Rachmaninov's Piano Concerto No. 2? She'd have to leap on him immediately . . .

She's biting her lip now, her mind racing as the small, shabby room with its faded floral wallpaper fills with beautiful music. *Possible outcomes if I kiss James: he likes it, it feels great, or he's completely horrified and pushes me off and explains – politely, of course – that I've totally got the wrong idea. Oh, what the hell. Do it, when he stops playing . . .*

James stops. Kerry senses her cheeks flushing as he turns to her. His eyes are *so* lovely and, crucially, he's not giving the impression that he finds her repulsive. Do it, just do it . . .

'Mummy!' comes the voice from upstairs.

Kerry flinches, then exhales forcefully. 'Oh. Sorry – hang on a minute . . .' She springs up from the stool and goes out to the hallway. 'Freddie?' she calls upstairs. 'What's wrong?'

'I'm not well, Mummy,' he wails.

'Okay, I'm coming . . .' She hurries upstairs, expecting to find him sitting up in bed, anticipating a cosy chat. But he's pale and sweaty as she places a hand on his forehead. 'Oh, honey, what's wrong? D'you feel sick or something?'

He shakes his head. 'Who's in our house, Mum?'

'Just a friend, sweetheart. We've had dinner . . .'

'Is it Brigid?'

'Um . . . no, it's a man called James. The one who gave us Buddy, remember?'

'Yeah.' He pauses. 'My ear hurts and there's stuff in it.'

'Oh dear. That doesn't sound good.' She clicks on his bedside light and peers into his ear as best she can. 'It does look red, Freddie, and there's a bit of sticky, leaky stuff here . . .' She touches it gently. 'It feels hot, too. I think you've got an ear infection . . .' He nods glumly. 'I'll take you to the doctor first thing in the morning. You can stay off school and have the day with me.'

Tears fill his eyes and he grabs for her hand. 'There's corns in it.'

'What?'

'There's corns in my ear.'

'What d'you mean, corns? People get corns on their feet, not in their ears – what are you talking about, Freddie?'

'Yellow corns,' he mumbles.

Kerry inspects his ear again – it's definitely gummy in there, and she can detect an odour – a sort of rotting-vegetation whiff. 'D'you mean you *put* something in your ear?'

'Yeah.' He bites his lip. 'I put yellow corn in it.'

'But . . .' Picturing James waiting patiently downstairs in the music room, Kerry shakes her head in disbelief. In fact . . . maybe he's *not* waiting patiently. Maybe he has already put on his jacket and quietly let himself out. 'I can't remember the last time we had sweetcorn,' she murmurs. 'I know you don't really like it.'

'It was at Nanny and Nonno's.'

'But that was last weekend! That's what, at least four days ago, five if you had it on Saturday . . .' Freddie nods, and Kerry shoots him an alarmed look. 'Are you sure you put it in your ear? You're not just making this up, are you?'

'Yeah. No. I'm not telling a lie, Mummy.'

'But why?' And now James will be walking home,

thinking, well, that's that. Pleasant enough meal, but Kerry obviously doesn't have space in her life for a proper, grown-up evening.

''Cause I don't like it,' Freddie says simply.

'Yes, and there are lots of things I don't like,' she exclaims, 'like eggs and mushrooms and tinned tuna, but I don't go stuffing *them* in my ear, do I—'

His bottom lip wobbles and she cuts herself short. Of course she doesn't; she's an adult and her son is a five-year-old, scared little boy.

'Oh, honey,' she murmurs, pulling him close. 'Does it really hurt?'

'Yeah, and it's stinky as well.'

'I know, love. I can actually smell it from here. Listen, I think I'd better take you to hospital right away.'

'Can the doctor get it out?' He is crying now, his cheek hot and wet against her face.

'Yes, of course he can.'

He sniffs and wipes a pyjama sleeve across his face. 'How?'

'Don't you worry about that,' she says. 'That's what they're for, darling. Now let's get you up and dressed.'

James is still there, amazingly, when she and a still-sleepy Freddie appear in the music room. 'You probably heard all that?'

'Yes, God . . . is there anything I can do to help?'

'Thanks but I'd better deal with it.' She smiles wearily. A few hours ago she'd felt like the old Kerry in her blue dress and lip gloss with her hair blow-dried; now, she's been pinged firmly back into Mum-land.

'I'd drive you,' James offers, 'but I've had half of that bottle of wine—'

'Yes, me too. That's going to look great in A&E, isn't it? Wine-breath mum brings in little boy who's had sweet-corn festering in his ear for nearly a week . . .' She laughs

251

mirthlessly. '*And* I'm going to have to wake Mia and bring her with me.'

'Well . . .' He frowns. 'You could call a cab and I could stay here until you get back . . .'

'That's really kind of you, but Mia would freak out if she woke up in the night and found you here.'

'Oh, of course . . .'

Kerry bites her lip. 'It's just that she doesn't know you . . .'

'My ear's still leaking,' Freddie whines.

'I know, darling.' She rubs her hands across her face, as if trying to erase the fact that this is actually happening.

'Shall I call you a taxi?' James asks hesitantly.

'Yes please. Phone's on the worktop by the cooker. You sit here, Freddie' – she indicates the armchair in the corner of the music room – 'and I'll get Mia.'

Minutes later she's lifting a sleeping Mia from her bed and gently feeding her arms into her red dressing gown, then carrying her downstairs and into the waiting taxi. She says goodbye to James – not even a peck on the cheek – and he's gone, slightly huffily she thinks now, but what else was she supposed to do?

'Shorling General?' the driver asks.

'Yes please.' She closes the car door and looks out at the inky night sky. It's nearly 11 p.m., the taxi smells pungently of Magic Tree, and she can hear Buddy barking fretfully in the house as the driver pulls away.

Serves me right, Kerry reflects, stroking Mia's hair as she rests her head on her lap, for having lewd thoughts in the music room.

Chapter Thirty-Eight

'Luke,' James says, 'I'm not coming into the shop today, okay?'

'What's wrong, Dad? Have a big night last night?'

'No, not at all. I was home by half eleven, which you'd have known if you hadn't been out spending our takings.'

'Yeah, and the rest. Dirty stop-out.' Luke sniggers and peers into the toaster where something appears to be incinerating. 'How did it go anyway?'

'It was . . .' James shrugs. 'It was nice.'

'Seeing her again?'

'Don't know,' he says briskly, unwilling to go into detail. In fact, he's only just starting to make sense of it himself. Dinner had been great, but being cajoled into playing the piano had unnerved him – does Kerry ask every man who comes round to play for her, like some kind of audition? Maybe he'd passed it, as there had certainly been a *moment*, after he'd played his song, when he'd sensed a distinct spark between them. But then the leaky ear thing had happened, and James had felt awful for being unable to help; plus, Kerry's sudden coolness towards him had suggested that, really, he shouldn't have been there at all. Who could blame her after all the horror of her cheating ex and his pregnant colleague? Sure, James was dumped too, but compared to Kerry's situation he feels – perhaps for the first time – that he might have got off pretty lightly.

'Are you going to do website stuff instead?' Luke asks, inspecting his handsome reflection in the shiny chrome kettle before pulling on a grey hoodie over his T-shirt.

'No, I'm having a day *off*. You know, the old-fashioned concept of not actually working every single day? And doing something for yourself instead?' It comes out sounding sharper than he'd meant.

'Er, yeah. All right, Dad.' Luke rolls his eyes.

'I might see a film,' James adds.

'Great. Something foreign and completely weird, yeah? Oh, and listen, I hope you don't mind but Charlotte's parents are off to their holiday house for Christmas – the one with the hot tub and a Jacuzzi. And she's asked if I'd like to go too.'

'What, for actual Christmas?' James's brows shoot up.

'Er . . . yep.'

'But that's, like, four days away!'

Luke shrugs, at least having the decency to look embarrassed. 'You know how it is, Dad. We've only just got back together . . .' *Yes, so I bloody heard.* 'And it'll save you getting so much food in,' Luke adds lamely.

'Yeah, I suppose so.' James musters a faint smile. 'I was hoping for a quiet Christmas anyway.'

'Great. Thanks, Dad. I knew you'd be cool about it and I'll only be gone a couple of days.' There's a quick hug from his son, then he's gone, leaving James regretting his grumpiness when Luke was being perfectly pleasant. And hadn't James told Kerry that he desperately needed some space? It'll be great, having Christmas Day all to himself. He'll be able to, um . . . what exactly? Watch so much TV and gorge on so many chocolate brazils that he makes himself feel ill? He has never spent a Christmas alone and now, at the ripe old age of forty-three, he'll have to figure out how to do it. If he still had Buddy, they could go for a long, festive walk that would at least give the day a sense of purpose and structure.

James makes a coffee and wonders what to do next. He's become so unused to having time on his hands that he is, literally, incapable of knowing how to fill it. Should he call Kerry to find out if they managed to excavate the sweetcorn last night? How would they do it – with a little suction device like they use at the dentist's? It seems rude and uncaring not to get in touch, but maybe it'd be a bit much to call right away. He's forgotten how to be with women, that's the trouble, especially one who's so attractive and intriguing, yet gives the impression that she doesn't actually need anyone very much at all. Not a boyfriend, anyway. James feels terribly out of practice with this kind of stuff. He's been single for nine months now, and the last person – Sarah with the pie-crust collared, libido-murdering nightie – wasn't what you'd call a proper girlfriend. She'd been a client; he'd built a website for her angel-channelling business. Then he'd sort of fallen in with her, or rather, fallen into her four-poster bed with its dreadfully-painted cherubs peering down from the canopy. It was disconcerting, having sex beneath the gaze of dozens of chubby little baby faces. Off-putting in the extreme. So James had retreated, deciding he was finished with women – until Kerry had appeared in the shop, oohing and ahhing over his chocolate brownie . . . Perhaps the cherubs/pie-crust-nightie combination hadn't killed his sex drive after all.

The thought of Kerry and the brownie has perked him up, and he heads out at midday, making his way to the town centre. An enormous Christmas tree stands proudly in front of the town hall, and the assortment of gift shops are crammed with Shorling-acceptable decorations: silver stars, paper lanterns and plain glass vases filled with fir-cone laden twigs. Nothing as crass as fake snow or tinsel around here. James stops outside the arthouse cinema – the one that sells proper coffee and carrot cake – and is drawn in through its beautiful art deco doors.

Why not see whatever is on, just for the hell of it? In typically arrested-development fashion, Luke still favours *American Pie* type trash, and Amy was always dragging him along to see terrible rom-coms which she'd weep over and insist on re-watching at home on DVD. A small realisation brings a smile to his lips: *he will never have to watch another Jennifer Aniston movie ever again.* Today, James reflects, he can do whatever the hell he wants, so he buys a ticket for a Hungarian movie he's never heard of, looking forward to broadening his mind. Two hours later, he blunders out, having watched a young woman with self-cut hair and smeared lipstick screaming in a hospital ward for pretty much the duration of the movie. He heads for the seafront, blinking in the sharp December sunshine, feeling as if he, too, is in dire need of psychiatric help.

And now he's on the beach, where everyone seems to have a dog except him. A girl in a sky-blue tracksuit jogs past with a poodle-type hound, its neatly clipped coat resembling her prim blonde bunches. A gang of excitable spaniels are bouncing around together on the sand, and there's that woman in the bright pink coat with the little white terrier – the one who took delight in dispensing unasked-for training tips for Buddy. *He must understand who's boss . . . You need to show him that you're the leader of the pack, and you MUST get a whistle and a Halti lead . . .* Yeah, yeah. He'd always thanked her politely as Buddy launched into a terrible display of barking and lunging at the sight of her (perhaps it was the pink coat, in a similar way in which bulls go mad for red?). She flashes him a quick smile now, glancing down at the space where Buddy should be. 'Oh, where's your dog today?'

'Erm . . . I don't have him anymore,' James says levelly.

'Really?' She frowns with concern. 'Nothing . . . happened to him, did it?'

'No, no, things just got too . . . hectic. Couldn't manage to walk him as much as he needs so I decided, sadly, that I'd better rehome him—'

'Does that piano teacher woman have him now?' she cuts in.

'Er . . . yes, that's right.'

The woman flares her nostrils. 'I *thought* it was him – your Buddy, I mean. Ruined my coat, had to get it dry cleaned and even then it didn't all come out, look . . .'

She points to a small, greyish mark a few inches below the collar. 'Oh dear,' James says flatly, then turns and walks swiftly towards the kiosk at the end of the beach.

He starts to feel better as he perches on the rocks and sips an Americano. The sky is a bright winter-blue, his rather watery coffee making a pleasant change from the fierce stuff they sell in the shop, brewed with freshly-ground Ecuadorian beans. Sometimes, he reflects, something ordinary can be pretty good.

James sees her then – or rather, he sees Buddy first, leaping to catch a stick. And there's Kerry, striding along in the distance with her two children – she must have kept them both off school today – looking quite the happy, well-functioning family. He sees the pink coat woman's white terrier doing a dump on the sand, and its owner glance around before quickly walking away. James is transfixed as Kerry clearly sees what's happened, and hurries over to hand the woman something – a little black poo bag, he thinks. The two women chat for a while, their dogs pottering about happily together.

The way Kerry looks so happy and natural with Buddy has triggered something else inside him: a fierce and sudden wave of missing Amy, as if it could be *her* over there,

257

walking their dog. To his horror, tears fill his eyes. He lost his wife, and now his dog – what is *wrong* with him? Or is it the prospect of spending Christmas alone, which now feels far from okay? He knows he should head across the beach to say hi, and ask if Freddie's fully recovered – but he can't, not when he's struggling to control his tear ducts. James gets up from the rocks and tips away the remains of his now-tepid coffee. He must leave the beach now, before Buddy spots him; if he does, he knows he'll come bounding over, with Kerry in pursuit.

'We've just grown apart, James,' Amy had told him. He's tried to forget her, but it's virtually impossible when her piano is gawping at him every day in the house. He's already dealt with the Buddy issue – should he make arrangements to rehome her piano too? James did everything he could to make Amy happy – God, how many of those terrible movies had he endured over the years? – yet she *still* left him. Dogs are different. You can give them away, as if they're just some musical instrument no one plays any more, and they'll still love you, no matter what.

Chapter Thirty-Nine

'So how were things at handover this morning?' Harvey asks Kerry as she makes coffee after his lesson.

'Quick and straightforward,' she replies, 'which is about the best I can hope for. It's better than the painful, sheepish-faced lingering thing he does sometimes.'

He chuckles, and she takes the seat opposite him, feeling the tension starting to ease after a particularly trying couple of days: the hospital visit, then blundering through yesterday, managing only a short dog walk in between catching up on an entire night's lost sleep. (The children were so exhausted she'd kept them off school. Last day of term, too – the fun day, with nothing but games).

'I don't know what's going on with Rob, though,' she adds. 'He says his mum's being really peculiar with him – keeps asking if he has something personal he'd like to discuss.'

'What could that be?'

'No idea. I just wish he'd get over this urge to share every little detail of his life with me.'

'Well,' Harvey ventures, 'he obviously still feels pretty tied to you.'

Kerry nods. 'And I suppose we always will be, at least until the children are grown-up. But he also can't help being disapproving, either, which is a bit bloody cheeky seeing as the sweetcorn thing happened when Freddie was in *his* care.'

'Really? He implied it was your fault?'

'Not exactly. But he did suggest that perhaps I should have checked sooner, just in case Freddie *might* have slotted something in there at some point . . .'

Harvey snorts. 'So what happened at the hospital?'

'Three hour wait in A&E. Mia curled up and slept on a plastic chair, and Freddie described the rotting mess in his ear to anyone who'd listen. And of course all the parents of children with fractured limbs were glaring at me as if to say, "Call yourself a mother?"' Harvey laughs, fixing her with his clear blue eyes. 'Then he was given a light anaesthetic,' she continues, 'and they managed to get it all out with tiny tweezers. Now he's on antibiotics to zap any lingering infection.' She stops herself. With no kids of his own, and clearly being a few years younger than she is, Harvey really doesn't need to be bombarded all this child-related info. 'Anyway, I'm being a mummy-bore,' she says quickly.

'No, you're not, and I work with children, remember. I'm not completely allergic to them.'

Kerry smiles. 'Still okay for Mia's party next Saturday? We'll have to miss your lesson that day, I'm afraid . . .'

'Yeah, probably a good idea. Might be a bit challenging doing our improv session with fifteen children charging around the house.'

'I do feel better, knowing you're going to be there,' she adds. 'Mia's given out the invitations but hardly anyone's RSVP'd to say they'll come.'

'Oh, I'm sure they will . . .'

'*Will* they, though?' She gets up to refill Harvey's mug from the percolator jug. 'What if there's only Mia, Freddie and my friend Brigid's little boy Joe, and acres of untouched food? Hiring you will seem completely over the top . . .'

'Kerry,' he says firmly, 'it'll be fine.'

She exhales loudly. 'This probably isn't even about the party, not really. It's just . . . I feel *guilty*, I guess, uprooting them from all their old friends just before their dad and I split up. It's all been too much for them . . .'

'But you had no idea that was going to happen,' Harvey insists. 'You moved down here for the best possible reasons . . .'

'Yeah.' She laughs mirthlessly. 'The "great schools" issue. God . . .' She gets up and swills out her mug at the sink. 'Anyway, Harvey, I have to say I still can't quite imagine you in the full clown outfit.'

He chuckles. 'I know it sounds a bit crap to say I'm just doing this to tide me over. I'm an actor really – at least, that's what I was trained to do. Things just went a bit quiet last year . . . well, *silent* actually.'

She turns and smiles at him. 'I guess being pelted with barley sugars is slightly preferable to eviction and starvation.'

He nods. 'Yes, just about.'

'Anyway,' she adds, 'you mean it's not the way you planned things.'

'Definitely not.' He laughs ruefully.

Getting up from his basket to perform an extravagant stretch, Buddy pads to the front door and whines insistently. 'Sorry, Harvey, but I need to take him out.' She lifts her jacket from the hook on the door.

'Mind if I come with you?'

Kerry smiles, suprised but pleased. 'No, not at all. I'd like the company.' And so they set out along the beach. As they walk, she learns about his flatmate Ethan who, at the ripe old age of thirty-three, finds it hilarious to leave sinister teeth marks in Harvey's cheese, and how he's having a hard time convincing his parents – churchy, conservative types up in Cumbria – that Ethan isn't his boyfriend.

'What about *your* parents?' he asks. 'Where are they?'

'Oh, they died when I was seventeen. Car crash on holiday in France.'

'That's terrible,' he exclaims. 'I'm sorry I asked . . .'

'It's fine,' she assures him. 'It's twenty years ago now. I do miss them of course but, you know . . . it's as if another life has happened since then. It's weird. They didn't even know me as a proper adult, not really, and they never met Rob.' Harvey nods, and although she has vowed to herself that she won't launch into a despicable-ex rant, she can't help blurting out, 'You know what, Harvey? The one part I still can't get my head around is that Rob says he can't remember a thing about it.'

'You mean sleeping with her?' He looks incredulous.

'Yes, the sex bit. The impregnation. Is that possible, d'you think?'

'Um . . . can't say it's ever happened to me, but maybe, I don't know – is there some kind of condition that makes people black out, y'know, mid-act?'

She frowns, considering this. 'I'm not sure. Doesn't *petite mort* mean orgasm? A little death, like a black-out . . .'

'Yes, well, I suppose that could explain it . . .' He gives her a quizzical look.

'. . . Or maybe that's her modus – inviting men to stay over and, when they've fallen asleep, she gets out her patented baby-making machine and syphons off their sperm . . .'

Harvey sniggers. 'In that case, he should have called the police to report a theft.' He checks his watch. 'D'you have any more pupils today, Kerry? I fancy a drink, don't you?'

'Love one,' she says firmly. 'I'm free the rest of the day but we'll have to sit outside, I'm afraid, freezing our arses off. Buddy doesn't like being left on his own.'

*

262

The day has panned out better than Kerry could have hoped. She has enjoyed her lessons today – a sparky nine-year-old who's hurtling towards grade three, followed by a pair of earnest teenage sisters who share a lesson; then Harvey, of course, who is learning the rudiments with endearing keenness. And now they're on their second drink – beer for him, wine for her – grateful for the patio heater which is doing an excellent job of making The Jolly Roger's beer garden a little less Baltic. In fact, Kerry isn't feeling the cold at all as Harvey regales her with Ethan stories.

'So he's gone out,' he tells her, 'which happens about twice a year – did you ever see that *Life on Earth* documentary about the cockroaches that live on a huge pile of dung and never actually leave their cave?'

'Oh yes, that's Freddie's favourite, the dung one . . .'

Harvey nods. 'So my parents come over and it's all nice, y'know, because my gay lover isn't there, which always makes them twitchy – until Mum happens to glance at the fireplace and lets out this awful scream because Ethan had been complaining about a draught coming down the chimney and, in his wisdom, has stuffed my spare wig up there.'

Kerry snorts with laughter. 'So it looked like someone was coming head-first down your chimney . . .'

'Exactly.' He grins. 'Like Santa, but with bright yellow hair and about six weeks early.'

The next hour flies by extremely pleasantly as the sky darkens and Shorling's silvery Christmas lights twinkle in the distance.

'So,' Harvey says as they head back along the coastal path, 'you've told me about Rob, but what about you? Are you seeing anyone at the moment?'

His blatant question makes her break into a smile. 'Nope. I did have dinner with someone a couple of days ago – the man I got Buddy from, actually – but it ended pretty abruptly with the leaky ear thing, and I think that's that.' She decides

263

not to mention that she's slightly put out that James hasn't called since, not even to ask about how things turned out with Freddie.

'What,' Harvey asks, frowning, 'because of the corn, you mean? Why would that put someone off?'

Kerry shrugs. 'Well, he has one grown-up son who seems really sweet and sorted, and I suspect he was horrified that a perfectly enjoyable evening can end up with us hurtling off to A&E. Anyway,' she adds quickly, glancing down at Buddy, '*he's* the only man in my life these days. I've decided it's a whole lot simpler that way.'

'Oh, come on. It's no fun going out with someone whose poo you have to pick up in a bag.'

'There are far worse things,' she says, smirking. 'I know he's not the most obedient dog – I mean, I can't see him trotting off to fetch my Saturday *Guardian* anytime soon – but apart from that, he's so undemanding and simple and at the moment, that's just what I need.'

'Undemanding and simple,' Harvey muses. 'So *that's* what you look for in a man.'

'Yes, although I don't mind if he rolls over for a belly tickle now and then. Anyway, listen – I'm starving and I know the cupboards are bare at home. I'd better pick up some supplies.'

Harvey bunches his hands into his jeans pockets. 'You're welcome to come back to mine if you like.'

'Oh, I don't know,' she says quickly. 'Buddy and I were thinking of having a romantic Saturday night in.'

'Ethan will be there,' Harvey adds, as if keen to convey that he has no intention of pouncing on her, 'and there's a lamb dansak I made last night, always better the next day . . .'

'Well, that sounds great,' she says with a wide smile. 'I'd love to come if you're sure that's okay. Just let me drop Buddy off at home.'

'You needn't do that. Just bring him with you.'

'But I thought you said Ethan was allergic to dogs?'

'He'll be fine for a while,' Harvey says with a grin. 'Anyway, it'll pay him back for his little prank with my wig.'

Chapter Forty

'Roberto,' Mary says, 'I need to talk to you.'

'Uh-huh?' He drags his gaze away from a fast-moving Swedish thriller which is impossible to follow without staring intently at the TV screen.

'Please listen to me,' Mary says, twisting her hands together.

He looks at her in her armchair with what he hopes passes for rapt attention. 'I am listening, Mum, but I know what you're going to say.'

Her brow furrows. '*What* am I going to say?'

With a sigh – no chance of figuring out who that guy in the alley was now – he flips the TV to mute and turns to face her.

'Look, I know it's been hard for you. I understand that you're really fond of Kerry, and when all this settles down there's no reason why you can't still see her as much as you used to . . .'

'It's not Kerry,' she says carefully, her neck turning mottled pink. 'Well, it *is*, and you know how I feel about all that, but you're a grown man and . . .' Mary shrugs sadly. 'You make your own choices in life.'

Rob nods. 'Look, I tried everything to sort things out, but she wouldn't hear of it . . .'

'Can you blame her, Roberto? The way I understand it—'

'Mum,' Rob cuts in sharply, 'I can't go into this now. I'm with Nadine and that's just the way it is. It's not ideal but it's happened, and we're trying to make it work.' He blinks at his mother, wishing his dad would bring the children in now; they're out in Eugene's shed in the back garden, a treasure trove crammed with model steam engines at various stages of construction, where his father whiles away much of his spare time.

'I'm doing my best, Mum,' Rob adds. 'You'll like Nadine once you get to know her. She's just young and she was nervous about meeting you, but she's a sweet girl really and she means well . . .'

Mary waggles a foot, allowing a sheepskin slipper to drop onto the ivy-patterned carpet. 'She's certainly very attractive.'

'Mmmm.' Rob can sense her peering at him as he picks at a fingernail.

'It all happened very quickly, didn't it? I had no idea you and Kerry were having difficulties.'

'Mum, *please*.' The credits are rolling on TV; final episode too.

'Does Nadine mind about this . . . this *thing* you have?'

'What thing?'

Mary inhales deeply. 'This thing about being born in the wrong body.'

'*What?*' Rob turns and stares at her. What is she on about now? He glances out of the living room window, focusing on the glowing window of Eugene's shed.

'I read about it in a magazine, Roberto.' She lowers her voice and casts a quick glance at the TV, as if the muted model in the insurance ad might be able to hear them.

'You mean . . . people who think they've been born the wrong sex?'

Mary shudders. 'Yes, and I know what you'll go through. It starts with hormones and you change shape and the beard stops growing and then . . .' She looks at him, her eyes wet and shiny, the tears threatening to spill over. 'And then breasts come.'

Rob stares at his mother. Her veiny hands are trembling on her lap as she fiddles with the pleats of her olive-coloured skirt.

'You don't think . . .' he starts.

She nods, unable to form words for a moment, then blurts out, 'They have surgery, don't they? To remove it, I mean. It's irreversible, Roberto . . .'

Her cheeks are flushed, fat tears coursing down her cheeks now as Rob lurches off the sofa and across the room to gather his mother up in his arms. 'Mum, it's okay, please don't cry.'

'But I read . . .'

'*What* did you read? One of those real-life stories in some stupid women's magazine?'

'No.' She shakes her head. 'On your laptop . . .'

'God, Mum.' Rob sweeps his hands over his burning cheeks. 'That's a column I do, a pathetic thing my new boss is making me write in the guise of a woman. *Jesus* . . .'

She looks up at him, blinking away tears. 'You mean it's not really you?'

'No, of course not,' he says, squeezing her bony hand. 'Not the real me anyway. It's just a stupid made-up persona.'

'Really?'

He laughs mirthlessly, not hearing his father stepping into the hallway with Mia on one side and Freddie on the other as he declares, 'Yes, *really*. Listen, Mum, I know you're

268

concerned about me right now, and I've been a pretty awful husband and father. There's a lot to be worried about – I realise that. But I can promise you that I am perfectly happy being a man.'

Chapter Forty-One

Harvey's curry has been eaten and pronounced delicious. Despite his warning about Ethan's naan-draping tendencies, he actually placed it very politely at the side of his plate, perhaps due to being in the Presence of a Woman. Kerry has enjoyed herself hugely so far, managing to avoid becoming too drunk due to consuming her bodyweight in carbs. And now Ethan – short, chubby, carroty of hair – is standing before them in the small, book-filled living room, having set up a flipchart on a stand.

'From my training days,' he explains, brandishing a fat black felt tip. 'I'm a failed actor like Harvey, you see.' Harvey shoots him a mock-exasperated look.

'What did you train people in?' Kerry asks from her curled-up position on the sofa.

'Teambuilding, motivation, making things happen – all that stuff.'

Harvey snorts. 'Making what sort of things happen, Ethan?'

'Oh, fuck off. Anyway,' Ethan continues somewhat tipsily, 'what I'm saying, Kerry, is that you need to view the situation objectively and list the pros and cons. Then you can make an informed decision.'

'What the hell is he talking about?' Harvey whispers to Kerry as she gives him a baffled shrug.

'So here,' Ethan says grandly, 'is Dog.' In the flipchart's top left-hand corner, Ethan draws an approximation of a small, droopy-eared hound. 'And here is Man,' he continues, sketching a scrawny person, then writing DOG and MAN beneath them, to avoid any confusion. 'So,' he addresses Kerry, 'give me some pros for choosing Dog over Man as your beloved.'

'Er . . .' She tears off a small corner of cold chapatti and chews it. 'Loyal. Cheery. Always pleased to see me. Cuddly. Sweet. Likes playing. Never moans . . .'

'Whoa, enough, hold on a minute . . .'

'Never comes home pissed,' Harvey adds as Ethan scribbles on the board.

'Doesn't try to broaden my musical tastes,' Kerry suggests, recalling Rob's unintelligible jazz phase when the house jarred with squawking saxophones.

Ethan frowns. 'Can we just put "good taste in music"?'

Kerry glances at Buddy who has arranged himself, rather forwardly, across Harvey's lap. 'No musical preferences,' she suggests. 'That's definitely a plus.'

'Now cons?' Ethan prompts Kerry.

'Poos on pavement,' she replies.

'Anything else?'

'Actually, I can't think of any. Can we move onto Man now?'

'Okay, Man: pros,' Ethan says bossily.

'Er.' She cannot think of one positive thing.

'C'mon, Kerry,' he smirks, 'there must be *something* the male of the species is good for.'

She shakes her head. 'Don't like Man. Man impregnate editorial assistant,' which has them all convulsing with laughter.

'Not your ex,' Ethan says. 'He sounds like a jerk. I'm talking generic everyman . . .'

271

'He's bloody lost it,' Harvey chuckles.

'Okay,' Ethan bellows, 'what can a man give you that a dog can't?'

She considers this for a moment, feeling slightly sleepy now, full of delicious curry and wine and thinking about the walk home – only fifteen minutes, but still, it's freezing out there. Anyway, the only pro she can think of to place Man above Dog is sex and right now, she doesn't really want to go there.

'Could I be cheeky,' she says, 'and ask for a coffee, Ethan?'

'What, not another proper drink? Come on, it's still early . . .'

'Thanks, but I'd better head home. It's been lovely, thank you, and you've really helped me to think about things . . . *objectively*.' She catches Harvey's eye and smiles as Ethan heads to the kitchen.

'Come and give me a hand, Harvey,' he calls back.

'I'm sure you remember how to operate the kettle,' Harvey mutters, but extracts himself from beneath Buddy anyway, who flops onto Kerry instead.

She sits there, looking at the flipchart bearing Ethan's wonky scrawlings. 'You embarrassed her,' she hears Harvey murmur, just audible over the low music.

'No I didn't.'

'Jesus, Ethan.'

'She didn't say the obvious, though – that a dog can't take her out to dinner . . .' There's a snigger, and Kerry can't decide if they don't care that she might be able to hear, or are just drunk and think they're whispering.

'*I'd* take her out,' Ethan slurs.

'Oh, shut up.'

'No, I would! Seriously. She's fucking gorgeous, Harv. You never said. I'd even put up with her dog – I could always take an antihistamine . . .'

'What *are* you on about?'

272

Ethan snorts. 'You come back from your lessons making her sound plain and dreary . . .' Kerry blinks down at her rice-speckled plate on the coffee table.

'No I don't,' Harvey mutters.

'Yeah, you do. I was imagining a middle-aged woman with chunky ankles and a lilac twinset stinking of mouldy rose petals . . .'

'Shut *up*, for God's sake.'

'And she's not, is she? She's hot. You never said!'

Kerry stares ahead, deciding to bolt down her coffee as quickly as she can without scalding her mouth. Or maybe she won't drink it at all. She'll invent some domestic emergency she must rush home for and attend to at once. An iron left on, or the horrible feeling that she left something in the oven . . . While the evening has been fun, she now feels faintly ridiculous for coming back to the home of one man she barely knows, the other a complete stranger, just because she didn't want to sit in an empty house on a Saturday night.

The sound of the boiling kettle has drowned out the two men's voices. Then it clicks off, and the whole flat seems to fall deadly silent as Ethan says, 'You know what, Harv? I'd love to meet a woman just like Kerry. But *younger*.'

Chapter Forty-Two

It was just an offhand remark. Kerry doesn't care if Ethan regards her as a well-preserved geriatric, the kind of woman you'd describe as 'good for her age' or – horrors – 'young at heart' (which, let's face it, means *old*). Yet, infuriatingly, his words are still playing over and over in her mind the next day, like the way she sometimes finds herself humming a *Cuckoo Clock* song in the checkout queue.

Just like Kerry . . . but younger. Bloody fantastic. Okay, she's four or five years older than Ethan and Harvey, but is it really that obvious? Glancing into the tiny flower-shaped mirror stuck to the fridge, all she sees are under-eye shadows and a blur of crow's feet. Shit. It's one of the downsides of being distinctly un-vain, she realises. When you can go for days barely glancing into a mirror, merely giving your hair a quick brush and stuffing it into a pony-tail, it comes as an almighty shock when you actually take the time to have a proper look. Maybe she should build up to it gradually, allowing herself just a casual glance before the full-on examination in what appears to be a *magnifying* mirror, she realises now. Ugh. So it's almost a relief when Rob's car pulls up outside. At least, now the children are home, she won't have time to ponder such a stupid, meaningless comment.

'Hey,' she says, trying to gather Freddie and Mia in for a hug as they charge into the house. 'Have a good time?'

'Yeah,' Mia replies distractedly, having pushed past her in order to bestow Buddy with cuddles and kisses.

'Nonno made us this, Mummy.' Freddie holds up a beautiful gleaming green and gold steam engine.

'Wow, that's amazing! Isn't he clever? You'll have to take it in to school after the holidays.' She glances at Mia, detecting a distinct lack of festive spirit. 'You okay, sweetheart? Have you enjoyed yourself this weekend?'

'Um . . . it was *okay*.'

Kerry frowns at Rob. 'What's wrong?' she mouths as Freddie dumps his model on the table.

'Can we play with Buddy in the garden?' Mia asks.

'Yes, sweetheart, as long as the gate's shut. . . .' As children and dog tumble back outside, Kerry fixes Rob with a quizzical stare. 'So what's up?'

'Er . . . they just overheard something when I was having a chat with Mum,' Rob mumbles. 'It's nothing.'

'Well, they both seem a bit upset, Rob.' She clicks on the kettle, dropping an ordinary teabag into a mug for Rob, and a chamomile one in hers.

'You've gone all Shorling,' he remarks.

'It's just herbal tea, Rob. It has been around for a few decades now. So, the thing they overheard . . .'

'Oh, God. It's going to sound awful but Mum read my column on my laptop last weekend – my Miss Jones one – and assumed it was some kind of fantasy thing, that I actually want to *be* a woman . . .'

'What?' She explodes with laughter. 'Like . . . have the full op, you mean?'

He nods, his mouth set in a firm line.

'You're not, are you?'

'For God's sake, Kerry . . .' He emits a withering laugh.

'And they overheard you talking about this? About having your, your . . . *dick* removed?'

'Not exactly,' he says glumly. 'Just that I was perfectly happy being a man, and I guess it's confused them. Like, there was a possibility that I might want to be a *lady* . . .'

'For God's sake, Rob,' Kerry exclaims. 'And they've been asking you about this?'

'All the way here, yeah . . .'

Kerry shakes her head. 'As if they haven't enough on their plate right now.'

'I know . . . and I'm sorry. I'm a complete and utter fuck-up, aren't I?'

She looks at him, assessing the man she could quite happily have slapped in the face just a few weeks ago. Now, though, her barely controllable fury has ebbed away to be replaced by a sort of . . . quiet disillusionment. It's less painful, certainly. To her surprise, a sense of something akin to *pity* has also begun to creep in.

'I can't believe your mum jumped to that conclusion,' she says, turning to tip out the kids' overnight bags, and stuffing their laundry into the washing machine.

'You know Mum. Makes worrying about me and Dom her life's work. She hadn't even been able to bring herself to tell Dad . . .'

'God. Poor Mary.' Kerry can't help smiling as she turns back to face him. 'Listen, d'you want to come to Mia's party next Saturday? I know she'd be delighted if you were there.'

There's a small pause. 'I'd really like that, if you're sure it won't be awkward . . .'

'Why would it be? You're still her dad, Rob.' Kerry's voice cracks a little, and she quickly clears her throat. 'It would mean a lot to her. We've spent ages planning it and I've booked a clown as a surprise.'

'Have you? Why?'

'To make it *fun*, Rob. That's what clowns are for, apparently.'

He winces. 'I'm not sure about clowns. Don't you think they're kind of . . . sinister?'

'Not this one. He's a pupil of mine. D'you remember you saw him when you picked up the kids last weekend? He's an actor really . . .'

'Oh,' he laughs witheringly, 'one of *those*.'

'Yes,' she says, deciding not to rise to the bait, 'one of those, but don't hold it against him, will you, and be all terse and tight-lipped while he's here?'

'Of course not,' he blusters, finishing his tea. 'I am perfectly capable of being pleasant, you know.'

She sniggers, taking a moment to savour the image of Rob and Harvey in the same room. As children's birthday parties go, she figures, this one might prove more entertaining than most.

*

Next morning, having underestimated the amount of gift wrapping she still has to do, Kerry ignores the small stab of guilt as she suggests Freddie and Mia watch a full-length movie while she 'gets on with things' upstairs.

'What things?' Mia wants to know.

'Christmassy things. Things you're not meant to see.'

'*Ohhh.*' Mia nods, eyes shining. 'Santa's busy as well, Mummy.'

'Yes, I'd imagine he is.' She puts on the movie, eager to tackle the pile of gifts currently stashed in her wardrobe.

'Mummy?' Mia has followed her out into the hallway.

'Yes, honey?'

'Is Father Christmas real?'

Kerry frowns, conscious of the seconds ticking by as she

scrabbles for the appropriate response. 'Why d'you ask?' she says lightly.

''Cause Audrey-Jane says he's not. She says her mummy and daddy don't believe in lying to children and presents just come from shops.' Mia blinks slowly.

'Why would they say that?' Kerry asks, feigning amazement.

''Cause Santa's a lie, she said.'

'Oh, Mia.' Kerry bobs down and brushes a caramel curl from her daughter's lightly freckled face. 'You know what? I think maybe Audrey-Jane just said it to be mean, to spoil the fun, don't you?'

Mia nods solemnly.

'Shall we put out Father Christmas's mince pies and beer now, and a carrot for Rudolph?'

'Yeah,' she says firmly. And that, thankfully, seems to satisfy her. While Kerry wouldn't wish her daughter to be speculating on Santa's existence at the age of fifteen, she is only seven, for goodness's sake. Anyway, does it really count as a lie? How *joyless* are some of the mothers around here? Briefly, Kerry wonders again how many of the invited children will actually turn up for Mia's party.

No time to dwell on that now, though. Upstairs in her bedroom, Kerry surveys the vast selection of games, books and soft toys – both children are still rather fond of their cuddlies, albeit secretly in Freddie's case – plus a dazzling array of stocking presents which she's been amassing over the past few months. Aunt Maisie, too, has sent alluring parcels for all of them, while the children's main gifts – new bikes – were ordered by Rob and are hidden in Mary and Eugene's attic. Then, for Mia's birthday in just five days' time, Kerry has bought an easel and enormous art set, including five hundred pens which she knows her daughter will store in perfect rainbow order (clearly, Mia has inherited Rob's organisational skills).

Momentarily distracted, Kerry picks up the carefully handwritten note from her bedside table, which had fallen out of Aunt Maisie's Christmas card:

Dearest Kerry, I know from your last letter that things have been incredibly difficult lately. Sending you all my love for a happy and peaceful Christmas and, who knows, perhaps you and the children will manage to come out to stay for some much-needed sun?

Kerry folds up the sheet of thin blue paper and slips it into her top drawer. She has tried not to dwell on how bizarre Christmas will feel this year, although it's clear from the enormous stash of presents still to be wrapped that she's tried to compensate for something lacking. Anita has invited them over for lunch tomorrow, then the children will be whisked off by Rob to spend Christmas evening at his parents' house, where they'll have Boxing Day too.

It'll be *fine*, she tries to reassure herself, biting off strips of Sellotape. After all, plenty of families manage Christmases like this. But what about the new year? Her resolutions are usually along the lines of 'start running, do stomach crunches, drink less wine'. Not 'divorce Rob'. A lump forms in her throat and her eyes suddenly fill with hot tears. She blots them with a corner of her duvet and focuses on wrapping the easel instead.

With the children now installed in front of a *second* movie – call the childcare police – Kerry tackles the last of the gifts, coming up for air three hours later to the sound of a sharp rap on the door. Buddy leaps from his basket with a cacophony of barks as she takes the enormous, cellophane-wrapped wicker hamper from the delivery man.

It is stunningly presented with flamboyant ribbons and bows, and filled with delicious things to eat. There are Italian wines, plus pickles, chocolates and cheeses: the perfect offering to take to Anita's tomorrow as a way of saying thanks. Blinking away more tears, Kerry peels off the tiny envelope and extracts a card. *To Kerry*, she reads, *still our beloved daughter. A very happy Christmas from Mary and Eugene xxx.*

She carries the hamper to the kitchen table and is untying its flashy red bow when her mobile rings. 'Kerry? It's James.'

'Hi,' she says, quickly wiping her eyes on her sweater sleeve.

'Just wondered how things are going. Um . . . are you all organised?'

'Yes . . . just about.'

There's a small pause. 'You sound a bit . . . upset.'

She exhales. 'A hamper just arrived from my in-laws – my *ex*-in-laws, I mean. It's a sort of ritual but usually, of course, it would be for all four of us. I didn't expect it this year.'

'Oh, that's sweet of them.'

'There's even some Camembert and Brie,' she adds, 'which they don't usually include – it's normally Italian goodies all the way . . .'

'Luke's test-running melted Brie with cranberries as a kind of seasonal special,' James chuckles. 'I thought it was a bit over-ambitious, even for around here, but it's actually proving quite popular.'

Kerry smiles. 'I might try that. I'm taking the whole lot to my friend Anita's tomorrow – we're invited for Christmas Day. What are you up to?'

'Um . . . I thought it was going to be a miserable little turkey dinner for one, but Luke's girlfriend's parents have asked me up to their holiday place in Norfolk. Bit of a mercy mission, I suspect, but kind of them, even if it means a board game marathon.' She laughs, then he adds, 'Sorry I haven't called, Kerry. It's been crazy in the shop. We've had orders for huge buffets from people who've been let down. A couple of sandwich places have gone out of business and it seems like all their customers have come flocking to us . . .'

'I'm glad it's going well,' she says.

'Um, I hope Freddie's ear's okay now?'

Hmmm. A little belated, she decides. 'He's fine, thanks. Anyway, enjoy your Christmas,' she adds, wandering through to the living room where the children are sprawled beneath blankets, looking cosy as anything on the sofa.

'You too. And, um . . . maybe we could meet up for lunch sometime during the holidays?'

'Sure,' Kerry says, 'that sounds great. Bye, James.' With a smile, she switches on the multi-coloured Christmas tree lights and places Mary and Eugene's note among the clutter of cards on the mantelpiece. Then she snuggles between her children on the sofa, the three of them basking in the glory of their undeniably tacky yet beautiful twinkling tree.

Chapter Forty-Three

'So you're not the editor of the magazine,' barks Jens, Nadine's Swiss father, across the restaurant table. 'Just the *deputy editor*.'

'That's right,' Rob says pleasantly, 'but I'm quite happy with that. It's actually through choice.'

Jens frowns in bafflement at Candida, his blonde, rather fragile-looking, English wife. If Nadine was taken aback when they called her from Heathrow this afternoon, having opted for a last-minute Christmas in London, Rob was downright horrified. He hasn't shown it, though. So far, he has been a study in charm and manners, despite being invited to dinner in possibly the only restaurant in North London which still seems to think it's 1976.

'And why did you choose this?' Jens wants to know, fixing him with small, rapidly blinking blue eyes.

Because I didn't want the sodding Steak Diane. 'I just fancied something light' – Rob prods his unyielding risotto with his fork – 'with that big Christmas dinner looming tomorrow.'

'No, no, I mean the deputy editor position and not editor.'

'Erm . . .' Rob forms a rictus smile. 'You see, on magazines the deputy tends to be more hands-on in the office, especially in a small team like ours. Whereas the editor has to be out there, schmoozing advertisers, being a figurehead . . .'

'And you don't want to be a figurehead?' Jens's startled expression suggests Rob actually said, *And you don't believe in wearing underpants?*

'Er, not especially, no.'

'But the editor is paid more?'

'Yes, of course, but I'd rather have job satisfaction—'

'Even when you have my daughter and a baby to support,' Jens cuts in, scratching his thick, pink neck.

'Dad,' Nadine says quickly, placing a small hand on her father's arm. 'Rob's happy. He's really good at what he does. Let's leave it, okay?' She casts Rob an apologetic smile which does nothing to thaw the chilly atmosphere. Rob already feels as if he has spent half of his adult life in this restaurant with its thick beige tablecloths and napkins folded into swan shapes, or possibly geese. There are too many wine glasses – four each, for some unfathomable reason – and a few feet behind him, Rob can hear the miserable dribble of some hideous fountain.

'I'm sure you are, Rob,' Candida says kindly. 'I think Jens is just a little concerned about . . .' she casts Nadine a fond look ' . . . how you'll both *manage*. That's why we came, to make sure everything's all right.'

Oh, sure. The caring vibes are overwhelming, Rob reflects, resorting to picking out a lump of stodgy rice that had become embedded in a molar. While Nadine gamely attempts to further boost his PR as fabulous boyfriend and father-to-be, he takes a moment to assess the curious family he's found himself plunged into. Jens is a large, fleshy man with a face that was probably once classed as handsome, but is now softened by several chins which wobble as he chews. Candida was clearly a beauty – all high cheekbones and kind, baby-blue eyes – but, being far too skinny, has a rather alarming, sinewy neck which, to Rob's mind, moves in an almost alien way as she speaks. Plus, she has the misfortune to be named after a yeast infection.

'So, what are your plans for tomorrow, Rob?' she asks pleasantly.

'Erm, I'm going to my parents' in Kent in the morning, then after lunch I'll pick up my children from my wife's – my *ex*-wife's – friend's place and take them back to Mum and Dad's.'

'Very complicated.' She emits a tinkly laugh.

'A lot of driving, yes,' he says inanely, 'but at least it'll keep me off the drink.' *Otherwise, you see, I'd be a raging alcoholic . . .*

'Hmmm,' Jens grunts. 'And you, Nadine – you say you're spending Christmas Day with friends?'

'Yes. Sasha and Harriet share a flat and neither of them are going home this year so, um . . . we thought it'd be fun to get together.'

'Are you cooking, sweetheart?' Candida asks.

'We're, er . . . having a sort of stir fry,' she mumbles, lowering her eyes and flushing pink. 'Rob did ask me to go to his mum and dad's but it's family time for him.'

Jens raises a greying eyebrow. 'So you have children already, Rob.'

He nods morosely. 'Just the two.'

'And they live with their mother?'

'Er, yes, on the south coast. I see them most weekends, though.' Jens scowls, as if not entirely sure that Rob is telling the truth, and a terse silence descends. 'So where are you staying in London?' Rob barks, too loudly.

'We're at Charles and Alicia's round the corner,' Candida says brightly, as if Rob should know immediately who she's referring to: *Oh, Charles and Alicia! Do give them my love . . .*

'Excuse me a minute,' he says, pushing away his vomit-like meal and bounding up from his seat. He strides across the sparsely-populated restaurant, wondering how, in one neat move, he's managed to transform Christmas Eve from being a lovely occasion, bubbling with excitement as his children set out Santa's mince pies and beer, to being grilled about his career prospects by a terrifying Swiss man. Rob doesn't even need the loo. He just craves a few moments' respite from Jens's booming voice and the creeping sense that his natural charm is faltering somewhat.

From inside the locked cubicle Ron hears someone coming into the gents and sploshing noisily into the urinals. He sits on the loo, hiding, until the man goes away, and decides he needs to think up some safe conversation topics. That's the only possible way he'll get through this dinner alive. Idiotically, in an attempt to establish some common ground, he had planned to announce that his own father is Italian, but realises now how lame that would sound: 'So you're from Switzerland, Jens. Well, my dad's from Verona. How amazing that you both come from other countries!' No, that won't do at all. Something about Switzerland then? Banks, mountains, being neutral during the war . . . Christ, Jens would probably stab him with his steak knife for that. It would be as crass as meeting an Austrian and asking if they like *The Sound of Music* . . .

What about cuckoo clocks? They could have a fascinating discussion about novelty timepieces. No, that's even worse. And now he's thinking about Kerry, who's probably in a flurry of last-minute wrapping right now, with a glass of wine at her side. His mobile rings, and he almost cries with relief when it's her.

'I was just thinking about you,' he blurts out.

'Were you?' There's an awkward pause.

'Yeah. I, er . . . was just wondering how you were getting on with things. Wrapping presents and doing the stockings and all that . . . have you put out mince pies?'

'For Santa?' Her voice softens. 'Yes, of course we have,

and a carrot. All the usuals.' She reverts to a more business-like tone. 'Anyway, I've just remembered, Mia really wanted gold pens in her stocking and I've forgotten to buy them.'

'Gold pens,' he repeats flatly.

'Yes, gold ink ones, I mean. Kind of rollerball things, you know? She's been doing these brilliant Tutankhamun drawings and wants to colour them in gold, so . . .'

'But she'll open her stocking first thing with you, won't she?'

'That doesn't matter. If you could get them and give them to her at your mum and dad's . . .'

He runs his tongue over his lips. 'Er . . . I'm sort of out at the moment.'

'Well, there must be a late newsagent's open, couldn't you just—'

'Kerry,' he interrupts, 'I'm out having dinner with Nadine and her parents.'

'Oh.' There's a pause. 'So . . . how's that going?'

Aware of the weirdness of conducting a phone conversation in a toilet cubicle, he lets himself out and inspects his waxy face in the mirror above the hideous scallop-shaped basins. 'It's absolutely fucking terrible.'

'Is it? Oh dear . . .'

'It's not *funny*. Her dad obviously hates my guts, looks like he'd happily smash the water carafe over my head . . .'

'And why would he hate you, Rob?' Kerry's voice trembles with mirth. 'What could this man, the father of a pregnant twenty-year-old, possibly have against you?'

'It's probably because I ordered risotto,' he snaps before ringing off, the gold pens request evaporating immediately as he steps out of the gents.

Rob pauses, taking a moment to examine his fingernails before rejoining the table.

'So you've found yourself a *zuckervati*,' Jens is declaring loudly across the room. 'He's twice your age, Nadine. A grown

286

man with a family he hardly sees. Children of his own he doesn't care about . . .'

Rob winces, rooted to the spot. What the hell does this man in his disgusting shirt – murky green with contrasting white collar – know about his family? He's just told him he sees his kids almost every weekend, for Christ's sake. He can hardly do more than that. Anyway, how dare Jens pass judgement on Rob's parenting when, as far as he can gather, he can only be bothered to shift his paunchy arse to visit Nadine about once a year?

'A *zuckervati*,' Jens repeats. 'I can hardly believe this is what you've settled for.'

Now, what could that possibly mean? *Zucker* . . . sugar. *Vati* . . . father, perhaps? Sugar daddy?

'Jens, *please*,' Candida hisses. 'Let's not spoil the evening.'

'It's not like that, Daddy,' Nadine murmurs. 'Age doesn't come into it. It's not relevant . . .'

Their table is obscured by an alabaster statue of a woman clutching an urn from which blue-tinted water is dribbling. Realising he must look bizarre, loitering by the loos rather than rejoining the happy group, Rob takes out his mobile again and pretends to check his texts.

'So is he divorced?' Jens wants to know.

'Not yet, Daddy, no.'

'Well, it would be nice to know if he's planning to marry you – I assume he's already living with you in the flat . . .'

'Um . . . we've haven't even talked about getting married yet,' Nadine replies wearily. 'And he's sort of between homes at the moment. He's mostly at mine but the sale of his house has got caught up in a chain so there's been a delay there. It should all be sorted very soon.'

'Hmmm.' Jens pauses. 'And what happened to the other one you were seeing?'

'What, you mean Eddy?' she asks. 'That was just a casual, on-off kind of thing.'

'At least he's closer to your age, and an *editor* . . .'

Rob can sense his blood coagulating as he makes his way back to the table. He takes his seat and snatches the menu that's the precise glossy orange of a cling peach.

'What d'you fancy, Rob?' Candida asks sweetly.

He can barely speak. So, Nadine had an *on-off kind of thing* with Eddy, did she? He glares at her, wondering if it was on or off at around the time he slept with her, and if there's a chance that the baby . . .

'How about sharing a crème brûlée, Rob?' Nadine suggests with a smile. 'Or a lemon sorbet?'

'Oh, yes, Nadine was telling me your father's Italian,' Candida witters nervously. 'You must have had some lovely sorbets in your time!'

Rob blinks at this assortment of ridiculous people with whom he has been forced to have dinner. He feels his upper lip sticking to his top teeth as he replies, 'Not really, Candida . . . in fact I think I'll pass on dessert. I really couldn't eat another thing.'

*

'I promise you, it was nothing,' Nadine insists, buttoned up to the neck in fleecy pyjamas as they lie side by side, without touching, in bed. 'It was just . . . you know. A friends-with-benefits thing.'

'Oh, for God's sake. This isn't a movie, Nadine.' Rob turns away sulkily.

'Well, what else am I supposed to call it? We were never serious. It was just . . .' She tails off lamely. 'A bit of fun.'

Rob glowers at his brown suede slippers neatly paired up on her lilac bedroom carpet, their backs worn shiny and completely flattened by his heels. He's almost living here now. As well as his slippers, he now keeps his dressing gown, some toiletries, six pairs of boxers and a decent Italian coffee percolator at her place. All of this – like them becoming a couple – seems to have happened without him considering what's actually going on, and whether he wants it.

'Who else have you shagged from the office, then?' he asks flatly.

'That's *completely* offensive,' she snaps. 'There's no need to be so spiteful.'

He presses his lips together, his heart pumping away at what feels like twice its regular speed. They travelled back in the cab from the restaurant in near silence, Nadine mistaking her father's rudeness as the cause of Rob's ill-humour.

'Have you done it with Frank?' he blurts out.

'*No!* Jesus, Rob . . .'

'That new post boy with the dyed yellow hair?'

'Shut the hell up.'

'It's just . . .' He pauses. 'I realise I know so little about your past . . .'

'So I've *got* one,' she barks. 'I'm young, Rob. I'm not forty years old, I don't look baffled if someone asks if I'm on Twitter . . .'

He breathes deeply, sensing what he managed to eat of the risotto shifting uneasily in his stomach.

'I just can't be bothered with stuff like that.'

'No. Fine, then don't. No one's forcing you.'

He lies there, overcome by a wave of desolation as he looks up at the ornate ceiling rose.

'So when did it finish with Eddy?' he asks.

She sighs loudly and sits up. 'There was nothing *to* finish. I told you – it wasn't a big deal.'

'Yes,' he says tersely, 'I understand that. I realise you weren't on the verge of announcing your engagement and popping into John Lewis to choose your dinner service.' He falls silent as they sit in a fug of ill-feeling.

'Er . . . it wasn't that long ago,' Nadine says finally.

'When was the last time, then?'

She turns to him and pulls in her lips as if faced with a tough calculation. 'It was . . . three or four days before the night with you.'

'Three or four *days*? Like, in the same week as me?'

'Yeah?' she says with a shrug. 'I was single, Rob. I told you, it was just—'

'Fun. Yes, you said.' He jumps out of bed and marches to the window where he stares at the skyline blurred by her white gauzy curtains. 'Can you be honest about something at least? Did we definitely do it that first night – you and me, I mean? Because it seems to me that this might not even be my child . . .'

'Of course we did,' she exclaims. 'D'you think I'd lie about that?'

He whirls round to face her. 'I've no idea, Nadine. I don't know what to think any more. Why didn't you mention you and Eddy before?' He feels sick now at the dawning realisation that he might have thrown his life down the toilet for something that never even happened. His marriage, his children, his new life by the sea . . . all as good as lost, for something he didn't even do.

'I told you, Rob, it was nothing.' She is hunched miserably on the huge white bed, picking at a fingernail.

He regards her dispassionately. 'Did you and Eddy have unprotected sex in the same week that we slept together?'

'Christ, you're like . . . like a scary policeman, interviewing me.' She laughs witheringly as he starts pulling on his clothes. 'You'll be shining a bright light in my eyes next and asking me to take a lie-detector test.'

'For fuck's sake, this is serious. *Did* you?'

She shakes her head, the silence stretching a beat too long before she replies, 'Listen, Rob . . . I'm *sure* the baby's yours.'

'Great. Fine. We'll be having a paternity test then, all right?'

'Okay! Go ahead,' she yells as he marches out of the room.

'I'm calling a cab,' he shouts back, 'and going back to Bethnal Green. I can't stay here tonight.'

Nadine doesn't reply or try to follow him. Rob calls a taxi, smoking a cigarette as he paces up and down in her living room – just let her dare come through and complain about the smell – until the driver toots outside. In what he knows is a rather pathetic gesture, he snatches the fairy lights from around her horrible abstract print and flings them onto the pink rug, crushing one of the plastic stars with his foot. Then he stomps downstairs and out into the chilly night, wondering what he'll do when his house keys are finally handed over to the new owners. *Then* he'll be screwed, not that he isn't already.

Rob climbs into the grotty cab with its ripped back seat, wishing with all his heart that he could say, 'Please take me to Shorling-on-Sea.'

Chapter Forty-Four

There are numerous 'firsts' after a break-up. That first online grocery shop, for instance, when Kerry realised she could now delete 'dark almond deluxe' from her favourites because, actually, she's secretly always preferred cheap milk chocolate. Or the first time she glanced down into the washbasin, noting that it was entirely free of those beardy speckles, and knowing it would remain so until either: a) Freddie sprouts into a hairy teenager or b) she invites an adult male to stay the night, whichever comes sooner (her money is on her son reaching adolescence). Other firsts are more difficult: for instance, that first conversation with Rob's parents post break-up, when Mary had cried even more than she had. And the first time (shamefully, not the *only* time) Kerry found herself obsessively Googling Nadine Heffelfinger at 2 a.m., and pored over her breathless book reviews on the *Mr Jones* website. (*Heffelfinger*. What kind of name is that? Sounds like a long-handled back scratcher. 'Ooh, got a bit of an itch below my shoulder blade. Luckily I can reach it with my Heffelfinger.')

This, though – the first Christmas without Rob – is a big one, and Kerry has laid down some firm rules for herself:

1. Do not get drunk.
2. Do not get maudlin.
3. No public crying *under any circumstances*. After all, this is Anita and Ian's Christmas, and six children will be present, not to mention Ian's and Anita's parents whom Kerry hasn't seen for years. And the last thing all these people want to see – apart from a suddenly traumatised Buddy, who appears to have added the premature bang of a Christmas cracker to his phobia list – is a weeping woman.
4. No reminiscing about blissful Christmases past because, in fact, plenty always went wrong. For instance, Rob commenting that perhaps the sprouts needn't have been boiling away since September, and murmuring to a put out Kerry, 'But I thought we weren't going to bother buying each other presents this year?' *Yes, but we didn't actually mean it, tightwad . . .*

In fact, it doesn't turn out that way at all. Christmas morning is a delight, with Mia exclaiming, 'Audrey-Jane was wrong. Santa *has* been!' as she and Freddie tear open their presents. More parcels, plus Mary and Eugene's hamper, are loaded into the car. The children pile in with Buddy, who only vomits once behind his metal grille during the forty minute journey.

At Anita's, the combined gifts form an impressive mountain range in the living room. As Ian shouts, 'Go!' the unwrapping begins, the room filled with so much fun and joy that no one would guess that the Tambinis' world had fallen apart just a few months earlier. Anita's pleasingly rowdy parents are getting stuck into the wine, and Ian's mother – immaculate in a pale mint twinset and pearls – is attempting to gather up mounds of ripped paper. Kerry unwraps a beautiful silk camisole and knickers from Anita ('Well, you never know,' she says with a wink), and Ian's dad helps Freddie to construct a robot (another 'first' for

Kerry: realising that Rob was *always* the one to build things). While Buddy shows zero interest in his new red leather collar, his bag of chocolate-flavoured bones proves a huge hit.

Lunch is a pleasingly chaotic affair, after which the adults spill into armchairs and sofas, apart from Anita's mother-in-law who demands a floor brush – why are some people so compelled to clean other people's houses? – despite Anita saying, 'It's fine, Helen, please just leave it, I'll sort everything later.'

'D'you have a duster, then?' Helen asks.

'Mum, sit down,' Ian teases. 'You're forbidden to dust, it's Christmas Day. Look at them.' He indicates Buddy and Bess who are gently dozing together like a sweet elderly couple. 'They've got the right idea.'

'She'll be trying to groom *them* next,' Anita's dad chuckles.

'I just like to make myself useful,' Helen says, sounding hurt.

'You can,' Ian says, handing her a glass, 'by drinking this. You too, Kerry, Come on – your glass is empty.'

More drinks are poured, the delicious contents of Eugene and Mary's hamper delved into and later, when Rob arrives to collect the children, he is clearly taken aback by the bubbling good humour in Anita's rowdy living room.

'Why can't you stay, Daddy?' Mia asks, clasping his hands in hers. 'I want us to all be together!'

He shrugs, pulling her in for a hug. 'That would be great, but listen – Nanny and Nonno are waiting to see you. We'll have fun there, I promise.'

Her brief disappointment soon fades as presents are gathered together and packed.

'So how was your dinner last night?' Kerry asks as they make for the door.

Rob pulls a mock-terrified face. 'Pretty dreadful but, you know – I coped.'

'Hmmm. I guess it wasn't going to be easy.' Having come out into the porch ahead of the children, Kerry opens the front door and inhales the crisp, cold air.

'Yes, well, there was something else too. Seems that Nadine was having a thing with Eddy until fairly recently.'

'Really?' Kerry glances back to where the children are exchanging reluctant goodbyes in the hallway. 'D'you think it's still going on?'

'No, not now, but . . .' He tails off.

Kerry studies him, not feeling sorry for him exactly, but realising that perhaps, in the grand scheme of things, he's ended up with by far the worst deal.

'Daddy!' Mia cries, charging into the porch to join them. 'Freddie says he won't come to Nanny and Nonno's!'

'Oh, he'll want to when he sees the huge present that's waiting for him there,' Rob says quickly. *The bikes are amazing*, he mouths at Kerry.

She turns back to coax Freddie outside, gathering up the carrier bags containing their gifts, and hugs her children in turn before they climb into Rob's car.

'Well, enjoy the rest of your evening,' Rob says.

'You too.' He smiles stoically and opens the driver's door. But instead of climbing in, he stops for a moment and, without warning, throws his arms around Kerry. Although she doesn't welcome the hug – it's too desperately sad, too out of the blue – she realises with a start that she no longer despises the very air he breathes. And that really is a first . . .

Anita appears at Kerry's side as she waves the children goodbye. 'You okay?' she asks hesitantly.

Kerry nods, remembering the rules: *no public crying* . . . 'I'll be fine,' she says. 'Just give me a moment.'

Squeezing her hand, Anita darts back inside as her name is called, followed by the announcement that a charades game is starting. Hanging back for a moment, Kerry pulls out her phone from her pocket. *Happy Christmas Harvey,* she taps out. *See u at Mia's party. I asked Rob to come! Grown-up & mature huh? But Dog still beats Man.*

Chapter Forty-Five

Although he's enjoyed the huge family gathering at his sister Melissa's, Harvey is more than slightly relieved to be saying goodbye. Spending time with his nephew Sam was great, and he gamely did a few balloon tricks for him (he'd brought a pared-down selection of his usual party paraphernalia). Yet he'd felt more comfortable when he and Sam had volunteered to walk Honey, Melissa's ageing Labrador, Sam regaling him with tales from the nursery frontline during their stroll through the woods.

'Will you do my next party, Uncle Harvey?' he asked as they headed back home.

'Yeah, sure. I'd love to.' They stopped to examine some paw prints in the light snow which had fallen that morning.

'Was it a fox?' Sam's eyes gleamed excitedly.

Harvey wiped snow from a tree stump so they could both sit down. 'Yep, it could have been.' More likely a dog, he surmised, but what was the harm in pretending if it made life more exciting? Like the whole Santa thing. As Melissa had cajoled him into planting floury footprints throughout the house on Christmas Eve, it had struck Harvey – not for the first time – that this was what he was missing: a purpose in life. And right then, it seemed to be about making another person happy, not because you'd been hired and paid to do so, but just because, well . . . what else was life about?

And now Harvey is leaving his family – it's just after lunch on a cold, wet Friday – realising he's looking forward to making a few changes when he gets home to Shorling. He must find a proper, grown-up job; what was he thinking, imagining he could make a living from prancing about in a yellow wig? 'Just a stop-gap,' he'd told Ethan at first, and when his flatmate had sneered at the ridiculousness of his idea, Harvey had become even more determined to make it work.

He has been thinking about Kerry over Christmas, too. With Mia's birthday party happening tomorrow he'd have had the perfect excuse to send her the odd chatty text. He'd left his phone in the flat, though, so that's been an opportunity wasted.

What does he like about Kerry exactly, he muses as he drives south. Well, she *is* gorgeous, though clearly doesn't know it – but it's her unusualness, mostly. The slightly shambolic house, the way she is with her kids – bit haphazard but obviously loves them to bits – and the fact that she launched herself into dog ownership with an open mind, despite clearly not having a clue what she was doing. He hears the crazy barking every time he arrives for a lesson – pretty normal behaviour, of course – and he sees how devoted Buddy is to her, curled up in the corner while she's teaching.

At Melissa's, he grabbed any opportunity to sneak off to play the piano in her grand, mosaic-tiled hallway – his sister's house feels like a small country hotel – feeling self-conscious at first, but then forgetting about his extended family listening in, and thinking only of impressing Kerry at his next lesson. And now he pictures her mesmerising green eyes, those eyes that hint that she's also capable of being fierce, if she needs

298

to be, and that honey-coloured, infinitely touchable skin that he can't help glancing at whenever she's demonstrating how to play a simple piece.

I'd love to meet a woman like Kerry . . . but younger. What had possessed Ethan to say something so insulting with her sitting just a few feet away in the living room? Had she heard? There'd been music playing, so maybe not . . .

Even so, the thought of that moment still makes Harvey sweat.

*

By the time he pulls up outside his neat 1930s block, it's gone midnight and the rain is torrential. Although it's only a few strides to the entrance, those few moments are enough to soak him and plaster his dark hair to his scalp. He's in the flat now, surveying what some might assume was the aftermath of a teenager's party, or even a burglary. Ethan appears to be out, which is unusual, even for a Friday night. Empty beer bottles are clustered on the floor by the sofa, and the coffee table is strewn with newspapers, dirty mugs, a foil carton containing a few noodles lying in an oily puddle, plus a red and white tub bearing the jaunty image of Colonel Saunders in his chef hat.

Ah, the famous Family Bucket: twenty-one pieces intended, Harvey supposes, for at least four people. An empty two litre plastic Coke bottle sits beside it. While Ethan isn't what you'd call tidy, it's not usually as bad as this. The difference is, Harvey has never left him alone in the flat for nearly a week. Kids' mess doesn't bother him; Melissa's vast living room is permanently strewn with plastic toys and plates bearing leftover snacks. No, there's something more sordid about the chaos adults leave in their wake, and Harvey can't live with it a second longer.

His irritation soon abates as he starts to clear away the detritus, slinging cartons and bottles into a plastic sack. It's doing him good, tearing into practical tasks after hours spent peering through a rain-lashed windscreen. Forty-five minutes later, the living room is not only tidy but also smelling of Mr Sheen and hard graft, and beneath an empty Doritos packet he's unearthed a scrap of paper on which Ethan has written: VICTORIA CALLED. Victoria? The only Victoria he knows is his agent, but Harvey hasn't heard a peep from her since November. In fact, he'd begun to fear he'd been dropped without having it spelt out to him. Weird. Well, he won't be able to call her until Monday.

With a shrug, Harvey tackles the vast pile of newspapers and magazines which Ethan insists he's 'not ready' to throw away, and by the time he's moved on to the kitchen – the sink piled with dirty dishes, unsurprisingly – he has decided to go ahead with what he was planning in the car. All he needs is courage, in the way that his timid mum hugged him before he left Melissa's, and said, 'Harvey, me and your Dad have been thinking. Next time you come up, we'll be happy for you to bring Ethan.'

He almost hadn't had the heart to tell her he wasn't gay.

Yet if his sixty-three-year-old mum can manage to do that – to come to terms with the fact that her only son might be in love with a short, podgy man who consumes fried chicken by the bucketload – then surely he can muster the courage to ask Kerry Tambini out.

Chapter Forty-Six

'Oh, a *bought* cake. Goodness.' Lara's eyes light upon the circular blue slab as Kerry sets it onto the table.

'Yes,' she says. 'It's not really my style but Mia wanted one like this. She said everyone has bought cakes.'

Lara winces. 'Well, yes, we tend to go to Dilly's Bakery, not the supermarket . . . but I suppose it's very . . . bright.'

Kerry suppresses a smirk as she glances down at the garish confection with its clearly factory-made decorations of fondant icing balloons. 'Sure is. I'd imagine it's stuffed with E numbers too. But what's the point of a party if they can't get all manically over-excited?'

'Hmmm,' Lara says, wincing visibly as Joe, his hair covered in fluorescent spray, careers into her as he charges past. Kerry had expected parents to drop off their kids and run, as they used to in London. However, most have stayed for the duration, casting amused looks over the birthday tea as if they have never encountered a Wagon Wheel before.

Beside her, looking as if she'd dearly love to cram a fistful of milk chocolate fingers into her mouth, Emily squints at the assembled gathering at the far end of the kitchen. 'Who's he?' she asks, meaning the striking, dark-haired man who's giving the distinct impression of being a million miles from his normal habitat.

Kerry crunches a cheese and onion crisp. 'Oh, that's just Rob, Mia and Freddie's dad.'

'Really?' Emily exclaims. 'He's very, er . . .'

'Good-looking?' Kerry offers.

'Well, er . . . yes!' She gives Kerry an inscrutable look as if to say, you snared *him*?

Pinching a strawberry from the huge bowlful, despite their blatant unseasonality and air miles accrued, Lara smiles patronisingly at Kerry. 'You two are very modern, aren't you?' she observes.

'What, being able to be in the same room for a few hours?' Kerry shrugs. 'We're both Mia's parents and she's delighted that he's here.' She smiles broadly, then busies herself by filling cups of juice, and calls the children through from the living room for cake-cutting.

'Well done,' she mouths to Harvey as he appears in the kitchen, flanked by excitable children. His act was even better received than she'd hoped for; instead of some feeble balloon-modelling routine, he brought along an array of battered old instruments – from xylophones to trumpets – and the whole thing had descended into a chaotic, yet hugely enjoyable improvisation session involving every child at the party.

'With everything she's got on her plate,' Kerry overhears a gazelle-limbed woman remarking, 'it's no wonder she doesn't have time to bake.'

Brigid sidles up to her, brash gold earrings jangling. 'There's a time for oat biscuits,' she whispers, 'and a birthday party isn't it.'

'Quite right,' Anita says, mouth full of Jaffa Cake. 'You've done a brilliant job, Kerry, and Harvey was great. Cute, too. You kept *that* a secret . . .'

Kerry laughs, casting him a fond look across the kitchen.

'Well, yes, he scrubs up nicely when the wig's off. I'm just relieved everyone's come, to be honest, and so is Mia.'

In fact, relieved is an understatement. Mia is obviously overjoyed that it's going so well, and beams delightedly as Tabitha announces, 'This is the best party I've ever been to. I'm never allowed food like this – *or* a clown . . .'

'Poor, deprived darling,' Emily mutters.

'Yeah – you're so lucky, Mia,' Audrey-Jane exclaims, while the birthday girl glows with happiness. And so the cake is cut, its unashamed syntheticness greeted with delight by the children, if not their mothers. And soon, festooned with party bags filled with tacky plastic jewellery and toys – 'We gave everyone a miniature cactus at Tabitha's party,' Kerry hears Emily remark – parents and children are beginning to leave. Anita is hugging Kerry, her children *and* Buddy (although not Rob, Kerry notes) before herding her exhausted offspring out to their car.

Soon only Brigid and Joe, plus Rob and Harvey – who are having a rather stilted conversation – are left in the trashed living room.

'How did you get into this, then?' Rob asks him half-heartedly.

'Oh, you know.' Harvey shrugs. 'Acting went a bit quiet.'

'What kind of things have you been in? Any films? TV?'

Kerry exchanges a look with Brigid as Harvey shrugs and says, 'Nothing you'd know. A few TV dramas ages ago, the odd play . . .'

Rob nods. 'Well, I hope things pick up for you.'

'Yeah, thanks.' As Harvey shifts position on the sofa and sips his beer, Kerry goes to the kitchen to fetch more drinks. While she'd quite like Rob to go home now, she doesn't relish the idea of Harvey and Brigid leaving just yet. Freddie, Mia and Joe have flopped in a tired but happy clump in front of a DVD, and Kerry isn't looking forward to an eerily quiet, adult-free Saturday night after such a fun day.

'Well, I'd better be off, I suppose.' Rob drains his mug of tea and hugs the children goodbye.

'You smell of bonfires,' Freddie announces, detecting a just-smoked cigarette on Rob's breath. 'You've got dragon-mouth, Dad!'

'Er, do I?' Rob pulls a comically innocent face. 'I don't know *what* that could be.'

'Hmmm, me neither,' Kerry says with a smirk.

'Daddy smoked a cigarette in the garden,' Mia crows triumphantly, causing Rob to look aghast and speedily make for the front door.

'Bloody hell, I've got to give up,' he tells Kerry outside. 'That's so crap, being spotted having a sly fag by your own daughter on her birthday.'

'I'm sure she'll cope,' Kerry says. 'Anyway, I'm glad you came. It meant a lot to Mia.'

He smiles. 'It was really fun and I have to say, you really pulled out the stops with that cake. It was even better than usual. More professional . . .'

'Er, I didn't make it, Rob.'

'Oh, God, didn't you? Sorry . . .'

She shrugs. 'Don't be. It was a relief, actually, not to be up till two in the morning sticking jewels onto a sarcoph-agus, although by the eye bags I've got, you'd still think I had.'

'Rubbish, you look great.' He stops suddenly as if real-ising it's no longer his place to compliment her.

'Erm, thank you, Rob.' She glances down at her red dress, the one she'd worn with those ankle-slicing shoes for the surprise visit on his birthday. Today, though, she has wisely chosen more practical flat boots.

'And your hair's nice, up like that,' he offers hesitantly.

'Glad you like it.' There's a pause as they both stand outside the house, in the dark, with the odd car going by and the steady swoosh of the waves crashing onto the sand.

''S'pose I'd really better get back,' Rob murmurs. 'It'll be gone ten by the time I'm there.'

Kerry studies him. 'You mean home, Rob. Not "there".'

He nods glumly.

'Doesn't her place feel like home, then?'

'Um . . . I don't know, Kerry. I don't really know what anything feels like anymore.'

She frowns. 'Is it this Eddy thing?'

'Among other things, yes. We had an awful row the other night and are only just about back on speaking terms.'

'You don't think . . .' She stops herself, wondering whether to go on.

'D'you mean . . .' he frowns '. . . that the baby could be Eddy's?'

Kerry nods. 'Well . . . is it possible?'

He shakes his head and opens the car door. 'I have no bloody idea. I've asked her, of course, and she's adamant that it's mine, but who knows? I think she's trying to convince herself as much as me.' He pauses. 'I'm sorry. I don't know why I'm telling you this . . .'

'I don't either, really.'

'I, um . . . I suppose you're still the one I want to talk to . . .'

She exhales, glancing over her shoulder to see that Brigid and Harvey have migrated to the kitchen.

'I'd better go back in,' she says quickly, relieved that she's the one returning to a party-mangled house, and not a child-free Baker Street flat.

Chapter Forty-Seven

Kerry isn't sure why she hadn't fully appreciated Harvey's handsomeness before today. Maybe, she concedes, sipping her first glass of wine of the evening, *all* clowns appear startlingly eye-pleasing once they've changed out of their terrible red and yellow diamond-patterned trousers, into a nice pair of Levi's and a black lambswool crew-necked sweater. Is that what's happening here? Having limited experience of party entertainers, she has no idea. But now, she decides as he chats to Brigid, he's sort of appealingly boyish and manly all at once. Something to do with the dark, wavy hair which has a bit of a mind of its own, that lovely, sexy mouth, and those blue eyes which are almost E number blue, as zingy as Mia's cake. As for the manly bit, well, she almost can't allow herself to dwell on how nicely put together he is – tall, strong-looking, exceptionally nice compact little bum, she happens to have noticed.

'You were brilliant today,' Brigid is enthusing, taking a big swig of white wine. 'I thought it was all going to fall apart at one point, but you were *so* clever, keeping it all together like that.'

'Oh, come on,' he laughs. 'They just wanted me to shut up so they could get on with that Egyptian mummy game.'

'Don't be bashful, Harvey,' she retorts. 'You're a very talented man. I didn't realise you were a musician too.'

'Oh, I've just dabbled about, it's nothing really . . .'

'Well, I must book you for Joe's party.' Brigid is drinking at an impressive speed, Kerry happens to note, as her friend drains her glass and refills it immediately from the bottle. The table is laden with leftover sausage rolls, pizza and sliced baguette, which they are all picking at absent-mindedly.

'I'm actually going to stop doing parties,' Harvey says, sipping a Coke, 'but sure, I'd be glad to do Joe's, if you let me know when it is . . .'

'Oh, really? That would be fantastic, Harvey, thank you.' Brigid scoops up a handful of chocolate raisins and crams them into her mouth, then wrinkles her nose. 'Ew. Has Buddy farted?'

'He does that sometimes,' Kerry sniggers. 'God knows what the kids have been feeding him today.'

Brigid swivels to face Harvey. 'As long as you don't think it's me, haha! That's the great thing about dogs, though, isn't it? You can blame them for all sorts of things.'

'Oh, I have a flatmate for that,' Harvey says with a grin.

'You have a flatmate?' she squeals. 'That's so sweet, so kind of . . . *nostalgic*.' As Brigid casts him a soppy look, Kerry wonders whether he minds her hand attaching itself to his arm like that, as if glued there.

'How d'you mean, nostalgic?' Harvey asks.

'*You* know, like those things you haven't thought of for years but remember fondly like, uh . . . Viennetta ice cream or Arctic roll . . .'

Harvey laughs, and Kerry tries to join in. Yet it feels stiff and forced, and the more the two of them banter about nostalgic desserts and the joys and annoyances of flat sharing, the more she feels herself melting further and further into Aunt Maisie's pale green speckled wallpaper.

From the living room comes the babble from the TV and the odd murmur of sleepy chatter.

'Oh, I'd better get Joe home,' Brigid says, checking her watch. 'It's half nine. I can't believe it's so late.' She tips the dregs from the wine bottle into her glass and knocks it back.

'Joe can stay here if you like,' Kerry offers. 'I can easily put a futon in Freddie's room.'

'Really? Are you sure you could bear it, after all the mayhem today?'

'Of course I can. It won't really make any difference, and anyway, Freddie will be delighted to have a sleepover. I'll go up now and get the room ready. My two should be heading up to bed now anyway.'

'I'll help,' Brigid starts, making no move to get up.

'Don't worry, it won't take a minute. Help yourselves to more drinks if you like – there are Cokes and wine in the fridge . . .' She heads upstairs, glad for a few minutes' respite from that scene in the kitchen. It's disturbing how easily Brigid and Harvey have slipped into cosy camaraderie. Kerry knows she's being ridiculous; so what if they become friends, or even end up having a fling, or getting together properly and making babies? Brigid is loud and lovely with her cheap jangly jewellery, *and* she's only thirty-one. Occasionally, Kerry has wondered if Harvey is vaguely attracted to her. But if she were him, who would she choose – the statuesque blonde who clearly fancies him, or the slightly hung-up piano teacher with a lurking ex-husband (who really is crap at small talk) and a flatulent dog?

Buddy has followed her upstairs. She crouches down to ruffle the extra-soft fur behind his ears while staring into Freddie's room. The carpet is faded – more grey than its original blue – and strewn with Lego and plastic railway track. So much for the wall unit with basket drawers ('The ultimate storage solution!') which she'd bought in a fit of

308

optimism, and had to build from flat-pack, a project which had brought her close to mental collapse. Prior to the break-up, Rob had done all the flat-pack, grudgingly but methodically, with minimal swearing and no losing of vital nuts and bolts.

Under Buddy's watchful gaze, Kerry drags out the futon from the airing cupboard and flings it onto the floor. As she makes up the bed she can hear Brigid and Harvey sniggering away in the kitchen together, no doubt planning how to break it to her that they're off back to her place for hot sex.

Kerry looks down at the futon, wondering if anyone would notice if she had a little lie down.

'Sure you don't want me to help, Kerry?' Brigid calls from downstairs.

'No, it's all done, thanks.' She smooths back the strands of hair which have snuck out of her messy up-do, then gives up and pulls out the clip.

'Oh, you've taken your hair down.' Brigid is standing in the hallway, eyes slightly squiffy as Kerry heads downstairs.

'Yes, it was starting to look a bit floppy, like the balloons.' She smiles resignedly and glimpses Harvey still sitting at the kitchen table, sipping his Coke. In the living room, the three children are still bunched up as one on the sofa.

'Okay,' Kerry announces, 'PJs on – it's nearly ten. If you go to bed now and settle down, I'll take you all swimming in the morning.'

'What, me as well?' Joe asks hopefully, face daubed with blue icing.

'Yes, if it's okay with Mummy.' She turns to Brigid who is lurking a little unsteadily behind her.

'Well, yes, if you're sure. But you've had a houseful of kids all afternoon, so if anyone takes them it should be me—'

'I'd actually like to,' Kerry says firmly. *Because if I don't, you see, it'll just be me, Freddie and Mia and an achingly empty, post-party day . . .*

Brigid grins. 'You're a star, you know that?'

'Hey, come on.' She squeezes her hand.

'I'm going to have a big lie-in tomorrow,' Brigid adds, slurring slightly. 'I *never* have that. Joe won't let me. He comes in and starts jumping all over my head . . .'

'You're long overdue it then,' Kerry says warmly as Brigid cuddles Joe goodnight, and the three children troop upstairs, debating who got the prime piece of birthday cake with the icing balloons on. In pursuit, and to avoid witnessing any more of Brigid virtually *drooling* over Harvey, Kerry supervises teeth cleaning, pretending her barely-used toothbrush is a brand new one she's managed to magic up for Joe. Over the sound of mass brushing she can hear Brigid and Harvey chatting in the hallway. Children are swiftly tucked in, lights turned off, and as Kerry goes back downstairs, she hears Harvey saying, 'No, of course I don't mind. It's on my way . . .'

Brigid tosses back dishevelled fair hair. 'I could get a cab if it's easier, or walk . . .'

'Don't be silly, I'll drop you off.'

'Isn't he sweet?' Brigid announces.

'Yes, anyway, safe home.' Kerry hugs Brigid and Harvey in turn, willing them to leave so she can drop the forced smile and be normal.

Harvey picks up several canvas bags containing his costume and a plethora of musical instruments. 'It's been a lovely evening, Kerry. Great party, too. I've really enjoyed myself.'

'Well, thanks to you, the kids loved it too. Are you sure you really want to give this up? You're really good at it . . .'

'This was different.' He shrugs. 'They're not usually this much fun.'

'And *you*, Kerry, are a marvel,' Brigid blares out as they

310

leave. 'Thanks for tomorrow, too. I'll drop off Joe's swimming things in the morning.'

'No need. There'll be something of Freddie's that fits him.'

'Hey, come on, Brigid, let's go.' Harvey touches Brigid's arm, a small, caring gesture that causes a lump to form in Kerry's throat.

When they've gone, she looks around the eerily silent kitchen. Buddy is asleep under the table, and every surface is littered with dented plastic cups and crumb-strewn paper plates. *What did I expect anyway*, she reflects, overcome by a crushing wave of loneliness as she pours another glass of wine, *when I've already told him I prefer dogs to men?*

Chapter Forty-Eight

The weird thing is, when she calls, James doesn't have a clue who she is.

'Hi,' she says, 'it's me.'

Jesus, he thinks, it's pie-crust-nightie woman with the scary cherub bed. 'It's *Amy*,' she says, sounding put out. 'Don't you recognise my voice?'

'Oh, of course I do,' he blusters. 'It's just a bit of a surprise, that's all.'

It's almost 11 p.m. and he and Luke have been spending a companionable Saturday evening discussing ludicrous sandwich fillings over a few beers. It's off again with Charlotte, and James is somewhat relieved; he'd lasted four hours at Charlotte's parents' place in Norfolk, just long enough to ingest a terrible Christmas lunch – some smoked gammon thing, not even a turkey – while her parents had bickered and sniped. He'd had no option but to feign a stomach bug and, luckily, Luke had been happy to leave with him.

'How are you?' Amy wants to know. 'And how's Luke?'

'We're fine. We're pretty good.' *Why are you calling?* he wants to ask, but can't bring himself to say it. The phone is in the hall on a small table beside the piano, and James absent-mindedly nudges dust off the keys with a finger.

'Well, I've got a bit of news,' Amy says. 'I'm moving back to Shorling.'

He scowls. 'Are you? Why?'

'To see our son, of course.'

'But you haven't seen him in two years,' he exclaims, relieved that the TV is on so Luke is unlikely to overhear. 'Why d'you want to make contact now?'

'It was Luke who didn't want to see me,' Amy murmurs. 'Are you surprised?'

'No, no, I don't blame him at all . . .'

The silence stretches uncomfortably. 'I've left Brian,' Amy adds.

Ah, the colourist. James had almost forgotten his name.

'So you're moving back on your own?'

'Yes. How about you – are you seeing anyone?'

'Sort of,' he blurts out without thinking, his finger slipping off a black piano key and striking the white one beside it.

'What was that?'

'Nothing. I just knocked against the piano.'

'Hmmm. So you've kept it, then.'

'Er, yes, of course.' *Don't read too much into that*, James thinks darkly.

'So . . .' Amy starts, 'who are you seeing? Sorry, I know it's none of my business, I just . . .'

'Erm, just someone, a piano teacher . . .' Hell, why did he say that? A tentative arrangement to meet up at New Year, that's all they have. It startles him, the way Kerry sprung into his mind like that.

'Been seeing her long?'

'Um, just a few weeks.' Another pause.

'How's Buddy?'

'I rehomed him,' James murmurs.

'You *rehomed* him?' she shrieks. 'Why?'

'Amy, listen . . .'

313

'You gave him away? Who to?'

'If you'd let me get a word in,' he says sharply, 'I'll explain what happened. Luke's set up a sandwich place in town . . .'

'Yes, so I heard . . .'

'. . . And it was going down the pan, frankly, so I'm working there most days and trying to keep the freelance website stuff going and I just didn't have time, okay, for the walks and all that. Plus, he turned into a bit of nightmare after you left. I mean, he was highly strung after Suzie died, but once you'd gone off with *Brian*' – he laces the name with distaste – 'he was all over the place. Barking constantly, peeing indoors, chewing anything he could get hold of—'

'He never did any of that when I was there,' Amy cuts in. 'He was a fantastic dog.'

'Well, then he *wasn't* such a fantastic dog and frankly, I couldn't cope with him. And it wasn't fair to leave him all day in the house.'

Luke has appeared in the hall and is looking quizzically at his father. *Mum*, James mouths, at which Luke looks aghast.

'So who's he with now?' Amy asks again.

'Just a friend.'

'Your girlfriend?' she asks, sounding choked.

Luke is showing no sign of going back into the living room, and James doesn't feel comfortable inventing a love life at forty-three years old. Nevertheless, he hears himself mumble, '*Yes*, he's with her. It just seemed like the best solution . . .'

There's a stunned pause. 'Well,' Amy says tersely, 'I'll be down in a couple of weeks. Maybe we could have coffee or something.'

'Er . . . okay.'

'I'd like to see Luke, too.'

James flicks his gaze at his son. 'Um, I'll see what he says.'

He hears Amy sniffing now, and wonders if she's actually

314

crying. 'I *am* his mother,' she declares before finishing the call.

James looks at Luke, and neither say anything for a few moments.

'Shit,' Luke says finally. 'What did she want?'

'To see us, I guess. She's moving back down here.'

Luke exhales loudly. 'Right. And what was that about, telling her you'd given Buddy to your *girlfriend*?'

James's cheeks flare. 'So you heard that.'

'Yeah. So . . . you're seeing Kerry, are you?' He waggles a brow.

'No, of course I'm not . . .'

Luke is helpless with laughter now as he wraps an arm fondly around his father's shoulders. 'You're a mental case, Dad, trying to make Mum jealous like that. How old are you again?'

Chapter Forty-Nine

Harvey hadn't planned for this to happen. But how could he refuse Brigid a lift when she'd asked him? And she *is* pretty pissed, having knocked back that bottle of wine as if she couldn't believe her luck at being out after dark, albeit in the aftermath of a children's party. In fact she's probably had more than a bottle – Harvey isn't in the habit of monitoring how much women drink. He just knows he wouldn't have felt good about letting her wobble off home by herself.

'Mum off the leash,' she giggles from the passenger seat, as if reading his mind. 'I've been so badly behaved, Harvey. You must think I'm such a lush.'

'Not at all,' he replies with a smile. 'We've all got to kick back sometimes.'

She snorts and, with no discernible logic, quips, 'You think all single mothers are up for it, don't you?'

'What?' He frowns and indicates to turn into her road. 'I didn't say that. I don't think that at all. Um, which number are you again?'

'Yes you do, they *all* think it . . .' She laughs a little insanely.

'Um, Brigid, which number—'

'Ninety-seven. I don't mind, you know. I don't care. God, I *never* go out, last time I enjoyed myself was . . .' Oh no, she's dabbing at her eyes now, and laughing at the same time. 'Sorry, sorry, sorry,' she exclaims as he pulls up outside her rather shabby bow-fronted house. 'I'm an idiot, Harvey, take no notice of me. I shouldn't be allowed out.'

'It's okay,' he says gently. 'You could probably just do with some sleep.' He turns off the engine and waits for her to get out of the car.

'Oh, so knackered old mother should be tucked up in bed with her Horlicks!'

'I didn't mean it like that. You just seem a bit upset . . .' Harvey can feel himself ageing rapidly as if time has fast-forwarded. He wants to go home now; no, what he *really* wants to do is turn around and head back to Kerry's and just sit talking into the night. It's so easy with her, and not just because of his ridiculous crush, which he *has* to get over. He's met the ridiculously handsome ex-husband now – big-shot magazine editor or whatever he is – and he saw the way he kept looking at her. Drooling, virtually, still clearly in love. Must be a nut-job for cheating on her. Still, Harvey bets she'll take him back. For one thing, the children obviously adore their dad . . .

Brigid is still showing no sign of saying goodnight, and Harvey can't exactly manhandle her out of his car. She's staring at him now, a little scarily with those wide grey-blue eyes and parted lips with most of her lipstick worn off (the slightly darker outline is still there, though: how does that happen?). Brigid is a good-looking woman, but far more Ethan's type than his: robust, almost regal, like the figure-head of a ship.

'Want to come in for a drink?' she asks suddenly.

'Er, thanks, Brigid, but it's getting late and I've been working . . .' He grips the steering wheel tightly.

'Yeah, right, getting a few children to rattle some tambourines.' She guffaws. '*I* don't call that work. Come on, just for a quickie . . .'

'I've got to drive, Brigid—'

'Yeah, two minutes up the road. Have a coffee then, or leave your car here and walk home, lazy boy. How far away are you?'

'Erm, just up by the golf course . . .'

'There you are then! Come on, I've got a lovely bottle of Prosecco in the fridge.'

Harvey turns this possibility over in his mind. She might be a little unhinged, but a quick drink *is* tempting. It's certainly more appealing than going home right now, as Ethan has invited his old friends Baz and Georgie over, and they'll all be lolling around drinking cheap lager and smoking copious amounts of weed. They'd spent much of the Christmas period there, too, Ethan admitted after Harvey had taken him to task about the almighty mess he'd come home to after his stay at his sister's. 'I told them to put their bottles in the bin,' he'd whinged, as if describing toddlers rather than enormous bikers in Anthrax T-shirts.

Brigid, who's been rubbing at a sore spot on her ankle, looks up and beams a hopeful smile.

'Okay, just a quick one then.' Harvey unclips his seatbelt, then gallantly unclips Brigid's for her and takes her arm as she wobbles along her cobbled front path.

Her house feels chilly as they step inside, as if she's intent on keeping the heating bills down. In the small, cluttered living room, ethnic embroideries hang on two of the walls, and a chunky brown and white Staffy stirs on its cushion.

'Sorry, Roxy, darling,' Brigid murmurs, coaxing the dog outside and chatting to her on the tiny front lawn. There's effusive praise for doing her business, then Brigid reappears and the dog potters back in. 'Didn't expect to be so long at Kerry's,' she explains, motioning for Harvey to sit down.

'Poor thing. Never complains, very undemanding. Anyway, I'll get us that wine.'

As she trots off to the kitchen, Harvey takes in the rest of his surroundings: pine fireplace cluttered with pictures of Brigid's little boy (the one who raised merry hell over not being given all the icing balloons off the cake), and a faded Turkish rug with children's books strewn all over it. Various ethnic artefacts are clustered around the tiled fireplace: a papier mâché cockerel, some gilt-edged tea glasses containing burnt-out candles, and a jazzily-painted plaster skull which Harvey assumes is one of those Mexican Day of the Dead accessories.

Brigid reappears with two glasses of Prosecco, plus the bottle, and a fresh layer of pinky-red lipstick. 'Here,' she says, grinning and handing him a glass.

'Thanks Brigid.'

'So!' She sprawls beside him on the sofa. 'What d'you think of Kerry?'

'Er . . . I think she's great. Why?'

'Oh, she is. She's an *amazing* person. So strong, after everything she's gone through.' Brigid jumps up and wends her way over to an ancient-looking CD player. 'We need music,' she declares, putting on some thumpy dance track and refilling his glass to the brim, even though he's barely drunk a third of it.

'Thanks.' He sips it, deciding he'll definitely be walking home tonight.

She casts him a slightly wonky smile. 'You're such a sweet guy. Kerry never said how *lovely* you are. Think she wants you all to herself, haha!'

'Oh, I don't think so . . .' He chuckles awkwardly, wondering when he might feasibly be able to make his excuses and leave.

'Kerry told me you used to be a model,' she adds.

'God, a couple of jobs about sixty years ago,' he says, cringing.

'Oh, come on! Don't be modest. Did you strut your stuff on the Prada catwalk?'

'No,' he laughs, shaking his head. 'More like a fashion spread in *Prima*.'

Her eyes are on him now, wide and vaguely glassy and he takes another gulp of wine. 'I wish there were more men around like you,' she declares, snuggling a little closer on the clapped-out sofa.

He doesn't know how to respond to this. Yet he realises that every second he sits here, doing nothing, brings him closer to the moment when Brigid will pounce. He just knows she will. There's something slightly *coiled* about her, like a cat, poised to spring on a mouse. He glances at the Mexican skull, which seems to be leering at him from the fireplace. Would it be so terrible anyway, to be lunged at? Christ, it's not as if he's awash with offers, and he can't blame it *completely* on clowning, or even Ethan, as they rarely go out drinking together. And if an attractive woman like Brigid wants to lunge in for a big snog, surely it would be rude of him to push her off? He has barely processed this thought before they're kissing. They fall back onto the sofa, snogging like teenagers, while Harvey tries unsuccessfully to place his wine glass on the stripped floor. There's a clonk as it falls over, causing the Staffy to flinch on her cushion.

'Damn, sorry,' he mutters, twisting round to peer at the floor. While the glass is still intact, a small Prosecco puddle has formed on the floor, which Roxy is now padding towards and investigating with tentative sniffs.

'Doesn't matter,' Brigid growls, waving a hand ineffectually in Roxy's direction in an attempt to shoo her away. 'That's the great thing about natural floorboards . . .' She's on top of him now, straddling and kissing him with such ferocity he's starting to fear for his teeth. He can taste her lipstick – honey-flavoured – and, although he tries to concentrate on the matter in hand, he's aware that Roxy hasn't

320

obediently trotted back to her cushion, but is standing there, watching. She's *far* too close for comfort. He can hear her breathing, for God's sake. The situation is ridiculous; he's kissing a woman just because she's there, and initiated it, and it seemed more appealing than going home to a living room filled with hairy-arsed bikers.

Brigid is pulling at Harvey's jeans now, unbuttoning his fly. Then they're off and cast onto the floor, followed by his sweater and boxers. Now he's clad only in a pale grey T-shirt while she grapples at his genitals as if playing the game where you have to stick your hand through a hole in a box and identify the mysterious objects by touch alone.

'Whoa!' Harvey cries.

Brigid's hand flies away. 'What is it?'

'Your *dog*,' he exclaims, turning round to face Roxy whose perky seated position suggests she's eagerly anticipating a matinée. 'She just prodded my hip with her nose.'

'Oh, don't worry about her,' Brigid purrs. 'She's very friendly.'

'Brigid, I don't really want a dog being *friendly* right now, thanks very much . . .' He's up on his feet now, pulling on his boxers and jeans and buttoning his fly securely.

She emits a deep, throaty laugh. 'You're far too sensitive.'

He laughs, shaking his head. 'It's just too . . . bizarre. I'm sorry.'

'Okay, c'mere, Roxy babe . . .' With an air of reluctance, Roxy trots after Brigid into the kitchen, where the door is shut firmly behind her. 'There,' she announces, reappearing just as Harvey has decided how appealing his lovely king-sized bed seems at this moment. 'She can't bother us now.'

'That's good,' he says tentatively.

'So now, could you do something for *me*?'

'Er . . . what exactly?'

'Go and get your clown stuff from the car.'

321

Harvey laughs involuntarily. 'You *are* joking . . .'

She sways a little and places a hand on the doorframe for support. 'No, I'm not. Come on – don't be a spoilsport, sweetie.'

'Brigid, I'm really not in the mood for showing you how to balloon-model or juggle or whatever.'

'No, not that. I mean your *costume*. I want to see you with it on.'

'But . . . you have, at the party,' he says uncomprehendingly.

'Yeah, that was different, though, wasn't it? That was party clown.' She raises a harshly pencilled brow, her unwavering gaze triggering a creeping sense of unease in him. 'The one I want to get to know,' she adds, 'is *naughty* clown.'

He blinks at her. 'Naughty clown,' he repeats.

'Yeah.' She sniggers. 'Please, Harvey. Just for me . . .'

'You . . . want me to do some tricks for you?' he says carefully.

'Yes!' She claps her hands together. 'Go on. I've always wanted to do this. Tell you what – I'll nip upstairs for a quick shower, okay? That'll give you time to get ready . . .'

She grins squiffily, and for a brief moment, Harvey wonders what Kerry is doing right now: if she's curled up all gorgeously on her sofa, or already tucked up in bed.

'Um, Brigid, I really think I'd better—' he starts as she turns and charges upstairs, missing her footing more than once.

'Oh, and don't forget to paint your face,' she yells back. 'There's a mirror in the downstairs loo if you need it. Go on, Harv. Be a good boy and get ready.'

He takes a moment to assess the situation. Of course, Ethan would leap at the chance of some no-strings, uncomplicated sex. He'd be slathering on the greasepaint and have the wig on by now. Christ, he'd probably be juggling, naked apart from the red plastic nose and oversized shoes if it meant the chance of a shag.

But Harvey isn't Ethan – he has better hair for a start – and hadn't he vowed to himself to retire from the clowning game anyway? He fixes his gaze on the skull while, clearly cheesed off at being banished to the kitchen, Roxy emits a pitiful howl.

Chapter Fifty

Kerry knows precisely what will be happening right now. Brigid will have invited Harvey in 'for coffee' and that'll be that. She's a striking woman with fabulous legs and swathes of blonde hair, and he's a young, single, attractive guy – of course he'll be up for it. What man wouldn't? If Rob couldn't resist a fling with a wedding ring firmly encircling his finger, what chance is there that Harvey will make his excuses and leave?

There is, Kerry reflects as she tackles a quivering spillage of pink jelly with a dustpan and brush, no way they're *not* doing it right now. Bloody hell. It had been lovely, that afternoon drink she and Harvey had had, with the patio heater roaring away in the pub garden, and she'd felt happier than she could remember as they'd strolled slowly back to town. Had he been interested then? Had she wasted an opportunity? Kerry curses herself for not only being unable to recognise whether a man fancies her or not, but also for resorting to that 'I'm just one of those batty pet people now' routine. Where the hell had that come from?

As Kerry rinses the jelly-gunked brush in the sink, she realises how ill-equipped she clearly is when it comes to – snort – 'dating'. She'd be no more up to speed if she were suddenly thrust into a biology exam and required to describe the process of photosynthesis. Plus, what made her think that brushing up jelly was a good idea? Throwing the sticky brush into the sink, she bobs down to peel a lump of blue fondant icing off the floor and rescues a spare party bag which appears to have been kicked under the kitchen table.

Tipping its contents onto the counter, Kerry glares at the sparkly plastic necklace and bracelet, the candy lipstick that turns your mouth bright cerise, and the temporary glittery butterfly 'body transfers' that Mia had insisted on including. She and Mia had chosen all of the contents together, and had a fun time labelling the bags. Brash jewellery, make-up and tattoos – was ever a party more slapperish? No wonder those mothers today – like the one who'd emerged from the downstairs loo, remarking, 'Gosh, that's a very *bijoux* bathroom' – regard her with blatant distaste. Kerry makes a mental note to include little packets of candy fags in next year's party bags, if such items are available within the Shorling postcode.

'*What's inside the cuck-oo clock?*'

The chorus from upstairs makes her flinch.

'*What's inside those lit-tle doors . . .*' There's an explosion of laughter from Freddie's room. Glimpsing her reflection in the mirror on the fridge – her make-up is long dissolved, her hair a study in limpness – she charges upstairs to find Mia in the boys' room, the three of them giggling hysterically.

'Come on, Mia, off back to bed,' she says firmly, 'and, boys, get to sleep if you want to go swimming tomorrow.'

Freddie eyes her from his bed. 'It's a bad song, Mum, everyone says.'

'Well, they might,' she says briskly, 'but it's for younger children, not your age.'

'I hate *Cuckoo Clock*.'

'Yes, I know you do.'

'It's crap.'

'Freddie! That's enough,' she says, drowned out by Joe's delighted laughter from the futon on the floor.

'It's the fat people in bird costumes I don't like,' Freddie adds helpfully.

'Me too,' Joe agrees.

'Why do they wear 'em?' Freddie wants to know.

Kerry blinks in the doorway, overwhelmed by a crashing wave of tiredness. Brigid and Harvey aren't trying to coax small children to sleep; they're in bed, naked, having one of those spontaneous nights you remember for the rest of your life. She's probably *orgasming* right now. Christ.

'It's just their job,' Kerry says levelly. 'Some people are doctors and have to tweeze bits of corn out of little boys' ears. And other people have to wear bird costumes.'

'I'd rather be a doctor,' Joe says, as if they are the only career options on offer.

'Yeah,' Freddie declares, 'birds are shit.'

'Freddie, that's *enough*.' Ushering Mia back to bed, and stomping downstairs, Kerry wonders where Freddie is getting his language from. It's ironic, really, that he's started talking this way – she's heard him telling Mia to 'uck-off' – since they relocated to Langoustine Land. She carries on de-partying the house until midnight, but even when she's finished, she still feels too riled to go to bed.

Brigid and Harvey. How will things be if they become a couple? Awkward, or fine once she's got used to it? It's amazing, she reflects, flipping from channel to channel on TV, what can seem almost normal once enough time has passed. Like Rob, Nadine and the baby . . .

Kerry's phone bleeps, and she retrieves it from the top of the TV. It's a text from James, saying simply, *Fancy that lunch tomorrow?* As if he knows she's sitting here, feeling dismal and alone.

Sorry, taking kids swimming, she replies, pausing before adding, *Some other time?*

Monday good for you? he pings back, and she wonders if he, too, is having an aimless Saturday night, finding nothing to watch on TV but a stupid quiz show and an ancient episode of *Minder*.

Monday is New Year's Eve. Clearly, he doesn't expect to be working or busy with other, New Year-ish things, which makes Kerry feel marginally better about her own lack of plans. Plus, the children are going to some art event during the day so, technically, she's free.

Sounds great, she replies. *Where shall we go?*

Glasshouse at one? I'll book. Ooh, the big, glassy cube where you glimpse the glossy and beautiful grappling crustaceans. Very chic, and cripplingly expensive, but what the hell. This has been – how should she put it? – a *challenging* year. And it seems somehow fitting that she'll spend the last day of it popping scallops into her mouth in the company of a kind, handsome, grown-up man. And not some *clown*, she thinks, with more than a trace of bitterness.

Chapter Fifty-One

Harvey perches on the edge of Brigid's Aztec-patterned sofa, wondering what to do. She finds the clown thing a *turn-on*? Could this really be happening to him, or was there something hallucinogenic in those bite-sized sausage rolls? His mind skims the possibilities of what's really going on: 1) Brigid wants him to dress up so she can have a laugh, maybe take some photos, then tell him it's okay, he can put his normal clothes back on now because she was only kidding; 2) She actually wants clown sex – i.e. to do it with him in costume. Harvey rubs his tired face and wonders if this is something he can participate in.

Granted, it's been a long time since he's done it with anyone, and no one needs to know. Casual sex has never been his thing, but maybe that's all that's on offer these days. He examines his fingernails, wondering why this isn't making him feel very fortunate indeed.

Harvey can hear Brigid pottering about in the bathroom upstairs, singing out of tune. She's taking ages, and it's so tempting to creep stealthily out of her house and head home. Wouldn't that be the worst manners ever, though? Plus, she's a friend of Kerry's, and what would *she* think? It would be so awkward at his next piano lesson. No, he must sit here and wait, as if anticipating an invasive and highly embarrassing medical procedure. Then, when she finally reappears, he'll explain, very politely, that this isn't really his sort of thing.

She's coming now, padding softly downstairs. 'Close your eyes!' she trills.

'Er, Brigid . . .'

'I'm not coming in unless your eyes are closed. *Are* they?'

'Yes,' he replies truthfully.

'Good boy.' God, he wishes she wouldn't address him like an obedient hound . . .

He hears her stepping quietly into the living room, her soft footsteps on the ageing Turkish rug. 'You're a naughty, naughty clown,' comes her husky voice. 'You're not in costume, Harvey.'

He opens his eyes, about to rattle through his rehearsed speech: *It's not you, it's me. And it's been a lovely evening but—*

'So what d'you think?' She does a little shimmy in her thigh-length white dress. At least, he assumes it's a dress. It's sort of gathered at the neck, like an outlandish silken napkin with three large fluffy black pom-poms down the front. There's a kind of ruff thing happening at the neck too, like something from the Elizabethan era, and her pale-painted face has been adorned with a purple teardrop.

'Er . . . what *are* you wearing?' he splutters.

'I'm a sad Pierrot clown! Don't you like it?'

Oh, dear God.

'No, no – you look *great* . . .' Sweat springs from his forehead as he glances towards the living room door, quickly calculating how many strides away it is. Perhaps he'd under-estimated how pissed she really is. Or maybe, unwittingly, he'd somehow given the signal that getting it on with a lady-clown would round off his evening perfectly. In a flash of optimism, he wonders if she's dressed up like this just to *chat*, or because she's thinking of going into the entertainment business herself and wants his considered opinion on her costume . . .

She's plonked herself beside him now and draped her arms around his shoulders. 'Go get your outfit,' she purrs. 'Get those funny long shoes with the bells on.'

'Brigid, look, I'm just not into—'

'Just the hat, then, with the bobble on top . . .'

He shrinks away, pressing himself into the back of the sofa. 'Erm, your teardrop's a bit smudged.'

'Never mind that,' she growls, leaning towards him and breathing hotly into his ear. 'Be a good clown and ravish me in your big top . . .'

He explodes with laughter. 'My big *what*?'

'Your big top! Oh, go on, it's just a bit of fun . . .'

'I don't actually have one,' he says, shoulders bobbing as he tries to contain his hysteria. 'I have a two bedroom flat next to the Carpet Warehouse. I'm sorry, I really have to go . . .'

'Pierrot's sad,' she exclaims. 'Pierrot's *crying* . . .'

Oh no. Now she's referring to herself in the third person, as if being trapped in a cluttered living room with a deranged mime artist person wasn't enough for one night.

'Sorry,' he says again, wiping the tears of mirth from his cheeks as he leaps up. 'Got a party to do first thing in the morning.'

'A party? In the morning?' Her nostrils flare a little and the effect – of an extremely *vexed* Pierrot – is reminiscent of a nightmare he can still recall from when he was off school with measles, aged seven. No wonder people joke about the thin line between circus people being entertaining and completely fucking creepy.

'Er, it's a *breakfast* party,' he blusters, at the front door now, already stepping outside into the bitterly cold night.

'Anyway, see you around soon, I'd imagine . . .' He hears Roxy whining and scraping at the kitchen door.

'But Harvey—'

'Good *night*, Brigid. Sleep well.' He plants a brief kiss on her greasy cheek and turns away.

He starts walking, past his car, past the scruffy bow-fronted houses to the end of her street. He doesn't care that he's freezing – he's left his favourite black sweater in there – or that, right now, his nice, tidy living room will be a fug of smoke and bikers' farts.

'Harvey, wait!' He whirls round. Brigid's out in the street now, marching after him with a small black bundle in her hand.

'What is it?'

'I said, wait!'

As he watches her approaching, it strikes him that, while she's thinking clown sex, he's concerned only about her being out with bare legs in the middle of winter.

'You'll freeze,' he hisses. 'Go back inside, you'll catch your death . . .'

Across the street, a smartly dressed couple has stopped to observe the proceedings. 'My God,' the woman sniggers. 'It's one of those scary clown movies come to life.'

'Watch out, mate,' the man cries. 'There's a freaky Pierrot after you . . . need any help?'

They convulse with laughter, clearly enjoying the show. 'We're fine, thanks,' Harvey barks across the road, willing them to move on.

'I *know* you,' the woman announces. On the plus side, at least she's stopped laughing. Less happily, she's now grabbed her partner by the hand and is trotting across the road towards them. 'You're Charlie Chuckles, aren't you? Remember I booked you for my daughter's party in the community centre – the one where you made the scary testicle dog from a sausage balloon . . .?'

'Er, yeah, yeah,' he says, not even bothering to correct her as Brigid gawps at him uncomprehendingly.

The woman sniggers. 'Isn't it sweet,' she says, turning to her husband, 'that he's got a clown girlfriend? To be honest, Charlie, I assumed you just shoved on your costume to make a quick buck, but you really immerse yourself in the part!'

They beam at a shivering Brigid. 'That's what I call method acting,' the man says with an infuriating whinnying laugh.

'Yes, well, nice seeing you again,' Harvey says quickly, putting an arm around Brigid's shoulders and guiding her back down the street towards her house.

'I wonder if he has an elephant as well?' the woman muses as they walk away.

Having shaken off Harvey's arm, Brigid is stomping back home at an impressive speed. 'You forgot your sweater,' she says sulkily, thrusting the soft black bundle at him.

Harvey takes it from her. 'Thank you.'

'You know what? You're no fun at all.'

Harvey smiles, pulling on his sweater as they walk and giving her a quick hug as they reach her front door. 'You're probably right. I always suspected I wasn't really cut out to be a clown. Now go back inside and see to Roxy, okay? She didn't seem too happy being shut in the kitchen.'

'Erm . . . I can't.' Brigid shivers and rubs her bare arms. 'Why not?'

She gazes up at him, her white-painted face looking chilled and faintly unwell under the silvery light of the streetlamp. 'I left my key inside, Harvey. I've locked myself out.'

Chapter Fifty-Two

While Kerry launches herself down the biggest slide in the pool – she *loves* flumes, the sensation of whooshing down a huge plastic tube – Rob is lying on a rather hard, leopard-patterned couch in his stockinged feet in a flat in Hackney. It's a damp Sunday morning and by rights he should be having a lie-in, drinking coffee and leafing idly through the papers – i.e. attempting to have a normal, couply time with Nadine. Unable to face anymore squabbling and bitterness, he has decided to accept her version of events – at least until the baby's born.

Yet even last night, they ended up bickering again. 'Oh, so you're smoking in the car now?' she'd announced, detecting a whiff as he'd let himself into the flat. 'The car I have to sit in and, more importantly, our baby will travel home from hospital in.'

'Yes, in five months' time,' he'd snapped back. 'I think the smell will have gone by then and if it hasn't, I'll buy a bloody air freshener.' And so it had escalated, a stupid row about how she had no intention of subjecting the baby to the disgusting synthetic fumes of a pine-scented thing dangling from the rearview mirror, and Rob alerting her to the fact that you can now buy ones that emit a new car smell, no matter how old your vehicle is. Which Nadine interpreted as him taking the piss, triggering her to make an urgent call to Jade.

Not merely one of Nadine's *best friends in the whole world*, Jade is also a qualified hypnotist. What did that mean anyway? Which university course in advanced mind-fuckery had she actually completed? Anyway, Nadine was adamant and, after a quick call, announced that Jade would be happy to 'treat' Rob the next day.

'You're lucky,' Jade says now, placing her cold fingers on his slightly clammy forehead. 'I'm chock-a-block at this time of year with everyone trying to give up something for New Year.'

Rob mulls this over as she stops prodding at his head and potters over to a wonky, cheap-looking unit stuffed with books and CDs. Is that what New Year is about, then – not looking ahead with a positive frame of mind (which he is desperately trying to do), but denying himself the one little puff of pleasure he enjoys twice, maybe three times a day? Okay, it has escalated to more like fifteen a day, but still . . . stressful times.

'It's here somewhere,' Jade mutters, grabbing a bunch of CDs from the unit and flipping through the plastic boxes.

Whale music, Rob decides with absolute certainty. Or someone singing in Sanskrit . . .

'Here it is.' Grinning, she holds up a CD entitled *Stop Smoking With Self-Hypnosis*. 'I wondered where it had gone.'

'But . . .' Rob peers at her from his prone position on the couch. 'Aren't you going to hypnotise me personally?' *I'm paying you fifty quid to put on a sodding CD?* is what he wants to say. *You're planning to leave me lying on this grubby couch while you fuck off and have a bath, or phone your mum, or go back to bed and eat cake?*

'This is just as effective,' she says. 'It burrows deep into the subconscious mind.'

334

'Mmm. Like a little rabbit.'

'Ha. You are funny.' She smiles unconvincingly.

'But, er . . .' Rob continues, 'isn't that what hypnosis is supposed to do? I mean, real hypnosis, done by an actual person?'

'Oh, you know a bit about it then?'

About as much as you do, probably . . . 'Erm, not really,' he mutters.

'The thing is, Rob' – she switches on the CD and plugs in some headphones, which she hands to him – 'you're bound to have your own, personal beliefs about smoking. Like, you think it makes you look cool . . .'

Cool? How old does she think he is, fifteen?

'. . . So the whole purpose of hypnosis is to forge a channel through all that and bore right into your brain.' Then, with a sugary smile, she clamps the large, not especially hygienic-looking plastic headphones onto his ears and trots out of the room.

Rob lies there, wondering what possessed him to think he could be cured of an addiction in a twenty-year-old's rather nasty living room. The smell of fried egg hangs in the air, and a solitary goldfish drifts in a bowl full of algae on the bookshelf. The voice has started, but Rob isn't listening because all he can think is, she reckons I smoke to look *cool*? No, he smokes because he's fallen into a fully-fledged relationship with a girl he doesn't love, who doesn't even know who the Wombles are, and in three days' time he'll have to go back to the office he despises and work for an arsehole who, until about ten minutes before Rob's 40th birthday, was also sleeping with Nadine. How terribly cosy. Is it any wonder he finds solace in an occasional nicotine rush?

. . . To help you achieve a state of deep relaxation, the man's voice drones on.

That's a laugh. Rob feels as if he hasn't been deeply

relaxed since he was about eight years old and tucked up in bed with *The Beano*.

. . . I'll help to loosen those nicotine ties that bind you, freeing you to a healthier, happier, longer life in which you'll experience no irritation, just a blissful state in which you no longer need poison surging through your blood. . . .

On and on he goes, regurgitating gobbledegook for what feels like weeks on end. Yet, perhaps due to being unable to sleep lately, Rob finds himself floating away from the leopard print sofa and depressed goldfish. And now he's no longer in a sordid Hackney flat, but Jack's, the private members' club he doesn't even belong to. It's his fortieth birthday. There is lemon cake and he's with Eddy and the crowd. Ava is there, looking like a corpse with lipstick, and everyone is making a fuss of him and telling him what a great bloke he is.

The scene changes, and they're at Nadine's flat. He's woozy – he actually feels drunk in his semi-conscious state – and it happens, it actually happens . . . she's there beside him on the sofa bed, this young thing with her hair like Kerry used to wear it when they first met. A little impish crop that shows off a slender neck and striking cheekbones. It happens, briefly, and there's a flicker of horror as Rob realises what he's done. He's had sex with Nadine – accidentally cheated on his beautiful wife – so he does the only thing he can think of. He fires off a drunken instruction to his brain to erase this moment, as if it has never happened, and when he wakes in the morning he'll go back to Bethnal Green, a little hungover but still a decent, grown-up man.

'Rob?' Jade's voice snaps him awake.

'Huh?' he barks, heart pounding.

'That's the end of the CO. Take your time before you get up, okay? You might be a little woozy.'

He opens his eyes and squints at her.

'How do you feel?' she asks, gnawing spearmint gum.

336

'Er . . . okay, I think. Kind of drowsy.'

Jade nods sagely. 'It's a very powerful CD.'

Yeah, he thinks, one I could have bought for £6.99 but never mind that now. He hands over five crisp tenners, bids her a terse goodbye and sees himself down the three flights of stairs and into the busy, dirty street.

The sky is the colour of pale ash, and across the road is a scruffy little newsagent's . . . a newsagent's full of cigarettes. He wants one as strongly as ever – no, *more* urgently if anything. His gums are tingling and he feels the slight light-headedness that only a big hit of nicotine can dispel. He crosses the road and stands outside the shop, studying its pitiful window display of packets of crayons and tennis balls. But he manages to walk on by, preparing himself to report that Jade's 'treatment' was indeed miraculous and that he has no intention of involving himself with another nasty, stinky cancer stick for the rest of his life.

First, though, he'll nip into the beleaguered mini-market by the bus stop and treat himself to his very last packet of ten.

337

Chapter Fifty-Three

'You're beautiful, Mummy!' Freddie cries from the hallway as Kerry heads downstairs towards him. 'You're like a queen, but nicer.'

'Oh, thank you, sweetheart. I'm so glad you think so.'

'I want to *marry* you.'

'You can't marry Mummy, stupid,' Mia retorts, appearing from the living room with a fistful of felt pens. 'Mummy can only marry a grown-up man.'

'Hmmm,' Kerry murmurs with a smile. 'Anyway, we'd better get over to the art club, okay? It starts in twenty minutes. You do remember I'm not going to stay there with you, don't you?'

'Yeah, yeah.' Freddie shrugs, affecting nonchalance.

'Lara will be there, though, and she says she'll look after you both.'

'Okay, Mummy,' Mia says brightly. Kerry is overcome with relief that, since the party, there's no doubt in her mind that her children have been accepted around here. Audrey-Jane and Tabitha have both been round to play, and were still enthusing over the contents of their party bags. There's even talk of a sleepover before the holiday's out.

338

'Is Joe going?' Freddie asks.

'Erm, I'm not sure, Brigid hasn't mentioned it. There'll be plenty of people you know, though. The idea is, everyone will be given part of the wall to paint and all the pictures will make a huge mural. So maybe start thinking about what you'd like to do.'

As she takes the children's coats from their hooks, Kerry wonders why Brigid was clearly not in the mood for chatting when Kerry dropped off Joe after swimming yesterday. Kerry hadn't particularly wanted a prolonged discussion, in case Brigid had felt compelled to deliver a blow-by-blow account of her nocturnal frolics with Harvey – but she'd also found her briskness a little odd. Kerry still feels pretty reliant on her for company, and anyway, she reminds herself sternly, it's none of her business who she – or Harvey for that matter – sleeps with.

As it turns out, Brigid is the first person Kerry sees as she and the children enter the church hall.

'Hi,' she booms, hurrying over with her hair scooped up prettily and an oilcloth apron over her sequinned top and faded jeans. 'Didn't know you were coming today.'

'Mummy's not staying,' Mia announces.

'Oh?' Brigid grins and raises a brow. 'Escaping, are you? I thought you were looking especially lovely today.' Kerry laughs, feeling suddenly self-conscious in a favourite corn-flower-blue dress from last summer, plus a black lace-knit cardi that's a little more decorative than her usual style.

'Just meeting a friend for lunch,' she says casually as Mia and Freddie rush off to join the other children. 'It's James,' she adds in a whisper.

'I *knew* it! Told you he was keen. He wasn't going to be put off by a bit of corn in an ear or us assuming he ran over his poor wife. So where are you going?'

'*Only* The Glasshouse . . .'

'Get you,' Brigid grins. 'Oh, and listen . . . I'm sorry I

necked all your wine the other night. Not terribly good behaviour at a children's party.'

'You were fine. Anyway, the kids' part had officially finished by then. Um . . . so did Harvey drop you off okay?'

'Yep, sweet man.' Brigid flushes slightly.

'Isn't he?' Kerry says in a teasing voice. 'Thought you two were getting on *very* well at my place.'

With a small spluttering noise, Brigid shakes her head. 'Oh, sure, he's lovely, but you know . . . not really my type. Bit young and flighty with no proper job and what sounds like a hopeless flatmate.'

'Oh, I know what you mean.' Kerry smiles.

'Anyway,' Brigid says briskly, 'off you go, have a lovely time and give me a full report later. I have a *very* good feeling about this lunch.'

*

Kerry has, she realises as the vast seafood platter arrives, become the kind of person who's hugely excited to eat in a grown-up restaurant that doesn't have colour-in place mats or anything crumb-coated.

'This looks amazing,' she exclaims, admiring the array of clams, scallops and langoustines on a vast granite board. 'Wow. I don't know what to try first.'

'You are funny,' James says with a chuckle.

'Am I? Why?' She takes a scallop and eats it. It's the most delicious thing she can remember tasting, but then she does exist on a diet of bog-standard child-friendly fare these days.

'I don't know . . . and I wouldn't want you to take this the wrong way. It's just . . . your enthusiasm, that's all. It's almost childlike.'

She smirks. 'Don't worry, I'm not going to start throwing food.'

'No, I mean in a positive sense. When I was doing my website work, I'd bring clients here occasionally and they'd just sit and eat, hardly taking anything in. They might as well have been in a Little Chef.'

'They're spoiled then,' Kerry declares. 'They probably eat like that three times a week whereas I probably have a scallop about once a decade.'

James chuckles. 'I can tell, the way you're hoovering them up. More wine?'

'Yes please. Better not have too much though. Can't be staggering back to the hall, you know: "Did you hear, Kerry Tambini dumped her kids at the mural-painting thing and went off and got plastered with a *man*?"'

'You'd be the talk of the town,' he agrees.

'Doesn't take much, does it?' She sips her glass of chablis. 'So, are you from round here originally, or did you do the escape-to-the-coast thing too?'

'Yep, pretty much,' he says, skimming over his North London childhood as they slowly devour the seafood, and explaining how one particularly lovely day trip here had been the trigger for he and a pregnant Amy to move.

'Same with us. It was flukey really, how everything felt so perfect – the sky just the right shade of blue, no one having their ice cream swiped by a seagull, and then my aunt deciding she'd had enough of England . . .'

'So it felt like it was meant to be?' he suggests.

Kerry nods, pronging a deliciously plump mussel. 'But of course, it turned out to be very, very wrong, although I didn't realise that at the time . . .' When she glances up from her plate, James is studying her. 'Do you ever speak to Amy these days?'

'The weird thing is, she called the other day, right out of the blue.'

'Oh?'

He pauses. 'Er . . . she wanted to tell me she's coming

back – moving back to Shorling, I mean. She's found herself a flat.'

'Really? Wow.' Ah, here we go. *It's been a lovely lunch but maybe I should have mentioned sooner that I'm on the verge of getting back together with my ex-wife . . .*

'Is that weird for you?' Kerry asks.

He shrugs. 'Not really. It's a big enough town for us both to live our lives without constantly bumping into each other. Anyway, I think she just wants to try and salvage something with Luke, now she's discovered the charming Brian has turned out to be addicted to internet porn.' He sniggers, his grey eyes sparkling appealingly.

'Ah, not good. What about you and her, though? Don't you suspect she's coming back for you too? Sorry if I'm prying . . .'

'No, not at all. I don't think that's part of her plan, though. We're completely over.'

'You sound so sure! How can you be certain?'

'I know myself, Kerry.'

'You've kept her piano these past two years,' she reminds him with a smile.

James shrugs. 'Yeah. Well, Luke might learn to play one day.'

'That sounds *really* likely.' She laughs, not sure she entirely believes him, but enjoying his company hugely. 'I've had the loveliest time, James,' she adds as they leave the restaurant. 'The food was fantastic and the place was so *grown-up* – in a good way, I mean . . .'

'We could go somewhere with laminated menus and ice cream sundaes next time if you'd prefer . . .'

'Well, it did feel a little odd not being given a pot of crayons. That's my only criticism.'

He laughs as they meander beside the harbour, and she's about to add another quip when he stops her, taking her hand in his. 'I've really enjoyed this, Kerry. It's been a lovely afternoon.'

'Well, it'll be my treat next time,' she says, her heart quickening at the sensation of his skin against hers.

'Great,' he says. She feels him studying her again, then, startlingly, he kisses her – a proper long, sweet kiss on the lips. Anyone could walk past and see – *'She'd better hurry up if she's going to be in time to pick up those poor children!'* But right at this moment, with the cool wind in her hair and the salty breeze against her face, Kerry doesn't care a bit.

Chapter Fifty-Four

It's surprised Rob, how he's warmed to Candida over the past few days. She's dropped by at Nadine's flat several times and has been easy, pleasant company. (There have been no further sightings of Jens, thankfully, although Rob half expects him to burst in unannounced and wrestle him to the ground).

'So you're still working with Eddy, Nadine?' Candida says over a gin and tonic one evening.

'Yes, for the moment,' Nadine says. Rob clamps his back teeth together as she gives him a quick, apologetic glance.

'Hmmm.' Candida purses her lips. 'I get the feeling he plays with you, darling, and I'm not sure I like it.'

'In what way?' Nadine asks.

'Well,' her mother says, 'what about the way he treated you on that *tawdry* little magazine you were on together?'

'You mean *I'm Hot?*' Nadine laughs.

Candida turns to Rob and flashes a mischievous smile. She is, he realises now, probably only a few years older than him. In her pale blue cashmere sweater and a swishy black skirt, with her highlighted hair casually pulled back, she looks far younger than she did in the restaurant.

'Yes, that one. Gosh, darling, I couldn't believe you were

actually working there. Remember you had to answer the phone, "Hello, I'm Hot"?' Candida laughs. 'And you said to Eddy, "Please can I say, "Hello, *I'm Hot* magazine", because everyone used to say, "Oooh, *are* you?" But he wasn't having any of it.'

'That's just what he's like, Mummy. He's an idiot.' She chuckles, and it strikes Rob that he rarely sees her relaxed like this.

'You can say that again.' Candida rolls her eyes at him. 'I'd call it ritual humiliation, darling . . .'

Rob is relieved when the conversation moves on to Nadine's childhood, and Candida's rarefied life in Zurich; he is amazed that anyone can fill up their time with little more than lunches and shopping. It's impossible to dislike her, though.

'I think you'll be a wonderful father to this baby,' she says warmly as he and Nadine see her off in a cab to the famous Charles and Alicia's.

'Thanks,' he says. 'I'll do my best, anyway.'

Maybe, he reflects, it wasn't that Nadine was more relaxed tonight, but that the grotto was so much nicer with Candida around. The fact that this is virtually his home now – and will be officially by the end of the week, when the house sale completes – is something he's not keen to dwell upon right now.

*

Nadine goes to bed early these days. Well, maybe not just 'these days'; perhaps that's always been her natural pattern, to change into her little tartan pyjama shorts and vest top at around 9 p.m. It strikes Rob, not for the first time, how bizarre it is that he barely knew her un-pregnant, when she wouldn't have known what stretch marks were, or that certain aromatherapy oils are beneficial during labour.

345

Tonight, though, he needs to talk to her, and feels that in bed – where she can't start pacing up and down and rearranging cushions – is the best place to do it. So by nine thirty he is tucked up beside her, pretending to read while reflecting that only children and the unwell retire to bed at this hour.

She yawns, places her magazine on the floor and clicks off her bedside light. She'll be fast asleep in a minute. Better make it quick.

'Er, Nadine . . .' Rob starts, twisting a corner of the duvet between finger and thumb.

'Mmm,' she says. 'Nice seeing Mummy, wasn't it?'

'Yes, it was. She's easy to have around.' *Never mind that. I need to know if you were telling the truth about there being no possibility of this being Eddy's child . . .*

She has turned away, and despite his lingering uneasiness, his hand comes to rest on her bump. Although he can't feel it yet, he can sense life in there, and movement too. According to Nadine, who pores over websites on foetal development, the baby is already the size of an avocado.

Nadine twists round to face him and kisses him lightly on the lips. 'That was nice of Mummy to say you'll be a wonderful dad.'

'Yeah.' Rob shrugs. 'Well, we'll see.'

'*I* think you will be.'

'I'll try,' he says sheepishly, allowing her to wrap her arms around him and pull him close.

She kisses him again. 'You'll be amazing, I just know you will. Oh, I'm sorry I've been so moody and horrible lately. I just can't help it, Rob. It's like I have no control over my feelings or the things I say . . .' Without warning her eyes fill with tears.

'Hey,' he murmurs, overcome with an urge to protect her. 'It's okay. Don't cry. It's all going to be fine . . .'

'I don't know how you put up with me,' she adds, wiping her wet eyes on the sheet.

Rob pulls her towards him, stroking her hair and kissing her until he senses her relaxing in his arms. God, though – she *is* beautiful, possibly even more so now she's starting to fill out a little, her angular little body acquiring soft curves. He touches her bump, leaving his hand there as she slips towards sleep. And he decides that this child feels absolutely his, at least for now.

Chapter Fifty-Five

Kerry tries to make sure her lessons are relaxed. She chats to pupils before and afterwards, rather than booking them back-to-back with no gaps in between; yet she can often tell more about someone from what's *not* said. For instance, she knows that shy Lucia wishes her mum wouldn't stay during her lessons, watching intently from the armchair as if at a concert. She knows, too, that Tristan and Freya – thirteen-year-old twins who share a lesson – are fiercely competitive, each watching intently as the other plays, and prickling with irritation when no mistakes are made.

And she knows that something is going on with Harvey, that he's not his usual, easy-going self. Although he has clearly practised, he plays stiffly as if just going through the motions. When she shows him some chords, then asks him to try them, it's obvious he hasn't really been listening. Buddy watches, subdued, from the corner of the room.

'So, next Saturday as usual?' she asks as the lesson ends.

'Um, I can't make next week,' he says, 'or the one after that, I'm afraid.'

'Oh . . . so you're still doing children's parties, then?'

He shakes his head and smiles. 'No, it's a job – a proper acting job. My agent called over Christmas. A producer she knows was about to start touring a play, and it had been through rehearsals when the lead actor fell ill, and then the understudy had some kind of personal crisis . . .'

'Wow. So you got the part, then?'

'Yes, well, Victoria, my agent, did a fantastic job selling me as the amiable young dad . . . at least, young-*ish*. You can get away with a lot on stage, fortunately. And the audition went well – better than I could have hoped for, considering how rusty I am. But then, they were pretty desperate by then.' He laughs self-deprecatingly.

Kerry smiles. 'I'm so pleased for you. So no more running for cover in a hail of barley sugars.'

'Yeah.' He smirks. 'I suspect it'll still be a pretty young audience, though. Children *and* animals – maybe I've lost my mind . . .'

'What's the play?' she asks, filling two mugs from the kettle.

'A new production of *101 Dalmatians* – with real dogs. Only six, though, thank Christ. I think that's what swung it at the audition – my natural affinity with the canine species.' Kerry laughs, relieved that he's dropped the guardedness he'd maintained during his lesson. She realises, too, how much she'll miss these Saturdays.

'So, definitely no more Harvey Chuckles,' she says.

'That's right. And when the play's finished, I'm going to be running some drama workshops with kids and teenagers at the arts centre.'

'More working with children . . .' She smiles.

'Yes, but at least they'll *want* to be there. Apparently, they've wanted to set up a drama course for ages. It's very Shorling, isn't it?'

'Sure is. Maybe I'll sign up Freddie and Mia. So . . . are you planning a ceremonial burning of the costume?'

'Nope, tempting though it is to have a huge pyre on the beach. But Ethan's taking over. He's done one already – turns

349

out he has a far more natural affinity for that kind of thing than I ever had.'

'I can imagine,' she smirks. There's a stilted pause, and she's overcome with an urge to find out what happened that night after Mia's party. Brigid's been a little awkward ever since, and Harvey definitely wasn't himself during his lesson. Are they seeing each other, she wonders, but aren't sure about telling her? She can't imagine why they'd keep it secret . . . 'Harvey,' Kerry starts, 'you know the other evening, after you'd been such a star at Mia's party . . .'

'Um . . . yeah.' And now he's fiddling with the sugar bowl on the kitchen table and won't look at her at all. What's going on?

'I . . . I don't want to sound nosey,' she adds, 'and I know it's none of my business but—'

'Kerry, it's all a bit embarrassing,' he says quickly.

She frowns. 'What – for you or Brigid?' She's being way out of order now, prying too much, but she can't stop herself.

'For her, I guess,' he mutters.

Kerry studies his face. 'I don't see why. I mean, we've all been drunk, haven't we? We've all launched ourselves at someone and regretted it, not that she *should* have regretted it with you, but maybe, if she'd been sober . . .'

As Harvey fixes his gaze on hers, Kerry detects the slightest hint of a smile playing on his lips.

'What's funny?' she asks, more intrigued than ever.

'Nothing. Nothing at all . . .' He splutters with laughter and clasps a hand over his nose and mouth.

'There is! What happened, Harvey? *Please* tell me. I promise I won't breathe a word. I won't mention it to Brigid that you've said anything – honestly . . .'

He rakes back his hair, convulsing with laughter now.

'You can't sit here in hysterics and not tell me!' she exclaims.

350

'Okay,' he blurts out. 'I will – but I feel crap about this. I'd never normally talk about something that happened. I'm not one of those guys who brags about—'

'Just get on with it,' she cajoles him.

He takes a sip of his tea and inhales deeply, as if trying to compose his thoughts. 'All right,' he says finally. 'The other night, I discovered that certain people are, er . . . attracted to clowns.'

Kerry regards him quizzically. 'Well, I suppose you do come into contact with lots of mums at parties. And you know what we're like, spending so much time with small children. We tend to get a bit overexcited in the presence of an adult male.'

'Er, yeah, I guess so.' He sniggers and blushes a little. 'But it's sort of more than that.'

She frowns. 'What is it, then?'

He grins then, pausing as if figuring out how best to explain it. 'Um . . . it would seem that some people – probably the *tiniest* percentage, I don't think official figures have been collated . . .'

'Figures about *what*, Harvey?'

'Er . . . about people who fancy clowns, like a fetish-type thing.'

'Really? You mean they want to . . .'

'. . . Do it with Coco in the big top.' He blinks at her, his shoulders trembling with mirth. 'Yeah, that kind of thing.'

'A sort of clown-shagging urge?' Kerry says, snorting with laughter. 'Are you serious, Harvey, or just making it up?'

He, too, is laughing hysterically. 'It would appear that it's a real thing, Kerry. Wig, face-paint, red plastic nose – the lot.'

'You're kidding! And Brigid likes that kind of thing—'

'Um, yeah . . .'

'You did it with your full outfit on?'

351

'No!' He virtually shouts it, causing Buddy to flinch.

'Well,' Kerry says, still dissolving in laughter, 'she *was* laying it on with you, and there's no shame in it, you know. God, you deserve some perks of the job after the crap you put up with from all those kids . . .'

Harvey grabs her arm. 'Kerry – truly, it wasn't like that . . .' He tells her then – about Brigid fluttering off to have a shower, having left firm instructions for the costume to be donned in preparation for her return.

Kerry is laughing so much, she fears for her beleaguered pelvic floor. 'And you absolutely, honestly didn't do it? Go on, *please* tell me. I won't breathe a word . . .'

'Absolutely not. I swear on my life. Listen – she reappeared wearing a Pierrot costume and virtually chased me down the street. And then she realised she'd locked herself out, so I had to get Ethan to charge over with warm clothes for her to put on over her skimpy little white tunic thing – all he could think of to bring were his jeans and smelly old duffel coat – while we waited for the emergency locksmith.'

Kerry takes a moment to process all of this. 'And you honestly didn't do it with her in costume?'

'No! God . . .'

She raises a brow. 'Come on, saucy clown man.'

'Stop it,' he sniggers. 'You reckon I'm desperate, don't you? You think that, even if it meant complete humiliation for me, I'd still do it because wearing a flashing bow tie is the only way I can get laid.'

'Of *course* not. Actually, I imagine it was probably a bit . . . *freaky*.'

'Well,' he says, grinning, 'let's just say I decided it was safer to sneak back at half six next morning, under cover of darkness, to collect my car.'

They're still giggling as Kerry sees him out, wishing him luck for the play, or rather that he should break a leg.

'When does it finish?' she asks.

'Not until early May. I'll be coming home for the odd few days here and there, but I won't be able to fit in regular lessons.'

'That's fine, just give me a call when you're ready to start again.'

Harvey smiles warmly, gives Buddy a goodbye belly tickle and briefly kisses Kerry on the cheek. As he drives away, it startles her to realise that she already feels a little bereft. She also wonders how she will possibly manage to maintain a normal expression next time she sees Brigid.

*

Six days later, as ten-foot waves smash up onto Shorling's seafront, Kerry opens the newspaper to see that Luella Hunt, a young English actress with a curtain of impossibly glossy flaxen hair, has been spotted stepping out in Manchester with an 'unknown friend'.

She studies the paper for long enough to satisfy herself that Harvey Galbraith looks just as fetching in a hastily-taken paparazzi shot as he does in the flesh.

PART THREE

Training

'Try not to show your frustration, even if your new friend doesn't seem to understand what you want him to do.'

Your First Dog: A Complete Guide
by Jeremy Catchpole

Chapter Fifty-Six

Four months later

It has been one of those seasons which will forever be entwined with another person. The spring of James, Kerry reflects, opening the birthday card he sweetly posted to her, despite the fact that they see each other twice or three times a week. The spring of visiting galleries, museums and going for long country walks with Buddy and the children, all terribly grown-up.

'James is just my friend,' she told the children in response to their inevitable question a few weeks ago.

'He's your boyfriend,' Mia insisted.

'No, sweetheart, he's not. He's a friend I like very much and enjoy spending time with.' Eugh. However she tried to phrase it, it sounded so horribly corny. Why couldn't she talk about James while still sounding like a normal person, instead of some dreadful self-help book? In fact, the thing she has with him – whatever it is – is deeply pleasant in a relaxing, warm bath kind of way. Perhaps because he's so mature and capable, diligently researching opening times and special exhibitions as they explore the Sussex coast, Kerry doesn't feel as if she has to put on a pretence of being some sort of alpha female. She is unembarrassed when they stop for lunch and she pulls out her purse, discovering it's smeared with an oozing chocolate coin because her bag had been resting against a radiator.

'That's what I like about you,' James joked. 'Always prepared for sudden famine.'

The coastal explorations are enjoyable, and at last it feels as if she has carved out space to do things for herself. *Me-time*, as the magazines smugly call it. *Cuckoo Clock*'s production company have moved her onto a more prestigious – and better paid – series of nature documentaries aimed at older children and teens, requiring atmospheric scores and no lyrics. So she feels justified in rewarding herself by taking the odd weekend day off to browse through sculpture gardens with James, or have tea and cake in the weak spring sunshine in the grounds of a stately home. At last, it no longer seems vital to spend her child-free weekends working in order to fill the hours.

Yet it also feels . . . slightly *odd*. Sometimes James says peculiar things, such as, 'I thought that went really well', as if willing her to agree, or perhaps in preparation for filing a report. Occasionally, she'd love him to exclaim, 'Have you ever seen a duller exhibition than that? I was actually starting to contemplate suicide in there. Come on, let's go and get smashed in the pub.'

And one breezy, blue-skied Sunday, Kerry feels a small stab of guilt as James drives them back to Shorling, having clearly plotted a far prettier route than the more obvious A-road. *Why aren't I appreciating this?* she wonders. *What's wrong with me? This is what grown-ups do. They have nice days out together and on the way home they discuss how enjoyable it's been.* There's nothing to remotely pick fault with because nothing ever goes wrong. Unlike those family days out when Rob was still around, she and James never arrive at a quaint country restaurant to be informed, rather tersely, that it's 2.45 p.m. and lunchtime is over. It doesn't even rain (or, if it does, it's not a problem because they are snug and dry inside a particularly beautiful church).

Perhaps Kerry's mild unease has nothing to do with any of that, but the fact that, despite the occasional hand-hold, or an arm placed affectionately around her shoulders, James doesn't seem to be remotely interested in sleeping with her.

*

'Well, he's gay then,' Anita declares, having escaped for a child-free overnighter in Shorling.

'Of course he's not,' Kerry laughs. 'That sounds awful, anyway – "He shows no interest in me sexually so he must only fancy men." And he was married, you know – in fact they've never got around to getting a divorce. *And* they have a twenty-two-year-old son . . .'

'Just because he's fathered a child, and been married, doesn't mean he's not gay.'

'Anita, he's not! James is *so* not gay. Anyway, if we're assuming that about any man who doesn't want to sleep with me, that's basically the entire male population of Shorling.'

Anita pulls a wry smile. In celebration of Kerry's birthday, they are somewhat thrilled at finding themselves in licensed premises after dark. They are drinking delicious mauve-tinted cocktails involving gin and a lusciously-named concoction called Creme de Violette.

'What about the lovely Harvey?' she asks. 'Heard much from him lately?'

'No, but I read that he's in a "close relationship"' – Kerry waggles her fingers – 'with Luella Hunt.'

'Really? That insipid little actress with a repertoire of one facial expression? Surely not.'

'Surely *yes*.'

Anita exhales. 'You never gave any sign that you liked

him, that's the problem. You've always been all *friendly-friendly* with men, even the ones you really like . . .'

'What's wrong with that?'

'Nothing, if you're really not interested. But when you are, you have to make sure you give off some signs . . .'

'What, so I should have launched myself at him while he was having a lesson?' Kerry snorts with laughter. 'I was his teacher. It would have been *unethical*.'

Anita shakes her head and sips her drink. 'God, these are delicious. Anyway, you know what I mean. You could have just been a bit more . . . playful. You do fancy him, don't you? He's so cute, great body and I love all that dark, wavy hair. And wasn't he brilliant with the kids at Mia's party?'

'Yeah, that did have a slightly aphrodisiac effect.'

'Anyway,' Anita adds with a shrug, 'maybe James is just a bit shy on the bed front.'

Kerry sniggers. 'Not gay, then.'

'Well, maybe not. And at least you do stuff together – all these outings along the coast . . .'

'. . . Which can feel a little like school trips,' Kerry cuts in, 'only without the children – or rather, without Freddie careering around a gallery while someone says really loudly, "I don't know *why* people insist in bringing small children to places like this."'

Anita laughs, ordering a second round of cocktails as Kerry's phone bleeps. 'It's James,' she says with a smile. 'Said he'd text me the full schedule for my birthday treat next weekend.'

'Read it out,' Anita commands.

'Okay: *Hi Kerry, all sorted, hope not presumptuous of me. Pls say no if you don't fancy it but have booked us dinner and b&b at that lighthouse we saw. My treat.* He's put *two* kisses,' she adds unnecessarily.

'Well,' Anita says, 'sounds like the tide's turning after all.'

'The Lighthouse Hotel. God,' Kerry exclaims. 'It's a *real*

lighthouse, perched on the edge of the cliffs. We passed it last weekend and I was going on about how amazing it looked.'

'He obviously took the hint then, didn't he?'

'That's the thing, I *wasn't* hinting. It's been so long since I've done anything like that, the possibility of staying in it overnight hadn't even crossed my mind.'

Anita crooks a brow and giggles. 'That tends to be the idea with hotels, Kerry. The staying overnight part.'

'Yes, I know, but—'

'Listen,' she says, smirking as their cocktails arrive, 'you've precisely one week to put it back *into* your mind, because this poor, timid man has obviously plucked up the courage to ravage you, at long bloody last. Make sure you wear some decent underwear, okay?'

Kerry guffaws and takes a sip of her beautiful violety drink. 'I will,' she says, 'but what if I've misread the signs, and he only wants to go because it's of architectural interest?'

'Well, I shouldn't really tell you, but that birthday present I left at your place should put paid to any of that.'

Chapter Fifty-Seven

She wanted a natural birth with no intervention. Nadine
had made that absolutely clear, waving her handwritten
birth plan in the face of some random woman in a dark
blue tunic when they'd arrived at the hospital. Although
Rob doesn't like to break it to her, he suspects the woman
wasn't listening; it might as well have been a shopping list
for all the interest she showed in it. Anyway, it's a different
woman now – or rather a girl with astonishingly fresh skin,
her dark shiny hair pulled into a sleek ponytail.

'Get the oil, Rob,' Nadine barks at Rob. 'Come on, I
thought you were going to *help*.'

They're in a bleak little room with an iron-framed bed,
walls the colour of rice pudding and her contractions are
coming thick and fast. Rob extracts the white box of bottles
from her enormous polka-dot kit bag – but which one out
of the set of eighteen does she want? She'd told him the
order in which they should be sniffed, to manage the pain
and make everything lovely, while the baby slipped out
effortlessly with a polite little peep. And he'd tried to mem-
orise it all, in the way that he'd valiantly learnt his French
irregular verbs and The Highway Code. But right at this
moment, as Nadine lets out an enormous groan – far bigger

than anything he'd have imagined could come out of such a tiny person – he can't remember a thing. Even at thirty-nine weeks pregnant, Nadine doesn't look remotely ready to give birth. Her bump is neat and compact, whereas Kerry's were vast, almost heroic, forcing him to migrate to the very edge of their bed. The midwife is a slip of a girl too, with childlike freckles smattered across her little snub nose. Rob feels too big, too clumsy – too *male* – to be here.

'My oil!' Nadine commands again, causing him to grab at the first bottle his hand lands upon. As previously instructed, he shakes a few drops onto a cotton handkerchief and wafts it under her nose.

'That's the wrong one!' she snaps.

'No, honestly, it's a clean hankie . . .'

'I mean the *oil*. That's rose, Rob, God. *Oooohhh . . .*' Another contraction is coming; he sees the sweat beading on her forehead as if being squeezed out of a sponge.

'Which one then?'

'Clary sage . . .' Her face contorts with pain.

'Two minutes between contractions,' says the midwife.

'What does that mean?' Nadine cries.

'It means the baby's coming, sweetheart,' she says, smiling and patting her hand.

Nadine is up on all fours now in her organic cotton T-shirt, twisting her head to face Rob. 'Clary sage, Rob, come *on . . .*'

'Sorry, sorry,' he mutters, feeling utterly redundant as the midwife utters soothing words, seemingly unfazed despite the fact that she looks, to Rob's mind, as if she's not old enough to drive a car, let alone deliver a baby. It's amazing, he thinks wildly, what they teach them at school these days . . .

'Clary sage!' Nadine shrieks, but Rob's mind has gone blank. *Who the hell is Clary Sage?* Oh, the oil, the oil . . . He grabs it from the box as she lets out another guttural moan, and the sound of her pain makes him flinch and drop the bottle. There's a tinkle as it smashes and leaks out onto the shiny yellow floor, filling the room with a powerful bitter scent.

'Have you broken it?' Nadine exclaims.

'Um, sorry . . .' Hell, should he try to mop it up? An image forms in his mind of a drawing of a hospital delivery room with all the dangerous things highlighted. And now he sees a huge red arrow pointing to the floor, with the caption HAZARD – OILY SPILLAGE.

'*Why* are you cleaning the floor?' Nadine shouts, causing Rob to leap up, still clutching a green paper towel from the dispenser.

'Don't worry,' the midwife says quickly as another woman arrives. 'If you need gas and air you won't be able to use your inhalations anyway.'

'I don't want gas and air. I wanted the water pool but you made me get out of it.'

'Yes, because your contractions were slowing right down.'

'And I wrote in my birth plan that I wanted Jade's hypnotherapy CD on – where did you put it, Rob?'

'I think we must have forgotten it . . .'

'But the breathing techniques,' she exclaims. 'The positive affirmations—'

She is stopped short by what seems to Rob like unimaginable pain that no human should have to go through, and he hears the freckle-faced midwife murmur to the other woman, 'It's a bit late for that.' They're both telling her to push, and Rob feels as if he's watching a terrible scene in a movie that he should walk away from, but feels compelled to see through to the end. The pushing isn't working; she can't get the baby out. Clary sage forgotten, Nadine sucks hard on gas and air, then it's pethidine and more pushing, pushing, and still the baby won't come. Rob feels helpless, as if he might cry. When he tries to mop her forehead with a

364

cold compress, she bats him away. If he murmurs encouraging words, like the midwives are doing, she cries, 'You don't know what this is like! I can't do it, I can't get this baby out . . .' And a terrifying thought fills Rob's brain: it's a freaky, massive super-baby and it'll *never* come out of Nadine . . .

'We're taking you to theatre, sweetheart,' the younger girl is saying as the room fills with people and urgent voices. And Nadine is no longer on all fours, barking and yelping in her sweat-soaked T-shirt, but on a stretcher, being taken away.

Chapter Fifty-Eight

The head of the Sussex Tourist Board couldn't have organised it better. Kerry and James have visited a nineteenth-century poet's cottage, a perfectly-preserved art deco house which is open only six days a year (naturally, today was one of those days) and watched a chamber orchestra performing in the manicured grounds of a castle. He'd packed a lavish picnic to nibble at during the concert (naturally, it has been a perfect, sunny May day with just a few wispy clouds streaking a pale blue sky) *and* researched the nearby town so they could skip the boring bits and head straight for the more interesting shops. Kerry isn't sure that a stop-off at the bottle museum was strictly necessary. But she's maintained a perky exterior, praising James for choosing all the right things, and never once suggesting that they might go off-piste and have a cup of tea in, say, some nondescript but perfectly nice cafe.

And now they're at The Lighthouse Hotel, which is also perfect, surpassing Kerry's expectations as she'd glimpsed it from the main road. Having dropped off their bags late morning, they are now in their room – an airy circular space with a curved wall separating off the shower room, and light flooding in through two original windows. The rough stone walls are white, the enormous bath – which sits, alarmingly, in the centre of the room – has elaborate claw feet, and the enormous bed has been made up with the most luxurious cotton sheets Kerry has ever felt against her skin. Only her bare feet are making contact with the sheets at the moment, as she lies on her side, flicking through the pile of information leaflets which James collected from the various places of interest today. Later, though, after drinks and dinner, it will be her naked body. With James's naked body next to hers, and followed at some point, she'd imagine, by sex. Sex in a lighthouse with James. Kerry would feel no more weird if someone had told her she must do it with the Archbishop of Canterbury.

She fans out the leaflets on the bed. 'James, you've put so much thought into today. I'm so touched you organised all this for me.'

James is carefully unpacking his clothes and placing them in the chest of drawers. 'I think we could probably have done without the bottle museum,' he says with a small laugh.

'Yes, well, the children will be impressed that I've seen every design of milk bottle ever made in Britain.'

He closes the drawer and comes over to the bed, lying down on his side to face her. 'I wanted you to have a really nice birthday.'

'Well, it has been already and we haven't even eaten yet. And you know how I love my food.'

He leans closer, kissing her softly on the lips. 'They do great gin and tonics here, I read in the reviews. Thirty-five gin varieties, the best one scented with wild flowers from the Orkneys . . .'

'*That* sounds delicious.' There's a pause, and she wonders if he's ever brought anyone here before. 'What did Luke think about us coming away this weekend?' she asks.

'Oh, he approved. Glad to get me out of his hair for a

367

couple of days, I suspect. He's jacking in the shop, you know. Says he finds it repetitive, as if making sandwiches was ever going to be anything else . . .'

'So he's going to sell it?'

'Nope, it's staying open for the time being – run by me.'

'Oh, so you're buying him out?'

'No,' he says ruefully, 'because he never put anything in in the first place. I mean, he didn't finance it – that was me and his friends' parents. He was the ideas person which, I have to admit, he is pretty good at. No, what I'm doing is allowing him to step away gracefully.'

'Ah, I *knew* you liked the shop,' she says, grinning. 'And it might be better, running it your way . . .'

'Yes, that's what I thought.'

'Would Amy get involved?' she asks. 'You mentioned she was looking for something local . . .' His ex-wife has moved into a tiny flat in the centre of town and, as far as Kerry can gather, she and James maintain a cordial, if slightly chilly relationship.

James is laughing now, swivelling off the bed and stashing his empty case in the wardrobe. 'We wouldn't last a morning, working together. Listen, we should get ready for dinner . . .'

'Yes, I could do with a quick freshen-up first, though, okay?'

'Bath or shower?' he asks with an entirely straight face.

Kerry blinks at the central bath which utterly dominates the room. 'Oh, a shower I think. I need something to liven me up.'

Chapter Fifty-Nine

Nadine is shouting for Rob; he can hear her through the doors.

'I need to go in,' he barks at the brick of a man with a pink, shiny head who's preventing him from being with her.

'There's too much going on in there, mate,' the man grunts. 'You can go in when they're ready.'

Ready for what? He's not about to miss the birth of his child. When Nadine yells, 'I want Rob!', he shoves his way past, surprised at the burst of determination that seems to come from nowhere and blunders into the room where his girlfriend is lying on a bed, her short dark hair plastered to her forehead with sweat. She manages a weak smile.

'Oh, you're *here*.' Like he'd been dawdling and only just made it in time.

'Yes, I'm here. Don't worry.' He grabs her hand and grasps it tightly.

'She's refusing to have a caesarean,' says a woman with an unyielding helmet of black hair.

'It's not in the plan,' Nadine wails.

'Who cares about the plan?' Rob touches her hot, damp cheek. 'It doesn't matter now. You've tried and done your best but it's not important. They have to get the baby out

369

safely.' He pauses, expecting Nadine to say something cutting, but she murmurs a weak, 'Okay.'

Then something in helmet-hair's mood changes. 'You can try one last time,' she says firmly. She urges her to push, and a man Rob hadn't even registered before takes what looks like a pair of tongs off a trolley – he's reminded of his parents' special-occasion salad tongs – then there's so much shouting that Rob has to turn away. He can't watch the tongs bit, it seems too wild and chaotic, not the way he likes things at all. It wasn't like this when Mia and Freddie were born . . .

With his back teeth jammed together, he tries to spirit himself away to a place where babies are delivered in a orderly fashion. Then he hears the man saying, 'Well done, well done, Nadine, it's a boy . . .'

Rob turns to see his tiny baby being held up and being placed, all wet, silky skin and dark hair, on Nadine's chest.

She looks at Rob and smiles. 'Look, it's our son.'

He nods, unable to find words while he studies the face, which is definitely *his* face – or rather, his father's brow and nose. For a moment, he wonders if there's something of Eddy too, around the mouth – although, actually, this perfect child really only looks like one person: Nadine.

The baby is whisked away, then returned all clean and alert, his dark eyes taking in his surroundings. The nurse hands him to Rob. 'Here you are,' she says kindly.

'Er . . . okay.' It's silly to feel nervous, but Rob hasn't held a newborn baby for so long that he's fearful of somehow breaking him. He is sweating a little, but after a few moments something in him adjusts and he remembers what to do, and it feels utterly natural to be cradling this tiny human being. Sod paternity tests and quizzing Nadine and night after night spent worrying. As Rob looks down at the baby in his arms, there is no doubt in his mind that this child is his, in the only way that matters.

Chapter Sixty

It's like that feature in *Mr Jones* – 'Your A–Z of foreplay' – which Kerry's eyes had lit upon in the dentist's waiting room. She'd almost convulsed with laughter when she'd spotted that it was written by 'Miss Jones' – Rob's alter ego – and had been unable to resist sneakily tearing it out of the magazine and slipping it into her bag. How she and Brigid had laughed at the way he'd written it. It was the way he'd suggested working through the proceedings in *alphabetical order*: 'a for areola', 'b for bottom', 'c for clitoris' . . . oh dear, oh dear . . .

Only now, it appears that this is happening to Kerry in real life. She's not averse to some things being alphabetised – her CDs have been a jumble since Rob left and his ultra-strict filing system broke down – but not this. Plenty of women would appreciate James's efforts and award an A-star for effort. But the more James gamely continues, and the more she tries in vain to participate – to feel *something*, in this perfect lighthouse room – the more she is conscious of a terrible rising hysteria in her, until everything he does is unbearably tickly and it takes every ounce of concentration not to cry with laughter. Was she always this tickly, or is it because she hasn't been touched in so long, and her nerve endings are over-responding?

'Sorry,' he murmurs as she flinches again.

'No, it's not you. It's fine – I've just gone horribly tickly. I don't know why. I'll be all right in a minute . . .' James pulls back, observing her with a quizzical smile. He's so handsome, she reminds herself. *Don't mess up this opportunity when you haven't had sex in . . .* well, she can't actually remember.

'James, I just need the bathroom.'

'Okay.' Mercifully, he removes his hand from her breast.

She slips out of bed, feeling conscious of her nakedness now, and perches on the loo. In fact, she doesn't really need to go. She's just buying some time while cursing herself for wasting this lovely man, this incredible room, this opportunity. Two bathrobes are hanging on the back of the door. They look like possibly the fluffiest bathrobes ever; James probably checked up on robe quality when he made the booking. She gets up and slips one on. When she emerges from the bathroom he is sitting up in bed, a particularly fine specimen of a man, his lightly-tanned body shown off to best effect by all the whiteness around him.

'Hi,' he says with a smile.

'Hi.' She pauses for a moment. Then, with the belt on her robe done up tightly – a little too tightly after that amazing dinner – she climbs into bed beside him.

'Are you okay?' he asks gently.

'Yes, I'm fine . . .' She's about to concoct an excuse, like she's eaten too much or doesn't feel well, but she can't bring herself to lie to him. 'I'm really sorry. I've had such a lovely time but, James . . . I'm not sure this is going to work.'

His mouth forms a firm line, and for a moment she wonders what the hell is wrong with her. 'You're right,' he murmurs, taking her hand in his. 'You're absolutely right.'

'I'm *really* sorry.'

James sighs. 'Yes, me too. But it's not your fault, you have nothing to apologise for.'

She looks at him. 'I do love our days together, though . . .'

He nods, and they fall silent for a few moments. 'It's just – Amy moved on,' he murmurs. 'She was with someone else. She got on with her life and I wonder if I ever will.' He turns to meet her gaze and she kisses him lightly on the lips.

'You're probably the most eligible man in Shorling, James.'

He chuckles. 'Good God. I very much doubt that.'

Kerry stretches out, grateful for the coolness of sheets against her skin, and hoping he comes back sometime to this very room, with a woman who appreciates it.

'It's been a perfect day,' she murmurs, feeling drowsy now, 'but . . . let's just sleep.'

Chapter Sixty-One

Rob is at his desk in the office, trying to write a Miss Jones column on the theme of women's sexual fantasies. It's Friday evening, way past home time, and he's finding it virtually impossible to squeeze a single intelligible sentence out of his addled brain. Every time he types something like, 'Sometimes I want a big dirty trucker man', a hectoring voice in his head bellows, 'For Christ's sake, Rob. You have an innocent baby at home. This has got to stop.'

He squints at his screen, his head aching and RSI tingles shooting up his right arm, willing the voice to shut the hell up. It's only work, after all, so why is he getting himself into such a stew? People do all kinds of crappy jobs just to bring in some money – what about that clown guy Kerry seems to have befriended? Anyway, Rob can't afford to show anything less than one hundred percent commitment right now, even though he's barely managing to restrain himself from slapping Eddy most days. Even when his boss quipped, 'God, Rob, you look knackered – rather you than me with this baby lark, mate!', he had to just smile benignly and get on with his work. Rob is now living full-time with Nadine and their beautiful baby son, and is acutely aware that he has two families to support.

He performs a quick calculation. By the time Rafferty

is, what, twenty-two and has finished university, Rob will be . . . *sixty-two*. That's perilously close to pensionable age, and at this rate he'll still be dashing off Miss Jones columns suggesting that it might be a good idea to dress up as a fireman once in a while.

'Just get on with it,' he mutters to himself, flinching as his mobile rings. 'Er, hi, Nadine, everything okay?'

'Yes, it's just . . . how much longer are you going to be? It's nearly seven and Rafferty's a bit fractious and I thought you might be home by now . . .'

'Okay, won't be long.'

'What's keeping you, Rob? I've been here all day, haven't talked to another living soul – at least, not one who can talk back . . .'

He exhales fiercely and glares at his screen. 'I've just got to finish this thing about women's fantasies. Then I'll be out of here, I promise.' He pauses and bites his lip. 'What kind of fantasies do women have?'

'Huh?' Her response hangs in the air like a bad smell.

'I mean . . . what kind of thoughts go through a woman's brain when she's, y'know . . . imagining her ideal scenario in a bed type thing?'

There's a burst of bitter laughter. 'You are fucking joking, Rob?'

He frowns. 'No. I just wondered—'

'Right,' she snaps, 'you thought it'd be a good idea to ask a woman who's barely recovered from having a baby yanked out of her vagina with forceps about what kind of sexual fantasies she has?'

He opens his mouth and shuts it again, relieved that everyone else has gone home. 'I didn't mean it like that,' he mutters.

'Would you be up for exotic scenarios if you had five stitches in your perineum?'

'Er . . .' He racks his brain, trying to recall what a

perineum is exactly, and whether or not he has one. 'No, I probably wouldn't,' he concedes.

He can hear Nadine's urgent breathing down the phone. 'The health visitor said, "Don't worry, Nadine, you'll be able to resume intercourse after your six week check-up." Ha!' she barks mirthlessly. 'Like I'll be ready then. God, the way I feel now, it'll be more like six *years* . . .'

'That's fine, it's not as if I feel like—' Rob starts, before realising that she has abruptly ended the call.

For God's sake. There was no need to take it like that. He despises his stupid column more than ever now; this would never have happened if he was still allowed to write the entertainment pages – the film reviews and celebrity interviews. He suggested swapping his Miss Jones page for a monthly recipe at the last features meeting – for busy dads with hungry mouths to feed – but was met with a gale of derisive laughter. Eddy has even taken the Style Tip of the Month page off him and given it to Ava instead.

In a fit of annoyance, he turns off his computer, grabs his jacket from the back of his chair and storms out of the office. At least it's Friday, and he'll be able to get stuck into baby-related duties over the weekend and relieve some of the pressure at home. Rafferty is adorable, but he has yet to learn to distinguish day from night. Nadine is convinced that his nocturnal howlings are due to the fact that she can't produce enough milk, yet when Rob suggested giving him the odd bottle of formula, anyone would have thought he'd suggested force-feeding him gin.

Hmmm. He *should* head straight home, he decides as he dries his hands in the gents. But would anyone blame him for having a quick drink, just to bolster himself before the onslaught of feeding and bathing and being spurted with baby sick? Maybe it would give Nadine time to calm down, so they'd have a nicer evening. He calls Simon's number on his mobile. 'Still in the office?'

'Yeah, unfortunately,' Simon replies.

'Just wondered if you fancied a quick pint . . .'

'Sorry, still a bit busy, mate,' he says distractedly.

'Oh.' Rob checks his watch – 7.20 p.m. 'Mind if I pop down for a quick coffee? That is,' he chortles, 'if you have coffee down there and not just Horlicks.' Why did he say that? He didn't mean to sound like a crashing snob. In fact, as he's never ventured down to the bowels of the building where the hobby magazines reside – no one from *Mr Jones* does – it wouldn't surprise him if they still used manual typewriters.

'Things are a bit full-on at the moment,' Simon explains, sounding echoey, as if in a cave. 'We're on deadline tonight and I've still got to pass the cover. But if you're around later, we're all off to Bill's retirement party . . .'

A *retirement party*? Lord help us. It's a short step from ordering trousers ('slacks') from the small ads in Sunday supplements.

'Er, I don't think I know Bill,' Rob mumbles, 'so I might leave it.'

'Oh, you *must* know Bill. He's our features editor, been working here for thirty-five years, virtually part of the furniture . . .'

'Oh, um, yeah,' Rob fibs. In fact, the *Mr Jones* team have always made a point of avoiding the likes of Bill. Rob once spotted Eddy flinching when forced to ride in the lift with one of the old blokes, as if close contact might somehow contaminate him or damage his suit.

'. . . Heading down to The Lounge,' Simon is saying. 'See you down there, if you fancy it. Should be a laugh.'

Right – as long as no one chokes on their false teeth . . .

'Uh . . .' Rob pauses. 'Okay then, if you're sure it's okay for me to tag along.'

''Course it is,' Simon laughs. 'They won't mind associating with a ponce like you just for one night.'

377

Chapter Sixty-Two

Nadine checks her watch. It's gone 9 p.m., and when Rob called again to say he was off for a quick drink with Simon, he promised he'd be home by eight. She didn't mind him having a catch-up, even though it had meant having to bath Rafferty all by herself – but why isn't he home now?

Since Rob went back to work, she has developed an aversion to being alone in her flat. It's manageable during the day, when she accepts that Rob has to be at the office, but come the evening, she's craving adult company so badly that she finds herself staring at the clock, willing the hands to whir round, and sometimes even takes Rafferty out to buy milk or bread, simply so she can talk to someone. The flat feels so small and cramped these days, and it terrifies her, being in sole charge of a baby who's not even one month old. Besides, she should be having her customary long, sudsy bath by now – her reward after a gruelling day – with Rob taking care of Rafferty in the living room. She'll still have it, she decides, popping the baby into his sling and carrying him through to the bathroom while she runs a bath. He can sit in his baby seat on the floor beside her. She needs to be clean and have ten minutes' respite: 'I *am* still a human being,' she blurts out into the tense, milky-scented air.

Leaving the bath running, and with Rafferty still strapped to her chest, she gathers together her pyjamas, dressing gown and a magazine. But by the time she returns to the bathroom, the roll-top bath is full to the brim, having reached the overflow, and is stone cold too. Brilliant. She must have used up all the hot water. She plunges in a hand and pulls out the plug, checking the time again on the starfish clock on the shelf: 9.47 p.m. Where *is* he?

Rafferty is whimpering now, so she feeds him and puts him to sleep in the cradle at the side of the bed. His eyes ping open immediately. *Waaaaah!* Nadine lifts him out, accidentally elbowing the revolving sheep night light on her bedside table and sending it tumbling to the floor. 'Oh,' she gasps. Its paper cylinder shade, onto which the little sheep are projected, is crumpled and torn. 'Daddy never liked it anyway,' she tells Rafferty, her heart thumping as she crushes its balsawood frame with her bare foot.

Stomping through to the living room, she perches on the sofa with Rafferty on her lap. What should she do now while her boyfriend enjoys his impromptu night out in Soho? She *won't* call Rob's mobile. Her father has always kept her mum virtually under surveillance and she won't lower herself to that. No, she'll watch TV instead so she'll be nice and calm for when he finally comes home. However drunk he is, Nadine is determined not to have a row, not in front of Rafferty. Her overriding memories of childhood are of her father's loud, bullying voice, and her mother trying to hold her ground, inevitably giving in and tearfully agreeing that he was right. Jens *always* wins an argument.

It's nearly 10 p.m. now and it'll be eleven in Geneva, but Nadine finds herself calling her parents' number, desperately hoping it's her mother who picks up.

'Mummy?' She almost weeps with relief.

'Sweetheart, is everything okay? Is Rafferty all right?'

'Yes . . . we're both fine. I'm sorry to phone so late. You weren't asleep, were you?'

Candida emits a small laugh. 'No, darling. Just pottering about – your father's out for the evening. So, tell me how things have been . . .'

Nadine wonders where to start. 'It was easier when you were here.'

'I know, darling, but I had to get back and didn't want Rob to think I was getting in the way . . .'

'He didn't, not at all. Anyway, we *are* doing okay, I suppose, but . . . it's hard work, isn't it? It never stops.'

'Oh yes,' Candida laughs sympathetically. 'I do remember all that, sweetheart.'

'And Rob's out at some undisclosed location tonight,' Nadine adds before she can stop herself.

'That's very rare, though, isn't it?'

'Well, yes,' Nadine says grudgingly.

'And he is very good with Rafferty. That was lovely to see.'

'Uh-huh.' It's true, he really is, so perhaps it's for the best that he's been through this parenting thing before. Every time she sees him tenderly cradling Rafferty in his arms, or managing to rock him to sleep when she's failed dismally, she reminds herself that it wasn't such a bad thing, to sleep with Rob to make Eddy jealous. In fact she hardly thinks about Eddy at all these days. He's made no contact since she's been on leave – hasn't even sent her a quick text, even though he must have heard how gruelling the birth was. She suspects that the enormous hand-tied bouquet he sent had more to do with Ava than him. Even so, she quickly tore off the accompanying card – which merely said 'Love from Eddy' – and threw it away before Rob could see it. 'They're just from work,' she explained when Rob had asked who'd sent the flowers.

As her mother chats on, reassuring her that she's doing

fine, Nadine's thoughts drift until she's barely listening. Right now, she isn't even sure she wants to go back to work, even when her maternity leave is up. When Ava dropped by last night, she told Nadine that sales have plummeted, and that some of the major advertisers are threatening to pull out because they don't like the new topless element that's snuck into such a 'respectable' magazine.

'Nadine?' Her mother's voice snaps her back to the present.

'Yes, Mummy? Sorry, I was miles away there . . .'

'You sound ever so tired, darling,' Candida remarks. 'Why don't you try and put Rafferty down now and get some sleep yourself?'

'Yes, maybe I'd better, or I might have a bath once the water's heated up. He's actually asleep now.' Oh no. Does this mean he'll be awake in two hours and screaming his little lungs out all night long?

'What did you say?' Candida asks. 'I didn't hear what you—'

'I said . . . I can't do it,' Nadine chokes out.

'Oh, darling, *what* can't you do?'

'This!' she exclaims. 'This . . . this looking after a baby thing. It's so scary, Mummy. I mean, it's forever, isn't it? It's irreversible. No one ever said . . .' Tears start to roll down her cheeks.

'Well, it is,' her mother says gently, 'but it's not always like this. It gets easier and more fun, too. It's just these early months that are the toughest . . .'

'*Months?*' It sounds like a life sentence. 'I look awful as well,' Nadine declares.

'No you don't. You're *lovely*. Just . . . just try to take things one day at a time, sweetheart. Ignore this ridiculous pressure that's heaped upon young mums to be perfect, to be rake-thin and not have stretch marks . . .'

'I've got those,' Nadine mutters, drying her eyes on her sleeve. 'The oils didn't work.'

'So what? You've had a baby and that's a beautiful thing.'

Nadine sniffs, no longer concerned about Rob being out. In fact she's glad, as she can't talk to her mother like this when he's at home.

'I've stopped breastfeeding, Mummy,' she says in a small voice.

'That's fine too. There's no law against bottle-feeding. I bottle-fed you, you know. Did you find it painful, or is it so you and Rob can share night feeds?'

'Er . . .' Nadine wants to say something – to tell her the real reason – but she knows it'll set her off again, and she doesn't want Rob to walk in and find her in floods of tears. 'I just didn't seem to have enough milk,' she murmurs eventually.

'Well, Rafferty is fine and thriving,' Candida says soothingly. 'I loved the pictures you sent me – you're obviously doing a great job. All that really matters is that you love him.'

'I do,' Nadine says, hurriedly finishing the call. It's true – she cannot believe how much she adores this little person who's now waking with stuttery sounds. She loves him more than life itself. Yet, when there's finally enough hot water, she is able to sink into a deep bubble bath while his shrill cries ring through the flat. Rafferty screams and screams, making himself hoarse as he lies on the sheepskin rug on the living room floor. Nadine focuses on the bathroom ceiling light and, instead of rushing through to look after her son, she tops up the tub with more hot water and closes her tired eyes.

Chapter Sixty-Three

Before he sees her, Kerry spots Rob amidst the crowds milling around outside the main entrance to London Zoo. He's with her, Nadine – it *has* to be her. Small, dark-haired and pretty, the baby strapped to her chest in a sling. There's a complicated handover of sling and baby, and Kerry's eyes flood with tears as Nadine kisses the child's head, then Rob's cheek, before hurrying away.

'What's wrong, Mummy?' Mia asks, looking up at her with concern.

'Nothing, sweetheart. I'm fine. Look – there's Daddy . . .'

'Daddy!' come Mia and Freddie's explosive cries as they charge towards him, giving Kerry a moment to arrange her expression into some semblance of normality.

It's the first time the children have met their new baby brother. Nadine has barely allowed him out of her sight, and according to Rob, she felt it would have been 'too much' to have Mia and Freddie in the flat, despite the fact that it sounded as if the place had been buzzing with her friends for the first couple of weeks. Anyway, who would have brought them to Daddy's new home? Perhaps Kerry could have gritted her teeth and done it, ushering them in through the door before rushing off to hide in a cafe somewhere. But, as it was, Rob had suggested they 'wait until things are a bit more settled', and Kerry agreed that it might be easier for Freddie and Mia to meet the baby on neutral territory.

'Mummy, come and see!' Mia yells, craning up for a better view of the baby. Kerry manages to propel herself forward. She is buffeted by an enormous cluster of foil helium balloons as she peers around the sling to get a look at the baby's face.

'He's beautiful,' she whispers truthfully. 'God, he looks like you, Rob.' She swallows hard, her vision blurring again as he clasps his hand around hers and squeezes it.

'Hey,' he says softly. 'This is really weird, isn't it . . .'

'It's fine,' she says quickly, blinking away her tears. 'Oh, he is lovely, though, Rob. He looks like your dad.'

'But Nonno's *old*!' Freddie retorts. 'Rafferty's a baby. Can I have a balloon please, Daddy?'

'Uh . . . not right now,' Rob says quickly. 'Let's get into the zoo and maybe you can have one later, okay?'

Kerry isn't sure whether it's because Rafferty doesn't do much yet, but after the initial flurry of interest, the monkeys are clearly more fascinating to Mia and Freddie than a four-week-old baby.

'So, how's it going so far?' she asks as the children point and laugh at a primate clawing at its rear.

'Okay . . . I think. Nadine's finding it tough. I don't think she had the faintest idea what it would be like.'

'Well, none of us do,' Kerry says coolly.

'Yes, but . . . you seemed more realistic. It didn't seem to shock you to the core like it has with—'

'Please don't compare us, Rob. I really don't need to hear that.'

'Uh . . . okay. Sorry.' She sees him flush and softens a little.

'Anyway, I promise you I *was* pretty shocked, the first

time at least. Maybe I was better at hiding it. So was Nadine okay about you coming out with us today?'

'Yes – delighted actually. She needs some time to herself.' He glances at Kerry. 'And I've been desperate to see you all too,' he adds. 'I've hated not being with the kids this past month, and them having to wait so long to see the baby . . .'

She nods. 'Well, you're both here now. They've missed you too, you know. But I do remember how all-consuming it is at first, so don't give yourself a hard time . . .'

A flicker of amusement crosses his lips.

'What is it?'

'Nothing. It's just, I had a bit of a late one last night . . .'

'You mean you were out at night? You *rebel* . . .'

'Yeah. Didn't make me very popular but it was one of those spontaneous things, the tram enthusiasts' party . . .'

'*What?*' she splutters.

'I know.' He's laughing too. 'I nearly didn't go. Just fancied a quick drink with Simon, but there was this thing going on – a retirement do for one of his team. And I thought, okay, just drop in for half an hour, it'll be a load of old guys sipping real ale and they'll all be ready to throw in the towel by nine thirty . . .'

'So what goes on at a tram enthusiasts' party?'

'Oh, you wouldn't believe. We went on a crawl of the diviest bars you've ever seen – places I didn't even know existed, that I'd have assumed would have been shut down decades ago. We ended up in some sleazy jazz place where someone happened to have a sax for Bill to play . . .'

Kerry raises a brow. 'So what time did you roll in?'

'About midnight, so pretty restrained, though I heard some of them were still at it at six a.m.'

'Rob,' Kerry says cautiously, 'you sound almost . . . jealous. Like you'd quite enjoy being one of the basement boys too.'

He grunts. 'Yeah, well, at least they have a laugh and aren't stuffed with self-importance. And at least . . . Freddie, get down off that fence!' He hurries towards him, stirring Rafferty from his nap as he grabs Freddie's hand, coaxing him back down from his vantage point by the monkey enclosure. Things escalate further when Freddie starts running away at any opportunity, hiding behind ice cream kiosks and leaping out, laughing uproariously.

'God,' Kerry mutters to Rob. 'He's being such a handful today. I think meeting Rafferty has really freaked him out.'

'But he had to sometime . . .'

'Yes, of course.' Thank God for Mia, Kerry reflects, who's clutching her ice cream cone and admiring the pelicans, seemingly unfazed.

They stop for lunch, occupying a picnic table while Rob bottle-feeds Rafferty. The sun has come out – it's a beautiful fresh May afternoon – and the day is panning out better than Kerry could have hoped.

'It's funny,' she says as the children wander over to inspect the owls. 'I'd sort of dreaded today. The thought of it was actually making me feel physically ill.' She smiles ruefully.

'Yeah, me too,' Rob murmurs.

'But . . .' Kerry starts, 'it's almost like old times, isn't it? Apart from this little addition.' She indicates Rafferty who is fully alert now, checking out the world with intense brown eyes.

'Yes, I'm relieved actually, that we can do this. Maybe, when he's a bit older, I'll be able to bring all the kids to places by myself. But for the moment it's good that you're here.'

Kerry studies him, still able to appreciate his striking face which, irritatingly, retains its handsomeness even after the tram enthusiasts' excesses.

'What would Nadine think,' she asks hesitantly, 'if we had the occasional day out together?'

386

He looks at her, then quickly pulls his *yes-I-am-paying-attention* face as Mia points out the snowy owl. 'Daddy look, look! He's *so* cute . . .'

'Yes, darling, I see him.' Then he turns back to Kerry and smiles. 'I don't see how she can object, can you? You are my family after all.'

Chapter Sixty-Four

When Rob arrives home after saying goodbye to Kerry and the children, the flat feels even smaller than when he'd left that morning. Nadine's fairy lights and *objets* look tacky and cheap now the place is strewn with baby blankets and bottles containing the dregs of formula. Rob sets about gathering them up, stuffing grubby babygros into the washing machine and giving the bottles a thorough scrubbing at the sink with the wire brush.

For such a small person, Rafferty seems to occupy an enormous amount of space, and not just due to his vast collection of equipment. It also feels as if they – he and Nadine, that is – are somehow contributing to the general stale airlessness of the flat, due to all the fretful pacing that goes on. In fact, Rob is building up to suggesting a move. The fact that this is Jens's flat makes him extremely uncomfortable, as if Nadine's father might show up unannounced at any moment and barge his way in, demanding to know why Rob isn't MD of the company yet. Plus, once Rafferty is up on his feet and toddling around, he'll really need a garden. It's all very well living in W1 but even in Bethnal Green Mia and Freddie had a backyard.

Rafferty has been snoozing while Rob has cleared up, and now he's wide awake and requiring attention.

'Hey, Raffie-boy,' he murmurs, picking him up from his seat and carrying him to the living room window. 'Did you enjoy the zoo? Will you remember any of that – the baboons scratching their bums and the lion doing a huge poo?' He smiles as his son's eyes seem to bore into him. 'Where d'you think Mummy is anyway?' he muses. 'Maybe she's gone shopping, or to meet someone . . . that's good, isn't it? Give her a break from us for a bit longer . . .'

Perhaps he'll start preparing supper – something he can heat up quickly when Nadine comes home. But when he peers into the fridge, there's nothing there but two bottles of formula, a packet of suspect-looking feta and a solitary egg.

A take-away, then, from the veggie Thai place he knows she approves of. That'll be easy, and they deliver too. Still carrying Rafferty, Rob goes through to the bedroom to fetch his laptop and Google their number. While he perches on the edge of the bed, he notices a sheet of A4 paper on his pillow.

Nadine's handwriting isn't the most legible at the best of times with her over-fondness for superfluous squiggles, but this is even harder to read than usual. He squints, gently placing Rafferty on the bed beside him as he deciphers her words.

Dear Rob,
I hope you all had a lovely day at the zoo. Of course I didn't mind you going – why did you think I would? In fact it suited me because I needed to do something by myself. By the time you read this I'll be on a flight to Zurich.

I'm going to stay with Mummy and Daddy. I can't do it, Rob – can't spend another day in this miserable flat pretending to be a proper mother. It feels so surreal. You're far better at it than I am. You're the only person in the world I'd trust with Rafferty and that's why I'm not coming back.

I'm sorry. I know this will majorly screw things up for you but I'm sure you'll cope. You're the most capable man I've ever met. And I also know that Rafferty is lucky to have such a kind and loving dad.

All my love,
Nadine

Rob doesn't know how long he sits there holding the note. Wondering if it's just a sick joke, he half-expects her to appear at the door, saying, '*Now* d'you see how hard it is for me?' When she doesn't, he tells himself it's just a blip, and she doesn't really mean it – a few days with her parents and she'll be fine. After all, doesn't everyone want to run away sometimes?

When he glances down at Rafferty on the bed, his son has fixed him with an unwavering stare. Rob picks him up, supporting his head and breathing in the sweet, milky scent of his skin. What if she does mean it, and this is *it*? Why the hell hadn't she said something? Perhaps she had, and he hadn't been listening. As Rafferty mews a little in his arms, Rob gets up and walks to the bedroom window, blinking away tears and simultaneously fishing out his phone from his pocket to call her mobile. Voicemail of course.

'Nadine, please call me,' he says, his voice cracking. His son seems unsettled, writhing in Rob's arms until he pulls back the curtain so he can see the cloud-streaked sky.

Rafferty has wisps of soft dark hair, and the warmth of the tiny body against his father's chest seems to fill Rob with a kind of strength. 'We'll be okay,' he murmurs, and as soon as he's said it he knows it's true. Together, they watch dusk settle over the city until streetlights glow silver against the night sky.

Chapter Sixty-Five

'The thing is,' the pert mother says, all bones and angles in Kerry's faded red armchair, 'we think Lucia should skip the early grades and whizz straight to seven or eight.'

'Right,' Kerry says, her mind racing ahead as she tries to formulate a diplomatic response. 'I think you're doing really well, Lucia' – she turns to address the wispy blonde girl who is seated at the piano – 'but sometimes, rushing things can create an awful lot of pressure, and it's better to do the grade that's right for the stage you're at.'

Lucia's mother emits a scathing laugh. 'But she's been playing since she was six! That's *three years*, and her old teacher said . . .' Here we go. The woman witters on, detailing the many ways in which Mrs Ferguson's teaching methods were superior. 'More formal,' she says, 'and structured . . .'

'Well, our lessons are structured too,' Kerry says, sensing a nerve flickering on her eyelid, 'but there's also room for flexibility, so depending on—'

'You see,' the woman barges in rudely, 'we *need* to keep tabs on what sort of progress Lucia is making week to week so we can ensure that she's practising correctly . . .' Kerry allows her to continue, this dreadful woman who seems hell-bent on putting her daughter off music for life, poor thing, sitting there meekly, staring down at her black patent Mary Janes . . .

'Would you like to do grade eight, Lucia?' she asks when her mother finally pauses for breath.

'I don't know,' she mutters, cheeks flaring pink. 'I think it might be a bit too hard for me.'

'Some people don't do formal exams at all,' Kerry adds, trying to keep her annoyance in check as she meets the woman's gaze. 'With some children – and adults too – they can actually be a turn-off. If it's a struggle, it comes through in the playing and I don't think that's how music should be.'

'Oh.' The woman frowns. 'So what *do* you suggest?'

'Um . . . I think we should let Lucia think it over and we can talk about it again next week.'

Kerry can tell, as they leave, that the woman is dissatisfied and, as she gathers together a pile of music from the kitchen table, she hears her sharp voice outside: 'You could go back to Mrs Ferguson, you know. She's out of hospital now. *She'd* put you in for grade eight . . .'

'Mum, I don't want to. I just want to keep coming to Kerry, okay?'

As their voices grow distant, Kerry checks her diary; there's an hour's gap before her next pupil. Rob and the children are at his parents' – he's back to spending weekends there, much to Mary and Eugene's delight – and Buddy needs a walk. Slipping her phone into her pocket, she clips on his lead and allows him to pull her forcibly to the front door.

She could call Brigid to see if she'd like to meet for a walk, but decides she'd rather be by herself today. Using the ball thrower, she strides along to the furthest beach – the dog-friendly one – sending Buddy's tennis ball flying in a huge arc. He leaps delightedly, catching it in his mouth as it falls. Keeping a close eye on the time, she throws it into the shallow waves. It's so pleasing – life-affirming really – to watch a dog running just for the fun of it. Kerry's favourite pupils are like that – the ones who play because they want to, because they love it, and not because they're forced to, or solely in preparation for an exam.

In the distance, a jogger is heading towards her, his face a violent shade of puce, and feet slapping wet imprints in the sand. When he draws closer she realises it's Ethan. Spotting her, he tugs his headphones out of his ears and grins. 'Hey, Kerry!'

'Hi. Didn't know you were a runner, Ethan.'

'Just these past few months,' he says, catching his breath and rubbing his shiny forehead against his T-shirt sleeve. 'Started as a New Year's resolution, and when I took over from Harvey – in the entertainment business, I mean – I realised I'd need to shape up if I was going to be able to cope with the little sods.'

She laughs. 'So is it going well in the, er . . . entertainment business?'

'God, yeah. Got double the bookings Harvey used to have. Focus, you see.' He taps the side of his head. 'He wasn't committed enough.'

'Right . . . so how is he?' she asks lightly. 'Still touring with the play?'

'Yeah, hardly see him these days. Suits me, to be honest. All that nagging about my personal foibles.' He rolls his eyes dramatically. 'Like living with your bloody mother.'

'I can imagine,' she says, breaking off to call Buddy when she spots the approaching spectre of the woman in the pink coat. He zips back towards Kerry, spraying both of them as he shakes off the sea water.

'And when he does have a break,' Ethan continues, 'he's always jetting off somewhere with Luella . . .'

'Oh, really?' She offers Buddy a biscuit from her pocket.

'Yeah.' He grins. 'She's loaded, you know. Got a place

393

in the south of France so they're often down that way, living the bloody life of Riley . . .'

'That's . . . that's great,' she enthuses. 'I'm really glad, and I've read some brilliant reviews of the production. Maybe I'll get tickets and take Mia and Freddie at some point.'

'Erm, you don't fancy a drink sometime, do you?' he cuts in.

She smiles. 'Um . . . thanks, Ethan, but I've kind of got a lot on right now.'

He nods and plugs his headphones back in. 'Ah well. Maybe some other time when things are a bit quieter, eh?' Before she can reply, he's dashed off at an impressive pace, dodging pink coat lady's terrier who tries to snap at his ankles as he hurtles past.

Chapter Sixty-Six

Whatever life throws at him, Rob likes to think he can somehow muster a smidgeon of optimism. Look at the fiasco at *Mr Jones*. Despite Eddy the Wrecker's disastrous editorial decisions, Rob has managed to keep his head, reassuring himself that something else will turn up and he'll be out of there by autumn. However, the Nadine situation is somewhat trickier. She's been gone a month now, and their phone conversations have been tense to say the least.

'So you can walk away from your son, just like that?' he'd snapped last time.

'There's no *just like that*,' she'd shot back. 'It's the hardest thing I've ever had to do, Rob.' He'd finished the call then, unable to continue a conversation with her. How could she walk out on them the minute motherhood became a little boring for her? Yet he knows, even as he formulates these thoughts, that something else had been happening – something he should have picked up on. Could he have been more hands-on? Would she still be here if he hadn't tagged along on that tram enthusiasts' night out? Ridiculous, he knows, but Rob is completely baffled. Her terse emails haven't helped to make things clearer, and now she has stopped replying to his texts and messages. Rob kept firing off the odd email about how worried he is, and how Eddy has been pretty decent about him working from home until he can find a suitable childminder. Then Candida called him, explaining ever-so-nicely in her tinkly voice that it might be easier for Nadine if he stopped contacting her now. 'She's just in a very delicate place,' she said apologetically. Even so, Rob is confident that Nadine will want to hear about Rafferty at some point, and maybe even come over to see him. He can't believe that anyone would wish to be parted from their child through choice.

And now, driving at a steady sixty as he indicates to take the Shorling turn-off, Rob decides that things could work out with Kerry too. Not immediately, perhaps, after all that's happened – but in a few months, if he is careful to say and do the right things. Rob is forming a plan and almost dares to believe it'll work. He just has to convince Kerry that it's the best thing for all of them.

First, though, he must eat. Kerry turned down his offer of going out for lunch – she has a piece for this nature series to finish, can't afford the time – and he doesn't want to risk getting off on the wrong foot by raiding her fridge. He's starving, though, having come via his parents' to drop off Rafferty. All he wants is a sandwich, so he parks in a side street and strides into the first place he sees, a little cafe called Luke's. There's a tall, amiable-looking man behind the counter, chatting to an attractive woman with swathes of highlighted hair and the requisite Shorling glow. She's reminding him about a big lunch order tomorrow.

'I've told you, Amy – it's all under control,' he assures her good-naturedly. 'God knows how this place survived before you rolled up to knock it into shape.' He turns to Rob and grins. 'What would you like?'

'Um . . .' Rob's spirits sink a little. There doesn't seem to be a sandwich on the blackboard that doesn't involve seared aubergines or melting Brie or liberal sprinklings of pine kernels. He doesn't want a great slab of a thing with oily fillings that'll fall out and stain the new pale blue shirt he's bought specially. 'Actually,' he says, already turning away, 'I'm just after a plain cheese sandwich.'

'We can do that,' the woman says brightly. 'Would you like a baguette, sourdough or . . . James, do we have any plain white sliced?'

'Uh, yep,' the man says.

'White sliced please,' Rob says, almost apologetically.

The man makes it quickly and hands it to him in a brown paper bag. *How sweet*, Rob thinks, glimpsing the woman planting a quick kiss on the man's cheek as he turns to leave the shop. It's obviously the couple's place. He glances back again and sees them giggling about something together. With the shop to themselves now, the man gathers her into his arms for a hug. Rob's mind starts to whir as he imagines he and Kerry being together during the day – him writing, her composing a score, meeting up in the kitchen every so often, or even sneaking illicitly to bed . . .

He devours his sandwich on a bench overlooking the beach, feeling entirely guiltless about skiving off work today. Why the hell should he? The early afternoon sun is warming his face and, as he watches a father and toddler kicking a beach ball on the sand, he wonders why he had such cold feet about moving here. What's not to like, really? Anyway, Kerry and the children are here, which means he needs to be here too. Rob still loves her desperately – even Nadine knew that – and he'll do everything within his power to put things right.

Chapter Sixty-Seven

'So you want to move down here with Rafferty?' Kerry needs to be certain she's got this absolutely right, and hasn't misunderstood Rob's announcement.

'Yes, I really do.' He rubs his tired-looking eyes. 'God, Kerry. I was such an arse when you wanted to move here. I know I went along with it, but then I got this terrible fear that I'd be missing out and feel as if I'd *retired* or something . . .'

'*I* haven't retired,' she says sharply, brushing a strand of hair from her face.

'I know! You're teaching and composing and keeping everything afloat and I want to be here, Kerry. I want to be a proper dad again. You can't imagine how much I miss Freddie and Mia . . .'

She observes him across her kitchen table, feeling oddly detached. 'Maybe you've forgotten it wasn't just about you developing a sudden allergy to the coast, Rob. You know, there was also that little thing about you having a child with someone else.'

His cheeks flame red. 'And now it's just me and Rafferty.'

'Yes, for the moment—'

'It's finished,' he says firmly. 'To be honest, it should never have started . . .'

She makes a snorting noise. 'And you're planning to resign from work?'

'Not resign – they want voluntary redundancies because sales are so poor. I'm sure I could sort it, I've never fitted in there anyway since Eddy arrived. It'd be, God, I don't know – how long have I been there? Ten, eleven years? I'll get a fortune, we could use it to extend the house, build a proper music studio where you can teach and write instead of being crammed in that dingy little room . . .'

'But I *like* my room, Rob.' She studies the man she once loved so much.

'Your life would be a lot easier,' he adds, 'if I was here.'

Kerry frowns, glancing out at the clear blue sky. 'You don't like dogs though, Rob. You'd have to wear some kind of metal codpiece to keep him from savaging your private parts.' She is only half-joking.

'Don't be silly. Jesus, a dog can't dictate how we live our lives. I could get into it actually, all the walking, getting fit after ten years spent hunched at a screen . . .'

She exhales, looking around the kitchen for Buddy, and wondering if she's wrong to dismiss Rob's proposal: that he moves here, renting a flat for the time being so as not to pressurise her, because he's not so presumptuous as to assume he can just waltz right back into her life . . .

'Buddy?' Kerry calls out, as a way of buying herself a few moments. She must think this over carefully because it's not just about her. Rob is Mia and Freddie's father, and what child wouldn't prefer them to all be together, like the smiling family all sitting around a cafe table in *The Tiger Who Came to Tea*?

Kerry is up on her feet, scanning the kitchen in case Buddy has discovered a new place to nap. 'Buddy!' she shouts again, a little unsettled now. He is never far away from her. Rob looks mildly irritated – he's come all this way, and now she's more concerned about the whereabouts of her dog – but it doesn't feel right, Buddy not coming when she calls. Perhaps he's lying down somewhere, feeling unwell, or someone's inadvertently shut him in the bathroom . . .

Buddy isn't in the living room, bathroom or any of the bedrooms, and when Kerry comes back downstairs she realises the porch door is open. Maybe he's in there, having a sneaky pee. For some reason, as far as Buddy's concerned, the tiny porch doesn't count as indoors, and several puddles have been deposited there. But when she goes to check, the front door is open too – Rob mustn't have clicked it shut properly.

'He's got out, Rob!' she cries, darting out to the front garden, then the street, where there are lots of ambling day-trippers but no scruffy black and white dog, as far as she can see.

'God. How did that happen?' Rob is at her side now, looking up and down the street.

'The door wasn't closed . . . *Buddy!*' she yells, even though she knows there's no point.

'I'm sure I shut it . . .'

'It doesn't matter – I'm not blaming you. I just need to find him. He has no road sense, he could be run over. God, he could be under a car right now . . .' Her heart is hammering against her ribs.

'Where does he usually go?' Rob asks.

'The beach, of course – this one and the far one too, the park occasionally and the golf course but only if the weather's bad and there are no golfers . . .'

Rob rubs his chin. 'Won't he just come back?'

'He's a dog, Rob, not a bloody pigeon. Come on – I'll lock the house, you check the beach and I'll head into town and search the park – make sure you've got your mobile . . .'

'What, um . . . you mean *now*?'

She glares at him. Has he no concept of what this means? '*Yes*, now.'

'And if I find him . . .'

She darts back inside, handing him the posh Christmas lead and stuffing Buddy's old frayed one into her pocket.

'Just bring him home.' She locks the door, already striding away. 'We've got an hour and a half before I need to pick up the kids from school,' she calls back. 'We'd better have found him by then.'

*

By 3 p.m., there's still no sign of Buddy. Kerry has scoured Thorny Park, giving every passerby a description of her dog, and marched up and down the steep slope where the children sledged last winter. She has also called Rob, instructing him to hurry home for the kids' swimming bags, letting himself in with the spare key she keeps hidden under a large speckled pebble. He must then pick up the children from school and take them straight to the pool for their lesson.

They'll blame her, of course, for letting Buddy escape. Not marvellous Daddy. Fathers can do no wrong, she thinks bleakly. While Kerry dutifully prepares their favourite meals, sneaking vegetables in her bologneses and chillis, Rob can fling them an omelette and be heralded as a culinary genius. 'This is *lovely*, Daddy,' Mia used to exclaim, on the rare occasions that Rob would fix a weekend lunch. 'Why don't you cook all the time?'

An hour later, Kerry parks herself on a bench and pulls out her mobile to call Rob again. 'You haven't told them what's happened, have you?' she asks.

'No, of course not. They're in the pool now. They have no idea . . .'

'Because they'll be in bits. Please, Rob – they mustn't know what's happened . . .'

'Kerry . . . we could get them another dog. I'd buy it for them . . .'

'What are you talking about?' she exclaims.

'I just thought, so they wouldn't be so upset . . .'

'You think we could replace Buddy and they'd never know?'

He emits an exasperated snort. 'No, of course not. I don't mean an *exact replica*. But . . . well, maybe they could choose one that's, y'know . . . easier to train. Less erratic . . .'

She takes a moment to process this. 'I don't think so, Rob. Just take care of the kids, okay? Bring them home, make them pasta or something. And tell them I've, um . . . gone for a long walk.'

Leaving the park now, Kerry considers going home to get the car and driving around town in the hope of covering more ground that way. But then, she won't be able to stop and ask people along the way. Instead, she makes her way back to the seafront which is milling with kids and their parents around a collection of stalls. 'Kerry!' comes a shrill female voice. She scans the women in their summery dresses – it's a sea of pink, lemon and mint – and sees Lara striding towards her, glossy bob swinging around her chin.

'We thought Mia and Freddie might like to join in with the tug of war,' she says with a bright smile. 'It's starting in five minutes.'

'Oh, they're not with me today. They're having their swimming lesson, then their dad's taking them back to the house . . .' She keeps scanning the area for a flash of black and white fur among the crowds. 'Buddy's lost,' she adds. 'I've been searching for hours. Didn't even know this was on today . . .'

'Oh, it's on all week – different events every day. A fundraising thing for the Beach Buddies. I think there's a dog show starting soon . . .' Lara's face softens with concern as she touches Kerry's arm. 'Listen, Emily and some of the other mums are here. I'll put the word round about Buddy, maybe they could announce something on the tannoy . . .'

'No, don't do that—'

'Could he have been picked up by the police, d'you think?'

Kerry rubs her tired eyes. 'I'm starting to wonder. Think I'll give it another half hour and then I'll have to head home. God, I'm *dreading* telling the children . . .' Without warning, her eyes flood with tears.

'Oh, don't cry . . .' Lara's pale blue eyes widen with concern. 'We'll find him, Kerry, don't worry . . .'

'Why didn't I have him microchipped?' she blurts out. 'I kept meaning to do it. I feel so stupid, so bloody incompetent I can't even keep a dog safe . . .'

'That's the *last* thing you are,' Lara exclaims, delving into her lime suede handbag for a packet of tissues. Kerry takes them gratefully and mops up her tears and snot. 'God, Kerry. You're not stupid. You're amazing, the way you hold everything together all by yourself. Everyone thinks so. Come here, you poor thing . . .' She allows herself to be hugged, and as she pulls away, she realises she's left a teary splodge on Lara's marshmallow-pink cotton dress.

'Look what I've done,' she wails.

'Are you crazy? I don't care about that. Here, give me your mobile number and I'll make sure everyone starts looking . . .'

Kerry mutters her number, marvelling at Lara's status in town, and the possibility that she might have the power to rustle up an immediate search party. 'What about the tug of war?' she asks.

'There are plenty of people there to keep an eye on the children. Go on – off you pop, keep looking, and I'll give you a call if we find him.'

'Okay – and thanks, Lara.' She blinks at the damp patch on her dress. 'I'll head up to the golf course – we often go for walks up there.'

'Good idea, darling. And don't worry – it'll all turn out okay . . .'

Oh for the confidence of the Shorling wife, Kerry reflects,

who even has pretty tissues (Lara's were turquoise and patterned with daisies, she couldn't help but notice). On the golf course now, she scans the vast sweep of lush green, asking every golfer she sees if they've noticed a runaway hound, and receiving apologetic shakes of the head in response. Having searched for Luke's sandwich shop on her phone, she calls the number. A woman picks up. 'Um . . . sorry to bother you,' she starts, still scanning the area for a flash of Buddy, perhaps having spotted a golf ball in motion and claimed it as his own. 'I'm a friend of James's and, um . . . Buddy's gone missing. I just wondered if he might have seen him—'

'Oh, he used to be mine,' the woman says when she pauses for breath.

'Who?' Kerry barks.

'Buddy. I'm Amy, James's wife . . .'

'I see . . .'

There's a stilted pause. 'Look, I'm just finishing up here. James has just gone home, I'll be seeing him later . . . we'll keep a look-out.'

'Thank you . . . and I'm sorry. I feel so bad.'

'Don't,' Amy says kindly. 'James told me he'd turned into a bit of a handful . . . I'm sure it wasn't your fault.'

Kerry finishes the call, wondering whether it had been easy for Amy to slot back into James's life. Could she and Rob do that? Is there a remote possibility that they could, in his words, 'try again'?

'Hello, Ethan?' She scans the thickly wooded area with her phone jammed at her ear. 'Listen, Buddy's run away. I'm at the far end of the golf course, by the woods. Just wondered, seeing as I'm so near to your place . . .'

'Of course I'll help. Give me five minutes and I'll be there.'

As the minutes stretch, she pictures Mia and Freddie starting to worry now, figuring that it's strange, both their mother and Buddy being out for so long. 'Oh – you're back,' she says, breaking into a smile as Harvey, appealingly unshaven and in a scruffy black sweater and jeans, appears with Ethan.

'Yes, I was going to call you . . .'

'Well, I'm glad you're here but, I don't know – it feels as if I've looked *everywhere* . . .' They spend the next half hour searching, with Ethan combing the perimeter of the course and she and Harvey checking the woods. She finds herself telling him about Rob's proposal, and how, after his little adventure, he's decided he wants to come back.

'What are you going to do?' Harvey asks. 'Could you trust him, do you think?'

She shakes her head. 'God knows.'

'He's devoted to you, though, isn't he?'

Kerry snorts, her heart lurching as a black and white dog comes into view, then plummeting again as she realises it's a spaniel on a lead. 'The fact that he slept with someone else would suggest he's not.'

Harvey puts an arm around her shoulders. 'Hey, listen – talking of devotion, dogs tend to bond with one person in particular – and that's you. So maybe, when he's had his little adventure, he'll decide that's enough fun for one day and come back, a bit sheepish and a bit embarrassed for all the hassle he's caused . . .'

'You think he'll just turn up at home?' Her mobile rings, and she whips it out of her pocket. 'Lara? Any news?' She pauses, emitting a great 'Oh!' of relief. 'I'll be there in five minutes. Yes, please grab him if you can . . .' She turns to Harvey and grins. 'Seems like Buddy's gate-crashed the dog show. We'll probably be drummed out of town after this.'

*

While Buddy had so far resisted capture, when he sees Kerry approaching, with Harvey at her side, he runs full-pelt towards her.

405

'You've had us worried sick,' she exclaims, grabbing his collar and clipping on his lead.

'If you'd wanted to enter him for the show,' a prim woman says, her frosted peach lips set in a terse line, 'you should have been here at four o'clock for registration.'

'No, I don't think it's his sort of thing . . .' Kerry glances around at the assembled crowd – a vision of immaculate grooming and high pedigree, dogs and owners alike. Although the woman with the black cushion dog is clearly trying not to laugh, she's forced to stop a splutter of mirth with her hand. Brigid appears, creasing up hysterically, and blushing only slightly as she registers Harvey's presence. A demure-looking Roxy and a giggling Joe are at her side.

'Well, he's kept us entertained,' Brigid says, giving Kerry a hug. 'We did everything we could to catch him but he thought it was a game, kept scampering off and tearing around in circles while the other dogs were being judged. I've left my phone at home, so thank God Lara had your number . . .'

'He ran off with a rosette,' Joe announces gleefully, 'and then he spat it out.'

'Did he?' Kerry turns to Harvey and cringes. 'What am I going to do with him?'

'Um . . . training?' he suggests, raising a brow.

'Don't do *anything* with him,' Brigid retorts, frowning at Harvey. 'At least he livened things up. This dog show's the same every year – isn't it dull, Lara? Same old primped pooches trotting round the enclosure for what feels like hours on end . . .'

Both mother and daughter murmur in agreement, and Audrey-Jane is still giggling as she takes a bite of her ice lolly.

'Oh, absolutely,' Lara declares, her face breaking into a grin as she turns back to Kerry. 'You and Buddy are like a breath of fresh air around here.'

Chapter Sixty-Eight

BlinkMedia Towers obviously wasn't designed with buggies in mind. As Rob didn't fancy trying to negotiate the revolving doors, he's had to buzz the normal door which you used to be able to walk straight through as easily as if it were Marks & Spencer's. Why the high security all of a sudden? He's already waited five minutes for the haughty-looking blonde on main reception to let him in. Maybe management are scared that rival companies will send people in to infiltrate *Mr Jones* and steal Eddy's fantastic ideas, haha. The last issue bombed, Simon told him gleefully. And now, due to the magazine's rapidly increasing boob count, it's been repositioned on newsstands away from the high-end glossies and among the soft porn. Yet as a sales strategy that's failing too. As it's not rude enough to satisfy the top-shelf lurkers, *Mr Jones* has found itself caught between a rock and a hard place, so to speak.

If only Eddy had listened when Rob pitched that idea of the History of the Brogue for the Style Tip of the Month page.

The blonde girl finally finishes sipping her latte and sashays over to grant him access to the hallowed towers. He half expects her to soften when she realises he has a baby with him. Astoundingly, though, she fails to acknowledge Rafferty in his buggy, despite the fact that, to Rob's mind, he looks especially cute today in his little Paul Smith Junior all-in-one.

'Sign in?' The girl picks up a clipboard from the reception desk.

'Er, no, I work here.' Rob laughs stiffly, awaiting an apology.

'Which magazine?'

'*Mr Jones*. Been on leave, looking after this little man . . .' He casts Rafferty a fond glance, expecting her to register him now. But no, she wrinkles her nose as if he has brought in a buggy of rotting vegetables.

'What's your name?'

'Roberto Tambini,' he says flatly.

She flicks through a great wodge of stapled A4 until she finds the *Mr Jones* sheet. 'Your name's not on it.'

'But I've worked here ten years!' His outburst makes Rafferty flinch in alarm.

'Well, sorry.' She shrugs. 'You'll have to sign in as a visitor and wear this.' And so he is finally granted access to the lift. The greasy-haired boy who's already in there presses himself against the metallic back wall, as if fatherhood might be contagious.

Rob exits at the third floor, already sweating as he manoeuvres out Rafferty's buggy, pushing open the *Mr Jones* offices' swing doors with his backside and blundering up to Ava's desk.

'Oh, he's gorgeous,' she shrieks, bounding out of her seat and terrifying the baby with her burgundy grin.

'Does he always make that racket?' sniggers Phil, who's swiftly joined by Frank and Eddy, all of them looming over the buggy while Rafferty howls.

'Look – haha!' Eddy jabs a porky finger at Rob's huge laminated visitor's badge.

'Yes, well, it seems to have gone a bit high security around here. That girl didn't even have my name on the list.' Rob picks up a writhing Rafferty and holds him to his chest.

Eddy smirks. 'Oh, Cassie's not the brightest bulb. Decorative, though. Anyway, you said you wanted a chat. What'll you do with Junior here? He stinks a bit, by the way . . .'

'He should be fine, I just checked his nappy in the loos in Starbucks . . .'

'Must be you then, mate,' he guffaws.

Rob hesitates, cradling Rafferty and registering that his shirt is already daubed with a small splodge of milky vomit. Figuring that, as a woman, Ava will welcome the opportunity to cuddle a freaked-out infant while Daddy talks business, he makes a move to hand him to her – but she shrinks away and hurries back to her desk.

'Nadine okay?' she mouths with a pained expression.

Rob shrugs, about to explain that he has no idea how she is, when Ava snatches her phone and makes a call. In fact, apart from Eddy, everyone else has scurried back to their own corners of the office, like mice scattering when a light is switched on.

'I'll just bring him with me,' Rob says. 'He'll be okay in a minute.'

'Oh, er, all right.' Eddy flares his nostrils and heads for his little glass cube.

Rafferty does, thankfully, quieten down. In fact, Rob decides that it's better that he's here; his presence will ensure that the whole business is wrapped up as quickly as possible. 'I'd like to put my name down for voluntary redundancy,' he begins.

Eddy frowns at him across an eerily empty desk. 'No, you can't do that.'

'Listen, I know I'm springing it on you, and you've been great since Nadine, um . . .'

'Sorry, your timing's not good.' He shakes his head firmly.

Rob repositions Rafferty so he can peer over his shoulder and watch Frank adding a saucy caption to the centrefold girl. 'Well . . . I'll work notice of course. It's just too difficult to keep everything going and I've decided it'll be better for us – for my whole family, really – if I move down to Shorling and go freelance.'

Eddy blinks slowly. His eyelashes really are transparent, Rob observes, like tiny fishbones. 'No, you see, the cut-off date for redundancy applications was a week ago.'

'Oh,' he says hollowly.

'Which is a bugger, mate, seeing as you've been here since the year dot. Would've been a fortune.'

'Mmm.' Rob inhales, detecting the sour odour coming from his shoulder. 'Can't I just apply late? Surely, with having the baby and Nadine freaking out and going back to her mum and dad's, the HR people would bend the rules a bit . . .'

Eddy shakes his head. 'Not a chance, Robster.'

'You . . . you do *know* about Nadine, don't you?'

'Yeah, mate. Bad news.' He nods and stifles a yawn, unaware that, if he weren't holding a baby, Rob would happily knock him flat.

Instead, he glances round at the office in which a decade of his life has drained away. Years and years spent at his keyboard, clattering with such speed and intensity that he frequently left with a flickering eyelid.

'I'll resign then,' he says.

'You are joking,' Eddy guffaws. 'You're needed here. You just need to find a decent nanny or childminder or whatever they have these days and get back to the coalface.'

'The *coalface*?' Rob repeats mockingly.

'Yeah, back in the heart of things. You've been stuck in that flat too long, that's the problem. Don't know how mothers stand it. No wonder Nadine lost the plot.'

Rafferty is wriggling now, tired of his view of Frank's

screen. Delving into the vast quilted bag at his feet, Rob pulls out a bottle of milk. 'I'm not coming back to the coalface, Eddy. I don't want to work here anymore.'

'But what'll you do?'

Rob shrugs. 'I told you. Go freelance.'

'Yeah, but times are tough. There no work out there, you know. You think you'll have this great career, jobs pouring in, but your only commission will be writing the instructions on the back of a bottle of Toilet Duck.'

Sounds appealing, Rob reflects, compared to being here. 'Maybe I will,' he says steadily, 'but I've been talking to Simon about heading up the digital edition of *Tram Enthusiast*, which I could do from home.'

Eddy roars with laughter. 'What d'you know about trams, Robster? Jesus . . .'

'D'you mind not calling me Robster, Eddy?' Rob glowers at him. 'Actually, you're right – I know nothing about trams. Not a damn thing. But if I can manage to write a column as a woman, then I'm sure I'm capable of getting my head around them.' He blinks at Eddy's stunned face. 'They're interesting actually – and eco-friendly. In fact, I think trams are the future.'

He is standing up now, holding Rafferty close to his chest, rubbing his back to wind him under Eddy's baffled stare. 'You *will* still write Miss Jones, though, won't you? You've got a big following now, and at least it'd be regular freelance work, keep the wolf from the door . . .'

'Thanks for the offer, but no.'

'But we'll be stuck—'

'Maybe *you* could do it then?' With a quick, terse smile, he leaves Eddy's office and gently places Rafferty in his buggy. Without saying goodbye, Rob marches towards the door.

'I'll need this formally in writing,' Eddy snaps after him.

'You'll get it.' He steps out of the office and calls the lift.

When it arrives, one of the finance girls is already in it, and she beams admiringly at Rafferty.

'How are you getting on, Rob?' she asks. 'Haven't seen you around for a while.'

'Oh, fine. Really great actually.' He smiles, sensing the little knots of tension in his back and shoulders beginning to untwist themselves already.

'You look it. You look *really* well. I thought new dads were meant to be completely wrung-out and exhausted.' She chuckles kindly.

He laughs bashfully, embarrassed that he can't remember her name. 'Huh. Thanks.'

When the lift arrives at the ground floor, she waits to let Rob and Rafferty out first.

'Well, good to see you,' says the pretty, sunny-faced girl. 'Your little boy's a darling. He's the absolute image of you.'

Chapter Sixty-Nine

Kerry is taken aback by the amount of practice Harvey has done these past few months.

'I'm impressed,' she says. 'Most people let it slip when they stop coming for lessons. You've come on a lot. What did you do – drag that old Casio keyboard around with you from hotel to hotel?'

'No, but I did buy a roll-out one,' he explains. 'I hadn't even known they existed until I started searching around. So I shoved it in my case and whenever I had a spare hour, out it'd come, and I'd go through my scales and pieces and stuff.'

'So what did Luella think of that?' she asks, keeping her tone light.

Harvey frowns at her. 'Luella? She didn't think anything . . . why should she?'

Kerry flushes, getting up from her stool beside the piano to find another piece for Harvey to play. She bobs down again, feeling suddenly hotly self-conscious. 'I just thought you two were an item,' she says with a shrug.

Harvey snorts. 'Yeah, for about five minutes at the start of the run.' He shakes his head and pushes back his dark wavy hair. 'How did you know about that? I didn't think you read the grubby tabloids . . .'

'Well, I just happened to have a quick glance, and then Ethan said . . .'

Harvey looks bemused now. '*What* did Ethan say?'

'That when you're not working you're off to Luella's place in the south of France, and how much he's enjoying having your flat all to himself.' She laughs, relaxing a little. 'He said sharing with you is like living with his mother, actually.'

'Cheeky sod. And a liar too. He knows I got out of the Luella thing as soon as I realised what I was dealing with. God, Kerry – he's pathetic. He was just trying to screw things up for me . . .'

'Really?' she frowns.

'Yes, really. I know what he's like.' Harvey's eyes meet hers, and she feels a fluttering in her stomach. Screw things up for Harvey *in what way*? With her, does he mean? They are sitting on stools, his at the piano, hers angled at the side. Her music room feels very still and quiet but she knows that, in twenty minutes' time, the children will burst in, having been looked after by Lara while she was teaching.

'So what happened with Luella?' she asks tentatively.

He smiles. 'Couldn't cope with the high-maintenance princess behaviour. I didn't care how often she had her hair done, as long as I wasn't expected to *up my standards*, as she put it. And you know me, I'm about as low-maintenance as you'll get.'

'Er . . .' She laughs softly. 'I don't really know you, Harvey. Not really.'

There's a pause. She studies his handsome face, the clear blue eyes and the lovely, kissable mouth. She could do it – there is no one else here. It would be terribly unprofessional of her but nobody would know . . .

'Kerry?' His smile makes her stomach flip.

'Yes?'

'I hope it wouldn't be horribly compromising for you – as my teacher, I mean – if I . . .'

She looks at him, and his eyes meet hers. Then, with her heart in her mouth, she leans towards him, her lips meeting his in a kiss. 'I've really missed you, Harvey,' she says softly.

'I've missed you too.' Pulling back to study her face, he wraps his arms around her. 'You're so lovely. I've always thought so, you know. I don't think anyone ever looked forward to piano lessons as much as I did.'

'Really?' She laughs.

'Yes, really.'

She kisses him again, her head swimming and her entire body tingling. It feels like mere moments before there's a rap on the front door, and Lara's sing-song voice calls out, 'Kerry? It's just us. We're back. Carry on if you're still teaching, we can hang out and watch TV . . .'

'No, it's okay, I'm finished . . .' She and Harvey appear in the kitchen where Mia, Freddie and Audrey-Jane are all whispering and sniggering.

'Good lesson?' Lara asks, beaming at Harvey.

'Um . . . it was interesting, yes,' he says with an entirely straight face. 'I learnt a lot today.'

'Bet you did,' Lara says briskly. 'She's the best piano teacher in Shorling – everyone says so. In fact, Kerry, I meant to mention it – Audrey-Jane is keen to start lessons as soon as you have a space for her . . .'

'I'm sure I can fit her in,' Kerry replies, suppressing a grin as the three children huddle together again and dissolve into high-pitched giggles. 'What's so funny?' she asks, bemused.

Lara rolls her eyes. 'I'm *so* sorry, Kerry. You're going to hate me for this . . .'

Kerry gives her a quizzical look as Mia turns to her and says, 'Audrey-Jane's got a new kitten. She's so cute, Mummy. *Please* can we have a cat?'

Chapter Seventy

Three months later

Villa Serra, Costa de la Luz, September 2

Dear Kerry, Mia and Freddie,
Just wanted to put pen to paper and say what a
wonderful surprise it was when you arrived last week.
I can't quite believe Barbara had managed to keep it
secret that you were planning to come – I shouldn't
say this about my oldest friend, but you know what a
terrible gossip she is! Knows everyone's business, even
out here. Anyway, Kerry, it makes me so happy that
you've settled so well into the house and Shorling too.
You made me laugh when you told me how the chil-
dren have become Shorling-ified – mad on seafood
now! Didn't they love that sushi place we went to? It's
a favourite of ours and great to see the children
enjoying it so much. As you said, Freddie doesn't even
refer to wasabi sauce as snot anymore. He's quite the
sophisticated young man, and Mia is both beautiful
and a delight.
*   But more than that, what pleased me the most was*
seeing you so happy, Kerry, with such a wonderful man.
I must admit, both Barbara and I are now a little in

*love with Harvey too. He's delightful – fun and inter-
esting with a real zest for life. He is wonderful with
Mia and Freddie and I can see how much he loves you.
I'm glad things are working out for Rob and his baby,
too, and it's obvious that Mia and Freddie like their
daddy living close by. I'm sure you've had dark
moments, but you've handled it all amazingly well.*

*I know Harvey is teaching at the moment, but I do
hope the film comes off – it sounds as if it's 'in the
bag' as they say, but of course he wouldn't admit that.
Anyway, whatever happens, when you do have some
time, please come out to stay with us again very soon.
Seeing you always fills me with pleasure because, as
you know, you're the daughter I never had.*

With all my love,
Aunt Maisie

Children and Dogs . . .

. . . Are they really that different?

Once upon a time, before I had a dog of my own, it would drive me crazy when people likened pet ownership to the care and nurturing of a young human being. When a (child-free) colleague came to visit soon after our twin sons were born, she exclaimed, 'Oh, you two look shattered! Been up all night, have you? It was the same for us when we first got Caspar.' I'm sorry, and I know there's the pooping and chewing of soft furnishings and all that – but acquiring a Labrador puppy is *mildly* less daunting than raising a child.

However, since our collie-cross Jack joined our family, I've discovered that, actually, dogs and small children have more in common than I'd realised . . .

1. **The ability to embarrass you in public.** My dog has leapt in through open supermarket doors and careered around the aisles – not unlike my children when they were younger. Fortunately, though, a dog will not throw a tantrum and scream for chocolate.

2. **A tendency to leap at visitors as they arrive, slobbering all over their faces and muddying their clothes.** Some friends find small children scary and overwhelming;

others are wary of dogs. The people who come back to your house more than once will tend to be the ones who enjoy the company of both.

3. **No decorum whatsoever.** Pawing guests, jumping onto laps and leaving powerful smells in their wake – it's all in a day's work for a child and his canine companion.

4. **Boundless energy.** Young children, like dogs, need to be exercised regularly. During my first ten years of parenthood, we probably had around three days when we didn't leave the house – and on each of those, I'd vow to myself, 'Never again.' Keeping small children cooped up indoors generally results in mess, chaos and bad moods all around. A good run-about does wonders for most small creatures – however, a dog is more likely to come back when called.

5. **A knack of being able to fall asleep anywhere.** On – or in – your bed being a particular favourite, especially when you've just changed the sheets. No matter how cosy his own bed/basket may be, your sleeping quarters will always be more alluring.

6. **An urge to snatch whatever is on your plate.** It's always so much more enticing than theirs.

7. **A love of cuddling up on your lap.** My three children – all teenagers now – don't tend to do that anymore, and I miss that physical contact sometimes. Perhaps that's what drove me to acquire a hug-loving hound (who will lie sprawled across my lap for *hours*).

8. **An ability to bring in incredible amounts of dirt, mess and even live creatures into your house.** However, only a child will expect you to show great interest in his find.

9. **A dishevelled appearance** (unless you're the kind of parent/dog owner who invests more energy into maintaining standards than I could ever muster). I have yet to meet a small child who enjoys having his hair washed – or a dog who relishes being sluiced down in the bath. Detangling and grooming can also prove challenging for both species.

10. **They're both, well . . .** *fun*. Both dogs and children give us permission to be kids ourselves again. Without one or the other, would you ever find yourself playing games in a park, running just for the hell of it or leaping around your garden with an assortment of balls and squeaky toys? Would you venture out in the rain, hail or blizzard? Or shove on your wellies and splosh across a flooded field? However tired or stressed we are, dogs and children still manage to make us laugh. Perhaps that ex-colleague with Caspar the puppy had a point after all.

My Inspirations for Pedigree Mum

Whenever I do readings or author events, someone usually asks, 'Where do you get your ideas from?' A book is often sparked off by a phrase overheard, an idea for a particular character, setting or theme, or events that have happened in the writer's life. Here's what inspired *Pedigree Mum* . . .

Acquiring a dog

We've had Jack, our rescue dog, for two years – we adopted him from Dog's Trust in Glasgow and my whole family is madly in love with him. As soon as he'd settled in with us, I knew my next book had to have a canine theme. In *Pedigree Mum*, I liked the idea of Kerry acquiring a dog almost as a way of getting back at her ex-husband Rob – as a sort of act of rebellion. The fact that her children had begged for a dog was based on my daughter, who'd nagged for one for years. And now I love the 'doggie' community – I've discovered that the world's loveliest dog sitters live virtually next door, and have befriended a bearded collie who can salute.

Moving to a new town

My husband and I left London fourteen years ago when our twin boys were toddlers. We moved to a small rural town in Lanarkshire, Scotland, which *isn't* like Shorling in the book – it's not snooty or remotely Boden-esque. But I still remember the feeling of being 'new', with young children, wondering how on earth I'd make friends – whilst desperately missing my old ones, of course.

I found myself eyeing up prospective new friends in the park, whilst not wanting to come across as a creepy stalker. When someone asked me round for coffee I nearly cried with relief. We did settle in and find our feet – but moving can be tough when you have a young family and feel pretty vulnerable.

Magazine life

In *Pedigree Mum*, Rob works for an upmarket men's magazine. I worked on various magazines from the age of seventeen until my early thirties (although never a men's one). I've always found it funny how there's an obvious pecking order amongst the magazines – and how, at industry awards parties, people from the posh glossies would rarely lower themselves to mingling with staff from the 'grubby' celebrity weeklies or – horrors – the hobby and specialist magazines.

Motherhood

I used to write about my kids' antics for various magazine and newspaper columns. However, as they grew older – and could read what I'd written about them – this became somewhat trickier. These days, I have to be aware of their privacy and rarely write about them at all. However, in fiction, anything goes . . .